The Kingdoms Divided

By G.K. Archer

ISBN Paperback: 979-8-9891922-0-5

ISBN Hardcover: 979-8-9891922-1-2

Cover design by: Alexandria Sullivan

Printed in the United States of America

Table of Contents

Part 1: The Ice

Chapter 1
Niya

I walked into the palace training ring with my sword strapped at my side. Taking in a deep breath of crisp morning air, I sighed a smile.

This morning was unusually brisk.

I tugged my sleeves down from my elbows and freed my gloves from my pocket to slide them on. The Kingdom of Kaldamir was bitterly cold with a beautiful blanket of snow covering it well over half of the year. Our court and grounds were normally warmed by our dark magic, but it did not seem to have reached the infamous ring today.

As I plodded my way through the chill to the ring, I thought to myself how much I looked forward to a good sparring match first thing in the morning. Arriving wet from the knees down from the walk, my gaze met with Alman's. He looked at me with a grimace as he pointed his sword disapprovingly toward me.

I whispered to myself, "So, this is how we're starting our day? Great."

Alman was both my parents' advisor and mine. He was also my trainer. The gods knew that without him advising me, I would most definitely be in worse shape than I was.

Alman was an older Faerie with sharply pointed ears hidden behind silvering hair. His black eyes hid a thousand secrets.

Alman was fond of executing the same routine during our training, but today seemed to be...different.

He would always say, "Consistency allows for natural and automatic movement on the battlefield. You don't always have the time for thinking and strategizing. It could save your life one day."

Consistency was the bane of my existence; therefore, it would cause me to die...of boredom.

Our matches were always rigorous and thorough, though. He was unwavering in his dedication to training me. Alman made sure that my combat aptitude was just as good as my mental one.

I narrowed my eyes with distaste, "What are you doing waving your sword around like you're upset with me?"

Alman shifted on his feet, "What do you mean, Princess?"

Irritated, I groaned, "Get that word out of your mouth, Alman. We both agreed that you would not call me that."

It was more like I threw a tantrum, and he decided it was in his best interest to just not call me that anymore.

"Of course," he bowed slightly.

I unsheathed my sword and smiled at him, "Hold on to your balls, you old male."

I lunged, dark magic rippling through my blade and pointed it at him.

Like the sun beating on your cold face in the middle of winter, my body warmed with the flexing of my magic. Our swords rasped, hissed, and clanged together in a cacophony. His sword seemed unwieldy in his hands, and he was stumbling more than usual. I knew he was getting old, but training was his forte.

We continued this pathetic and tedious sparring match and I noticed there was something very wrong.

Is Alman drinking again?

Knocking the sword from his hand and forcing him to his knees, I pronounced, "Submit."

Quickly, glancing at our respective positions, I looked over my bearing and glared at the various small cuts on my body. Alman did not normally nip me this much.

My eyes widened with the realization that this...this was not Alman! My mind started racing, replaying the many, now obvious, signs. Alman never fought sloppy and NEVER tried to hurt me. Alman was precise and coordinated.

This fae was just *not* him.

Reaching my foot over to the fallen sword, I kicked it as far away as possible from the imposter posing as Alman.

Furrowing my brows and reaching out with my dark magic, I felt for a glamour and found one. Immediately, I dispelled it. I took a half step back when a dark-haired fae with a bedraggled and feral appearance glared at me. He whipped a dagger out from behind his back. Almost before I had registered the threat, he lunged toward me. In my temporary disbelief, the male separated me from my sword and stalked closer toward me.

I feigned cowardice and slowly extended my reach downward toward my trouser leg, pulling out my onyx bone-carved short knife. I sidestepped his ensuing blow and sent out my magic in dark clouds encircling him. He froze, eyes wide, and gaped at me. I slowly closed my hand, and my magic increased the tightness on his chest in response.

"Who are you?" I demanded, forcing him to the ground with my onyx knife to his filthy throat.

The male's eyes shone with terror as I held his life in my hands. The "ruthless" fae could only continue staring at me with eyes wide and watering. I snapped my fingers, allowing just enough relief from pressure for him to talk.

"Nobody. Somebody. Everybody." The unsettling male rasped.

I tried so hard to hold in my laughter, "What do you want?"

"To kill you." He choked out, tears streaming down his cheeks.

I toyed with my short knife, incredulous, "Well, that's very forward of you. You can try, but you will fail."

Who was this fae to say something so bold? If his statement were true, it meant that I must have pissed someone off. I do not remember doing such a thing but then again...I do have a tendency of making a fae or two angry.

Glancing down, I saw a darkening stain growing in the crotch of his filthy leggings.

I scrunched my eyebrows together and released my hold on the male. The fae lunged at me and my much quicker reflexes sliced into his throat.

Oops.

Black ooze started flooding down his wound onto his tunic and soggy leggings as well as...all over me.

Gross.

I backed up and examined this strange, dark liquid spilling onto the floor around the imposter. Neither Unseelie nor Seelie fae bled black.

What in all the realms?

I reached out to try and touch the black sludge. Before I had reached it, a hand wrapped around my arm and pulled me back. A deep voice grunted at me, "Don't."

Twirling around and shoving back from his grip on my arm, I announced, "Don't touch me, Garrin." I snapped my arm towards the dark pool on the floor and continued, "What *is* that?!"

Garrin, who was the head of our royal guard, looked toward the spectacle on the floor before us, puzzled. He gazed at me warily, "Princess Niya, we will take care of this. You are being summoned by your parents." He made a quick assessment of my sorry state. "Maybe wash up before you see them, yes?"

I would kill Garrin if he so much as looked me over as if I were a child one more time, "Who was that male? Why weren't any of you aware of his intrusion into our home? Where is Alman?" I barked out, wanting to talk to someone that actually knows their head from their...

Shrugging his shoulders, Garrin retorted, "You consistently snipe at us when we follow you around. In fact, you threaten us with our lives when we try to protect you. Why would we have assumed today would be any different?"

See, perfect example of making someone angry.

I did this to myself, really.

I glared at Garrin. Throwing my arms up in exasperation, "Don't be daft. Leave the body here and send Alman out to examine him." I held in my anger and turned on my heel, heading back to the castle.

Walking hastily through the drafty corridors and back to my room in the west wing, I was greeted by castle staff bustling about and muttering under their breath. Self-conscious from the black ooze all over my front, I tried to avoid eye contact and began to almost trot.

Nothing to see here, folks; just a little assassination attempt and a thoroughly ruined outfit. Nobody need be alarmed.

I slammed the door to my room behind me and let out an adrenaline-fueled sigh. I slid down the thick, timber door and put my forearms on my knees. I took in a deep breath...and let it out.

Sahriah would know what to do in this sticky situation. I needed to swing by the club and ask her for her sage, bartenderly advice.

The sound of running water interrupted my thoughts. My whole body pricked to attention. Bolting to my feet, I armed myself with my onyx bone-carved knife and slowly stalked to the bathroom.

Chapter 2
Niya

I flung the door open, and Rose screamed at the top of her lungs. She whirled around to me with her hand on her heaving chest, "My gods, Niya. You scared the shit out of me! I mean I heard you slamming the door, but I did not expect you to come in here like a blonde jungle cat ready to pounce..." Rose swatted one arm in my direction for emphasis.

I looked at my surprised visitor in utter disbelief and slowly placed my short knife back in its protective sheath.

Rose was a common fae whose fate was to be dealt a tragic childhood. Her parents were killed by the Seelie sentries during a skirmish on the border of The Great Divide when she was a child. Her parents' death led Rose to find sanctuary at our castle. She had no other family, and she was so young. Upon stumbling with exhausted little legs to our home, she begged to swear her allegiance to my parents. My parents, in return, requested that she swear allegiance to me, through a blood oath, instead.

Blood oaths were something that Kaldamir did not take lightly. If broken, the result was death. Rose knew this when she sliced her palm open to me in acceptance. She knew that if she were to ever betray me, she would die. Not because I would kill her, but because our blood sealed our bond and now our lives would be entwined.

Besides her allegiance to me, she had also taken it upon herself to take care of me. Rose was there every time I cried, punched a wall, or dodged my parents. She even helped me with an alibi a time or two...or more. She was not only acting upon her oath of allegiance, but she was also my friend.

My best friend.

The one person I could go to for everything.

Grumbling to myself and softening my posture, I replied, "Rose, you scared the shit out of *me*. I was not expecting anybody in my room. But now that you are here..." I grimaced, "You would not believe what happened in the ring this morning."

Rose turned off the water and sat on the vanity, "I need to hear all the details. Did you finally kick that old fae's ass?"

By "Old fae", she meant Alman, and by kicking his ass, she meant me finally being able to win a sparring match with him. That would have been noteworthy, for sure.

"No, that greedy bastard is determined to never let me win," I paused for a moment, frowning and casting my gaze downward before continuing, "It turns out," I said in a conspiratory whisper, "that we had an unwanted visitor *masquerading* as Alman."

"What?" Rose perked up and her eyes widened as if questioning if she needed to be concerned about a breach.

"It's okay. He was no match for Celeste," Lifting my foot a little to show my dagger; my face beaming.

Rose broke out in uproarious laughter, "I cannot handle you sometimes. I'm sure Celeste did a mighty fine job this morning. I will need to properly thank that weapon sometime." Rose stood up and walked towards the egress, "We will talk more later. I know your parents have requested your presence and I thought starting your morning routine for you would help speed up the process. You know, blood oath and all. I got your back."

"Rose you know I —"

"—It is my honor to care for you. Even if you hate it when I do." Rose cut me off and smiled, "I will see you later for a proper conversation and hopefully, some hot goss. Make sure there is plenty of wine!"

Rose closed the door behind herself. I tugged off my bloody clothes preparing to slip into the prepared bath. Getting in, I sank my body all the way under and stayed beneath the water until my lungs burned and I had to come up for air. The water was so warm I could have melted into a happy little Niya puddle in the bottom of the tub.

Trying to relax, I thought that maybe I should just keep to myself today and not socialize. I needed to do more research on black blood and what it meant. But, on the other hand, if I go against my parents' wishes by not showing up for breakfast, they would probably kill me. I grabbed my vanilla and jasmine hair cleaner and scrubbed my scalp. After a wonderful head massage, I worked on scrubbing my body with the same scented body soap starting with my shoulders and working my way down.

As I scrubbed my right arm, I noticed little shadow-like swirls dancing up it. I tilted my head, puzzled. I scrubbed my arm harder in hopes that it would come off, but the shadows did not budge. In fact, the more I scrubbed, the more prominent the shadows appeared. After several attempts, I frowned and dropped my soapy hand in the water in defeat.

Rinsing off the suds, I got out of the bath and wrapped a towel around my body. Looking at myself in the reflective glass, I snatched a hair towel and sat down squeezing out the excess water.

Pulling my hair away; it fell to the middle of my back in loose waves. I brushed through the silvery blonde strands, and I used some of my wind magic to carefully dry it, taking care to keep the curls intact. When I finished styling my hair with strands delicately braided, loose wavy pieces peaked out over my pointed, yet dainty ears. I inserted ear-cuffs to my right ear and dual earrings on both. I applied light makeup around my eyes and deep crimson color to my lip. I placed my onyx tiara atop my head with a marquise ruby crystal at each of the three peaks.

Frowning at my clothes, I thought about how I absolutely detested wearing formal dresses. But I didn't have a choice but to look "presentable". I had to look the part of Crowned Princess of Kaldamir.

I slid on a floor-length silk dress. The swath of fabric on my chest left little to the imagination and displayed the curve of my breasts, leading the eye of the observer into a tightened back sinched with silk string. The stringed mock-corset fit my hourglass shape perfectly. I was never athletically slim, but I did always have muscle in my well-curved body. I strapped my short knife onto my left thigh and straightened out my dress to cover it. The slit was beautifully tantalizing.

I looked over these newly formed shadows now twining around my arm and shrugged off the thoughts of what they could mean.

Making my way to the dining hall, Claude opened the main hallway entrance and announced my arrival. I examined the room to find faces full of concern and irritation. I sat down carefully making sure to be as pleasant as possible.

I looked over at my parents.

My mother with her deep brown eyes and black hair with severe, wine-painted lips; her black crown sitting elegantly on her head. My father, with his golden hair and icy blue eyes, looked regal as always with his black, long-sleeved tunic resting on his imposing figure. Both just stared at me with irritation on their faces.

"Would you care to tell us what happened?" My mother, High Lady, and Queen, Ravyn Blackbyrn of Kaldamir, tapped her fingers on the table; her intense stare boring into me.

I sank into my chair and put two fingers on my temple, "There was a breech in our fighting ring. *Somehow* a fae glamoured himself to look like Alman and he told me he was going to kill me. So, I returned the favor," I tried to hide my smile after that comment.

"Niya," my father drew out. I looked down and dropped my head to the table and groaned.

I whined quietly, "I hate this so much. I am not a child anymore. I can handle myself."

Everything I'd done at this point in my already long-lived life was never good enough for my parents. I was not a youngling anymore; I had lived decades in this castle and in these walls my parents built for my brother, Vallynn, and myself.

I was so done with the life they wanted me to live.

Honestly, I was suffocating.

I groaned again and closed my eyes, choosing my words ever so carefully.

Slowly I stated, "Look, I am more than capable of handling myself even with the intrusion that happened this morning. However, I don't appreciate having some random common shifter disguising himself as Alman." I lifted my head up off of the table to look at my father. "I mean, where was our security?"

"That's it? No explanation for why you had to kill him? You didn't think to hold him for questioning? Niya, this is getting out of hand. He was one of our citizens. You cannot just go around killing whomever you please. Not only does that look distressing for the crown; it looks bad on you, darling. We are the Unseelie, we already have an ugly look on us, let's not make it worse."

I gritted my teeth. I knew better than to challenge him, "Yes, father."

Vallynn and Alman walked in with black blood all over them. They stopped in their tracks, surprised to see me. I did not normally eat with any of them, but since my parents had requested me...

Vallynn gave me a distasteful sigh as he looked over my wounds. It's not like he had not seen my body messed up in a fight before. In fact, he was the one who would normally heal me. He had a gift that most Unseelie didn't have.

Healing.

Walking over to me, Vallynn started pushing his healing powers onto my wounds, mumbling scornfully, "You really need to learn how to harness light magic."

"Okay Vallynn, let me just waltz into the Seelie court and ask their priests to teach me their light magic. That will go over swell, brother."

Vallynn cut me a glare, "You haven't heard?"

I stared at my brother, bewildered, "First of all, why are you looking at me with that tone? Second, heard what?"

Vallynn smirked, "Your favorite person is coming to visit."

"Who is my 'favorite person'?"

Vallynn's eyes rolled to the back of his head, and he scoffed, "King Adryen is coming."

Blinking blankly and then curling my lip, "Ew."

He had to be joking about this. There was no way my mother would ever invite the King of The Seelie fae here to Unseelie territory.

Alman sat down next to me. Cutting my conversation short with Vallynn, Alman uttered quietly, "Someone disguised as me, huh?" He had a little smirk on his sweet, familiar face.

I looked up at him and nodded. Alman added, "So he was devilishly handsome and an amazing swordsman?"

"Something like that," I shot back, smirking and nudging his knee with mine, hinting to him that I was not about to get into any details with him right now. "Can we talk later?"

Alman shrugged his ascent.

Vallynn finished his healing and headed to his seat just as breakfast was being served.

After eating a very light meal, my mother dragged her eyes over to me and made a quick gesture with her head to follow her towards the exit. I politely excused myself and followed her out to the hallway. She led us down to the foyer that connected the ballroom to the throne room.

I looked up at the high-arched, cathedral ceilings and watched the grounds workers gingerly placing decorations around the room with their magic. It was definitely a sight to behold. It looked like a little, well-choreographed dance. I have never seen them so happy doing anything.

Their talents were being wasted here.

Chapter 3
Niya

We don't decorate.

"Why are we decorating? What's the occasion?" I blurted.

My mother turned around and smiled benignly at me.

"It is time for you to take your rightful place on the throne. With the prophecy coming close to its nulling and your father and I done with ruling, what better time than the present?"

She was absolutely avoiding my question.

I watched several stewards and stewardesses bustling about with my favorite sweets and canapes. I grabbed a chocolate-covered strawberry and bit into it. Juices tickled my taste buds as I closed my eyes and savored. Gods, strawberries were absolutely divine—

Wait—

My attention whipping back to what my mother had just said with a crack, "You are fucking joking, right?"

My eyes widened with my mother's as those five words projected for everybody to hear with the fine acoustics of the hall. It was an accident, but there was no going back now. The workers whirled their heads at me in shock.

My mother frowned slightly and then walked towards the dais where two huge, finely shaped, black marble thrones sat at the top. One had a tall and thin back built for beauty and comfort with intricate carvings along the arms, legs, and crown; the other, built more powerfully than the other, boasted massive carvings of wyvern heads, claws, and wings. Between the two symbols of power was a dainty side table that the both of my parents shared.

Queen Ravyn darted her hand out to my shadowed arm and pulled it up between us, "Does this look like I am joking? Your magic is manifesting into something darker. If you want to continue living, you need to do what the prophecy apprised."

And in that moment, I swear if looks could kill...

My parents were tired of ruling? That was the most ridiculous excuse I had ever heard. They had been ruling for centuries, and everything had been going just fine. An old prophecy should not change anything.

Being the first-born meant that I had no choice but to step up after they abdicated.

My mother was suddenly concerned about this mysterious prophecy which I didn't fully understand. She had never mentioned her concern about it before.

Why now?

Looking at the shadows on my arm, I wondered if it was truly my prophecy awakening. These shadows did not hurt, but I could feel them locking into my arm like a python coiling around its dinner.

"I was given that prophecy as a child, Mother." I tugged back my arm and continued, "What are the chances of it calling to me now?" I began fiddling with my dress, suddenly feeling both claustrophobic and exposed. This could not be happening. I was perfectly fine living my best life with my books, hobbies, and training with Alman.

I did not want to give any of that up.

She glared at me, "The time is now. The shadows appearing on your arm prove that." She stopped, then continued with a light sigh, "My dear, your father and I cannot rule forever. You are over a century old; stop acting like a child. The first-born reigns in every high fae bloodline; you know that. You are not the exception." Sitting on her throne now, the queen snapped her fingers for a guard to open the ingress.

"Why did you decorate, Mother?" I repeated due to her prior deflection. I grabbed a flute of champagne from one of the many ornate trays of delectables and started to gulp it down.

"Oh," she stated flippantly, "I have invited all of the royal families to celebrate your coronation announcement. They will be here for a couple of days and then be back before the solstice to watch you ascend."

My drink spewed out over my lips onto the marbled floor, "You—what?!"

The solstice was only a couple of months away!

Wiping the bubbly champagne off of my lips, I looked at the guests flooding in and finding places to stop and socialize. So many faces that I both do and do not recognize. The faces that I do remember vaguely, I assume must be the lords and ladies of Kaldamir. I needed to revisit our books on governance and public policy to place these faces with names. It had been too long since I'd sat down and studied our kingdom and its townships and personages.

All of these unfamiliar faces reminded me how gargantuan our kingdom was compared to the tiny Seelie Kingdom of Haldonia. I doubted my mother had been the one that invited the Seelie fae to this gathering. Our relationship with the Seelie Kingdom was tenuous at best and had been for many, many years. They wanted more land, and my parents refused to cede any to them.

It was the same old story.

Somebody always wanted more and somebody else didn't want to give it to them. Contentions were strung tighter than a bow with a drawn arrow.

"You could have told me of my own celebration, *and* coronation, mother.*"*

"Niya, even if I had warned you prior to this very moment, would your reaction have changed? I know you, daughter. You are strong willed. You do not accept what you do not want. I know you do not want this, but you do not have a choice. It is time."

And with that, I spun around, looking for anything I could use as an excuse to escape. Entering the throne room now were many fae males and females. All beautiful and all boring.

Belligerently, I lifted my head up in response, "I am not having a coronation on the solstice or any other time. Vallynn can have the crown. He'd be a great ruler; imagine all the wonderful things he could accomplish!"

The queen abruptly burst into laughter at my proposal. The throne room suddenly grew unsettlingly quiet. Not one voice or breath was made as I examined all their unimpressed faces.

I tried to sink so far into myself that I might disappear altogether.

Is it possible to die from embarrassment?

Ravyn cut her laughter, "You know as well as I do that Vallynn is not fit to rule."

"Whatever do you mean?" I derisively intoned as I looked back up to her through lowered and batting lashes.

Ravyn frowned, "Niya, we are not getting into that right now," she looked me over and a smile crept up her wicked face, "I need to pull one more thing from my satchel of surprises."

I absolutely loathed it when my mother willfully avoided my questions. As I had gotten older, it seemed like she had left me more and more in the dark when it came to my queries...and come to think of it, anything and everything that had to do with this kingdom and her motives.

Maybe that was my fault for being so absent.

I just couldn't help myself. I had no desire to be a part of the politics of this kingdom, or even this family at times. My parents were ruthless rulers, and the people of our kingdom knew it. One step out of line, and they knew there would be severe consequences; consequences that some would not walk away from.

I didn't want to be like them; I wasn't like them.

Grabbing a fruit pastry from a little rotund server, I started to eat through my feelings.

"And what is that surprise?" I replied to my mother, with a mouth full of delicious pastry.

The throne room's entryway unceremoniously slammed shut drawing me and the entirety of the grand floor's gaze to the last guest that pierced the room. A towering, sun-kissed, well-muscled male strolled through the crowd and scanned the atmosphere. The guests murmured with various facial expressions at this male's conspicuous entrance.

The male's presence exuded power and confidence. This was someone of nobility with that golden, antlered crown sitting jauntily on his head. The crown circled the apex of his head with the points facing inward toward eachother. His loose chestnut hair peaked out in front with a loose sweep across his forehead.

My mouth full of pastry and crumbs in my cleavage, our eyes locked, and he smiled sideways at me taking in my deportment. He stopped one of the waitstaff and swiped a glass of wine for himself before bowing slightly and beginning to slowly filter through the crowd to network.

My brain started reeling, my eyes grew wide, and my hand came up to my mouth with the full realization that this male had, in fact, seen my cleavage crumbs.

Damn.

I absentmindedly swiped the crumbs off myself while I stalked this impressively handsome fae with my eyes.

This was not anybody I had ever seen in our kingdom before. Our high lords do not usually wear crowns, let alone one made of gold. I rifled through my internal directory of fae and could not put my finger on who this male was. Either way, he seemed very into talking to all the females in this palace. Considering he had this natural godlike beauty with that tall, built frame, I did not blame them.

I would try to bed him, too.

I swallowed hard; that last bite had turned into a hard knot as I brought my attention back to my mother.

Before I could speak, Queen Ravyn pressed a hand on my shoulder, "The surprise is that I have invited the King of Haldonia to your coronation and he is expected today."

My eyes blazing, "We are on the brink of war with the Seelie Kingdom. Why in all the realms would you do such a thing? Are you asking for—"

"—I am asking for you to be flexible, daughter. If you would participate in regular courtly duties, you would know that this is a chance for an alliance."

I scoffed, incredulous, "You want me to ally...with the enemy? He is probably only here because he wants our land."

The King of Haldonia was a killer. Our border was breeched by him and his court a couple of years ago which decimated my sprite sanctuary. He killed them and destroyed their home. Very few sprites made it out.

∞∞∞∞

I hadn't even made it twenty feet into the sanctuary before Tallulah, a water sprite, came flying into my face.

She was hyperventilating and struggling to speak.

Lifting my hand to let Tallulah land, I peered into her blue eyes, "What is it, Lulu?"

"The lagoon!" She pointed towards the sanctuary, "It is ruined! Haldonia invaded and they wrecked our home! Niya!"

She was screaming at me, and I could do nothing. I felt useless and panic filled me.

I'd built the sprite sanctuary for both water sprites and woodland sprites several decades ago when I saw them wandering close to the castle. They were very mischievous and very emotional magical beings that did not take kindly to the destruction of their home.

"Niy, it is terrible!"

I dropped my hand and sprinted to the lagoon, Tallulah trailing me. I saw...nothing. There were no trees, no more lagoon, and the waterfall was gone. Panic rose in my chest. This had been a sanctuary; for the sprites and for me. It was the place that I could relax and watch the sprites play and chase each other in harmony and peace.

Out of breath, I panted, "What in the hells happened?"

"The King of Haldonia sent an army to our side of the border; I don't know what happened! There was noise and smoke, Niya. Your mother's

sentries did not make it in time to protect us. When they finally arrived, they saw what remained of our beautiful home and...left. They did not even check on us. So many perished." Tallulah shook her head, sadly.

I breathed, "Where are the rest, Lulu?"

At that point I could not afford to worry about the fallen sanctuary. I needed to know if all of the sprites were accounted for; and bury the dead.

"I don't know, I think they all," she choked up, "I think they are all gone. It's just me."

"Lulu, you can't survive without water, you will need to relocate for now."

Tallulah, still hovering in front of me, screamed, "No! I can't move again. I can't take it!" She buried her face in her tiny hands and began to weep.

Closing my eyes, I whispered, "I will stop by as often as I can to help rebuild; but you cannot stay here, Lulu. Look at me," I said and her tiny eyes, filled with tears, looked into mine. "Look for as many sprites as you can and get to Cleome. Let Delilah know you need to stay for a while, per the Princess of Kaldamir. She will give you refuge."

Tallulah wiped at her watery face and kissed my cheek, "Please don't forget about us."

I whispered, "I won't."

∞∞∞∞∞

My mother turned me around to face her completely, pulling me from an extremely vivid memory, "I want you, Princess Niya Blackbyrn, to act your ripe old age of one hundred and two. Prove to me you can at least take the time to get to know him before assuming his place here in our court."

"So, what you are saying is that you want me to ignore the fact that the Seelie King destroyed *my* sanctuary and the majority of the sprites living there? *And* you also want me to get to *know* him? I can't even believe you, mother." I spat out, disgusted, "What exactly do you get out of this?"

So many questions rolled through me.

Annoyed and uncomfortable with a sprite murderer being here, I bared my teeth at my mother, ready to pry out her hidden agenda; when a deep sultry voice interrupted us, "Hello, Your Majesty."

Whipping my entire body in the direction of the voice with my teeth still unfortunately bared, I saw that the golden-crowned male I had locked eyes with moments ago was standing next to me and hovering a foot above.

I snapped my lips together.

My eyes trailed over his muscular physique again. Honestly, he looked like he could be a model for underclothing. Putting anything more on that body should be a crime against all fae kind. This sculpted creature had the tanned skin of someone that spent a lot of time working outdoors, but I had a feeling he hadn't done any kind of manual labor in his life. He must've been doing something to get all those beautiful muscles, though.

My naughty mind started to trail off in places it should not be going.

My gods if I could touch that body.

I bit my lower lip and smiled in appreciation.

I will do more than touch this male.

I want his entire coc—

The male in question cleared his throat uncomfortably and my sexual fantasies with him and me tangled together dissipated. His cornflower blue eyes met mine and a twinge of desire shot right through my core.

I shifted on my heels, backing away so I could comfortably take all of him in.

Another round of champagne passed close enough to me that I stopped the server, downing one of the flutes. Placing it back on the tray, I grabbed another and pounded that one as well.

I will not embarrass myself or my kingdom.

Staring at my already empty glass, I frowned.

Well, shit.

"Hello, King Whitebourne," my mother crooned.

The Seelie King.

Haldonia.

My wine glass shattered on the floor and the throne room went quiet. The gasping breaths of everyone seemed to echo as I froze, agape. The tattoo-like shadows swirled on my right arm sending distinct heightened emotions through me: lust, anger, and embarrassment. I could feel my face flushing and my eyebrows pulling together horrified at what I just heard ringing through my head.

I should have known this fae was the Seelie King. He just *felt* different than everyone else in the room.

I raised my voice in distaste and concern, "King *Adryen* Whitebourne?!"

The crowd took my exclamation as a hint to continue mingling and minding their business. My body surged with anger and kinetic magic that flowed through me.

A muscle tensed in my jaw.

I take back everything I'd just thought.

This male was absolutely disgusting, and I wish he would glamour himself to look more like his ugly inner self.

Maybe a troll.

I thought Vallynn was joking about the king being here.

I guess the joke was on me. The joke *was* me.

"Please forgive her tone, Your Majesty. She has forgotten her manners. We are pleased to have you here." My mother announced with the ease and diplomacy that I would never have, dipping slightly to the king.

"No need for forgiveness, I have not yet had the pleasure since all of my communications have been through Vallynn or yourself," Adryen countered, "If you have a moment, I have some business I'd like to discuss with you," motioning to the queen with a sweep of his hand toward the dais.

I raised my eyebrows at both my mother and the Seelie King, scoffing, "Business? Are you going after the dryads next? Maybe the old and infirm?"

A lanky steward passed us with a variety tray of wine and more chocolate-covered strawberries. I grabbed both and dismissed myself into the foyer and stormed out to the gardens.

My mother's eyes trailed after me as she entered into conversation with the most beautiful male I had ever seen.

Chapter 4

Niya

Exiting onto the garden landing, I snatched my smutty book I had stashed behind the flowerpot. I looked around for a quiet, and isolated spot to read. I just *had* to find out who *Lynora* ended up with.

Light footsteps trailed behind me, and a whiff of birch and eucalyptus tantalized my nose. I slid my hand towards the slit of my dress to unsheathe my dagger. I gripped its handle, swung around, and pointed it at the King of Haldonia's throat. Balancing my blade in one hand, and my book in the other, I curled my lip.

The King's hand flew to the pommel of his resting sword, ready to defend.

My eyebrows furrowed, tightening my grip on the handle. Moving my onyx blade closer to his tensing neck, "I left the throne room to be alone. Leave."

He winced at my blade digging into his throat, "I did not mean to frighten you, Princess." A droplet of crimson welled on his neck.

"Do I look frightened, King of the Seelie?" I stared scornfully into those bright blue eyes.

He chuckled under my blade, "No, but I can hear your heart racing. Do you care to share *why* that is?"

I dropped my blade arm and placed Celeste back in through the slit of my dress, adjusting to hide her again in her sheath. I gripped the fore-edge of the book and jabbed the spine toward him with each word, "No. Go. Away."

"Now, that is no way to talk to your guest." The Seelie King put his hand to the little slice on his neck and light poured out of his fingers, healing his wound, "Especially a guest that you just threatened, and made bleed. A guest who happens to be of higher ranking than you, you viciously beautiful female."

"I do not care about your rank. You aren't even of this kingdom. If you do not leave, you will lose more than a droplet of blood, Your Majesty," I said with a mock bow.

He chuckled and snatched the book from my hand touching every finger before pulling it away from me, "I would like to see you try."

I jerked my hand back as his fingers glided through mine. I wanted to punch him in the face for having the audacity to speak to me and...touch me.

The Seelie King looked at the cover of my smutty book and his eyes glowed as he read, "*Eternal Lovers,*" He smirked and ran his hand through his loose chestnut hair, waving the book at me, "This is a very bland book. Chyann kills his mistress, Lynora, in the end. The sex is mediocre, and the lovers are subpar."

My mouth gaped open at what he had just done and groaned, "Next time, I will make sure I slice deep enough into your throat so you can no longer speak, or maybe even live. You do not get to ruin a book for somebody like that!"

I attempted to grab the book back and he pulled further away from me, and smiled.

"I am not playing games with you, Your Kingliness."

"Aren't you a feisty one?" King Adryen moved in closer to me. I backed up with every inch that he gained.

He looked down into my eyes, "We are going to have so much fun getting to know one another."

Pressing my lips into a thin line. I rolled my eyes and turned on my heels headed into the gardens.

That stupid twat of a king.

This was not even worth my time. I did not want to get to know this male. He was the king of a kingdom that had been nothing but trouble for the last hundreds of years. He, himself, had been more than enough trouble for uprooting my sanctuary and killing off the entire land around it.

King Adryen was here for a reason, and it did not seem to be for this coronation my mother had planned. We all know the tension between kingdoms, so why did my mother bring him here in hopes of an alliance?

Something did not seem to be adding up.

The luscious black tulips lined the walkway to the endless rose gardens our court had worked diligently on for as long as I could remember. The Unseelie castle grounds were so very dreadful and received many complaints from the courtiers about the landscape. My mother decided to have the gardens warmed by magic so all sorts of flowers, herbs, and shrubbery could thrive here. This was truly my favorite place. When I would read and catch up on my studies, I would spend hours here just lazing and enjoying the sun's rays.

I grabbed another stashed book from a potted shrubbery and weaved my way through the labyrinth of roses, searching for a place to settle into. I picked a lovely stone bench and plopped down, forcing myself to slog through the study of healing.

$\infty\infty\infty$

I woke up in a panic, looking around. Hours must have passed because the sun was now shining on the opposite side of where it had started.

Gods!

I missed lunch.

I got up and hurriedly made my way back to the castle, my stomach grumbling. A couple of feet from the entrance, my brother suddenly became corporeal in front of me and smiled. Vallynn and I were the only ones in our family that could transverse. As long as we knew the location, we could relocate ourselves into a new place, unscathed. There had been fae who would attempt spells and would fail and die in the process of jumping between two points through the void. This was a dark magical gift that should not be trifled with in amateur spell-making.

I looked at Vallynn.

It was uncanny how much we didn't look like each other. Vallynn was the spitting image of both of my parents. He had our mother's onyx black hair and my father's icy blue eyes. His facial features were a perfect mix of the two: strong jawline, high cheekbones, and full lips. He smiled at me and gestured for us to walk inside.

It was probably time for dinner and the meeting and greeting of the Seelie kingdom that had arrived.

Vallynn talked to me quietly, clasping his hands behind his back, "Permission to speak freely without getting a verbal lashing?"

I looked at him puzzled and stated slowly, "Sure."

"I know you hate this ascending the throne and prophecy bullshit, but hear me out. Wouldn't it be convenient if King

Adryen and you could form an alliance of a more personal nature? Niya, he holds a lot of magical power that you do not; you could use that. Plus, the prophecy would be fulfilled, and you could use that to your advantage."

Interesting that my living was the afterthought—and he was delusional.

"You are not serious, Vallynn, are you? How could making an alliance fix anything between our lands and my prophecy?" I glanced down at my inky shadows dancing up my arm, "Thank you for healing me. Again. What am I to do when mom and dad marry you off?" I said dramatically as Vallynn smirked. I double patted his cheek.

He held my hand on his cheek, "They will marry you off before me, sister," and chuckled.

My face snapped in seriousness, "What?"

Vallynn changed the subject, "What are those shadows on your arms?"

"I dunno. They popped up while I was washing this morning. It started as a little smudge and now it's full-blown swirls around my arm," pausing, "I can feel them."

"Weird. You should go to see Ca'Themar. He may be a crazy old man, but he *is* a priest and has enough experience to know what to do about whatever that is," Vallyn pointed at my arm distastefully.

I shrugged, "I kind of like them."

We continued down the hallway to the ballroom. Vallynn stopped me at the door where the guards waited for the command to open, "I want to warn you, Niya. There are a lot of eligible high lords here for your hand. Try not to obliterate them with your tongue and vocal cords."

I looked at my brother, dumbfounded.

He didn't even know what I did with my tongue.

Vallynn nodded at the sentries. They opened the double entryway, and we walked inside the ballroom that had been completely transformed since this morning.

I glanced around, taking in the spectacle. My parents never threw parties or balls. That was just something our kingdom never did. Kaldamir was known for brothels and orgies throughout the kingdom and lands. We were a singular kingdom as it was, there was no need for formalities.

I surveyed the decorations and bustling servers. Black sheer drapery flooded the high ceilings and walls of the throne room. There were tables arranged in delicate ivory silk with place settings fit for royalty.

The ballroom was filled with male and female fae alike. All dressed to their specific courts. There seemed to be a lot more vibrant color from the Seelie Kingdom than Unseelie this evening. I frowned, taking in the sights of vibrant purples, yellows, and pinks adorning the bodies of the light fae.

"Enjoy your night, Niya. I am going to enjoy bedding these Seelie females tonight. I might never have a chance again!" Vallynn smiled excitedly and slipped into the crowd.

Shaking the already intruding thoughts of Vallynn and any female, I slowly circumambulated the dais where my parents sat on their thrones. They had changed their attire for this evening, wearing much nicer clothing than myself.

Shit.

I should have changed.

Maybe it was not too late, and I could escape and just not *do* this whole social hour altogether.

As I reached the corner of the dais in thought, I quickly turned around to head back to my room when my mother said curtly, "Darling, where are you going? You just got here."

I stared blankly at her, realizing there was no way I was going to be allowed out of here. I huffed a sigh and glanced around into the crowd. There were so many people here. I had no idea who was who. I continued scanning the crowd when I locked eyes with those of stupid cornflower blue.

Murderous asshole.

Grabbing my attention back, my mother continued, "King Adryen has been inquiring about you since he arrived. He is quite the charmer." Ravyn raised her eyebrows at me solicitously.

I scoffed, "Oh, okay; charmer is not the word I'd use for him. Maybe a giant pest. He found his way into *your* gardens today. I'll make sure to tell the grounds keepers to spray out there." With a wicked smirk, "Maybe I could find a fire sprite to burn him to ashes."

My mother lowered her lashes, "Niya, I would try to play nice around the Seelie guests. The King of Haldonia is needed," she looked at me, "Maybe you will get lucky and have more than just an alliance with him."

"I want nothing to do with this frilly light-wielding king. He is not *needed*. I don't want to get 'lucky', nor do I want an alliance with him." Anger filled my blood.

My thoughts were obliterated when my father touched Ravyn's hand and looked at me, entreating, "My two rare and perfect gems, please; we have guests."

Alman shifted on his feet as he was trying his best to mind his business.

"If you want an alliance, mother, you will have to leave me out of it. I cannot believe that you are even participating in this travesty! I refuse to even consider it."

Trotting down the dais and to a petite female carrying wine on a service tray, I snatched two flutes from her tray and started downing the first glass of bubbly wine. I placed the first emptied flute back on another tray filtering through the crowds.

My lips touched the second champagne glass and the first guests started to approach me.

I tried with all of my willpower not to roll my eyes.

This was going to be a long night.

Sometime later and about two more glasses of wine in, I started to feel comfortable being surrounded by people that I absolutely wanted no business associating with. I talked to many eligible high fae, and did a pretty good job pretending to be interested as instructed—or warned.

I watched as King Adryen weaved his way toward me from the other side of the room.

Deciding now was a perfect time to leave, I hastily filtered made my way through the crowd to the exit.

As I opened the door to leave the throne room, I smelled that familiar scent of birch and eucalyptus.

How did he get here so fast?

The King closed the door behind us and continued walking behind me in the direction of my room.

"You should have stayed at the party, Your Highness." I waved towards the door.

King Adryen grabbed my wrist and pulled me towards him, "Call me Adryen."

My eyebrows pinched as I snatched back out of his grasp, "Don't you *ever* grab me like that again, *Adryen*." Disgust and disdain coated my words.

Adryen bared his teeth showing his elongated canines, "What did I ever do to you, Princess?"

There was no way in all the realms that the male, this king, did not know what he had done.

I challenged, "You think you can just walk into my castle, my kingdom, and not have any remorse for what you did?!"

The King's voice lowered several octaves, "What did I do?"

I screamed in frustration, "You are a fucking asshole! You killed the sprites at the lagoon. It was their home and one of the very few places where I could go to feel some sense of peace."

Adryen stood there, shock adorning his face.

"I had been looking after them and watching the little ones grow. Then, one day, *you* breech the wall and destroy everything and left the sprites that escaped to die! I hate you, Your Majesty. You ruined such a great thing in my life! One of the *ONLY* things."

The door to the ballroom cracked open and Alman entered the hallway. He looked at me warily and then at Adryen, "Is everything alright out here?"

My cheeks were red, and I avoided eye-contact.

"You are missed at the party, Your Majesty," Alman directed to Adryen. He then turned to me, "Niya, might I have a moment?"

Haldonia's King glowered at me for several moments. Then he dipped his head slightly and slipped back into the ballroom.

Alman grabbed my upper arm and pulled me further away from the ballroom, "What the fuck, Niya? Are you trying to get yourself killed? Do you have any idea what you're doing?"

Actually, no. I did not.

"What am I doing, Alman? He can't just waltz into this castle like he did nothing wrong! Besides the stupid land issue, he killed the sprites!" I started to screech.

Looking into my eyes, "Go change, and compose yourself. I will meet you outside to train." Alman stalked away from me.

I huffed and ran up to my room, changed into more comfortable clothing, and transversed outside the castle.

I was glad to be out of that dress and the reset was already helping me. Alman gave me a nod and we walked together towards the training ring; the same ring where I was duped by the imposter.

The ring where Alman brought me as a child to teach me how to hold my first sword, throw my first punch, and work through my anger and other high emotions.

Alman sat in the middle of the ring, groaning on his way down.

I sat in front of him, "Are you getting too old for this, you ancient fae?" I winked.

Alman shook his head back and forth, "Do not start with me, Niya."

"Fine," I wiggled around, trying to get myself more comfortable.

"Stretch and don't talk. We are going to do hand-to-hand."

Nodding, I pulled my arms above my head and pushed them in front of me, stretching my entire back. I followed this same routine to stretch every muscle in my upper body. I moved onto my legs and spread them out stretching them from the ground. I pushed up from the palms of my hands and produced a couple lunges to wake up my body up.

Ready to go, I balled up my fists and we started our combative training.

I threw a punch at Alman and asked, "What is up with the black blood on that fae this morning?"

Alman glared at me, deflecting my punch, "Stop talking."

I took my other hand and struck him in the chest, "Were you able to figure it out?"

Alman rubbed his chest and coughed, "What do you not get about stop talking?"

I shrugged my shoulders, and we spent the next several minutes punching and blocking.

Deciding that I was done messing around, I did a leg sweep, and he lost his footing and dropped to the floor.

"Tell me, Alman. You have lived forever; you have to know something."

Alman struggled getting up. I placed my hand out in front of him, and he grabbed it, allowing me to help him up.

He groaned and held his back, "I think we are done for tonight, Niya. I actually think you are trying to kill me." I smiled and patted him on the shoulder, victorious for the first time.

We walked back to the castle, which was eerily silent. I needed him to tell me about this fae and the black blood, otherwise it would gnaw at me.

Hoping enough time had passed, I stated again, "You have to know something."

"I do," was all he said as we reached my wing of the castle, "The black blood could mean two things. One: a bond with the vampires, or, two: a blood oath with a human. I am going to guess this was a blood oath with a human. The fae might have strayed a little too far from its bonded human and lashed out on the first person it saw."

"That does not explain why it said it wanted to kill me; and why it had glamoured as you."

We stopped at my door and Alman let out a frustrated sigh, "Niya, I really don't know. There have been a lot of strange occurrences happening in our kingdom in the last couple of months. I am just trying to pick up the pieces and puzzle them back together the best that I can. It is not always simple."

I squinted at him, pensively, "Okay."

"It's handled, don't stress about it."

I gave my tutor a tight-lipped smile and slipped into my bedroom to ruminate some more before going to bed for the night.

Chapter 5
Adryen

I excused myself from the ballroom several hours after talking with the Princess of Kaldamir. Her very confusing outburst left me agitated well after I had left her. The courtiers of her castle were kind; suspiciously so.

Growing up, my parents had always told me that the Unseelie fae were sneaky and mischievous; if not malevolent. I did not see anything like that tonight; maybe a little bit with the princess. I had no idea what she was talking about, but she was spitting venom and it seemed to be only for me. Despite the fire that was inexplicably lit under her ass, she was not terrible.

She was beautiful, actually.

It was a shame she wanted nothing to do with me.

I walked into this castle's gardens planning to leave. I pushed out my power, conjuring a crackling portal to take me back home.

The remainder of my people that joined would return home using the bracelets that my mechanics had devised for the occasion.

The portal sizzled and sparked as it waited for me to pass through.

Coming here was a bad idea right from the start. I knew the queen's proposition would be challenging considering what my spies had told me of Niya. I knew that her sizzling personality would be a task in itself.

But her implication that I'd killed living, healthy creatures...

She could not possibly believe that I would be capable of that.

There was no way I would ever kill another creature, especially sprites.

Who would ever intentionally kill the little things?

I shook my head to myself trying to remember if I had unintentionally done what she'd accused me of, but just couldn't remember doing anything like that. I had no recollection of sending any of my units out to the wall, let alone making it over The Divide to Kaldamir's territory.

Why would I?

I leapt through the portal and landed at the foot of my castle in Haldonia.

Cracked steps and a crumbling foundation greeted me.

I groaned.

I had to find my queen, my other half, or there would be no castle; there might not be a Haldonia.

Finion greeted me when I entered the castle. I asked, walking through the entrance, "Do you remember me sending out guards into Kaldamir's lands a couple of years ago?"

Fin tilted his head and questioned, "What do you mean?"

"Do you remember me signing any papers about sending our troops to Kaldamir?"

"I mean, yes, you did. We came back victorious. Why?"

"Oh, shit," I whispered.

Finion replied, "What's wrong, Your Majesty?"

"What's wrong is the fact that I don't have the faintest idea as to why or how this happened."

Fin shrugged his shoulders, "I don't know."

I furrowed my brows, "Show me the papers."

"What?"

"Show me the damn papers I signed, Finion!"

Panic taking over, I trailed behind him as we made our way to my office. I slammed the door behind me, afraid that he would find something that I was not ready to see. Finion started filtering through papers and pulled out the culprit.

I snatched the paper from him that showed full details of the events just as Niya had described.

Running my hands through my hair, I suddenly felt very hot. I reread the paper several times and nothing came back to me.

Nothing.

I was so young, and a lot of my early years of ruling were a blur of decisions. I would have remembered something like this, especially if I'd initiated it; wouldn't I?

I spoke quietly, "I fucked up. I need to fix this. How do I fix this?" I shot a look at a terrified Finion. "I feel terrible. I don't remember any of this, but I need to apologize to the princess for destroying something so incredibly valuable to her."

I dropped the paper onto the desk, sat down and placed my elbows on both sides of it, holding my head in disgust and shame.

"I am unsure what was 'valuable' to her, but okay," he shrugged, "I need to speak with you about more important matters. Can we discuss the poplar problem?"

I rubbed my temples; this never ended. It seemed like there was always something I had to fix or a decision to be made. I was so tired of having to clean up mess after mess.

I needed a break.

"Can we discuss this tomorrow?"

"Lady Delilah is requesting an audience, Sire."

Groaning, I firmed my voice, "We will talk *tomorrow*, Finion."

Finion bowed in concession and walked with me back to the entrance of the castle. I bolted up the three flights of stairs, flung open the door to my chambers, and turned the shower far to the right, hoping it would get hot enough to remove the taint of the day off of my skin.

$$\infty\infty\infty$$

The sun shone through the massive windows, and I rubbed my groggy eyes awake. I stretched out a yawn and went through my morning routine of styling my hair, brushing my teeth, and getting dressed.

I strapped my scabbard around my waist and tightened the leather belt, securing the sword in its place.

I trudged down the stairs to see Finion waiting for me at the end of the staircase. He blurted, "Hello, Your Majesty!"

"Hello," I replied.

"I was going to tell you last night, but you seemed frustrated enough," Finion started, "But, Lady Delilah would like to see you today."

I barked, "Today?!"

"Yes, Your Majesty."

"Why?"

Finion drew out, "Well..."

"If you don't know why I am needed, then I don't need to go, Finion."

Delilah was a hamadryad that lived in Kaldamir. She reached out to me several years after my parents passing, asking for refuge on my side of The Divide. Little did either of us know that because I had allowed this, my kingdom was now overrun and in dire need of more space. I needed to mention this to her; there were just too many poplars.

They were taking over my castle grounds.

I stared blankly at Finion, who was of no help whatsoever, "Sometimes I wonder why you are even my advisor, Fin. I really don't understand. If you talk to another fae, especially not of this court or kingdom, you need to be much more thorough."

Finion pushed his eyebrows together and frowned, "Yes, Your Majesty. I will do better next time."

I was going to have to visit her anyway, no matter what she needed me for.

We walked outside and I pushed my powers out, making a portal large enough for two.

I gestured for Finion to go first, and he stared at me, "You want me to go with you?"

I lifted both eyebrows in surprise, "Yes. You always come with me."

Finion shuffled his feet, "I'm afraid I might need to ask you to go alone, Your Majesty. I have business to attend to here."

I clapped him on the shoulder, "Why didn't you start with that, Finion?"

He looked at me sheepishly as I traveled through the portal entering Cleome.

Cleome was breathtaking.

It was a city built inside, and made of, the forest.

I walked through the bustling crowd to Lady Delilah's cot. Not one of the citizens of Cleome looked at me. It was almost as if they'd been given orders not to.

I felt uneasy.

Cleome and Haldonia had a fairly neutral relationship with one another. I would say that it bordered on pleasant since I had allowed Lady Delilah's people to portal into our lands to enjoy the milder weather.

I had never felt such a variety of emotions from so many at one time. Unfortunately, none of the ones I felt were of the positive variety.

The least they can do is acknowledge my arrival.

A smile.

Anything!

Delilah strolled out of her cot, arms wide, and greeted me with a hug.

"Hello, King Adryen. I hope your travels were well and safe," Delilah crooned.

I let out a breath and chuckled, "It was as smooth as could be expected, Lady Delilah."

"Come, come, let me get you some hot nectar," Delilah opened the door to her cot and we walked through.

Finding a seat by the empty fireplace, I sat down and waited for Delilah to reenter the room.

After a short time, she came out with two saucers and teacups. Pouring the hot sugar water, which she called nectar, Delilah released a wary sigh.

I slowly sipped, trying not to offend the Lady of Cleome. Sugar water was an acquired taste...and I had not acquired it.

"It's so wonderful to see you, Your Majesty," Lady Delilah chirped, "Tell me, how have you been?"

I took another sip of the warm sugar water, "If I am being honest, not great."

"Oh, child," she placed a hand on my knee, "It will get better. Do you think us getting divided from our home, your kingdom, was easy for us? You are doing the best you can. Better than any of us could have ever expected. Considering..." She smiled down at her nectar and took another sip.

I closed my eyes and took a long, slow breath of the steam coming from my cup. Every move I made as king was not bad "considering." Considering that my parents had died, and my brother was gone, and that I was still so young.

"Adryen," she drew out, snapping me out of my own head, "Your lands are dying; why didn't you tell me? I did not realize how dire things had gotten. One of my younglings had to reach out to us with her roots to send the message."

She was not wrong.

It *was* dire, and my land *was* dying.

I replied, swallowing hard, "I could use some of your assistance with asking your poplars to pull back into your city, Lady Delilah." I didn't want to accidentally show the lady any disrespect. She continued listening to my plea with an interested tilt of her head.

I continued, confidence building, "I would provide shelter and safety for the youngest of your poplars until they are strong enough to withstand the colder climate of Cleome. They will travel back here when they are ready." I attempted to quickly list all of the things I would do for them before she could get upset with me for asking this of her people.

"I will help them as much as I can," I said, finally, placing my cup and saucer on a nearby table.

"I understand." The lady of Cleome's response was so calculating that I wasn't sure if she had agreed with me or wanted to hurt me.

I let out the breath I had been holding, "Lady Delilah, it is truly okay. It is not too much of a hassle," I said, backpedaling. This hamadryad had me sweating all of a sudden.

She smiled and placed her emerald hand on mine. I jumped at the startling contact.

"You will find your other half, King of the Seelie. I know this burden you hold." She looked up at me, "And when you do find her, and see her for who she truly is, it will be a breath of fresh air; a new beginning."

What is happening right now?

"Wha—pardon?" I choked out, disconcerted.

She had a way of knowing things, and it was uncanny.

"I can see the look on your face. Let me tell you a story, Your Majesty."

I inclined my head, ready to listen.

She spoke softly, "When The Divide formed, my mother had just become the lady of the dryads, officially. My family had always been in charge, but to the Seelie court, we were just 'the dryads'. Just creatures, not worthy of any entitlement. My mother eventually withdrew herself from the kingdom altogether and kept herself and her people in this city you know as Cleome. But when the Unseelie court found us, they bestowed on us a title, acceptance. From this bestowment, they arranged a marriage for her; with an oracle, Calchas," she took a sip of her tea, "And had me. So, the look you gave when I spoke the vision, is not uncommon."

Calchas.

That was the name in all of the history books.

He was a powerful oracle.

"Thank you for sharing your story. I would have never thought that Calchas was your father. I thoroughly enjoyed reading about him growing up."

She glowed, "To me, he was just my father. Someone who loved my mother and I deeply and fearlessly."

I leaned in and hesitated for a moment before speaking barely above a whisper, "Who is she?"

Her lips quirked up at the corners, "You are a curious one," the lady winked, "She is silver fire, wind, and ice. She is somewhat unexpected, difficult at times. Above all, she is and forever will be your home. You *will need* each other."

I choked, "Need? Each other?"

Delilah stood up and patted my shoulder, "Yes, child. Need."

I took the last sip of the sugar water known as nectar and placed the teacup back down on its designated plate, "I should go. Thank you again for your hospitality, Lady Delilah."

"No, thank you. I have a feeling that we will become great allies. Always remember that you are doing the best that you can until you can do better. That is the kind of leader that you are." She looked into the empty fireplace and back at me, "You know, your parents never even looked twice in our direction when they ruled."

With a sudden sense of purpose, I rose from my seat and we walked to the entryway together. Bowing slightly, "I am not my parents, Lady Delilah. I hope to make amends on their behalf."

She smiled faintly, "You already have." She gave me a little wave goodbye.

Walking out of her cot, I closed the door behind me and turned around to see long, familiar hair bouncing through the crowd with a woodland and water sprite at her side.

Chapter 6
Niya

Sander, one of the very few woodland sprites that made it out of the attack a couple of years ago, kicked me in the shin.

I hissed at him, "What the hell, Sander!"

Cleome had become the sprites' new home after the destruction of their previous one at the lagoon.

Tallulah was able to find some of her friends. There were only a few, but it was enough.

Sander barked from below, "Would you look where you are going! I am trying to talk to you."

I bent down and placed my hand on the earth for him to walk up, "If I had known you wanted to talk, I would have picked you up; like now."

Sander was a petite, very tan wood sprite with short, curly red hair. He wore leaves to cover his most private areas.

He placed his hands over his chest and his minuscule translucent green wings twitched. Sander was the only woodland sprite to make it out of the lagoon alive, which resulted in him becoming very surly.

"We need our lagoon back, Niy. You know we do. We miss the peace and quiet. Cleome is too busy," Sander waggled his fingers and scrunched his tiny face in disgust.

I sighed, "I know, Sand, I am trying. It is just so—"

Sander cut me off, "So what, Niya?! It has been years!"

My eyes shifted away from him with guilt. Tallulah, who had been splashing in a small puddle nearby, flitted up next to Sander, "We need you now. Listen, Niy, you have done a great job taking care of us, but we need more. We need our home back," she begged, placing her hands sternly on her hips.

I blurted, "Would you please!" I glided my hand through my hair, "Please, I need a moment."

I needed to take a moment to breathe. I had tried several times to heal the land; it *refused* nourishment and mending. It felt impossible. I hadn't been taught healing magic, but it almost seemed like there was a taint on that piece of land.

"Niy niy," Tallulah squeaked, "We love you; we really do. We just want to go home."

The tinkling sound of Sander weeping drew my attention. I looked at him resting on my hand in a rolled-up ball.

Even though he was usually grumpy, he could also be melodramatic.

"I am trying," my voice was low, "Please just be patient with me."

The scent of birch and eucalyptus tantalized my nose, and I dropped my hand, sending Sander fluttering to the ground.

He cursed under his breath from the forest floor. I clenched my fists and furrowed my brows, looking for the source of that scent.

The male was beelining toward me.

I shot a glance at both of the sprites, and they flitted away in haste. I turned on my heel and pushed through milling dryads trying to avoid the Seelie King.

I heard the rustle of leaves behind me. I spun around to see those stupid blue eyes watching me.

"Fancy seeing you here, Princess," The King of Haldonia smiled broadly.

"Are you stalking me, Your Kingliness?"

"Please, call me Adryen," he paused, incredulous, "I would never stalk you. That is creepy."

I flared my nostrils, "That's hard to believe considering your history."

Adryen raised an eyebrow, "Considering my *history?*"

"Yes, your history of murder. Did you stalk my lagoon before you demolished it?" I shot with utter spite.

He did not reply; he did not move. He didn't even send a lick of emotion.

We stared at each other for a long while without blinking.

An eternity passed, and the king finally replied, "I am not an intentional killer, Niya. It was not supposed to go that way, I did not know what I was signing off on. I am truly sorry. Please, forgive me."

His facial features softened and in reaction, so did mine, "Adryen," I grabbed his hand and he winced under my palm, "I—"

Wow, he was really upset about what I said. I dropped my hand from his and his expression went neutral, like he was here, but he wasn't.

"I am not a killer," he looked down at me, "I have witnessed death firsthand. I would never take another's life. It just isn't in me."

Thinking about this carefully, I questioned, "Then why did you sign off on something like that?"

"I just started ruling, my advisor did a lot of the the heavy lifting while teaching me at the same time. I had no clue until just recently what exactly I had signed off on. I learned my lesson on this, though."

He couldn't have been *that* terrible of a king, considering that he had so many supporting him now .

"Can we agree to just leave each other alone?"

He placed his hand on my cheek and my emotions sparked in surprise when Adryen whispered, "I will never leave you alone," and snapped a portal to life in front of us.

"Then you will have to chase me," I winked.

He chuckled and said to me before leaving, "Challenge accepted, Princess."

I rolled my eyes so far into the back of my head, they probably could have stayed there.

I watched Adryen's crackling portal disappear and transversed myself back to the castle.

∞∞∞∞

I charged into Rose's room, still reeling; she stared, agape, at me from her midnight black leather chaise. Book in one hand and an empty wine glass in the other she noted, "Why do you look like you are about to kill someone?"

I plopped on her luscious velvety black bedding and fell backward onto the bed hugging a pillow and trying to catch my breath, "Because I am!"

"Spill. Wait—we need more wine." She shook her glass.

Rose set her book down on the floor and I snapped my fingers, distractedly. A whimsical, galaxy-like entryway portal appeared in front of me. This was my favorite magic. Little portals to hidden places in the castle that I had created for secreted items. I slipped my hand through and grabbed two bottles of wine from the cellar.

As I placed the wine bottles on the bed and closed the portal, Rose squealed. "That gift is *amazing*. Teach me your ways," she fawned exaggeratingly. She got up off of her lounge and grabbed another wine glass from her nightstand. She was either expecting company and I had interrupted, or she knew I would be up here.

I shrugged, "I wish I could. You know these powers just come naturally, Rose. As long as the land is under my feet, my magic holds true. "

"I have never seen powers like yours, or your brothers. They are so substantially different than most Unseelie. It's crazy. Either way, I still hate you for being so perfect." Rose pouted her small mouth.

Smiling at her rather discomposed, I took the proffered empty glass. Rose held both of her eyebrows up at me and the open bottle ready to pour. Figuring this was her way of indicating that if I don't spill, neither will she.

"Anyway," I began with a deep breath, "The Seelie King was at Cleome today." I paused, looking at a wide-eyed and open-mouthed Rose. "I had stopped by for my regular visit with the sprites and he was just *there;* walking out of Lilah's cot. It just made me so angry. I don't even know why he was there, but I wanted to punch him. My rage shot up from one to a thousand. I forgot to ask why he was even in Kaldamir."

Rose stopped pouring. I tilted my head and scrunched my brows, "What?" I took the forgotten bottle of wine from my friend's hand and continued pouring us both a hefty glass.

Regaining her power of speech and finally blinking. "What did you say to him?"

Rose sipped from her wine glass and continued, "Did you rip him apart?"

I thought about it for a moment and scrunched up my face. Rose repeated, "Well, did you?"

"No. I mean, yes. I—I don't know. He seemed apologetic about the lagoon situation and claimed not to have remembered it. He said he would not have cleared his sentries to attack like that. I don't know; how does a king not know what he is signing off on?"

Rose, mouth agape like a fish, "Well..." shrugging her shoulders, "He is so *hot*! You should just forgive him," Rose squealed and that was my cue to chug some wine as she continued, "And do *not* say he is not hot, because I met him when he was here, and I swear...if his beautiful blue eyes hadn't made me wet, his wavy chestnut hair, tight ass, and trimmed facial hair topped with voluptuous lips did...you need to have sex with him."

"Wh—," I choked on my wine, managing to continue I blurted, "What in the gods? Are you done?"

"Girl, I have not even started," Rose mused completely seriously. "Niya, if you do not claim him, I will." She plopped back on her chaise and sunk into it like a cat nestling into bed for the night.

I thought she might start to purr.

"You know you can't claim him," I countered, a little offended.

"Fine, party pooper, just ruin the fantasy. He is still eye candy, and I will not stop looking at him," Rose finished off with a little nip of her teeth to the air between us and sipped some more of her wine.

My eyes wide and shaking my head, unboggling my mind, I decided on changing the subject, "Was I the only one who did not know this was happening? I feel really stupid for being so excluded."

"Know what was happening? King Whitebourne coming to Kaldamir?"

I gaped at her, "You know damn well I am not asking about that. Why was I so clueless as to not knowing about my own alliance slash arranged marriage?"

"Um, well..." Rose trailed off.

"Well, what?!" I took another big gulp of my wine.

"The Queen told us not to bother telling you. By us I mean, well, everyone. She knew you would not take it well and would even try to stop your own coronation. I really did not have any say in it. It was your mother, father, and I think Vallynn making the decisions about these next events leading up to your coronation."

"Vallynn helping with decisions?" I laughed at the thought that Vallynn was involved in this whole situation. I distinctly remember when he asked me if I'd heard something. I should have questioned him more then.

Sneaky bastard.

As close as we were, Vallynn did a lot more in the line of courtly duties than I did. I knew that, at some point, mother had him traipsing about the realm getting information on the Seelie Kingdom and its moves towards our border. I'd never really cared to take those matters into my own hands. Dealing in political matters was not my cup of tea but, that will soon have to come to an end.

"Yes, he was actually the one that suggested Queen Ravyn to invite The Seelie King. Vallynn thought it—"

Putting the pieces together, I realized Rose must have been doing some unsanctioned snooping. Rose was my spymaster within the walls. She was so incredibly sneaky and loved to snoop around in places she should not be. Rose was very good at being invisible when needed.

"—How?"

"I, uh, I was walking by the study a of couple weeks ago —"

"—A couple weeks ago?! Rose!" I let out a huge, annoyed, sigh, "You didn't care to tell me?"

"I'm sorry, My Lady," Rose slightly bowed her head. Rose only said this when I upset with her and she did not want to make matters worse.

Calm down, she is your friend.

There was probably a reason.

"Your brother caught me sneaking and threatened me," Rose continued.

"Threatened you, how?" These new shadows on my arm tightened in rage. I needed to figure out what the hell this was.

Later.

Rose looked up at me, "To have his parents wed me off to High Lord Morelli, so I would be dismissed from my services to you."

Angrily, "You will never be dismissed from my services Rose...we have a blood oath. High Lord Morelli has not set foot in this castle in decades. Why would Vallynn threaten you with a withered up five-hundred-year-old fae? He has no authority to even say such a thing to you. Let alone the fact that you cannot just be wedded off to whomever."

"Oh."

Lord Morelli was one of our oldest ruling landowners. He controlled the majority of the south eastern lands called The Silver Expanse. This land is mostly inhabited by vampires and other bloodsucking creatures. This land also housed most of our mining and ironworks.

I had not seen Lord Morelli since he came begging my parents for funding to forge in The Wastelands. Of course, my parents refused, and he refused to come back sense.

Rose studied me, "You know he does have that authority. All of you do, you are the high ruling family in this land. He could say as much as 'kill her' and the sentries would have to oblige."

Rose was frightened about Vallynn's threat; I could feel her heart racing through our blood oath. I tried not to tap into our bond, but sometimes when emotions are high, we sort of broke the warded barriers of our bond in the most inconvenient of times.

"Do you still feel safe here, Rose?"

Rose did not answer for several minutes. I slowly sipped the last of my wine and got off of her bed. I stumbled, buzzed, over to Rose. Sitting on the chaise next to her, "You do not have to answer that." I hugged her tightly, "I love you, and I will not let anything happen to you. Vallynn can suck it. He will not threaten you again, I will make sure of it."

Rose smiled, "I love you too, Niya, now ward our bond again. I do not want you feeling my emotions anymore."

"You practice it. I showed you how to put up your mental wards. I will tell you when I cannot feel your emotions anymore."

Rose closed her eyes and her cheeks flushed as she started putting up the mental wards.

I tilted my head at Rose in amusement, "If you focus any harder, you might shit yourself." I chuckled at her attempt and our bond fell to silence, "You did it!"

Rose's eyes glittered, "Yay! That only took like so much of my magic. Next time, you just do it. Your magic seems never-ending anyways. Common fae aren't as lucky as you." Rose yawned and pointed at the wine bottles, "Leave those here when you leave. I want to hide those for a special occasion; like a Tuesday."

Standing up, feeling dizzy, I stumbled to the door. I took Rose's yawning as a hint she was done for the night, "What is happening on Tuesday?" I turned around to her one last time.

"When I work up the courage to invite the Seelie King back to my chambers next time he is here, and attempt to seduce his beautifully carved body into my bed," she rambled off as I backed into her doorframe.

"What does that...you know what, sleep, Rose. I will see you tomorrow."

Not thinking straight, and a little too drunk myself, I staggered and listed my way back down the stairs to the west wing, where my comfortable bed awaited.

Chapter 7
Niya

Waking up the next morning, I let out a luxuriant yawn and stretched.

Last night with Rose was nice. A girlfriend night was just what I needed.

I glanced over at the clock and stopped. It was midmorning!

Oh shit.

I'd missed Alman's training session.

A little note swirled from the void into view, and I read:

Training is cancelled. You come late again, and I will double your workload and make you cry.

-Alman

Oh, mother above.

I needed to set an alarm on my clock; or maybe just not have so much to drink.

Rushing to get ready for another day of bullshit courtly duties, I zoomed through my shower, hair, and makeup. Gliding to the closet I threw on a fitted mauve cowl neck gown with a revealing slit. Adjusting my crisscrossed spaghetti straps, I fenagled my dress over my chest. Placing my feet into nude slingback heels I tightened the straps. Looking over myself, not happy with how this dress was sitting on me, I frowned.

A knock sounded at my door and a small voice announced, "Niya."

Striding over to the door and cracking it open, Rose blurted, "Wow, you look stunning! You should dress like this more often. Your working clothes are such a drag."

I looked down, not knowing whether that was a compliment or an insult.

I said flatly, "I can't fight in a dress, Rose; but, thanks, I guess."

"Maybe you can wrestle King Whitebourne in that one!" Rose eyed my chest.

"I am starting to think that you are obsessed with him, Rose."

"Yeah, I am," Rose pined.

Making a retching sound, I closed the door to my room as we advanced toward the dining hall.

Crossing the threshold, I realized that Rose came to my bedroom for a reason. I asked, "Rose, I totally did not ask why you came to me this morning. What did you want?"

"Yeah, about that," she snapped back to her mundane court duties. "Breakfast was just cleaned up. Your mother sent me to check in on you since the courtiers missed your entrance this morning."

I flung my hands in the air in frustration that I would not be having breakfast today. So much for the blood-oath of a best friend.

Fuck.

I scowled, "When are these courtiers leaving again? Why didn't the Queen just send you to wake me up earlier?"

"Hopefully this afternoon. She is currently indisposed, but before leaving breakfast, she mentioned she had business matters to attend to with your father. So, she asked me to grab you from your room to give you some instructions for today."

"And mommy dearest did not care to feed her poor, starving, darling daughter?"

Rose shifted on her heels, and I waited for her to continue, "Please don't shoot the messenger," she paused for my reaction and then continued, "Your mother has sort of a list of things to do today with the guests. It started with breakfast—that you missed—and continues on from there."

"Rose, get on with it," I was getting irritated due to *food* not being forthcoming.

"Sorry, Niya. She is expecting you to give The King of Haldonia the grand tour today until about dinnertime."

"Grand tour! Like around the entire city?"

Rose curtly stated, "Yes."

I mumbled, "Fine. But I am only doing this because I don't want to piss of the Evil Queen."

Rose giggled in response "That she is. Oh—," she stopped smiling now, "I have sent for the first in command to guard you while in the city."

"Garrin?"

"Yes."

I groaned, "Thank you Rose, I will grab something quick to eat and get this tour done and over with."

Rose dismissed herself, striding in the opposite direction.

Walking towards the kitchen, I looked down in deep thought.

The scent of eucalyptus hit my nostrils and flowed down the back of my throat. Before I could look up, I slammed into him catching myself before falling backwards.

I peered up.

Adryen was wearing gray trousers and a light blue buttoned down shirt that accentuated every toned curve. He had a couple buttons undone on the top showing off his broad neck and a dusting of hair peeking out. His wavy, chestnut hair was neatly combed with a couple of loose strands falling in front of his forehead.

His cornflower blue eyes stared deeply into mine, "Hello, Princess."

"Don't stare at me that way," I growled.

"Stare at you like what? I swear I can't win with you."

I shrugged my shoulder, "You get used to it."

King Adryen chuckled, "You are absolutely adorable when you are angry," he said as a sexy smirk appeared on his face.

I looked up from the floor at his comment. His eyes trailed down my body, examining me. Adryen taking in every ounce of me on display, made me shift my weight uncomfortably. My breasts tightened unexpectedly at his lingering gaze.

"Please stop. This day is already going to be long enough; you don't need to make it worse."

The king proceeded, "So, despite your proclaimed hatred of me, I brought you a pastry. Consider it a peace offering."

Adryen placed a wrapped pastry in my hand and gave a gentle smile, "I noticed you liked them."

Vallynn should have taken him on a tour of the city. I was not in the right mental headspace to do this right now. I needed to just walk away before I dragged this gorgeous male to an alcove somewhere and stabbed him to death...or thought of something else to do to him.

I raised an eyebrow to myself, damn, I am really vicious today.

Adryen raised an eyebrow at me, "What are you thinking about?"

I decided to have some fun with the Seelie. I wanted to rattle his cage a little; unsettle him. I cooed, "About how much I want to take you somewhere private and fuck you until you scream my name."

"I...well," Adryen cleared his throat, eyes darting around, "That was forward of you."

I laughed at him, "I am Unseelie. Everything I do is 'forward,' Your Kingliness." I took a bite of the delicious berry and spice pastry and my mouth watered.

So delicious.

"If you think I am being serious, you need a lesson in irony."

Heavy footsteps trailed behind us, and a deep voice rumbled, "Your Highness."

I turned my head at Garrin who had his hand on the pommel of his sword waiting for my reply, "Let's go, Garrin. Apparently, I need a babysitter to accompany me into my own city."

Garrin grunted at my remark, "The tension in the air leans more toward chaperone duties, Niya."

I closed my eyes and breathed through my nose. Facing forward to continue walking, I scowled to myself, "I don't need you to protect my virtue, you brooding sentry. Don't make me kick your ass."

Garrin raised an eyebrow as if he wanted to challenge me.

Adryen chuckled at us, "I would *love* to see that."

I glowered at the both of them, "Let's go. I don't have all day."

We walked out of the castle toward the front entrance.

We began the tour with one of Kaldamir's more impressive cities. I'd always loved the city of Khine. Towering buildings shielded us from the rising sun as I slid my hand along the iron gates with calm contentment. Our kingdom was broken into several smaller lands we call districts. These districts all had qualities that made them unique yet equally enchanting.

Garrin opened the gates leading us to the frenetic city.

Adryen's face was beaming as I peered over to him, "This is your kingdom?" He said, mouth agape.

Giggling, I replied, "No. I will show you the city of Khine. Our kingdom would take weeks to tour, and you only have what? Just today here?" I asked with trepidation.

"Just today, I head back home this evening, but I should be back in plenty of time for your coronation," Adryen frowned a little, peeking back out to the charming city.

His somber mood turned spellbound as he glanced up at the massive buildings and crowds of patrons and merchants astir in the streets. I stared at Adryen's wonderfully pure and guileless countenance, and despite myself, my heart flipped a little.

Rose was right, he was fucking gorgeous.

Damn her!

King Adryen looked entranced, "Hold on, just what we see here is Khine and no other city?"

"Yes, this is our business district. Merchants and business owners from all around Kaldamir meet here to trade and sell their wares."

"It is breathtaking," He trailed off, "I have never seen Khine in person, but the books I have read about your kingdom do not do this city any justice. The buildings alone..." He trailed.

"Yes, it is," hiding a small smile and fighting the urge to reach out to him.

Walking on for a while and conversing about Khine and some of the history of how this city came to be, Adryen stopped.

We paused our walk-in front of Lord Zahar's merchant stand selling flowers and I thought back to Adryen frowning when we entered the city, "Why did you look displeased when I asked when you were leaving?"

He huffed, "Heh, well would you believe me if I told you?"

"Uh, try me."

I was genuinely not shocked that he would ask that. After all, we hadn't exactly had a history of open and honest communication. I would think that he would have several reasons to doubt my willingness to believe him.

"Well, I would like to stay a couple more days and continue to get to know you before I have to to go back to my kingdom tonight. Unfortunately, duty currently makes it impossible to extend my stay," Adryen paused, and it looked like he was thinking about his next words, "Seeing this beautiful city and being able to spend time with you, without you screaming at me is something I want more of. I have never been filled with such awe," his eyes dropped back to mine.

I started to think that maybe I *should* try to get to know this male.

My mind wandered back to my mother mentioning an alliance. I was of a royal Unseelie bloodline, and he is of royal Seelie blood. We were born enemies.

I asked, "Why are you so forthcoming with me? Aren't we supposed to be doomed mortal enemies?"

"Well, as you already know, I want to form an alliance with you when you ascend your throne. Being 'forthcoming' is the only option, Princess."

I shook my head in confusion and frustration that I had been so removed from the politics of our kingdom, "Why?"

Adryen said straightly, "Haldonia is dying. My cities are overcrowded, and we do not have any more room to grow. I am using my magic to help as much as possible with the needs of my court and its peoples, but..." he trailed off, "My magic can only go as far as the land itself. Same with yours. Knowing how massive your lands are, I accepted your mother's invitation to this event and to your coronation in hopes of her granting Haldonia some of the land back that Kaldamir took."

Took?!

That was not what happened.

"So...you want to try to make things better by coming to my mother and trying to charm her into giving you land? Adryen, you are so naïve. Queen Ravyn is clearly playing you! She will not simply *give* you *our* land. Do you not know what happened centuries ago with our families?"

My mind was flipping through historical documents on the Blood Wars.

"I know enough that this has been going on for too long. My people need more space and I need your help." Adryen paused, then continued, "I am also here because I need to find my counterpart. My people are getting restless with only one ruler on the throne. Being Seelie, our magic feeds from a king and a queen. Without a queen, my people cannot fully thrive."

He was here to try to take back land and find a mate.

No...queen.

Finding your mate, the other half to your whole, is uncommon. With our kingdoms divided, there had not been a mated pair in many centuries. The last mated fae that I had even read about was the Unseelie King Zephry Blackbyrn and his Queen Isabella Whitebourne.

This was an unwanted mating bond that led to pure chaos in our realm. Both their magic and politics were so divided that they caused the Blood Wars, causing a cataclysmic divide in the land. Since then, both royal families had kept their magic tied to their perspective lands causing The Great Divide to sprout up from the earth between the two. Its thick thorny edges were like the wall they'd used to try and protect their hearts with.

We continued walking through the merchant stands and I pondered Adryen's words of finding his 'counterpart', "Why not just find someone in your own kingdom? You are what? Forty years old? There are probably so many females waiting for your hand in your own court. There is one of your many problems solved."

"There are no eligible high ladies in Haldonia...I am twenty-eight and my other problems will be resolved when your mother and I come to a satisfactory agreement."

Holy mother of gods, he was so young.

"Agreement? What agreement?"

"If I marry you, she will give me more land," Adryen said with all transparency.

I put my hand on Adryen's forearm, stopping him. Turning him to face me so we could see eye to eye, I bellowed, "I am sorry, but are you saying that you came here in efforts to expand your lands by *courting* me?"

"No, I came here to acquire more land and make you my Queen. I am a King, I do not *court* females."

"What the fuck, Adryen?!"

Adryen could not possibly be this blinded by Queen Ravyn's motives and about the ease with which he could win *me*.

Adryen looked at me, baffled, "This can be a mutually beneficial agreement," his head lowered, peering at me through dark lashes.

My rage started to build and the shadows on my arm lashed out and grasped Adryen's neck. I snickered at this fresh new magic flowing through me, "I do not want any arrangements with you; business or otherwise...*King*."

I refused to be used as a pawn in someone else's game.

I closed my eyes and my shadows tightened fiercely around his neck.

The King of Haldonia choked, "Niya—please, I don't want to hurt you."

My eyes snapped open, and I bared my teeth at him, "Go home King Whitebourne. If I so much as see your face here again, I will rip your spine out and dangle it from a thorn on The Great Divide for everyone to see."

Adryen growled at me and grasped my shadows and ripped them off of his neck. They scurried back to me, and a slight twinge hit my arm as he roared, "No!"

Stunned, "How did you..." I trailed off. Adryen just grasped *my* shadows and pulled them away like they were nothing.

He was incredibly powerful.

That was kind of hot.

No, no it was not.

He wanted to use me, and *that* was not okay.

I twisted my head over to look at Garrin as he gripped tightly to his pommel, ready to attack or defend. The nosey group of people surrounding us stopped and gaped at our quarrel. Snapping my head back to Adryen, I grabbed his wrist and started to transverse us just outside of the city where the forest lay open and private.

"I will not *deal* with you in front of my people," I seethed.

"Niya!" Garrin shouted as we vanished.

Adryen hit the floor on all four limbs and vomited.

"Sorry, I guess I should have warned you to close your eyes and think happy thoughts before I transversed us," I smirked.

Adryen continued to puke up his guts. A satisfied chuckle escaped me despite my rage.

Looking at his unkempt appearance, I continued, "You freaking prick!"

"What!" Adryen managed to say over his puking.

He wiped his lips with the back of his hand, and I knocked him over onto the snowy ground and planted a spiked heel onto the middle of his back so he could not move.

He held in the rest of his stomach contents, and I completely unhinged. I reached for Celeste to try to kill this fucker, but she was not sheathed to my thigh.

Fucking perfect.

Baring teeth, I shouted in frustration, "Tell me exactly why you have business here."

Adryen spun and grabbed my ankle as he flung me to the ground. My head hit the outskirts of the forest where the snow bunched up and I groaned in pain.

Hovering over top of me, Adryen growled, "I already told you. My magic is tied to the land because of my bloodline. Since I am the Seelie King, it is my duty to uphold the needs of my people. Oh gods!" Adryen held up one finger and paused looking like he was going to retch again.

Deciding he wasn't going to spew for the moment, he opened his mouth again to continue, "My kingdom is overpopulated and in order for me to continue using my magic I need more land and a queen. And for me to be able to have more land, I need to marry *you*. I get both with one agreement."

This time, Adryen's efforts to stave off his retching failed, and he turned to the side and released the rest of the contents of his stomach.

My fists bunched with clumps of dirt and grass as I reached for his face as if wiping off a string of saliva and vomit, "Here, let me just get that for you."

I rubbed my hand down to his jaw leaving a dark smudge across his face, "Much better."

My smug satisfaction hidden, "I will not marry you, King Whitebourne and there is no 'agreement'."

Thoughts started churning in my head. My coronation date and the onset of my courtly duties were no coincidence. It was strategically placed so I could meet and greet all the eligible fae males at once. Knowing that Adryen was King, and what my prophecy stated...

That cunning raven. She had some master plan, and I would have to enlist my spymaster to help me expose it.

"Niya," Adryen got on his feet and continued, "This could be something spec—"

"—I will not be coerced into marrying someone like you!" I ran my fingers through my hair fully, regretting everything that just came off my lips.

Adryen put his rough index finger to my lip snarling under his breath, "Let me finish, vexatious beauty."

I slapped his hand away and stood up off of the forest floor, wiping my lips on my bare shoulder, "You just put your filthy puke-covered finger on my perfectly clean lips!"

"I could put something else on those lips if you would like, Princess," Adryen retorted.

Oh, shit.

Wiping myself down as much as possible, I started to pace in psychomotor agitation, thinking of how I was going to get out of this; first starting with leaving here and then ending with possibly killing Adryen out of pure hatred of him.

I reached for Celeste again out of habit, and she *still* was not there.

Fuck you, you stupid whore of a blade.

I exhaled in frustration. Adryen looked at me extremely concerned as I crossed back and forth in front of him like a caged cat. I could not transverse again so soon; I would look like Adryen did several minutes ago on the floor retching if I did it again now.

I only have one option.

Looking down at my gorgeous heels in concession, "Damnit, I liked these shoes," Backing up further from Adryen, I bolted into a full sprint back to the castle through the forest.

I had to get away from him, from my family, and from this path that had been chosen for me. I ran on the balls of my feet, wending through the trees back to the castle. This was going to be a long journey home in the cold. The warming magic stopped at the city line, and that was far behind me now. Snow pelted my face as I tried to create a greater distance between The King of Haldonia and myself.

I couldn't hear anything behind me. I turned my head as I ran to see where he was. Just then, I sensed a huge *whoosh* directly above my head. The wind striking my head and shoulders suddenly froze me in place for a moment. I looked up and nothing was there. I should have taken my chances with transversion.

The ground rumbled as a puff of hot moist air hit my neck and chin. I snapped my head around and what I saw made me fall backward, slamming into a thick blanket of snow. Shock and fear rolled through me as I wriggled on my bottom backward, staring at this massive beast hovering over me.

Familiar cornflower blue eyes glowered down at me.

Adryen.

This terrifying blue iridescent dragon-like creature with two faded midnight blue legs and large leathery scales growled at me, inching closer. I shrieked and tried to get to my feet. My whole body went numb from the cold and it was hard to move. There was nothing I could do but try to outrun him. I was not afraid of Adryen the fae, but I *was* afraid of Adryen the wyvern.

My feet ached, and my breath shook.

I settled my hand into the plush snow and created a solid ice longsword. Wrapping my hand around the hilt of my newly manifested sword, I aimed it at wyvern Adryen, and shouted, "Back off," trying to keep the shake out of my voice.

It was not a real sword, but it was pointed enough to pierce and made me feel slightly better than being wholly weaponless.

We stared at each other for what felt like an eternity. Hot air blew out of both of our mouths as we waited for the other to make a move. My body pricked with bumps as I just stood there, entranced yet frightened by this alluring creature.

The longer I stared at him, however, the less terror I felt.

Wyverns were extinct but, I was staring into the eyes of a creature that was very much not.

I advanced with my icy sword and Adryen pushed hot steam out of his nostrils at me. My sword melted to a dull weeping pole. My body engulfed in this warm steam; my legs gave out.

No.

Dropping to my knees on the ground, I had decided that there was only one thing I could do to escape.

Void, please be kind to me.

Squeezing my eyes shut, I transversed back to my mother's wing of the castle, leaving behind the wyvern, Adryen.

I burst through my mother's chambers wet and disheveled. She was sitting at her vanity, brushing her onyx hair. She jumped a little at the slamming of the door behind me.

She frowned into the mirror at my appearance, "You look like shit. Did you and The King of Haldonia wrestle, darling? You were just supposed to take him on a tour."

Bile rose up into my throat and I keeled over, heaving up a liquid mess into a nearby can. I immediately felt my body with my hands, making sure every part was still attached and in the right place. Everything checked out perfectly, except for my aching feet.

Oh, thank the gods, I am still in one piece.

My mother batted her brush at me, "I would take that as a yes; I hope that means I will be attending a wedding soon."

Oh, if she only knew.

Adryen was a freaking extinct creature! I could not wrap my mind around it.

I continued, "I did take him on a tour, mother," belching, trying to hold back my stomach contents, I murmured, "I learned *so* much new information! When were you going to tell me about this 'alliance' being an *arranged marriage?*"

Struggling to get to my feet, I backed up closer to the door, leaving room for a quick escape if I needed it.

"Oh," she allowed herself a quick laugh, "I was not planning on telling you at all until the papers were signed by the King and awaiting *your* signature. Vallynn did a rather fine job of getting the king to come here in efforts to that end."

I opened my mouth to reply, and she chimed, "Yes, Niya, I was planning an arranged marriage for you; since you ask and, no, I am not going to give Haldonia any of our land; just you."

"Just me! Are you kicking me out?"

"It's not kicking you out if you have had your coronation, now is it?" A cunning grin crossed her face, "My plan is to have you ascend, marry Adryen, and then kill him so we can have the entire realm to ourselves again." She snapped her fingers and the entryway to her chamber swung open, almost hitting me on my back.

Yelling, I spewed, "WHAT?!"

"Get out; we are done."

I glared at her and scowled, "No!"

Darkness covered the room and my mother's eyes turned a dark blood red, "You will do as I say, child. If I want to marry you off, I will. If I want to kill you, I will. You are not any different than any other subject in the realm, Niya. You will marry Adryen, and then you will kill him. Not only will it benefit us as a kingdom, but it will also save you, my dear."

I know I said I wanted to kill him because of the sprite sanctuary, but I did not really mean it. Not literally. I really didn't like him, but I did not want him dead. This new information about Adryen being a wyvern really changed my views of him. He was a creature our kingdom had not seen in centuries.

He must be protected.

At all costs.

My lip curled and I snarled at her, "You can't do this! There has got to be another way to avoid my prophetic fate. I will not marry him."

"Yes, you will," her eyes faded back to their normal irises, "In the meantime it is time to start your courtly duties. You have put them off long enough."

I tried to calm myself by taking in a deep breath before stalking out of Queen Ravyn's room. My thoughts and emotions were a tornado. My mother's intentions were duplicitous, while Adryen's were simple and transparent.

Adryen didn't deserve this.

I placed the palms of my hands on my forehead and yelled out into the air.

I needed to leave.

Now!

Chapter 8
Adryen

The utter terror in Niya's eyes when she beheld my true form sent me unraveling.

I felt kicked in the gut.

I had hoped that when she found out, we would have already formed some sort of trust and even relationship. I had wanted to show her that I was not here to manipulate or use her. When she ran away from me, I panicked, and my wyvern just reacted.

Ugh, I am an idiot.

I had waited so long to meet her; I felt like I knew everything about her. Haldonia had spies sent by my parents to learn about Kaldamir. They were always trying to find a way to help our kingdom. Everything they wrote about Princess Niya was true.

She was a goddess.

Despite her family background and how she grew up, she was fun and playful. Something I was not expecting at all from the Unseelie royal family.

I knew she would not want to marry, let alone try to create some sort of treaty with my kingdom but, I had to try. I did want to help Haldonia and its people, but I would be lying to myself if I said that the idea of meeting and possibly marrying Niya wasn't of strong interest to me as well.

She was amazing.

She was everything I could have ever wished for and more.

She was irreverent and strong; she was beautiful and bawdy; she was sweet, and she had a warrior heart.

I gave myself a running start and flew back to where I had placed my clothes. Landing hard on the ground, I shifted back into my fae form. Bumps surfaced to my skin from the cold, and I slipped my clothes back on.

I couldn't be here anymore.

Not only was this damned place too cold for me, but I had officially fucked up everything for my kingdom. The sprite sanctuary had been the first strike, and this...this was the second.

More land, and a queen was very much off the table now. All that land not being used or reconstructed. I shook my head in disgust.

Walking back to the palace in the dark, dejected, my stomach started folding itself inside out from hunger. I didn't know how long it had been since I'd last eaten. I entered the foyer and looked around; I saw no one. I was glad that I didn't have to see or talk to anyone.

What time is it?

Glancing over to this enormous grandfather clock, it stated eleven forty-five. It took me more than a couple of hours to get back to the palace.

Walking by the reflective glass that hung on the wall, I noticed a dark smudge on my jaw in the same spot that Niya suspiciously touched in the guise of wiping off the remnants of my puking.

"I should have known" I chuckled wiping off the grime, "I would expect nothing less."

My heart sank a little at the thought of her now.

She hated me. She hated me for something I did not fully take part in. Or, better yet, did not remember. Or care to remember.

I don't know.

I hurt her, without even realizing it and, in turn, that hurt me. I thought about whether I should approach Niya before I left.

Don't be ridiculous.

You have done enough to upset her; no need to open that wound.

But I couldn't help myself. Something was calling me to her. I felt the insides of my body tighten at the thought of having her full lips touch mine again and those beautiful green gold-flecked eyes staring into me; seeing me.

I shook my head, getting rid of those thoughts.

A short time later, I created a transference spell and walked through the crackling portal to my castle gates.

Arriving at the gates, I felt like I could breathe a little deeper.

Home.

I looked around and spied shadows dancing underneath a nearby Bougainvillea tree. With a deep, purifying breath, I closed my eyes and turned my face to the sun, hoping for it to wash away the frost built up in my bones. Sensing my arrival, the castle gates opened for me, welcoming me home.

I took my time walking up the path and took in all the beauty. The grounds were manicured, with pops of color everywhere: purples, pinks, red, and yellows. There were creeping and flowering vines clinging to the castle walls, bringing the eye all the way up to the castle spires at the top. Coming to one of the stone benches near the side entrance, I sat, head in my hands, not being able to get my mind off of *her.*

Looking up at the sound of boots on gravel, I was greeted by my advisor, Finion. His brown eyes stared at me, "Your majesty, it's late. We were expecting you earlier."

I would had been here earlier if I did not need to worry about my damned wyvern in the open...that close to Kaldamir.

"Welcome home," he paused then continued, "How did the tour go? Were you able to speak to the princess about the agreement and the lands?"

We trailed into the castle, and I responded, "Fin, it was terrible. I fucked up."

"I am sure you didn't, your highness. It is hard for someone like you to mess up. Of course, besides the sprite incident."

I glared at Fin, who smirked in return.

"I think I might have caused more friction between our kingdoms. I said way more than I should have to both the queen and her daughter. I was being played, Finion. The queen does not want to share land. I think she just wanted to marry off her daughter to me for plans of her own."

"What does that mean?"

"I don't know what the Queen has in her plan. I have addendums to them. We need to figure out how to expand our land and fast."

My service staff bowed deeply towards me as Fin and I made our way into the common room. I reached for the brandy and poured myself a glass.

Slumping down into a seat, I asked, "Do you have any ideas?"

"Well, you could always trick the princess into falling in love with you and seal in your fates that way."

I gawked at him, "I am surprised you would think I need to trick someone to fall in love with me, Finion. Only the Unseelie would deceive someone like that."

"You could use Niya's prophecy to your advantage."

Her prophecy.

Niya's mom explained that once the princess taps into her darker side of magic that her body will manifest into something otherworldly and possibly die. She would not be herself anymore. Usually, prophecies disclose how to remedy them but, her mother didn't care to tell that part to me.

Apparently, familial fealty means nothing to the Unseelie.

"How would I use her prophecy to benefit us? It's just about how much power she will attain. If she holds too much at one time, she will die."

"Exactly."

"I do not want to mess with Niya in that way. She is not to be harmed, by anyone."

"Did you catch feelings?"

I lied, "No; who could love an Unseelie fae," and took a sip of my brandy, averting my gaze, "Especially her. She has made it very clear that she has no intentions of starting anything with me."

"Well, then we should have no problem with this plan."

"Finion, if you want to keep your tongue, I suggest you shut the fuck up."

He got the hint that I was done discussing this with him. Fin bowed deeply and excused himself from my presence.

Running my fingers through my hair, I gulped down the rest of my drink, feeling my very foundation crumbling beneath me.

Chapter 9
Niya

Turning on my *wonderful* shower, I waited for the steam to roll up to the ceiling before stepping in. I stood under the warm and calming water and let out a long breath that I felt like I'd been holding in for hours. Warm rivulets of water ran down my defrosting body and I scrubbed the affairs of state off of me. When I'd finished, I wrapped a plush towel around my body and another, less fluffy one, on my hair and sat down at my vanity.

Closing my eyes for a moment and rubbing at my temples, I let out a puff of air and a groan.

I needed to go see Sahriah and have *several* drinks.

I painted my face to look like a lady of the night: dark, smokey eyeshadow, red satin lips with a touch of shimmer. I led myself out of the bathroom and to my closet. I slid on a tight, strapless little sable dress that revealed way more than even I normally would. Looking at my shoe options, I pulled out matching platform stiletto heels with bows on the backs. Lacing them up, I thought how much I really needed an escape.

Maybe I would get lucky and find a handsome fae at the club.

I sprinted down the stairs of the castle and out the front entrance. Strutting towards our industrial shop, I entered the towering metal building and heaved the steel door open.

Bellow, our mechanic, stood and nodded to me.

I asked, "How is my baby doing?" I was concerned about Blackstar since my last trip to Khine.

"Well, Niy, considering you were drag-racing down Khine's motorized roads with a bunch of damned idiots...I would say he is doing a lot better. I had to replace your charging amulet though," Bellow looked at the bracelet hanging from the handlebar of my slick black motorcycle, "Amulets do not just spontaneously regenerate, Your Highness. Please be careful with this new one. It would take me months to acquire another."

I examined Blackstar and he looked good as new. Fully treaded fatty in the back allowing for a killer traction control, that I managed to subvert one night in Khine. Bellow did a fantastic job repainting and fixing the concrete marks left from the drag race.

I ran my fingers down Blackstar and grinned, "Thank you, Bell."

"Anytime, Niya. Just be careful; anymore crazy stunts and I will have to build a new cycle for you and Blackstar will have to be laid to rest." Bellow answered, wiping his greasy hands on his shop towel.

I squealed with excitement and snapped my fingers. A pure blackout aero tuned shelled helmet with a blackout eye shield landed in my hand. I slipped the leathery bracelet on my wrist and activated the purple amulet to start the bike. Shuffling my hair behind me, I slipped on my helmet.

Blackstar roared awake as I revved him up.

I hopped aboard and bolted out of the shop towards The Silver Expanse.

Parking in front of the club, I deactivated my amulet and stepped off Blackstar. Pulling off my helmet and fixing stray strands of hair, I took in the view of my most prized acquisition: the Nyte Club.

The Club was an old historic building that came to life every night with males and females looking for some fun. This club had everything any fae could want: a luscious bar, huge dance floor, lots of places to sit and socialize and, of course, private rooms.

I found this hidden gem many years ago when I'd decided I'd wanted to start a business. After so many years of living, I'd had to come up with some creative ways to keep myself busy.

This club was one of them.

I purchased it for my own, renovated the entire building and opened it up for the citizens of Kaldamir.

I glanced at the unusual, broody, and brawny elf, Leer. He winked at me as I walked closer to the club. Leer had long, straight, fire-red hair that he somehow seemed to beautifully braid and always keep tidy.

Leer was probably the only elf ballsy enough to stay and live here in The Silver Expanse for as long as he had. Elves were not known to dwell in the iron district. They usually live in the other districts like the business district or Metrika Bazaar, where they could use their magic to create elixirs and train in our armies.

With glowering forest green eyes, Leer looked at me and mumbled gruffly, "Haven't seen ya here in an incredibly long time, sweetness. I don't think y'will be happy with the changes made by yer staff."

I stated acutely, "I've been busy with courtly duties. Also, my staff have every right to change what they need to accommodate the club's population, Leer."

Leer smirked, "Welcome back, m'lady," he gestured inside, and I walked past him into the glittering lights and pounding music of the club.

Fighting my way past dancing bodies and too-close encounters, I sat myself at the bar and watched my old friend, Sahriah. I hadn't been here in a couple of months, and she had not reached out to me with any concerns. Sahriah turned her head towards me and squealed in excitement.

She was stunning.

All vampires were.

Sahriah glowed with her deep golden eyes, and plump, ebony-painted lips that hid her long fangs. Her finely shaped ears that came to a delicate point peaked a little out of her cropped midnight-black pin straight hair.

Sahriah pulled out elixirs and made my usual concoction for me: ecstasy, a muscle relaxer and some sort of purple liquid that made my insides warm in a way that always ended in a really good night or a really terrible one.

Her drinks were divine.

I was not sure how she curbed the elixir taste, but I had learned not to ask questions.

She was the best and *only* bartender for this club.

I took the shot and said, "I missed you!" By the time I'd finished my sentence, she had my second drink ready for me.

"I heard," she frowned, "about your mother's wonderfully devious plans. The whole kingdom knows. I am shocked the high lords haven't been knocking at your door, asking for your hand."

Wow, news travels fast, and I seem to be getting the tail end of this bullshit.

"The only one that has is Adryen Whitebourne," I raised my glass in the air in salute, and downed my second drink.

"The King of Haldonia is in Kaladmir?" Sahriah tilted her head in amusement, "What a treat. Hopefully he does not get killed by the Unseelie courtiers."

"*Was* in Kaldamir." I looked back at Sahriah, "Make me one more drink before I lose my mind, please. Can you add something to make me forget today? I had to entertain the king by taking him on a tour. Yay me. I do not know how much more of this I can take."

Sahriah smirked at this, "Yes...I can, but you need to tell me everything I missed in the last couple of months; including this business with the Seelie King." I smiled and told her everything. From my studies to the smutty books that I read. I also told her about my training in the ring and my tour with Adryen.

Sahriah gently placed her hand on my forearm at this last admission and looked at me, head down and eyes up, "Are you serious right now? Do you know what that sounds like, sweetie?"

Sahriah paused, letting a heavy sigh out, "A perfect life."

I blinked slowly, allowing her comment to sink in.

I continued before we spent any more time on the subject, "The King of Haldonia is a wyvern."

"I believe it."

I tilted my head at her response, furrowing my brows, "I also have these weird shadows that have shown up on my arm. My mother says it is because of my prophecy but I wanted to see if you could help me with both this and the king being a wyvern."

Drying a cleaned glass, Sahriah spewed, "Forget the wyvern situation. Show me your arm, now!"

I lifted my arm, and she backed up from me continuing, "What the hell is that?"

"My arm; you asked to see it." I looked around nervously.

Sahriah fiddled around under the bar mumbling to herself and dragged out a ginormous book that thudded loudly on the table as she dropped it. This book had to be at least four inches thick, eighteen inches tall, and twelve inches wide. I didn't know how she could even lift the thing.

"Normally, shadows on any fae are a shadow bond, but I do not think this is that scenario. They look different; darker," Sahriah stated, pulling out her tiny half-moon glasses from thin air and placing them on her button nose. She opened the book and waded furiously through the pages.

I leaned over to watch her, and she hissed, "Do not *look*. Do not *touch*. Do not even *think* about this book."

I threw my hands in the air, "Okay fine; sheesh. Is there anything about wyverns in there?"

"Stop asking me about your wyvern," Sahriah shot back. She looked at me above her halfmoon reading glasses. "You don't know what magic has gotten its mark on you."

"He is not *my* wyvern. He is far from that. I don't want anything to do with him. I just want to know how the hell he *is* one."

Scrolling vigorously through page after page and running her delicate finger down a particular one, "Ah, here," She stopped and pointed at the tiniest of script.

I squinted my eyes, trying to read what she was pointing at, and failed.

Sahriah continued, "When a fae starts manifesting shadow magic...she will seize and die...and she will become drunk as fuck tonight if I give her something to forget what she did today. Oh! And if she asks me about this wyvern one more time, I might *literally* throw this book at her face."

Sahriah slammed the book shut and tucked it away under the bar.

I gawked at her, "Seize and die?! Sahriah, I hate you but love you at the same time."

She smiled, "I know. Give me time to research this and I will see what I can do. I might not be able to find anything right away so you might want to seek out Ca'Themar in the meantime while I look through my resources."

This is now the second time that crazy old priest had been mentioned. Maybe I *should* go see him. I shuddered at the thought of going to the temple.

That place is beyond creepy.

Making another shot for me, Sahriah placed it in hand's reach.

I prodded, "What do you know about wyverns? Kaldamir has not housed a wyvern since before The Blood Wars. The Seelie Kingdom killed all our shifters off, leading to their extinction."

Sahriah let out an annoyed breath of air, "You are *relentless*, Niya. Well...wyverns are an extinct breed. Here. In Kaldamir. Usually, only high males of royal blood carry that gene, like your king. However, there are rare cases where royal females carry that gene as well. It is very uncommon."

I shifted uncomfortably at her statement again, "He is not *my* king."

"Oh, come on Niya, you know better than anybody you already have that male wrapped around you so tight."

I shrugged my shoulders, "I doubt it. I have been very unkind to him."

Sahriah raised her eyebrows, "You, Niya? Mean?" She burst into ironic laughter.

"Maybe I could have the king as my pet wyvern. I would need to figure out a way to get to him." I narrowed my eyes.

"You could always puncture a hole in The Divide."

I raised my eyebrow, incredulous, "How?"

"Use a combination of your fire and ice magic," she shrugged. "It would wither the thorns and they would die...have you been practicing with those elements in between all of your courtly duties lately?"

I thought about the simplicity of her saying that and responded, "That seems too simple. And yes, actually. I have!"

"Is it simple, though? I mean, to you it is. But Niya, you are incredibly powerful."

I ignored her statement, "I've been learning how to manifest objects of fire."

Sahriah raised an eyebrow, "Like entirely made of *just* fire?"

"Yes."

Sahriah nodded approvingly as I smirked at her and snatched the shot glass in front of me.

I downed it and winced at the taste. That one was not so tasty, "Sahriah, that was disgusting. Don't torture me like this."

She laughed and shrugged as she walked away to help another fae. I reached over the bar top and grabbed a bottle of liquor waiting to be opened. After a moment she pranced back and I interrupted her before she could reprimand me for stealing alcohol, "So, tell me about these changes you made. Leer said I would not be happy."

Sahriah was my top staff member; my right hand. She ran and operated the Nyte Club when I had prolonged absences. She looked at me and frowned, "Leer can shut his trap. He does not help in the decision-making process, broody elf. This Nikolaj fellow has kind of set up camp here for his business meetings and affairs. So there have been changes in *that* aspect."

"Nikolaj? Like High Lord Nikolaj Morelli of The Silver Expanse?"

"I do not know his last name or where he affiliates. I just know he handles his business here and leaves with countless women."

That couldn't be the old fae that Vallynn had used to threaten Rose with.

Sahriah tried to snatch the liquor bottle back from me and sighed in frustration, "Put the alcohol back or you will be drunk within the hour," she paused; then continued, knowing I was not letting this wonderful bottle go, "He is here tonight, Nik, if you would like to meet him."

"Is he causing anybody any harm?"

"Just the ladies' male partners."

"Then no, I would not like to meet him."

Sahriah hesitated, "Do you want me to kick him out?"

"I trust you will handle this appropriately."

Sahriah shrugged as I took another swig of the liquor and stood up, leaving it on the counter. Feeling pretty good at this point, I saluted her goodbye and threw my arms up, swaying onto the dance floor. Bumping and grinding by myself, a sultry vampire made eye contact with me from the bar. I glanced over at a frowning Sahriah and he quickly appeared in front of me. The mysterious male roughly slid his hand up my neck and held it to face him straight on.

My insides jumped at the dominance this male emanated.

The shadows on my arm danced with glee as my hand slid up his taut forearm feeling every toned muscle.

"Hello, gorgeous." The vampire said in a deep, husky voice. He grabbed me by my waist and pulled me closer, asking, "Are you looking for a distraction tonight?"

"I don't know, what do you have?" I said with a sexy and solicit expression.

I smiled at him seductively. Lost for words, I glided my hands through the vampire's perfectly messy blue-black hair and gleamed into his silver eyes. He must be a higher-ranking vampire. Only the highest vampires possess those silvery eyes. At least, that is what Sahriah had told me.

Slipping my hand through the rest of his hair, I grabbed onto the back of his neck pulling his face closer to mine. My heart started racing as I took in his distinctive mahogany and dark oak scent. Gods, this fae smelled divine. I could have this vampire for breakfast, lunch, and dinner without any complaints.

I gave a gentle peck to his throbbing neck and asked, "What is your name?" His neck tightened under my lips, and I smiled, kissing up to his chiseled jawline. He chuckled deeply and before I could blink, shadows engulfed us and we were in the corner of the club.

Vampiric magic was fast and efficient.

A slight panic rolled over me and I looked around at the new scenery. The dance floor had to be at least fifty feet away now. Before I could blink again the vampire sat in a booth and pulled me down next to him.

The handsome male simply stated, "Nikolaj."

I snapped my head so fast to face him.

So this was the miscreant who thought he could handle his business in my establishment.

I quickly trained my face to express admiration, "Oh, I heard that you are the one to know around here."

"Some have gotten the pleasure to know me; especially the females," Nikolaj responded with wink.

Twirling the bottom of my curl, I chirped, "Can I call you Niko?"

"Not unless you want your throat ripped out and fed to my employees."

My smile dropped, "Oh, okay. I guess you are not into the shortening of names."

"Well, I like Nik. So, you can call me that. Or lover. Either will do; just plan on screaming it."

"What do I have to do to be allowed to call you lover?" I cooed, putting on my best debutant voice.

Niko started kissing his way up my arm and I pretended to be putty in his hands. My body did have an unexpected breakout in goosebumps, though, which was disconcerting; and he was sexy. Maybe I would have to try him on for size; I didn't have anything else to do.

He stopped at the base of my neck and whispered, "I will enjoy you anytime," and continued kissing up my neck and stopped at the base of my ear, "Anyplace," and continued kissing until his lips were practically touching mine and stopped for the last time, "Anywhere."

He smirked and his fangs showed through his strong tightening jawline.

I stand corrected.

Breakfast.

Lunch.

Dinner.

Dessert.

Midnight Snack.

I moaned to myself at the thought of having him at all hours of the day. My insides swelled and I started to breathe a little harder. I would be damned if this fantasy did not come to life. I grabbed Nikolaj's hand, and he stood up with me.

Getting ahead, Niko beelined his way through the crowd to Sahriah at the bar.

Arriving immediately behind, I tried to covertly make eye contact with the bar manager. Sahriah cut me a glance and raised her eyebrow not looking away, "What do you want, Nik?"

"Key to the—"

"No." She interrupted him and our eye contact broke.

Nikolaj frowned and bared his teeth, "You are not going to deny me a room again, Sahriah. I am funding this place."

Wait.

WHAT?!

I stifled a giggle at the thought of both of them bickering with each other about this so-called *funding.* They both stole a glance at me and I looked away, trying to hide my smile.

"Fine, but you'd better return it as soon as you are done." Sahriah slid a key to Nikolaj and he quickly snatched it from the bar.

"Can I have another drink?" I slurred, with a wink.

She groaned and shook her head in dissatisfaction.

I saluted her again and Nikolaj guided me upstairs.

Chapter 10
Niya

We circled up the staircase and eventually made it to the hallway where room seventeen lay. Nikolaj turned the key in the lock and the door popped open with a creek. I took in the immaculate view. This room was one of our newly remodeled ones and a fan favorite.

Walking through the entryway, I clicked on the light and crimson red walls with a black assortment of paintings and decorations greeted us. The bed placed right in the middle of the room boasted an ornately carved wooden frame with hanging sheer curtains. The bed sheets were silky white with hues of marbled ebony.

In any other establishment, I would avoid the bed at all costs. But here, knowing what the staff were expected to do when cleaning the rooms, I would lay in this bed daily with no trepidation. I had hired a handful of house pixies who get paid handsomely to clean up thoroughly after each patron to keep the rooms in top shape.

Nikolaj smiled seductively and ran both his hands through my hair stopping at the nape of my neck. I pulled on his shirt collar and guided us to the wall for support.

This male looked *delicious*.

The lighting in the suite was significantly better than the bar room floor where we had just left. Now I could see every sculpted line on his bulky yet taut, body. He wore a tight, black, button-down shirt with his collar undone just enough for me to see his tattoos creeping up his neck.

His silver eyes were all business as he watched me. I ran my gaze further down his commanding body to find his equally tight, matching black pants. I started to explore his body with my hands until I stopped at his hard cock bulging from his pant leg.

My nipples tightened at the sign of his arousal.

He slammed his hand above my head onto the wall and I was suddenly startled out of my thoughts.

Nikolaj leaned in closer and smirked, showing a little bit of his left fang, "Do you like what you see?"

"Do you?" I countered.

He had to be a foot taller than me.

I was easily taller than most fae females and him towering over me just intensified the lethal attraction.

Nikolaj slid his fingers adoringly over my breast and down my side, stopping at my rear. Gripping it hard and moving to where our bodies were now touching, "I would say yes, I do like what I see."

My breasts brushed his upper stomach as he leaned his head down to get a better look at me. Niko took his free hand off of the wall and trailed it down the other side of my body. His hand explored from my neck down to my chest, running a thumb over my taut peak, and across the curve of my stomach to the other half of my rear.

Nikolaj hauled me up to where we could see eye to eye.

Oh my ever-loving gods.

No one had ever hauled me up like that before.

I wrapped my legs around his hips for support and he leaned into me, pushing me harder against the wall. Those silver-flamed eyes stared deeply into mine and I wrapped my arms around his shoulders and snaked my fingers up the back of his neck into his hair. Pulling him in closer for a tantalizing kiss, I bit his lower lip playfully and pulled away, teasing him.

He groaned, "If you want to back out, now is your chance."

My only drunken reply was, "I'm good," and then, sharply, "Stop talking and fuck me, Nik."

Nikolaj's expression went from languid to wild. He electrified at my words and with a deep sensuality, breathed, "Call me Lover."

I kissed him passionately, introducing my tongue into his inviting mouth. Nikolaj slipped his tongue in, entwining it with mine. I raked my fingers through his hair, pulling his lips from mine. Nikolaj continued kissing me in all the right places; down my neck, up to the delicate tips of my ear, and back down to my jawline. I moved his face to meet mine and slipped my tongue to glide over the sharp tip of a fang and tore open a small, welling spot on my tongue.

His eyes shot open and dilated as he smelled my blood. His kisses grew fevered as he began sucking at my tongue, pulling the coppery liquid through our kiss. Moaning with inebriated lust, I leaned my head back and against the wall supporting us.

Nikolaj pulled me away from the wall and started to carry me to the bed; my legs still wrapped around his hips. He slipped one hand down my back and unzipped my dress while balancing me in his other. I tried to steal kisses in between but he was struggling to get me undressed. Lessening the distraction, I pulled my dress off the rest of the way.

I went in for another kiss as he dropped me onto the mattress. I shrieked and laughed with surprise and then I lay back, placing my nearly nude body on display for him. He scanned me with predatory intent. I placed my heeled foot on the center of his chest inviting him to undo the lace. He grabbed my ankle and kissed gingerly, licking, and teasing the joint.

I giggled, "That tickles."

His eyes darkened as he growled, "Fuuuck," and lowered his body next to mine, "leave them on."

My insides turned liquid as Nikolaj placed my foot down and slid his roughened index finger down the center of my body stopping at my chest and unclasped my bra with a quick snap of his fingers.

He leaned his head lower, kissing the space between my arched mounds. I bowed my back in the little pleasure as my fingers curled into the sheets. He bit onto my lacy underwear and slid them off of my body in one graceful movement, not even struggling past my heels.

Nik beamed as his hand slowly walked its way back up my stomach to my aching breasts, desperate for his attentions. I was now naked as the day I was born, except for the shoes, and this vampire was still fully clothed.

Nikolaj tweaked one of my hardened peaks and I sucked in a breath. The dark and dangerous male huffed a laugh and said, voice low, "I'm sorry, lover; let me kiss that for you and make it all better." After an unhurried kiss to the injured nib, I growled in frustration at his leisurely pace.

Scowling, I sat up and rolled myself over on top of him. I began to unbutton his shirt as he reached out and dragged his thumb over my achingly hard and abused nipple. I shuddered with the pleasure and pain as he touched and played with me until I finished with his last button. He threw his shirt off and I gaped at his magnificent form below me. His entire torso was swathed in beautiful swirls and whirls tattooed on his sculpted and tanned body.

Not taking the time yet to fully undress, Nik flipped me onto my back and spread my legs wide before him. Nikolaj bit his lip in clear satisfaction and moaned, "You are *so wet,*" as he moved his hand down to cup my sex. Sliding a finger down my slick center, he elicited a sharp intake of breath from my lips.

Gods, yes.

His thumb pressed down onto the bundle of nerves at the apex of my thighs while he slipped a finger inside me. All of my nerves were shocked to life at the touch.

Nikolaj said gruffly, "I am going to make you scream and beg for more; I'm going to make you cum so hard, you'll forget how to form words."

I whispered, "Yes; more—please," I begged as I rocked my hips against his magical hand.

With my eyes closed in pleasure, I quickly unclasped his pants and slipped my hand gingerly into his them. Nik groaned and bucked against me. I could barely wrap my hand around his thick, rock-hard cock.

I pumped my hand a couple of times and then watched in satisfaction as he slid his pants all the way off for ease of access.

Craning my neck to get a better view of him, I surveyed what was now on full display down below, salivating at the sight of him.

Gods forgive me, because I am about to sin.

Nikolaj watched my face in amusement when he saw my delight. He slipped his fingers back to their positions on and into my throbbing center and began moving in and out, the movements growing harder and faster until he was pounding into me, adding another finger.

I arched my back as he sunk his teeth into a spot on my breast. I let out a small shriek and then moaned as lightning rolled inside of me. This feeling was magic and *hot*. It was a mixture of heat, electricity, and pure sex.

He began sucking from me and my vision began to blank in spots. I have never been bitten before and what I was feeling was on another level. I grasped onto Nik's hair and tightened my grip, pulling him more onto me.

With his fingers still working me and his mouth still on my chest, I came closer to the edge of that sweet release.

Too fast.

My head was swimming and all I could do was feel his hands and mouth. He felt like he was inside, outside, and through me all at once. Working on him and rolling in the sweet abyss, I screamed in pleasure as a powerful climax swept through me.

Nikolaj chuckled as he trailed his lips, wet with my blood, over to my other breast and flicked his tongue over my pretty pink point.

My body was on fire.

My legs felt weak, and my head was full of fog.

Gaining some semblance of coherence, I placed my hand on his chest and laid him back on the bed and straddled him. Barely able to keep my eyes open, I kissed and licked down his chest to his abdomen.

I stopped when I got to his rock-hard length. I placed one hand on his muscular abs and another on his thigh.

I leaned down and it all faded to black.

Chapter 11
Sahriah

Nikolaj swept down the stairs, shirtless and disarranged. Wiping blood off of his lips, he made haste over to me and dropped the key.

"As requested," trying to sound nonchalant as well as victorious.

The club was shut down by this point. Niya and Nik had been upstairs for at least an hour doing the gods knew what. I held on to the glass I was cleaning, trying not to shatter it in rage.

If Niya is hurt in any way, I will kill this male!

I pursed my lips, staring up at him angrily, "Where is she?"

"Who?" Nik smirked condescendingly.

I glared at him and slammed my fist on the bar watching him lick his fingers.

The glass shattered below my hand, and I hissed at him.

Nik threw his hands up, "Okay fine, you possessive little bat, she is in the room where I left her; breathing."

I decided right then that this was the last time this reprobate would darken my doorstep.

Nik started coming around shortly after Niya left a couple of months ago. He had set up camp here, making business arrangements and agreements on what I could only assume was illegal trade across the border.

Nik was sketchy and was treated with trepidation and he seemed to lean into his reputation. I used this to my advantage and started charging him a renter's fee for spending so much time here in Niya's bar. I should have given her a better warning about Nik so she could throw his ass out for me.

Niya needed to get home. Blackstar was waiting for her in the front, but she would not be in any kind of shape to ride home. I would make sure her bike made it home. The emotional attachment she had to that dangerous thing was unfathomable.

"Sayge!" I screamed behind Nik. A young vampire squirmed out of the kitchen and glanced at both Nik and me.

"Yes?" Sayge shifted uncomfortably when he saw Nikolaj.

"Can you please go check in on room seventeen. There is a silvery blonde fae more than likely naked and sleeping. Try to wake her up. I need you to drive her home."

Nik looked relieved that the female would be taken care of and that he would be free to leave.

"Yes, ma'am," Sayge responded quickly as he headed up the stairs.

Thank the gods for loyal staff that don't ask questions.

I was unsure if Niya had disclosed her identity, but I did not want to cause a scene if she hadn't.

Nikolaj, gaining some composure, turned on his irreverent charm.

"Sahriah, I have business meetings here tomorrow; it would be greatly appreciated if the club stayed closed to the public until..."

I pointed my finger at him with a wolfish grin, "Didn't somebody say they owed me money?"

Turning away from me and slipping his hands into his pockets, Nik strolled to the entrance of the club shouting behind himself, "I'll see you tomorrow, Sahriah."

As soon as the vampire was out of earshot, I roared at Sayge, "Well! Go get Niya, pup! I don't have all night, damn it!"

Sayge scrambled up the remaining stairs to the occupied room. Several moments later, he had Niya's arm wrapped around his shoulder helping her walk down the winding staircase. Sayge was struggling to get down those steps, and Niya looked like a dead weight.

Niya's head was down, and she was moaning with every step they took.

Fucking damn it, she looked like absolute shit. I should not have given her that last elixir. She probably blacked out between that and Nikolaj's bloodletting.

A deep voice interrupted my thoughts, "Should I be concerned 'bout our princess is bein' assisted by yer barback?"

I glared at Leer, "I don't see *you* helping. Shut up and go home, elf," already exhausted.

"Fine. Next time, get me instead. I am better built to help her, and she will probably respond better to me. Sayge is a wee too feeble for her." He put his hand on my shoulder and turned to leave.

"Wait!" I shouted, having a great idea. "Why don't you help instead of just running your mouth?" Leer turned back around, walking over to Niya and Sayge nearing the bar.

With a huge grunt, Sayge and Leer helped Niya to the bar seat. I cupped my hand under Niya's chin and lifted her head to where I could see every angle.

No bite marks that I could see.

Leaning over the bar to inspect the damage, Nik's missing shirt was poorly buttoned on Niya's curvaceous frame and little droplets of blood stained the breast. With a deep, exasperated breath, I rolled and then closed my eyes when I noticed that she wore no underwear, but her shoes were still laced perfectly on her delicate feet.

Fuckity. Fucking. Fuck.

"Sayge, Get my amulet from the kitchen. You two are taking her home in the extended bed. Make sure you put her bike in the back." I motioned for Sayge to grab my chained amulet from the kitchen.

Sayge gently released his hold on Niya momentarily as she leaned onto the table for stability.

Leer waited patiently for his services to be needed again, but a small muscle ticked in his jaw belying his calm.

"Sahriah, my chest is throbbing." Niya garbled.

I will kill him.

She probably had Nik's venom flowing through her veins on top of the however many drinks she had. I sniffed her scent, cringing at the fact that Nik's mahogany and dark oak lingered all over her.

I softened my gaze, "Oh, sweets, are you alright? Do you remember anything?"

She shook her head back and forth on the table, "Remember what?"

"The Vampire? Nikolaj."

"Oh, *that* vampire?" Niya giggled drunkenly.

Sayge ran in, out of breath and interrupted our conversation, "I'm ready."

I ordered, "Get her home to the palace quickly without getting her caught. She will need to enter on her own. Stay with

- 108 -

her until she is at least able to walk independently and come back to me immediately after. I will wait here for your debrief."

Sayge nodded and started to help Niya back up. She laughed and stumbled, arms around both Sayge and Leer, out the back door.

When I heard the back door snick shut, I leveled my hands on the bar, trying to calm my anxiety and frustration. I balled my hands into fists and slammed them as hard as I could. I should have never let her go with him. Nikolaj was a manipulative vamphole.

Niya did not seem to care that he was here, but I did. That lusty male was up to no good and if Niya got tied in with him...

Nikolaj had to go. This was where I was drawing the line.

Tomorrow, I would be cleaning house; starting with Nik.

He was no longer welcome at the Nyte Club.

Chapter 12
Niya

A brain-jarring slam jolted me awake as Alman swiftly moved to the curtains and flung them open. My body instantly tightened, and I winced in pain. I held my palm to my throbbing head as Alman stared at me, shaking his head with disgust.

I squinted my eyes and groaned, "What the fuck, Alman? What time is it?"

"It is time for you to get your ass up and train after the stunt you pulled last night. You really thought that you could run away, and you would not be brought right back? It is a good thing that Sahriah is a true friend."

Looking down at my new, strange shirt, I mumbled, "I guess. I had a good time last night, at least."

Alman stalked to my closet and ransacked my wardrobe pulling out an assortment of clothes. Alman pulled out a lacy piece of lingerie and blushed, throwing it back in like it was contagious.

Alman scowled, "Get dressed; you have five minutes," and glowered as he escaped out the door.

The fact that this old fae still got uncomfortable touching underclothes, I considered to be a little boon for my *already* terrible morning. I scanned through the mess he made and pulled out tan leggings and an emerald bishop-sleeved shirt. I forced my feet into my dark leather battle boots and put my hair in a loose braid at my nape. I placed my dark leather scabbard and long sword across my back, tightening it across my chest.

Grabbing Celeste, I placed her exposed on my thigh.

I rubbed my throbbing head one more time and begrudgingly walked to the kitchen. Jayce had a lovely assortment of delectable fruits, protein, and juice. I swiped a handful of chocolate covered strawberries and dipped out of the kitchen to the training ring.

Alman was standing there with his arms crossed over his chest and a foot tapping a rhythm.

I snarked, "What song are you making with your foot? It's not very catchy."

"You go out and get trashed last night, then wake up in somebody else's clothes; make *me* search for *your* clothes; and then stop by to see Jayce on your way here when you *knew* I was waiting?!"

"You did not have to search for my clothes; that was an Alman choice."

Alman shuddered, "I have to get the thought of your tiny female underthings out of my brain."

He unsheathed his sword inviting me to fight with a slight tug upward of his lips. In his hands was his infamous battle sword that I had only heard about and thought of as only legend.

I pulled out my long sword, smirking, "Is that what I think it is?"

Alman cocked his head to the side, "You didn't think I would go easy on you, did you?" His stance and the gleam in his eyes told me that he would go very *hard* on me today.

I did a slow blink and breathed, "You know, for a second there, I kind of did; yeah."

Alman started a slow, stalking circle, looking for a weakness. I held up my sword and turned it horizontally in front of my face, looking at the reflection of the parts of the room that were behind me. I had learned that one does not have to accept what is in front of them; but they can take advantage of things the opponent doesn't see. Battle is won by those that could use what was around them, especially if the opponent didn't look for such opportunities.

I didn't wait for Alman to make the first move. I lashed out, and when he blocked, I blocked his block.

I was pissed.

How dare he make me feel like I did anything wrong last night.

I had been grown for a long time now.

My lack of focus gave him the weakness he needed, and he kicked out at my gut, forcing me three feet backward; my sword flying out of my hands. As I acted like I was bracing myself to get up, I faked and gripped a nearby stool with my feet, kicked it up into my hands and began using it to parry his attacks.

Alman laughed at my innovative fighting and redoubled his swiftness and power. I threw the stool at him and rolled to grab my sword off the floor next to me. He paused; I paused and smiled. I worked; beating back this old fae, slightly concerned that I had underestimated him.

My head started to pound and sweat poured profusely from me.

I hadn't noticed.

I didn't think that I had rehydrated myself after all the drinking last night and my brain was starting to feel foggy.

Alman's sword zipped through the air and an unblocked lunge sliced my upper arm.

Damn it!

I had to get my head together. He was not giving me a break.

I spun, trying to get more force behind my blow, but Alman knocked me down with great speed. I didn't know he could move that fast.

Had he been holding back before?

My decision to spin was a very bad one. My head swam and I had no more fight left in me as Alman took the two steps to tower over me.

Alman relieved me of my sword and pointed his blade at my throat, "This is what happens when you're irresponsible and don't get a good night's rest, Niya."

I furrowed my brows at Alman besting me. I was already beating myself up over the fact that I should not have done what I did last night. Nik was a mistake. I was not going to continue to be a spoiled party princess. I had duties to uphold and if my mother ever found out what I did on my free time, she would be the one pointing Alman's sword.

"Are you done with her, Alman?" A sharp tone came from behind me.

I turned my head from Alman and a squeak came from me when I saw my mother.

"She is all yours, my queen. She clearly is done," Alman retorted.

Alman reached his hand down for me to grab ahold. I went to connect, but my foot had other intentions. I kicked his shin in frustration, "I am done when I say I am done, Alman," and continued to get up off of the floor without his assistance.

Alman let out a fatherly chuckle.

I wiped the invisible dirt off of my shirt as I turned to face her.

"Your training looks like it is not benefiting you anymore," my mother paused, "Which reminds me, you will be doing a royal tour of the kingdom soon. Your schedule has been cleared. You will begin the tour at The Divide and travel south-east to The Silver Expanse. I have invited Adryen to reconsider our offer of alliance. Expect to have papers awaiting your signature upon your return."

Queen Ravyn turned away from me, waving her hand in the air, cackling.

She stopped in her tracks and looked behind her shoulder, "Oh, and Garrin is officially your royal guard. He will follow you everywhere; to your chambers, to your hobbies, and to all social events. You will no longer be alone. It is unsafe with your immanent ascension. I would hate for anything to happen to you, darling."

She smirked and disappeared from the ring. I did not understand how my training related to a tour of the kingdom, but I was not about to ask any more questions.

I could take care of myself.

Garrin, would not like being my newly appointed companion.

Alman broke the silence, "Well," he patted my shoulder, "I will pray to the gods for you."

I frowned at Alman, thinking back to all of our training together through the years. I was going to miss fighting with him.

My mother was truly unbearable.

"Can she do this, Alman? I have been training with you my entire life," silver lined my eye, and I tried not to let it slide down my face. Ignoring my wishes, it did anyway.

Alman brushed it away and kept his hand on my cheek, "Unfortunately with how close you are to your ascension, yes. The queen may do or ask of you whatever she pleases," he paused, "Just know I am still here for you, Niya. I always will be."

The queen just ripped out a piece of my entire being. This was the end of an era.

Alman put his hand on my upper arm that he sliced open and healed it with his magic. Warmth tingled over me, and magic poured into my wound. I hugged him tightly, "When did you learn how to heal? I am finding this unsettling that both you and my brother both can harness Seelie magic."

"Vallynn has been very useful in that area, when he isn't busy with all of the females. I do not think it is just the Seelie that can harness it. I think it's more of your affinity to manipulate the light."

I slowly nodded my head at Alman like I knew exactly what he was talking about, "Thank you."

Walking back to the castle in silence, shoes scuffed behind me.

Garrin maintained five steps behind me and kept pace.

I moaned, "Garrin, I don't need your assistance right now. You are dismissed."

"I'm sorry, Niya. It is your mother's orders. I will be with you every step of the way."

I closed my eyes and breathed heavily through my nose, "Fine."

I made my way to Rose's room and turned around to face Garrin, "Wait outside, please. You can guard the door."

Garrin grunted and put his hand on the pommel of his sword, turning around to put his back to the entrance, "Gladly, if that means that I don't have to listen to your gossip."

I snorted a laugh and opened the door to see Rose was a mess. Paint was splattered all over her face and clothes with a paintbrush placed between her lips in deep thought.

I inquired, "Have I interrupted your quiet time?"

It took Rose several moments before she realized I was standing in the doorway.

Shutting the door, I silently maneuvered to her bed and plopped down, "Rose!"

Her wet paintbrush dropped to the floor, "Huh? Oh, what are you doing here?"

I looked over at the new stain on the floor and raised an eyebrow, "I need to talk. Are you busy?"

"Of course, I am busy; I am painting!"

I batted my eyes, "But, your best friend in all the realms needs you."

Rose turned to me and her eyes beamed, "Okay, let me finish this. I am almost done."

Rose was such a gifted painter; a master artist. The way she worked with all assortments of paint and brushes was mindboggling. She made sure that each of her strokes had such precision and intention. If she ever made a mistake, nobody would ever know.

Rose set her brush down on her easel and turned to me, "What do you think?"

I tilted my head, peering at the hues of colors. Such vibrancy across the canvas, "It is not Kaldamir."

"I read some books on Haldonia and this is what I envisioned the king's palace to look like," a little smile crossed Rose's face.

I stared into the painting longer, looking at every loving detail she put into it. There was this massive white castle with dark accents on the windowpanes and flowers creeping up the sides, giving off the beautiful aesthetic of the foundation of the place. I replied, "It's magnificent, Rose."

"Thank you! It probably looks nothing like Haldonia, but I tried," she plopped on the bed beside me, "What's up?"

"I think I went too far last night," I squirmed, remembering last night, "I drank too much, and kind of did something I regret. I slept with a vampire. Or I think I did? I kind of blacked out."

"Niya..." Rose trailed, "I thought the last time was the final 'get drunk at the club' visit. You said no more *then*."

"I know, but I was really exhausted yesterday and couldn't stop the self-sabotage. I feel like I left things very unsettled an—"

"—Niya, are these feelings I am sensing, from you!" Rose squealed in excitement.

I gaped at her in bemusement, "I thought going to the Nyte Club and getting with a handsome fae would help!"

Stopping, thinking about my next words, "I feel worse."

I told Rose everything that happened between Adryen and I after our last encounter where I left him in his wyvern form. She was shocked initially at the fact that Adryen was something we knew as extinct, and then pissed that my mother would do such a thing to me and to someone else.

I didn't hate him so much to where I wished he would die. I could tolerate his existence. Adryen was a wyvern, a majestic beast. I could not fathom death greeting him solely because my mother was selfish.

Forgiving him for what he had done, though, might take a little longer.

"Well," Rose let out a huge sigh, "Considering your mother wants to murder him, maybe it is best you two go your separate ways. Despite this guilt you seem to be feeling."

"I am being forced into signing papers to seal our alliance. That is not an option. I must form some sort of bond with him to get him to trust me beyond his probable suspicion about the queen's motives. I don't want to kill Adryen like she has planned, but I do want to try to help him and his people."

I was shocked at what had just come out of my mouth, but I knew that it was true.

It felt *right*.

Reflecting more, I frowned deeply, "I don't see the need for us to have all this land, and nobody to live on it. Maybe I could give him a sliver to connect his border to The Wasteland."

"Is it because he is a majestic beast? I know how much you love wyverns."

I smiled and pinched my index finger towards my thumb, "Maybe just a little."

The Wasteland was this deserted land of just pure nothing. Nothing and no one lived there long enough to set down roots; the tundra was harsh on anything that tried.

Rose countered, "That's very optimistic coming from an Unseelie Princess...you seem like you want to truly help him, Niya. I believe you will find a way to save him and yourself from your mother. Maybe you will get lucky and you two will actually become friends."

I needed to mend things with Adryen.

Despite not planning to marry him, especially now that I had probably ruined any chance I had had with him with my bullshit from last night, I still needed to smooth things out between us.

Rose put her hand on my forearm and gently stated, "You will know what's best for you, and this kingdom," She paused and smiled, "Just do not forget us common folk who helped push you in the right direction."

Rose nudged me on the shoulder, and I smiled, giving her the same gesture.

Chapter 13
Niya

The next morning, I woke up and dressed for the day. Quickly zooming through my morning routine, I slipped out of my bedroom and toward the kitchen where Garrin ran into me.

I huffed out a sigh, "You again? You are like a lost puppy, Garrin. I don't need you following me."

Garrin grunted, "You think I don't know that, Niya? I am very aware of how much you don't need or want me around."

"Fine."

Garrin closed his eyes, "Fine," and breathed out a heavy sigh.

"You know, Garrin, we could make this something special," and smirked.

"Here we go," he muttered.

I glowered at him, "Oh, come on!"

Breaking my glaring contest with Garrin, I glimpsed over at Jayce who was mid-chop, watching our stare down and trying not to laugh. I let out a soft cough and he blinked once, quickly going back to his chopping.

Frowning at Garrin, I pushed through him and walked toward Jayce.

"Good morning, Your Highness," Jayce, our head chef, bowed deeply, "What can I cook for you this morning?"

I smiled faintly at Jayce and replied, "I am just going to take an apple this morning, Jayce, but thank you. I have a full day of duties ahead of me."

"Ah, well," he paused, "In that case, I will make sure snacks are readily available for you, Your Highness."

Jayce bowed slightly. I exited the room, with my apple, on the way to the library.

Garrin, again, stalked five steps behind me.

Our library was massive. There were several levels of books on shelves and endless amounts of tables for studies and research. I opened the door with my elbow and looked over my shoulder at Garrin, "Stay out here," as I pointed to the floor in front of him.

If Garrin had been allowed to roll his eyes at the royal family, he would do it the most with me. I could sense that he was trying his best to keep himself in check before I zipped out of his sight, slamming the library doors shut with my conjured wind.

Alman sat on a vacant table with his hands on each knee staring at me. I took my first delicious bite into the crisp fruit, as he snarked, "You're late."

I threw my hands in the air, "I needed something to eat, Alman! You want me to starve?"

"It is not ideal, no. But you have no excuse for being late. A queen is never late."

I huffed, "A queen is what she says she is, Alman. If I appear late, then everybody else is just early."

"I don't think that's how that works," Alman's lips pressed.

I took another, more aggressive, bite of my apple and chewed.

Alman ignored my antics, "Today we have three things on the agenda: etiquette, socialization, and magic craft."

Coughing on my apple, I attempted to swallow without spitting anything out, "Socialization?"

He gave me some side eye and replied, "Yes, socialization."

We just stared at each other, and I finally worked up the courage to ask, "Why are you teaching me these lessons? Shouldn't it be our historians or royal tutors? *Literally* anyone else?"

Alman nodded, "Well, I am your royal advisor, after all, my knowledge is greater than anyone else's. Finish that," he pointed, "we need to get started."

A couple of minutes passed, and I made sure to cherish every bite of that apple until there was nothing left. Alman crossed his arms, staring at me in great dissatisfaction. Done wasting time, I threw the core in the trash and walked over to Alman, putting my hands on my hips, "I am ready."

"Perfect; sit down."

I sat down and he tsked at me, "Stand up."

Pushing myself up off the chair I stood up.

"Sit down."

I huffed and rolled my eyes; I obeyed and sat.

"Stand up."

"Alman!"

He seethed, "Stand up, Niya."

I rolled my eyes, again, and stood up.

"Now, sit down."

I plopped on the chair and crossed my arms in annoyance, "What is your problem?!"

"This time when you stand up, don't get up like a brooding male would. Queen's stand up in grace and beauty. When have you ever seen your mother use the table, or her lap to help her get up?"

He was right.

I *had* never seen that female use anything but air to help herself up. I attempted to stand without the use of the table or my lap and stumbled forward.

We did this for *several* minutes before I finally got it and Alman smiled, "Very good. This will need to become second nature; instinct. When you tour soon, your guests around the kingdom are going to expect a soon-to-be queen. Not a petulant child."

I crossed my leg over my thigh and leaned my head back to stare at the ceiling. I don't want to be queen.

This was not me.

"Oh hells, Niya."

I snapped my head at him, "What now?!"

"The way you are sitting is dreadful. My gods. A queen does not sit like that."

I gritted my teeth and seethed, "Alman."

He shook his head back and forth, "This will not do," and plodded toward me, pulling my leg down and reorganizing my legs to sit like I was wearing a dress. My legs were closed and the only two things crossed were my ankles.

Alman and I spent the majority of the morning with him criticizing everything about me, and then telling me how to fix myself. If I'd had poor self-esteem, I'd have been crying by now.

Jayce stopped by to bring some snacks and I grazed from the metal platter before moving forward to the "socialization" Alman had on the schedule.

Chewing on a pastry, I asked, "Why do I need to have proper socialization?"

Alman cuffed a finger under my chin, and I swallowed hard.

"This is why. You do not talk with your mouth full. Where are your manners?"

I whispered, "Yes, mother." I groaned, "I have had enough for today."

"Sit down."

I plopped in the chair and realizing what I just did wrong, I screamed, "Fuck!"

Alman groaned and I returned the gesture.

This was going to be a long day.

Hours passed of combining both socialization and etiquette. At one point, I was at the door ready to dismiss myself and Alman refused. He was dancing on a thin line and I was ready to *shove* him over it.

I dropped my head to the table and sent a silent prayer for deliverance.

"We are going to work on your magic outside," Alman commanded.

Thank you gods, for answering my prayers.

I trailed behind him, and Garrin, as usual, was not far behind me. I was a little worried, not knowing what to expect. I was not physically tired, but my brain felt exhausted.

Alman guided the three of us out to the grounds, where magic was no longer providing warmth. The snow was freezing, and my pant legs were already getting soaked from the excessive amount of walking.

Finally arriving, we stopped in a tiny circular patch of grass that did not have any snow or ice covering it.

"Interesting," I announced.

"This land is a lot like your sanctuary, Niya," Alman looked toward me with a smile, "It's an anomaly. When I stumbled across it on a morning stroll, I decided this would be a perfect area to channel your powers without the worry of it damaging anything...or anyone."

I kneeled to touch the grass and my body radiated heat.

It was pure, raw power.

Exactly like the home I'd created for the sprites.

These random patches of land were hidden gems and unknown to most of the realm. There was no explanation as to why the cold did not infiltrate them, but they seemed like power reserves for fae. These locations provided many things: near unlimited power, healing abilities, and meditation.

All of which the lagoon had provided for the sprites and for me.

"I thought the lagoon was the last elemental piece in our kingdom."

Alman replied, "It was, until more started popping up in the last couple of years. I think the goddess, Dreya, has blessed our lands again."

Garrin placed his hand on my shoulder, "I am sorry about your sanctuary, Niya."

I looked at Garrin solemnly, "It's okay. I just wish I knew how to rebuild there. I have tried everything, and nothing is working."

Alman interrupted, "I would love to continue socializing, but it is almost dinner, and I am hungry. Niya, join me," he reached out a hand.

I grasped his hand and my powers felt like they were truly waking up for the first time in years. Since the last time I was at the lagoon.

My eyes widened and Alman smiled broadly, "Close your eyes."

I closed my eyes, and my vision went black.

Alman echoed through my ears, "Think of what makes you the happiest, and lock into that. I want you to create a fire animal, or an ice animal. Whatever element you choose."

"Alman," I kept my eyes closed and questioned, "Why is it that I am the only one that can harness the elements?"

It was quiet for a long time before he finally replied, "I am unsure."

I pulled the power from the ground and in one hand a created a beautiful fire-maned lion in my right hand. I opened my eyes, and it skittered above the ground, being careful not to singe the grass. Garrin chuckled behind me as the fire lion ran and played around Alman, who was sitting on the ground.

Alman laughed, "Very good, can you make it larger? Life-sized?"

I raised an eyebrow and called the lion back to me. When the lion touched my hand, it roared to life and quadrupled in size. The fire lion stood next to me, ready to attack as its newly formed eyes locked into Alman's.

He moved closer to the lion and hovered a hand over the fiery animal, "Magnificent, Niya. Your powers have come a long way."

I perked up and smiled, closing my hand, making the lion dissipate into the air.

We went through all of the elements I was able to harness and practiced drills. We created elemental shields, weapons, and animals for defense. After several hours, I was soaked, and now *physically* tired.

My powers had felt never ending; but, when using them to practice and train, it drained a lot faster than normal. The land could only regenerate so much before it needed to rest as well.

Alman put his hands on his hips, "I think we are done."

I whispered, "Oh thank the gods," and fell on the ground staring up at the darkened, starry sky.

"Niya, we need to head back to the castle; it's well past dinner."

I thought for several moments, "I think I just want to stay out here for a couple more minutes, Alman. Go on without me."

Garrin entered the conversation, "I guess we will wait a little longer, Alman. I will make sure she gets home safely."

I scoffed and continued gazing up at the skies.

Footsteps moved toward me, and Garrin kneeled down and lay on the ground next to me. A little smile escaped from my lips as he just laid there, staring up at the skies with me.

Garrin became head of our guards shortly after The Blood Wars and had been around ever since. Despite the huge age gap between us, he still looked incredibly young, like all fae did.

"Garrin," I looked over at him. His wavy, shoulder length ash brown hair glowed in the moonlight.

Looking at me, he replied, "Yes?"

"I know you don't want this, and neither do I. But, can we just agree to make this work? I don't want to continue fighting with you." I paused and waited for a reply.

When it didn't come, "You are going to see things and learn things...about me, that I have kept hidden from my parents. I need to know that I can trust you."

His gray eyes looked into mine, "I would never do anything to make you lose your trust in me, Niya. I have watched you grow up. I don't think anything you do will come as a shock to me."

A warm smile crossed my lips, "Thank you, Garrin."

He stood up and held out a hand, "It is time to go."

I grasped it and he pulled me to my feet. We walked back to the castle, together. For the first time, he was not five steps behind me, but beside me.

Chapter 14
Niya

The days passed with Alman training me and teaching me my royal duties. The days blended together in a blur. I needed to get out, and just have a day of fun and peace.

I pulled out tightly fitted black pants and a white v-neck shirt from my closet. Strapping on my hiking boots, I flung open the door and smiled at Garrin, "We are going on a trip today."

Garrin placed his hand on his forehead and let out a huff, "I don't know if I should feel scared that we are going off schedule or concerned for your mental state."

"Well, Garrin," I placed my hand on his shoulder, "Today is the day that we find out!"

I powered my magic to create a prismatic, whirring portal for us to jump through, "Hold on, and try not to puke, okay?"

Garrin groaned, "I would not have that issue if we would just walk."

"Nope, not today," and grabbed Garrin's hand, dragging him through the portal.

We landed roughly on the ground and Garrin puked in his mouth, trying to hide it.

I gawked at him, "I said try not to puke, Garrin."

He growled, "Well if we had just walked like I said!" He covered his mouth with a hand and looked away for a moment.

We walked on a bit toward where the lagoon had once been.

As we entered the old sanctuary, rubble and torn and burnt grass started to become more apparent. What once used to be a beautiful waterfall flowing into a limpid pool was now broken stone and snow-covered dirt.

I put one arm out toward Garrin's chest and stopped him from walking.

"Do not approach him," I murmured.

Garrin grunted in acknowledgement.

I glared into Adryen's annoyingly bright blue eyes.

Adryen stood by the destroyed waterfall and empty lagoon, looking into the wreckage.

I had wanted to check in on the lagoon to see if I could come up with any new ideas to take back to Tallulah and Sander.

I had known that this place was not going to be easily fixed, not with my powers. Something kept calling me out here; tugging me.

The Seelie King was the last person I would have thought I'd see here answering a similar call.

"Why are you here?" I blurted, forming a fire ball from my hands, knowing full well I would not hurt him.

Scare him, maybe.

He mournfully stated, "I wanted to come visit the destruction I'd inadvertently caused." Adryen stared at me, contrition on his face. "I am so sorry; I did not realize how bad this was."

I looked to the earth and slid my foot over the snow, digging into the dirt. His apology was sincere, and meaningful. He took time out of his schedule to look at the collateral damage of this forgotten battlefield.

"I am not mad about it anymore, Adryen. I just want it fixed. The sprites are not in their ideal home right now and they can't thrive." I lifted my chin to see that he had moved closer to me.

Garrin cut in between us, causing Adryen to back up.

He spewed, "What are you doing? Back up."

Adryen choked, "What? I'm not going to *hurt* her."

Garrin snarled, "I don't care what you think you are going to do; it will not be getting any closer my princess."

I backed up a couple of inches and he continued toward me. I pointed my fiery hand at him, "Don't come any closer; Garrin is not joking."

Garrin smiled a warning and backed away, hand on the pommel of his sword, "I would be very careful with your next move, Your Majesty. I do not believe that the princess would appreciate getting your blood on her shoes."

As soon as Garrin moved, Adryen advanced towards me and gripped my enflamed hand, causing him to wince. Ignoring his burned hand, Adryen pulled me closer and I stumbled towards him. I diminished the flame, in hopes of not causing him anymore pain.

I glanced at Garrin, who moved in closer, ready to unsheathe his sword.

I put my hand up telling him to withdraw and stand down, and Garrin obeyed.

Garrin knew his job. Adryen was not a threat to me, and I believed Garrin knew that as well.

Adryen's nose scrunched, "What is the awful smell on you?"

"What do you mean? All I smell is your burning flesh, Adryen."

He pulled me even closer to where my chest was touching his. I craned my neck back to see his face wrinkled in disgust, "You smell disgusting, like dark oak and," he paused, "and mahogany."

I chuckled, "What are you talking about?"

Adryen crossed his arms over his chest and tilted his head, "I think you're very good at lying, Niya."

I looked over at Garrin who was glowering at Adryen, fully involving himself in this conversation with his hand on the pommel of his sword, relaxed, but ready.

I knew exactly what he was talking about, but I tried my damndest to lie.

I mumbled, "You're hurt."

Almost like I snapped Adryen out of a trance, he blinked and looked at his locked hand around my wrist. His arm glowed gold and he instantly healed the burn marks from his hand. He let go of his hold and my hand dropped, leaving me to back up a couple of paces.

"I'm sorry," he trailed his fingers through his hair, "Can we start over?"

Looking at him confused, "What do you mean?"

"I did not make a good first impression, clearly," He waved around to the deadness of the lagoon, "and I want a chance to redeem myself."

"You don't have to do that, I said I was not upset with you anymore."

"Do you forgive me?"

"I haven't forgiven you," I let Adryen really hear those words and I could see they panged his heart a little bit, but continued, "yet."

Adryen raised an eyebrow, "I can work with 'yet'."

He smiled and I couldn't help but smile back. I wanted to build something with him. Not sure what yet, but I was trying to be optimistic.

I stuck out my hand to him and reintroduced myself, "Hi, I am Princess Niya Blackbyrn of Kaldamir. First born to Ravyn and Edmund Blackbyrn. You may call me Niya. *Just* Niya."

Adryen stared at my hand aloft in the air between us and wrinkled his forehead in contemplation. This is what he'd wanted; a chance to start over.

I started to lower my hand, confused, but he quickly grabbed it back up and replied, "Hi, Princess," and closed my fingers into his palm and kissed my knuckles, "I am King Adryen. Just Adryen. Of Haldonia. It is a distinct pleasure."

I really looked at him this time and just gazed into his pure natural beauty. He was breathtaking. I placed my hand on his strong, stubbled jawline and my body warmed as his cheek nuzzled into my palm.

"Can you help me?"

Adryen's eyes were closed like he was thoroughly enjoying this. I would be too, if I was not so concerned about this lagoon.

"Hmm," was all he could get out.

I dropped my hand, and asked again, "Can you help me?"

Adryen opened his eyes and looked at me, "Help you with what, Princess?"

I walked toward the empty lagoon and shuffled my hand into the snow. I closed my eyes and pushed my powers out, trying to rebuild it. The rocks of the waterfall shook but did not move. The water deep within the ground refused to rise to the surface as I strained my magic.

A hand was placed on my shoulder, and I snapped my eyes open to see a little glittery reflection of what looked like water. I shot up and gasped, "How did that," I looked behind me to see Adryen removing his hand from my shoulder and shouted, "Garrin!"

Garrin ran to me to look at the little puddle of water and his gaze went to Adryen.

I stuttered, "T-the taint, it's you."

Adryen backed up and looked at the success of what we created, "The taint?"

"Adryen," I grabbed his wrist and pulled him closer to the lagoon, "When your sentries attacked, they uprooted the magic that was stationed here, leaving this place in ruins. I don't know how that happened, but it's gone. Everything magical about this place was obliterated."

"I don't know how much more I can apologize before it turns meaningless to you."

"No, that's not what I am saying, Adryen. I was just trying to send out my magic, and nothing was working until you touched my shoulder. You are the missing piece."

I turned to face Adryen, "Can you help me fix the sanctuary?"

Adryen placed his hands over his broad frame, "I don't think that was me doing that, Niya," he sighed, "but I promise to help you fix this in whatever way I can."

I could kiss him right now. But instead, I squealed in excitement and blurted, "Thank you!" and hugged him tightly.

Adryen wrapped his arms around my waist and tightened our hug, "You're very welcome, Princess."

"Adryen," I inclined.

He hummed, "Hmm?"

"How long can you stay?"

He pulled his head back from me, "I can't stay long this time, Princess." The corners of his lips turned down. Dipping his head to look into my eyes, "When I come back, we can continue looking for a solution...together."

A smile crossed his face, and he kissed my cheek, "Have a good evening."

I put my hand to where his lips left me, and my cheeks heated.

Adryen created a crackling portal and walked through it, leaving Garrin and me behind.

I felt the loss of him as soon as he was gone. Maybe I could have inquired more about his wyvern to make him stay longer. That thought was so strange to me. Why did it matter that he had to leave?

Garrin cleared his throat, disrupting my thoughts, "Well, that was...interesting."

I inclined my head, "Yes it was." Trying to ease the knot in my chest, "Can we go home now?"

"Are we taking the portal or walking?"

I groaned, "Fine, we can walk."

Garrin grinned, "Good, let's go."

He turned away from me and headed in the direction of the castle. I followed urgently behind him, "Don't tell my mom about my encounter with him."

"Niya, I told you. Your secrets are safe with me."

I nudged his shoulder, and he nudged me back, playfully.

Chapter 15
Niya

Standing in front of the Nyte Club, I closed my eyes and breathed in the crisp air of The Silver Expanse. I needed this break tonight. I had been working and training for several days without nearly enough rest.

Tonight, would be a good night.

Garrin, behind me, "What is this place?"

I'd forgotten he was there. Responding over my shoulder to him, "This is my Nyte Club."

"Like, a *literal* club?"

I turned to face him, "Yes, Garrin! A club," gesturing towards the old, bricked building.

"So, are we here to meet a lover, or are we here to actually *club*? Well, *you* club and *I* stand in the corner, watching."

We?! Oh my gods above, I needed a break from Garrin.

"I am slightly offended you would assume I would have a lover, Garrin," I sighed, "We *dance* at a club, Garrin. We don't *club*. *Drinking* happens in a club as well. You do not get out much, do you?"

Garrin hummed his annoyance, and I rolled my eyes as per my usual.

"I don't take lovers," determined to have the last word.

"She just takes one-night stands," a smooth, deep voice interrupted our argument.

I whipped around to see silver eyes meet mine. Nik seductively grinned with his brawny arms over his muscled chest.

Garrin stepped in front of me, unsheathing his sword. Pointing the tip at Nik's throat, "Back the fuck up, vampire!"

Nik put his hands in the air and backed up, being careful to put distance between Garrin's sword and his neck.

"Oh, is *that* what it was?" I raised my brows behind Garrin.

Nik lowered his lashes and frowned, "I did not know you had a personal guard. You must be someone of great importance."

"Who I am is none of your business, Nik."

Nik growled, "Can I speak to you, privately?"

Garrin shot a look my way and I nodded in approval.

Garrin grunted, "I am going to walk away now," He looked between the two of us in warning, "and let you two 'talk'. If I even *think* that I sense any sort of aggressive words, tone, or body language, *Nik*, I will rip your beating heart from your chest. Are we clear?" Garrin waited for nodded understanding from Nik. I was compelled to nod as well; Garrin was hard to ignore in his current state. He walked toward Leer who was tentatively watching the scene from the door.

I whispered, "Wow, that was very aggressive."

Garrin was not normally like this. He must know Nik, somehow; and it was clear that he didn't trust him.

I charged for Nik, ready to lambast him. Before I could speak, he grasped my neck, pulling me closer to him as he whispered, "I could be more than a one-night stand, if you'd let me."

- 138 -

"Ew, no thank you," I responded, pushing him away, "You were fun and all, but my thirst for vampires has been slaked. I am all good now."

His brow arched, "Really?"

"Nikolaj, we should just be friends; or even acquaintances. I would not mind just forgetting what we did that night."

"Ouch," he replied, "That's a shame. We could have been a power couple."

"You don't even know my name," getting agitated. "What do you want that you needed to talk to me about *privately?*"

Nik deflected, "What *is* your name?"

I looked him up and down, appraisingly; then I turned on my heel and dismissed myself. Standing a foot from Leer and Garrin, I turned around to a perplexed Nik, smiled broadly, and flipped him a very vulgar gesture. I walked into the club leaving Nik to the bustling crowds outside.

Garrin spoke behind me, "Who was that?"

"Nikolaj Morelli."

"That is not Lord Morelli," Garrin spat.

"No shit, Garrin!" I spewed, still reeling from my encounter outside. Garrin backed up a step from me with a hurt look on his face. Realizing how that came out, I apologized, "I'm sorry. It's just. I need a break, but coming here, I have realized I probably shouldn't have bothered."

"I am just trying to figure you out, that's all." Garrin spoke to me as if he was trying to calm a wild animal.

Suddenly drained, I simply replied, "I am going to the bar then to my office to sit in solitude. You can choose to stay down here or walk with me to the top floor."

Sahriah made eye contact with me and smiled, showing her fanged teeth. She was already preparing a drink for me by the time I'd gotten to the bar.

I grasped the drink, "Thank you," and took a sip, "Did you find out anything about my arm?" I waggled my forearm at her.

She shook her head, "Negative. It looks like meeting with Ca'Themar is your next step."

"Do I have to?"

She sighed, "You know he is a walking encyclopedia. He will know what is going on with you, Niya."

"He is mean."

She shook the contents of her shaker, eyeing me with pursed lips.

"Ugh, fine. I will go see him first chance I get."

She smirked, "Good. Now that *that* is settled, go upstairs and get that paperwork done. You're incredibly behind and the bills don't pay themselves."

"Shit," I whined, "paperwork."

Sahriah tightened her lips and firmly replied, "Go!" She made a shooing motion with the shaker and her other hand.

I waved my hand, "Yes, yes. I *know*," I looked over at Garrin, "Let's go, Garrin. I have work to do," and we both trudged up the swirling staircase to my office.

I opened the heavy solid oak door and allowed Garrin to walk in first. Following behind him, I looked at the stack of papers on my desk and let out a deep groan.

"How long has it been since you've done paperwork?" Garrin asked, eyeing my stack, concerned.

"Several months. Maybe a year. I don't really know," I sighed. Practicing Alman's skills on etiquette, I sat down as daintily as possible. Garrin stifled a smile at my attempt of grace.

As quickly as I'd made the attempt, I gave up and placed my heeled shoes down roughly on the desk. I leaned back in the swivel chair and stared at the ceiling, "This is going to take ages."

Garrin sat in the chair adjacent to me and asked, curious, "How long have you owned this club?"

"Fifty years," I grabbed a stack of papers and started filtering through what I needed to keep and file; what needed to be paid; what was urgent; and what was garbage.

"And how long have you been running it?"

I glanced over the papers to stare at Garrin, "Fifty years."

"Holy shit, you have done a great job keeping it private. I am shocked the patrons don't know who runs it."

"Oh, they know. They just don't deem it a necessity to share it," I continued sorting through the papers meticulously.

The process felt like it took an entire afternoon.

Garrin was to the point of fiddling with the pommel of his sword and leaning backwards in his chair, balancing on it.

Not looking up from my paper, I stated, "When you fall backwards in that chair, I am going to laugh at you."

Garrin let out a huff and put the chair's legs back on the floor, "Can I help you, at least?"

"No, you are my personal guard, so continue," I waved my hand, "guarding me; or whatever you do."

I stopped at one particular piece of parchment that looked different and set the rest on the desk beside me for later perusal.

It was a signed paper with Nikolaj and Sahriah's signatures.

I raised a concerned eyebrow and mumbled, "What in the hells?"

Garrin shot a glare at me, "What?" He straightened in his chair, ready to defend.

Sayge cracked opened the door and announced, "Niya, you are needed downstairs."

Setting the paper down, I asked, "Why?"

"Um, I think it is just better you come see for yourself."

I grumbled, "Fine," and got up, walking towards the door.

Garrin, a foot behind me, followed me down the circling staircase and I stopped in my tracks looking at Leer in between two vampires flailing their arms out at each other.

Closing my eyes and breathing through my nose heavily, I turned to Garrin knowing full well he was about to handle this situation, "Let me handle this, Garrin. I don't need a bigger scene. Stay where you are," and walked toward the bickering males.

I walked composedly toward Leer who was restraining two bellicose males. As I approached, Garrin trailing me, the two brawlers shouted, "What do we have here, Leer? You bring your little sister in here to have tea with her little dollies?"

Leer smiled a knowingly.

"What seems to be the problem, gentlemen?" My voice and demeanor calm and in control.

"This bastard tried to steal my queen, so I threw a barstool at him," the pale vampire with jet blacked hair seethed.

The other male, lashing out, "Which *hurt,* you vamphole. I didn't even steal her! She came onto me!"

I cringed inwardly. It was always the vampires...honestly.

Such possessive bats.

So sensitive.

Leer barked gruffly, "These two 'gentlemen' saw fit to vandalize yer club. There are several broken stools and bar glasses." I looked around at the damage indicated. "Sahriah tried her best to talk them down before it came to blows, but I stepped in before they could cause any more damage. They were at each others throats ready to rip each other to shreds."

I was quite annoyed even though I kept a benign look on my face. I looked at Sahriah who was staring at me with wide eyes. Leer shifted on his feet and looked down to my hands and whispered, "Sweetness, your hands."

"I am sure that these two have had enough excitement for one night, right boys?" Smiling an attar's grin, I looked back and forth at their faces as they stared agape at my hands. "Why don't you accompany me to the exit, hmm?"

Leer let the two miscreants go and, quick as lightning, one of them shot out from under Leer's elbow and ran out of the club door. The other, feeling slighted and disrespected by Leer's "little sister," decided that he wanted to have a few more words before he left.

"Who do you think you are, little lad—" Faster than a blink, I reached up my glowing hand and grabbed the vampire's delicately pointed ear and began calmly dragging him to the door.

The pale vampire shifted into a bat, trying to escape my grasp, and I growled with the fight growing in my veins. I grasped his entire body in both of my hands and motioned for Garrin and Leer, quick on my heels, to follow me outside.

I chucked the bat to the ground, "You *both* owe me new furniture and glasses. I will be sending an invoice to the both of you. You had better see it paid!"

The stunned bat turned back to its fae form and said, "You can't do this."

I seethed, "Oh, but I can. *My* club, *my* rules."

"I am not paying you for what that vamphole started."

"Do you hear yourself? You sound ridiculous," I put my hand on my hips.

He shot up and jogged into the crowd, bumping into others as he looked back to see if I was following him.

I swiveled around to see Garrin and Leer just gawking at me and I sneered, "What!?"

Leer finally spoke, "Nothing, just, you can be such a wild card sometimes, you know that?"

Walking past both of them, flipped my hair off my right shoulder behind me and smoothly stated, "I know," and walked back inside.

"Garrin!" I called behind me, "I need to get my paperwork done now. I think we leave tomorrow for our tour, right?"

Garrin caught up to me, "Yes, we do."

Feeling feisty I replied, "Could you stand by the door and make sure nobody bothers me until I am done?"

Garrin, lost for words, just nodded and that was that.

I went back to my office, closed the door behind me, and spent the next several hours finishing the piles of paperwork.

Standing up, ready to go home, I picked up the signed letter between Nik and Sahriah.

Attached was a check to the orphanage.

Chapter 16
Niya

The next morning, I packed two weeks' worth of clothes and necessities needed for the tour around Kaldamir. I organized my dark leather luggage into sections of pants, blouses, dresses, socks, and undergarments on one side. On the other I placed two pairs of shoes: flats and a small, heeled shoe. Within the luggage there were little compartments to put my bathroom soaps, supplies, and makeup. Zipping up the stuffed luggage, I pulled the leather strap over to pin it altogether.

Our court emblem shone bright metallic red under the faelight. Three knots intertwined with each other met in the middle with a three-point crown sitting on a skull's head.

I was fully dressed to ride a horse. I wore tan slacks and knee length dark cordovan boots. My long sleeve blouse was covered with my royal blue floor length hooded cloak.

I refused to ride in a carriage like a stuffy royal. That went over swell yesterday with mother; lots of arguing to eventually her submitting and letting me do at least one thing for myself. This next week is going to be all for her, and Kaldamir.

The first thing I was going to do as queen, is change this hideous royal crest. I grabbed my luggage and walked downstairs with Garrin to meet his second in command, Claude. Garrin nodded at our arrival as Claude took my bags.

"Princess," Claude bowed deeply.

"Oh stop, Claude, you know better than to use those formalities with me," I nudged his upper arm playfully before taking my leave of the two sentries.

I single-mindedly made my way into the stables and quickly shooed off the help. I headed straight for Nero; my heart happy in my chest.

He was *magnificent*. I lovingly stroked down his neck, forelock, and muzzle; talking to him and praising him for being so brave and beautiful.

This horse was the mightiest beast one could behold. Pure glossy black coat and muscular frame. Piercing black eyes stared at me as he huffed a breath through flared nostrils. I greeted him with lots of pats and rubs. I finger-combed his tangled onyx mane and braided several pieces. Once satisfied with his look, I tacked up Nero and waited for Garrin and Claude to get everything ready for our departure.

Walking out of the stables with Nero, I noticed Garrin and Claude standing back from their horses looking accomplished.

I questioned, "Why is nobody else coming with us, Garrin?"

Garrin shrugged his shoulders, "I guess the queen trusts us enough to get you through the kingdom in one piece."

Eyeing Claude, he made the last adjustments to his horse, securing all of our belongings to the small wagon attached behind.

I countered, "I am not sure I believe that, but okay."

These last couple of days had been very confusing. I know my mother's stated motives, but she does not seem to care at all that I was not okay with her plans. She knew that I would not follow through with them, yet she continued to push the matters. Killing Adryen was not ideal. It was a means to an unnecessary war.

Garrin mounted his horse and asked, "Are you ready to go to the border and visit Lady Delilah?"

"I suppose so. I haven't spoken with her in a long time. I am sure she is still doing well. Our border villages are quaint and quiet. I suspect it is all the same."

I slipped my foot into the stirrup and swung over to sit astride Nero. I grabbed hold of the reigns and clicked my tongue for him to walk.

My tour had officially started.

Lady Delilah's village was a couple hours ride from here when I was not riding my motorcycle or transversing. The snow was chilling, and I could feel my cheeks chapping from the wind. I should have just taken a carriage.

Or Blackstar.

We would have gotten there so much faster.

About halfway into our journey, my bladder was starting to ache.

"Garrin," I moaned in pain.

He looked over to me and smirked, "I thought you wanted to tour on your horse, Niya."

Mumbling, "Yes, with breaks."

Garrin, "We are halfway there, do we really need to take a break?"

Gawking, I retorted, "Yes, Garrin! My ass hurts!" I hauled Nero to a stop and stiffly swung off. My knees gave out and I tumbled into the snow.

I groaned, "Ooooowww."

Jumping off of his horse and rushing over to me, Garrin hauled me up and brushed the snow off of me, "Very graceful, Niya."

I rolled my eyes.

Garrin let go of me and sighed, a little puff of smoke billowed from his lips, "I am giving you five minutes and then we are getting back to our travels."

"Ten. I need to relieve myself."

Garrin shook his head, and I stomped past him to look for a private area. After beginning the process, I looked around and realized that I had nothing to wipe myself with. I let out a huge sigh and wiggled myself dry, pulling my pants back up my freezing thighs.

Chills rolled down my body that was trying to reheat itself.

Feeling a thousand times better, I found my way to the little carriage and pulled out a bag of dried fruits and nuts. I threw a couple handfuls in my mouth and jumped back onto Nero, "I am ready; let's get this first village done with. I am already over it."

Garrin chuckled and we continued our long trek to Lady Delilah. Lady Delilah was a dryad. Her physical appearance was unlike any other fae within our kingdom. She had lived by The Great Divide for as long as I could remember. Her lifestyle was perfect for what we'd expect of border living. She provided intelligence about trespassers and, in return, we made sure her forest was left untouched.

We finally arrived at the village of Cleome. Beautifully sculpted homes were built on the forest floor and towered well over twenty feet above me. Every house was built from some different variety of tree: birch, beech, and maple; wisteria and poplar abound.

We dismounted our horses and gave them to the stable hands as they'd expected our arrival. They bowed quickly and scurried away as we made our way into the heart of the village.

The dryad villagers were a gorgeous pallet of moss, pistachio, and mint—every shade of green one could imagine. Each of them stopped what they were doing and bowed deeply as we walked to Lady Delilah's cot.

Mere feet away, Lady Delilah burst out of her home and greeted me with a painful hug, "Princess Niya, it is so wonderful to see you again!"

Most dryads were shy, but not Lady Delilah.

She was a pure delight; a golden ray of sunshine.

I hugged her back and smiled, "It hasn't been so long, Lady Delilah. I was just here visiting with the sprites."

We let go of each other and I got a better glimpse of the dryad. Her jade skin radiated under the sunlight with several little wood branches swirling up her body and onto her beautiful face, creating a leafy crown. Flowers were placed delicately across her hairline to accentuate her natural beauty. Her eyes beamed in their aquamarine color.

"Yes, but you have not come to see me, child. I am honored that we are the first stop on your tour. Please, come in. I have made some nectar," Lady Delilah motioned for us to enter her cot.

I kept my expression neutral as she mentioned the sugar water they called "nectar." Dryads could eat food and drink water like the other fae. But dryads preferred to eat more natural food like dirt, honey, and berries. Hydration was different as well. Fae, who were not dryad, would normally drink regular water but for fae like Lady Delilah, sugar water was ideal.

Ideally sweet.

Garrin, Lady Delilah, and I walked into her cot while Claude stayed behind to stand guard.

"Your home is wonderful, Lilah," I smiled as warm scents of cinnamon and cedar hit my nose.

We took a seat on her wooden furniture in front of an empty fireplace. I would never understand why these homes even had fireplaces.

No dryad used them.

Delilah responded, "Thank you, Niya. We have been working on renovating our homes to better suit the needs of visitors and guests. Will you be staying for the festivities tonight? It is our celebration of the forest."

She poured us hot nectar from her magic-infused warming kettle my parents gifted her for last year's celebration and sat on the chaise across from Garrin and me.

I shivered under my cloak as the warmth of the sugar water slid down my throat, "I would love to."

Delilah smiled as I started to make myself more comfortable. I took my heavy winter coat off and slid up my sleeves. I have no idea what was in this water other than sugar, but I was suddenly very warm.

Delilah stared deeply into the shadows on my arm and whispered, "Niya, those are powerful shadows swirling around your arm. Have they manifested yet?"

"What? What do you mean manifested?" Sahriah was joking at the bar about shadow manifestation but had not elaborate any further.

A slight panic began to rise in me.

I shifted in my seat and Delilah quickly got up and backed up to the wall, "We do not play with your dark magic, Niya. I can feel your powers growing and becoming too instense. They signal a great deal of death and destruction."

I attempted to cover them with my hand, suddenly feeling very uncomfortable.

Dryads were often weak in dark elemental magic like fire, ice, and shadow. It made me curious to hear that Delilah had such knowledge on this matter.

"Lilah, I—"

Several screams billowed from outside as dryads across the village scurried past Delilah's cot.

Claude banged on the door and yelled to Garrin, "Get out here, sir. There has been a breech!"

Garrin stared at the door, than back to me, "Get out of this village, now!" His vociferation clanged against my skull.

"You can't just leave me here, Garrin! Let me help you!" I shouted as he ran out of the door, slamming it behind him.

I glanced over at Delilah, and she was now one with the foundation of the home, disguising herself inside the walls. I looked at her in her fear and vulnerability and knew that I had to do something.

I unsheathed my sword, escaping out the back door.

Not one villager was to be seen as I looked down the pathways.

Running between homes, I heard the grunts and screams of Garrin and Claude fighting off a dark shadow figure. I stalked around the periphery of the battle and tried to keep my eyes on the villain hovering above the ground. Claude valiantly attacked and counterattacked the massive shadow with his useless sword.

The figure slashed its dark fingers out and into Claude's chest. The mist like shadows' spikes turned substantial as its fingers protruded from Claude's back.

I shouted, "No!"

Claude dropped the the floor, lifeless.

I didn't know what was happening. Crimson eyes stared directly at me through the black haze. My body and mind locked up. I was like a deer confronted by a predator.

Garrin whipped around from the figure and yelled, "Niya, run! Get the fuck out of here!"

The red eyes did not release their hold on me. I walked slowly backward towards the stables as the shadow stood there, unflinching. A familiar horse neighed, and I grabbed his reins from behind me. Breaking our gazes, I hoisted myself onto Nero and kicked him into a run.

Nero and I bolted as far and as fast as we could and tried our best to maneuver away from the village and further into the forest.

Toward The Great Divide.

Dense fog started to cover the forest floor as Nero wended his way through. I looked behind me and not one trace of anything was following me. Nero neighed and bucked me off of the saddle. I went flying onto the snow-covered ground and Nero hit, sending wet icy soil my way. The shadow let go of Nero's front leg as it creeped towards me.

I rolled away from Nero and my own shadows tightened on my arm, squeezing me. I grabbed the arm in reaction and tried to rub the pain away. My magic surged and emanated off of me in furious pulses.

I got to my feet and started running. If this shadow figure could keep up to Nero, I would have no chance.

I continued running anyway.

I briefly halted, trying to figure out my escape route. If I go right, I will hit The Divide. Going left will send me further into the forest.

Not quick enough in my panic, the shadow figure grabbed my wrist and started to envelop me. Shades of gray and black devoured me as I was pulled into its darkness.

I pushed myself backward with my wind and tumbled out of the shadow's embrace and onto my rear. I closed my eyes, creating a fire rope in hopes of trapping the creature. I threw my fiery rage toward it, but it seemed to be fighting off my magic easily. I had to find a way to stop it. I struggled and was able to finally engulf the shadow in my rope, pinning it where it stood. I closed my grip, making it harder for the shadow to move. Wiping the sweat off of my face and clenching my teeth, I tried to push more of my magic into crushing this thing.

I was starting to strain, and my power felt like it was rupturing. This shadow was incredibly powerful. My ability to harness dark magic was great, but I was trying to keep control of the power that I was not yet fully comfortable wielding.

My heart stopped.

I pulled from deeper within my magic and my own shadows shot out of me in a burst toward the figure. An ice-cold jolt went down my spine.

Crimson eyes locked on mine.

In this moment, I remembered my studies on shadowed entities. I needed to grab this shadow and take the glamour off. Most of the time, this type of creature came from a Fae doing a spell wrong. I crawled to the figure, retracted the rope so I could grab what looked to be the shadow's hand.

The shadow seemed to wince at my touch.

A huge gust of air blasted me, pushing me several feet from it. My shadows came racing back to be.

I screamed in pain as I fell back.

Looking at my arm, my shadows were no longer shadows. They were permanent, like a tattoo. Dark black swirls frozen in an ethereal dance peaked up past my shirt to my shoulder blade. I looked up and the shadow figure laughed mischievously as it rippled a piercing finger across my abdomen.

A scream bellowed out of me as I cupped my bleeding stomach. A gust of wind pulsed past me. I looked up and an azure wyvern landed by the shadow, engulfing it in flame.

The shadow shrieked as the glamour wore off and the fae burned to ashes.

Adryen stalked over to me in his shifted form, and I squirmed backwards. He had just annihilated this thing and now he was going to kill me. I did not know if he had control over his creature and I was in a very vulnerable position bleeding my guts out.

I attempted to heal myself with no real knowledge of how to do so. I slammed my body back in frustration and kicked the ground like a child, knowing that was useless.

"You tried your best," Adryen laughed as I looked up at his perfectly toned naked body.

Offended, I countered, "And you came way too late you stupid wyvern! I thought your species was supposed to be majestic! All you did was burn the damned thing."

I was starting to get dizzy and little white and black dots flecked my vision.

Adryen turned back into his wyvern and trotted closer to me. I gasped and then winced as his face drew inches from mine. I could look at this form of his for hours, but I was bleeding profusely and was probably die.

"Help me," I whispered as I lowered my hand to my wound; his cornflower eyes followed the movement down to the wound spilling blood.

A penetratingly territorial growl rolled out of Adryen as he beheld my mutilated stomach. I threw my head back, writhing in the pain and my eyes closed, as I gave in to the darkness.

Chapter 17
Adryen

"I had no other choice but to bring her here, Fin." I hustled past him, carrying Niya in my arms into the castle.

She is breathing too slowly for what I'd thought normal. When I saw that wound on Niya's stomach, my blood started to boil. I had never felt such rage and need to protect before; not even with my own family.

I could hear Finion's footsteps behind me, "But sire, her parents will think we've kidnapped her and that will spoil any plans that we have. I—"

I stopped in my tracks and turned to face my advisor, "You are dismissed, Finion. I will handle this myself."

I quickly turned back around and hurried with Niya in my arms to my quarters on the third floor. Arriving, I pushed the handle down with my elbow and the white, wooden door swung open. Entering the master suite, I set Niya down on my bed and ripped the rest of her shirt, exposing her wound.

My breath caught at the sight.

Blood was still oozing from her abdomen, and I had to fight the black encroaching on my vision as I examined her.

It was deep; I didn't know if I could heal it.

I sent my golden light of healing into Niya, easing the pain the best that I could. I had never experienced such an injury before; I was fighting the panic and struggling to hold myself together.

Going to the bathroom I grabbed a clean cloth, cleansing solution, and warm water to gently clean and sanitize her wound. Once sterile, I produced a thin, tough thread of magic to sinch the damaged tissue. My power wove the thread through the edges of her wound, binding the flesh back together.

Moments later, I'd finished my stitching and tied off the healing thread. I exhaled a breath that I felt had been held for days. The wound was deeper than I had anticipated. My thoughts and emotions were all over the place. What if I hadn't gotten to her in time? I convinced myself that once the healing threads started doing their work, she would be fine.

She's going to be fine.

Please, let her be fine.

My body drained of magic, I stood up grabbing a loose flannel shirt, undergarments and tan pants from my closet. I slipped them on and knelt at the foot of the bed placing my head on the footboard. I should have noticed her wound immediately. I was too focused on killing that thing. I could hear—no; I could *feel* her scream from my side of The Great Divide.

It was an ice spike in my heart.

I walked back to the bed and looked down at Niya's sleeping body. Reaching over the foot of the bed, I felt for breathing. I moved in closer to Niya, placing my first two fingers to the side of her neck to feel for a stronger pulse. I sighed in relief at her stabilized heartbeat.

Thank the gods.

A light knock sounded at the door, and I walked to it, cracking it open.

"Your Majesty," Daphne bowed, "I saw that there was an injured female in your arms when you arrived. I wanted to see if I could be of service."

Daphne was my mother's attendant. She'd followed my mother everywhere making sure her needs were met and that she had company.

Daphne was probably around Niya's age, but I had never asked. When my parents died, Daphne took a step back into manual labor around the castle grounds to keep her busy. She was a very quiet and loyal subject. I'd wished I had something more productive for her to do.

"Thank you, Daph, but I don't think so." I idly finger-combed my hair, and she bowed and started to walk away, "Actually, I *could* use your help," suddenly coming to my senses.

Pointing to Niya's recovering body on the bed, "She will be here for at least a couple of days, and I am not going to be able to watch over her as much as I would like to. Would you be able to help me out and make her feel comfortable? My chambers are hers until she is healed."

Daphne smiled and nodded her head, "Thank you, King Adryen. I look forward to being of service. I will do my utmost to make sure she is happy and comfortable." Pausing and looking around me to the bed, "Who is she?"

I looked out at Daphne's translucent, rosy wings twitching with anticipation. "Niya," I said.

Daphne's pupils dilated as she asked, cautiously, "Like, *Princess* Niya?"

I nodded my head and opened the door to leave. Daphne squealed with excitement. Closing the door behind me, I walked past Daphne and looked back at her, "Yes. She will need your help, so please do whatever you can to make her want for nothing while she is with us. I would prefer the talks of our kingdom to happen with me, and me only," I paused, "Niya is...curious and stubborn. I want to make sure our kingdom is seen in the very best light, and I would like to be there in case she finds something not to her liking."

I nodded my head to Daphne and headed to the stairs and made my way down to the throne room.

Part 2:
The Warmth

Chapter 18
Niya

I t was dark and I was running through the forest. A blurred entity was chasing me and I kept looking back to see where it was. It was always right there no matter how fast or how far I ran.

I screamed at it to leave me alone.

Please just leave me alone...

The shadow figure reached out to me, grabbing my waist, and pulled me closer. Its fingers sliced at me, and I jolted awake.

I clasped my hands together where my heart threatened to pound out of my chest and looked around. I did not recognize any of this. The room was bright and had a plethora of windows. Cream curtains adorned them, blocking out some of the harshness of the sun's rays.

I looked down and felt the white silk sheets beneath me.

Where was I?

This room was massive.

I could fit two of my own rooms into this one. The bed was big enough to fit four fae. I sat up and a jolt of pain reverberated through my stomach. Sucking in a breath, I glanced down at the area of the sharpest of the pain and I saw these strange golden stitches glowing there. Fingering them cautiously, I felt little zings through me up to my wrist.

Realizing that I didn't know if I was with friend or foe, I reached for my longsword—that was no longer strapped to my back. Panic filled me and I rolled off the bed. Trying to catch my feet and failing, I fell knees first to the floor.

"Damn it," I whispered and moaned as I rubbed at my bruised knees.

The door squeaked open, and I darted a glare in the direction of a small voice that echoed into the enormous room, "Oh, hello Princess," she said was caution behind her tone.

I peeked up from the bedframe and looked straight at a pixie. The female had gorgeously long, loosely curled, blush-pink hair with matching wings. Her attire matched both the color of her hair and wings.

She looked like a little sweet on a party tray.

Russet brown eyes met mine, "Oh goodness, you are probably so confused," She shuffled around the room coming closer to me, "I am Daphne. I am here to help take care of you while you heal in our kingdom."

I shuffled up from the floor as she continued toward me, "Kingdom? Where am I?"

Daphne giggled, "Haldonia. Where else?"

My eyes widened as I remembered how Adryen had come swooping in his wyvern form to save me from the shadow thing.

I didn't remember how I got *here,* though.

"No, I can't be here," I rubbed my hands vigorously over my face, "Daphne, show me how to get to The Great Divide."

Daphne held her head down and knelt next to me, "You are in no shape to leave yet. Adryen placed stitches on your wound to help you heal. If you leave the kingdom, they will disappear, and you will bleed out. His magic is tied to the land."

I pulled my shirt up and looked down at the stitches again, "Adryen did this?"

"Oh yes, he is quite the healer," Daphne paused, "Amongst a lot of other things."

Daphne grabbed my hand and helped me up. I winced at the pain and sat back on the bed. This couldn't be happening. My mother was going to kill me. This tour was my opportunity to prove I was ready to ascend; not only for myself, but for my family and people, too. This was going to look terrible when I got back.

I questioned, "How long will it be before I am healed?"

Daphne answered, "Probably a couple of days or longer. I do not know how deep your cut was. The deeper the cut, the longer it will take to heal."

"Will it scar?"

"No, Adryen is very good with his hands."

A low growl escaped me in response.

Daphne, her tone changing to wary and eager, "Anyways! I will need to get your measurements so our tailor can get some clothes ready for you. Do you prefer dresses or casual clothes?"

I attempted to get up, "That is very kind, Daphne," I said through clenched teeth. "I am only staying for a day or two. I can wear whatever leftover clothes you have stored away."

Daphne giggled and motioned for me to lie back on the bed, "Don't be ridiculous!" She continued, "You are royalty, I will not allow you to wear anybody's left over garments. I had to argue with the king over what you are wearing now."

"Oh" I looked down to see loose stretchy pants and a very loose shirt sitting on me. I did not even realize I was no longer wearing the clothes I left in.

How long had I been out?

Suddenly feeling very uncomfortable I stated, "I don't know my measurements."

"That is no problem," Daphne chirped as she pulled out a measuring string, "Try to stand up for me. Move slowly so you don't disturb the stitches."

The pixie was really getting on my nerves. Sit down...stand up...I haltingly got back up on my feet and Daphne sent the string to measure around my entire body with her magic.

A notepad and pen appeared as she watched the string take my measurements. It started at my neck, then my chest and moved all the way down to my feet.

"The tailor is going to *love* these measurements. He has not made any clothing for a woman of your stature before," Daphne's eyes brightening.

My blood started to boil, and my permanent shadows coiled, "What does *that* mean?" I asked through gritted teeth.

Daphne was either socially inept, or she was trying to piss me off.

"Oh. Um." Daphne trailed off and then backed away from me calling her string back, "I did not mean it like that, Your Highness. It is just that you have the *perfect* shape. You have a perfectly curved hourglass figure..."

Daphne blushed as she trailed off.

I sighed, "I am sorry. I didn't mean to lash out."

She bowed her head slightly, "I will send these measurements to Doogan now and he should have something ready for you within the hour. Please, feel free to walk around the castle as you wish. Just, don't go into any rooms. The king likes his privacy."

An hour?!

I wish our clothing designers would worked that fast. I would have an endless supply of clothing.

I stated, "I will be here waiting, I guess," looking down at my side. "Thank you, Daphne."

She smiled and slipped out of the room. I looked around and got another view of this monstrous place. The bed was set against the back center of the wall with two accompanying mahogany nightstands.

This must be Adryen's royal chambers. There was no way this was a guest suite. He should have just put me in the hospital ward, where I belonged. Unless the Seelie are just that talented in the healing arts that they didn't need one.

I walked over to the nightstand on the right and pulled a drawer open. I grabbed an umber binding with metallic letters on the front.

A Lover's Crusade by Violet Vivienne.

Smiling, I opened the cover. The first page was inscribed with beautiful script:

> May you find love as powerful as these two.

I raised my eyebrow and laid my back on the bed and, propping my legs up, I started skimming the pages.

Not sure how long had passed, I closed the book at chapter ten as a rough knock sounded at the door. Before I could get up, blue eyes met with mine. Adryen's entire figure entered through the door; I was speechless.

Adryen was more stunning than I had remembered. Azure-tipped ears shone in the light of the room and my head tilted.

Curious.

When I met him, his ears were normal, not speckled to blue tips.

His tapered chestnut hair irreverently tossed strands over his forehead. Adryen's golden antler crown sat regally on his head.

He wore this linen-colored button-down cotton shirt with pewter slacks. Seeing him here felt like a sigh in a weary realm.

"Hello," Adryen smirked.

I slammed the book closed and sat up slowly, straining my lips at the tension from my stomach. Before I realized it, Adryen was next to me helping me sit up comfortably.

"How do you move so fast?" I winced.

He chuckled, "I don't know. It is just something I have always been able to do," Adryen paused, looking at the book I was now trying to hide, "Are you sneaking through my things?"

"No?"

Adryen quickly snagged the book from me and stared at it, "This was my mothers."

I looked down, "I'm sorry; I was trying to keep myself busy. I just—"

"—No, it's okay," Adryen smiled, "She gave it to me when I turned eighteen. I have read it several times. It's one of my favorite romances. You could borrow it, if you would like."

I peeked over at the book, "I wish I could. I don't have the time anymore," and then I looked up at him, "How long have I been here?"

Adryen fiddled with the book and then put it back away in the nightstand, "I don't think I should tell you. You might go crazy on me and transverse again."

I couldn't transverse. I was still very unfamiliar with my surroundings. I needed to figure out where The Divide was so I could create a jumping point.

Adryen didn't need to know that, though.

Squinting my eyes at him, I shook my index finger to him, "Tell me. Now!"

Eyes darting around the room looking for rescue, "Two days."

I jumped up and pain shot through me. I grabbed my stomach and yelled furiously, "What! You are telling me I have been asleep for two days!"

"Niya, please."

I started to pace back and forth, "I need to go home, Adryen. I shouldn't be here!"

Adryen frowned, "Well, you *are* here. And I would like you to stay until you are fully healed. It took a lot out of me to create those stitches."

"How long until I fully heal? Daphne told me a couple days. I need a definitive answer."

Adryen got up, irritated, and started towards me, "You know, a thank you for saving your life would be perfect right now. I could have left you by The Divide to die."

I glared at him, "But you didn't because you need me, right? You need me to marry you so your people can thrive."

As I walked by, I bumped into his arm. Adryen grabbed my hand, turning me to face him, "Niya—I. It is not like that anymore. At the lagoon earlier and just then, when I saw you hurt and felt you scream."

His voice trailed off into sorrow, and my eyes blazed, "You're saying that you *heard* a scream through thick thorns of a wall."

"I said felt, Princess."

Screaming was, as far as I knew, a sound, not something you could feel.

"You can't *feel* a scream, Your Kingliness." I pulled my hand away from his, wincing from the sudden movement, and made my way to one of the too many windows.

Adryen whispered, "I could feel your pain in my entire soul. It wrecked me," he trailed behind me, questioning, "You are not afraid of my Wyvern, are you?"

I looked out from his colorful terrace, wondering how the hell something like this could have happened.

The awe-inspiring kingdom made me want to cry with joy. I was confused and angry, yet I felt peaceful and at home at the same time.

Slowly and carefully, I replied, "I am not *afraid* of you, Adryen. I never have been. You just...took me by surprise," I turned to face him, and I could feel his heat radiating into me, "I think your wyvern form is magnificent," a jolt of electricity shot straight to my core at the realization of that.

I slid my hand up his jawline, without thinking, and reached up to touch his beautiful, cerulean-tipped ears.

Trembling, Adryen placed his thumb on my chin and curled his index finger under it. He leaned in closer to me, "I would be very careful when touching a wyvern's ears, Princess," he smiled lazily as he came in for a kiss.

I smiled back seductively, pulling his neck into me, still not feeling in full control of myself.

A knock sounded at the door and Adryen stopped in his tracks, looking over at the sound. I dropped my hand from him as he backed up, giving more space in between our almost caressing lips.

Daphne opened it to see us; the tension palpable, "Oh gods. I am so sorry, Your Highness."

She shut the door and Adryen and I looked back at each other and moved even further away, trying to look otherwise occupied.

I needed to put space between us, so he did not get the wrong idea. I didn't want to toy with his emotions—or my own. I needed to check myself.

Putting more space between us, I cleared my throat, "Your room is quite immaculate, Your Majesty."

Winking at Adryen, I walked out to meet Daphne, leaving him where he stood, smiling at me.

Chapter 19
Niya

Daphne was a beam of light as she cheered, "Your dress amongst other things to wear for today are ready, Princess. Doogan would like for you to meet him in the sewing room."

I grumbled, "Do I have to wear a dress?"

"Would you like to wear nothing?"

I raised an eyebrow, considering it, but then thought better of it. I did not need to show off my body to people who had no business looking at it.

Resigning myself, I gave Daphne a small smile and we walked down the seemingly endless flights of stairs to the bottom floor. We passed by several closed doors that sparked my curiosity.

Adryen's castle was colossal.

If I walked around by myself, I would get lost for sure.

My lips quirked at the thought of looking into every room this palace had to offer, despite Daphne saying he liked his privacy.

Daphne cut my thoughts short, "We are here!"

Daphne hurried to the door and opened...the sewing room.

Peaking my head in, I beheld a masterpiece of chaos. String and ribbon; thread and bobbins; sheers and bolts and bolts of fabric were taking up every inch of the walls and tables. In the middle of the menagerie was a tiny dais for a male or female to stand while the seamstress or tailor did their job. There were so many colors snagging the eye.

There were no windows in this room; for a change.

"So, you are my model?" A rich-toned male bellowed from somewhere inside the room.

I perked up and advanced toward the voice, shutting the door behind me.

"Hello, darling. You must be Princess Niya," Doogan glided to me with ethereal grace and held out his hand, palm down, "It is a pleasure to meet you."

He grabbed my outstretched hand and kissed my knuckles, bowing deeply.

Grinning, I bowed deeply back to him, "And you must be the tailor."

"Best one in the kingdom, darling," He winked at me and whirled around to indicate the kingdom in question.

Doogan wore very colorful clothing with his royal purple pants that tightened at the ankles and a pink and orange paisley patterned vest. He would fit in perfectly in our fashion district. He would *love* Metrika and they wouldn't know what hit them.

"I am only here for a couple of days," I started, "This really isn—"

Doogan cut me off, "Absolute nonsense. Let me work my magic, darling. Get on the dais and prepare to be in love."

Not sure that I was quite ready for *that* level of commitment to a dress, I hesitantly moved to the platform and stepped up standing with my arms crossed over my chest, "This is unnecessary."

"Darling, please. What is unnecessary is the ensemble the king brought out for you to wear," flapping one hand at me with his nose in the air. Doogan snapped his fingers and my clothes disappeared, "He would have such terrible style if it wasn't for me," pausing for a moment of silence for Adryen's terrible fashion sense.

I groaned at the thought of being completely naked in front of this male. I covered myself self-consciously as Doogan barked out a laugh.

I bared my teeth, "If you are laughing at me, I will rip your voice box from your throat."

"No, darling" he continued laughing, "I am *laughing* at the fact that you think I care what body parts you have on display. Honey, I have seen it all. Put your arms down so I can assemble your dress."

I dropped my arms tentatively and stood there waiting for Doogan to work his magic. He went to a rack in the corner of the room and pulled out a lavender tulle dress. My eyes squinted and my mouth quirked incredulously.

I didn't know if he was joking.

Doogan handed me the pretty purple thing and I dubiously slipped it on. The silhouetted princess-cut dress accentuated my ample chest reverently as I slid my arms through the off-shoulder tulle sleeves. Doogan came behind me and zipped up the back, adjusting the sweep train and the pleats that hugged my waist. I hefted the heavy tulle skirts and noticed... *oh my gods; it couldn't be*...the perfectly placed slit on Celeste's side. A smile beamed from my face.

I examined myself.

Stunning.

I would never have worn something so frilly and large. I continued studying myself, grinning at the thought of Adryen seeing me in this. I pushed my leg out of the slit, admiring the exposed leg.

Doogan looked at my expression in the mirror, "King Adryen told me you liked slits. He said something about a weapon?"

Heat rose to my cheeks as the thought of Adryen's kind gesture took purchase in my heart, "Yes, well almost all my dresses have slits. It makes it easier to move around."

"It seems as though the king has thought of everything," Doogan replied knowingly.

My stomach tightened.

I twisted around to peak at the back; it was low cut and revealed my shoulder freckles. I turned back and chuckled, "I love this dress so much, Doogan. I would have never thought of a dress like this for myself. I wouldn't have even considered that light colors like this might look good on me," and floofed it dramatically, "It is so *fluffy*!"

Doogan moved to stand in front of me, as pride swelled in his chest, "Damn, I did it again! I have not had the pleasure of making a dress like this since..." He went silent.

I saw Doogan's smile grow somber, "You don't have to tell me, Doogan. I appreciate you letting me wear your designs. May I take it home with me?"

"Absolutely! Any designs I make for you, are yours. They are customized to fit your exact measurements."

I looked down at Doogan, "How do I send you the money for them?"

"You don't. The King has paid for all of your clothes."

Doogan moved behind me as I trailed my fingers down the wonderous dress, feeling every tulle strand and pleat on the bodice and not paying attention to anything else.

Paid for my clothes? I could afford my own designer clothes. If Adryen insisted on paying for them, I would have to owe him yet another debt.

I said, frustrated, "Help me take it off, Doogan. I will not wear it if I cannot pay for it."

I reached for the zipper and a rough hand stopped me; the smell of birch and eucalyptus hitting me hard. The hand slowly lowered the zipper, with his remaining fingers trailing the skin left exposed. Once the hand had the zipper down to my rear, my back on full display, his other slipped inside, grabbing me by the waist and pulled me closer.

My body heated as blood rose to my cheeks.

I whirled around and Adryen stepped up on the platform with me leaning over and whispered, "Are you mad?"

I pushed Adryen's hand away from me and curled my lip, "What are you playing at, King?"

Adryen kissed my cheek, "Nothing; I just thought I would do something nice for you."

"Too big of a gesture, Your Majesty," I confided.

"Funny. I've never gotten complaints about the size of my *gestures* before," he smirked and leaned in.

I stepped back trying to get away from his kiss.

Forgetting I was on the platform, I fell backwards towards the floor. My body tensed in reaction before Adryen caught me and pulled me back up to him.

Pain zipped up to my stomach and blood began to bloom on the front of the dress.

No...I just ruined this gorgeous dress.

Overwhelmed, tears welled in my eyes as I stammered, looking into Adryen's then at Doogan eyes, "Doogan. Oh, my gods. I am so sorry." I fumbled for the shoulder sleeves to slip the dress off and fingers snapped, removing the blood-stained dress from me.

Adryen put his hand to my stomach and mended the opened wound. Warmth and tingles shot through my body as the blood dissipated. He frowned as he looked down at me, sweat beading on his forehead.

Healing my wound must have taken a lot out of him to be showing such signs of distress.

I tried to cover myself from Adryen, but he pulled me into him.

He was holding onto my bare body. Adryen tightened around me, being respectful, and not looking down. A tug of desire wrapped around me as I shifted my weight. Doogan handed Adryen a bundle of clothes. I snatched them away and moved away from Adryen, covering myself up with them.

"Turn around, both of you," I shrieked.

Adryen and Doogan looked at each other and shrugged their shoulders, turning their backs towards me.

Doogan smoothly stated, "I mean, we both just saw you naked."

"No, *you* have just seen me naked. Thankfully, his majesty has some decency."

I could feel the smile on Adryen's face as Doogan elbowed him on the forearm.

I rolled my eyes to myself.

Slipping on the white blouse, lacy black thong, and buttoned the black high-waisted trousers over my stomach, I looked at

Doogan, who already made himself busy taking the blood stain out of that gorgeous dress.

Sighing, "I am so sorry, Doogan. I will make sure money finds its way to you to replace the cost of the dress and the clothes I am wearing now."

I rushed out of the room with both their backs still turned and closed the door behind me. I looked around at the common room searching for any exit. I moved swiftly around the far edges of the room in hopes of finding a knob, or something.

The number of windows in this home was ridiculous.

There was no privacy!

A paned door stood majestically at the corner of the room, and I bolted towards it.

As I was running out to the open, the warmth of the sun beat on my face.

Warmth.

This kingdom was so warm compared to home, in so many ways.

My senses alerted to the sound of splashing water that clapped and crashed somewhere behind the castle; I cautiously advanced to peek around the corner.

A shore lay half a mile away from where I stood.

I hadn't seen open water like this, ever.

I ran barefoot, full of childlike abandon, as fast as I could to the water. I stopped at the shore's edge, huffing, and out of breath. Cool water hit my feet and the combination of the water, bubbles, and strange dirt overwhelmed my senses. I started to laugh.

I closed my eyes and embraced the wind blowing through my hair and the water flowing through my toes. I moved backwards and sat on the uncommon, dry dirt, looking out into the endless watery expanse.

I could live here and be happy, forever. Kaldamir was so cold and so dreadfully lifeless in most places. I pulled my knees up to my chest and rested my head on them.

A nagging sense of obligations unmet and sundry negative thoughts started to fill my head.

I needed to find a way home, despite the amazing hospitality Adryen had provided. My mother was probably furious as to why I had not tried to contact her. It had been two days and Garrin had most likely notified her of our attack and my disappearance; unless she thought I was dead.

That led me to other thoughts; would she mourn over me if I were? Would Ravyn wring her hands and keen or would she go on about her life as if nothing had happened? I wasn't sure I wanted to know the answer to that question.

I didn't know for sure how far away The Divide was from here so I couldn't pinpoint a transversing site for myself. I could always just ask Adryen, but he would probably refuse to aid me and reiterate what Daphne had said earlier about the magic only working here.

I pulled my blouse out of my pants and looked at the golden stitches again. They glittered in the sunlight as I pushed my fingers through them, the powerful magic keeping them together warmed against my skin. I glanced over at the swirls on my arms, and they started to turn golden with every touch I proffered to them.

I tilted my head curiously at the golden hue taking over my arm. Dropping it back to my side, the gold quickly disappeared from the swirls, turning them back to the inky black.

So strange.

Magic should not transfer like that.

I tucked my shirt back into my trousers and looked back out to the ocean.

Maybe I could stay a couple days and heal. I shook my head at the thought.

Ugh. I *really* couldn't stay; my mind warring with itself like a prudent parent and a petulant child. I left Garrin and a very dead Claude in the village. Garrin had probably made extreme haste back to the castle to let my mother know what had happened, but I had to find out.

Either way, I couldn't stay here, but I couldn't go back to my kingdom.

Not yet.

∞∞∞∞∞

Hours passed as I sat watching the ocean waves, feet submerged, and I just took in the view. I had never felt so serene.

The sun was setting on the horizon. I got up from where I sat and lazily walked to the retreating water, spreading my toes to let the water flow through them again. My heels sank into the wet and the bottom of my trousers became soaked with the water. Bending over, I stroked and caressed the water with my fingers, inviting the coolness to envelop me.

"Princess," a female voice interrupted my reverie.

I twisted around to see Daphne smiling warmly.

"Please, call me Niya," I insisted.

"It's time for supper...Niya," the petite pixie continued shyly.

"I'm going to go upstairs and change first," wiping my hands on my damp pants.

"I will walk you up," she continued.

I waved my arm in front of myself indicating that I would follow, and we began the hike back to the palace, leaving the beautiful scenery behind.

I took in the full view of the kingdom.

Rose's painting is a perfect representation of Haldonia.

Better, in fact.

We made our way up the staircase and onto the third-floor landing to Adryen's room.

Daphne smiled at me and curtsied, "I will check back in a little bit to escort you down. I pulled out a more relaxed outfit for you that Doogan made. New pants and a nice blouse." I nodded my understanding and dismissal and slipped into my new temporary quarters.

Entering the room, my footsteps halted abruptly just inside of the entry, blood running cold. My eyes scanned all around me in shock and disbelief. The ginormous glass windows had words written in drying blood all over them. One giant letter covered each window: D-E-A-T-H. I jolted back; my body thudding mercilessly against the wall next to the doorway.

I groaned in pain, thinking, this wound is never going to heal with my constant movements.

Something wet dripped in front of my face from above. Blood covered the floor at my feet. I had slipped in it and hadn't even noticed as my eyes took in the windows. I wiped my bloody feet several times on the unblemished floor next to the puddle.

With dawning realization and terror, I slowly looked up to behold a slaughtered and mutilated animal hanging above me.

I recognized the need to check for the intruder that did this; too late if someone was still there. With renewed caution, I grabbed the heaviest, blunt object I could find nearby and started scanning the room, clearing every corner and dark entryway.

Nobody was there, thank the gods. Kneeling on all fours in front of the closet, I rummaged and threw behind me every old, battered piece of clothing piled there until my hand hit metal. I grabbed Celeste and examined her for damage.

Perfectly attached and untouched.

I sighed in relief.

Walking back over to the animal and looking closer, I was less afraid.

It looked like a goat.

Some sort of sacrifice?

Oh, no.

Running to the bathroom I grabbed a face towel and soaked it in warm water. Hurrying to the windows, I scrubbed every blood marked window until, many trips later, nothing was left but wet streaks. I made many more trips to rinse the towel as I cleaned the sticky floor beneath the animal next. I stepped back, wiping my brow, and examined the hanging goat again.

A knock sounded at the door, and I jumped in surprise, "Just a minute!"

Not knowing what else to do, I created a portal above the goat and pushed it upwards, sending the bloodied animal to the shore where I spent most of the day.

I guess I'm not going back THERE.

The animal disappeared as I closed the portal and placed my hands on my knees leaning over, exhausted.

Another knock sounded with a voice, "Niya, are you okay?"

Blurting again, "Just a minute!"

I threw my disgusting, bloody clothes off and put on the ones Daphne left for me.

I had never been to this kingdom before.

Who could possibly want me dead?

I could not tell anybody about this. Whoever did this would show their hand and then I would strike. Resolved and armed with my mask of confidence and nonchalance, I strapped Celeste to my thigh and walked out of the bedroom to Daphne waiting for me, her eyes beaming.

Daphne flitted next to me, chatty and lively on our way back down to the first-floor common room, through a hallway into the dining room.

Chapter 20
Niya

I looked out from the massive floor to ceiling windows as they exhibited the darkening sunset on the ocean's horizon. Entranced by the view, my feet had a mind of their own as I moved closer, ignoring Adryen's presence.

I was quickly by the window glancing out into the darkening waters and chills ran down my spine, "Your kingdom is stunning, Adryen."

I turned around to see Adryen looking awfully comfortable. He was leaning on the table with his hand on his chin, staring at me admiringly.

Daphne released a small cough and dismissed herself from the dining room as I made my way to where Adryen sat.

I plopped down into the chair next to him and winced, "Why do you look so happy?"

Adryen shrugged his shoulders, "This just feels right."

My day had shown a good amount of *wrong*.

I raised my eyebrow, "What feels right? Please elaborate because I am not sure I'd agree."

"You being here feels right, Niya. Do you not feel it?"

I felt the need to slap him, but that was beside the point.

Looking away, I whispered, "Is it a Seelie thing?"

"What? Being nice?"

I lowered my eyelashes, "No, being so quaint."

Adryen shrugged his shoulders, as a server came out with two dishes. He placed them in front of us and bowed walking away. He brought back a bottle of wine and inclined the wine to my glass.

I shook my head and pulled the glass away, "Oh, no thank you. I'm okay."

If I drink anything after what I just encountered, I will not wake up tomorrow.

Adryen arched an eyebrow in surprise, "Just a water, Stone. Thank you."

Stone nodded and went back to the beverage bar and busied himself getting a pitcher of water ready to bring back. I looked at the plate of food and started to salivate, not realizing how hungry I had been.

Working my fork and knife into the meat, I took a bite. Closing my eyes, chewing slowly savoring every taste. Bursts of new, and exotic flavors engulfed my mouth as I moaned in pleasure.

Ruining my moment, Adryen laughed, "I don't think I have ever heard or seen anybody enjoy a piece of meat like you do."

I pointed my fork at him, "Do not ruin my dinner, Adryen."

"Or what?" he inclined.

"I will fight you."

Adryen set his silverware down and entwined his fingers, "You really do like threatening violence, don't you?"

Pointing my fork at Adryen, "It's not a threat. I will fight you, and I will win." I pulled my fork back to the delicious meat and continued eating.

"Okay. Fine. I'll bite," Adryen grabbed his wine and swirled it in his glass, "I will say that I am rather skilled with hand-to-hand combat."

I smirked, "Hmmm. How about you show me what you got; tomorrow."

Adryen laughed, "You think I will let you ruin the amazing work I did on your stomach? Absolutely not."

Lips tightening and eyebrow raised, "When?"

"When you are healed. We will have a proper match."

I relented, satisfied, "Fine."

He smiled and took a sip from his glass. As I took the last bite of my meal, I pushed the plate away and slouched back in the chair, "Well, I am stuffed," caressing my food-baby.

Stone returned to retrieve our emptied plates and brought them back to the kitchens without a word. I sat back up in my chair and placed my elbows on the table disregarding everything that Alman had taught me, "How are you able to keep your kingdom so warm?"

Adryen looked out of the window and back to me, "The Whitebourne bloodline has used their spell-making to make and keep the land warm the majority of the year. We get a slight chill at winter solstice."

I took a sip of my water and asked, "What will happen to the warmth if something happens to The Divide?"

"I would assume either we will be suffocated with the cold, or your kingdom will melt and become warm. I do not foresee the lands staying two distinctively different temperatures."

Stone came back out with a little chrome tray and cloche; setting it between us, he said, "Enjoy."

Adryen inclined his head to me as he lifted the cover and four chocolate-covered strawberries sat on a dainty white plate.

I put the palm of my hand on my forehead and whispered, "Are all Seelie this observant? Or am I just always eating, and everybody can't help but notice?"

Adryen grabbed my wrist and pulled it off my head, "No to both. I am just the Seelie that is trying to impress you."

I grabbed a chocolate-covered strawberry with my other and beamed, "It's working," taking an intentionally slow and sensual bite.

Adryen backed up from the table and out of his chair, encouraging me through my gripped wrist, to get up with him. I moved out of my chair and stood up, pulling myself from his grasp.

"I want to show you something," Adryen walked towards the exit and motioned for me to follow him.

Maybe Adryen set that stuff up in the room and is now leading me to my death. I had no idea where we were going.

This was all a charade.

It must be.

I felt for Celeste, just in case, as we walked through the common area and up two flights from the grand staircase. Walking down towards the left, we entered a narrow hallway with a single closed door at the very end.

Fae light hung in between handfuls of pictures.

I looked at the gold-framed pictures and tilted my head at one in particular. This one was of a chestnut-haired, regal woman sitting on her throne, wearing a simple, golden crown and gold dress. I moved closer to her portrait, realizing she looked familiar. I reached up and felt the ridges of the woman's hair, eyes, and lips, a sudden understanding dawning.

A deep, whispered voice came from behind me, "That was my mother."

I dropped my hand and turned around to see Adryen's sorrowful face. As much as I did not have a close familial bond with my family, I could not imagine them being taken away from me.

Kaldamir knew that his family had died, but we were not told the details.

Adryen continued, "She was this kingdom's light. It is terrible how she and my father were taken from us," He paused then continued, pace quickening, "I want to show you something. It is going to make me extremely vulnerable to you, but I need you to understand my history in hopes that you grow to understand me better. To understand Haldonia."

I looked at him puzzled.

Adryen held out a hand gesturing to me to take it and continued, "I have sensory projection, let me paint you a quick story of my last ten years as ruler of my kingdom."

I hesitated, "I don't know what sensory projection is."

"It is a type of light magic that the Whitebourne family has possessed since the beginning of our rule. It sort-of replays personal memories into someone else's head through contact and intent."

I blinked stupidly at him, "Does it hurt?"

He laughed, "No. I would never do anything to hurt you."

Lies.

How could something like what I'd walked into earlier happen in his own kingdom? Something was off here.

But I felt this tug of trust between us.

Would Adryen ever intentionally harm me?

He had saved me from the shadow figure.

I grabbed his outstretched hand hesitantly and a brilliant yellow sparkling cord wrapped around our forearms, locking us in.

Oh gods, I felt instantly mesmerized and then my irises rolled to the back of my head.

Vivid pictures of Adryen's parents dying in front of him flooded into me.

So much blood.

His brother was using his magic and it backfired and killed both of them. Or maybe the magic had powers of their own. It was very difficult to see, considering I was on the outside looking in.

Adryen was able to protect himself fast enough with a shield, but not his parents. He was just a boy and had never considered that anything could ever happen to his parents.

I squinted my brows in despair as he jumped around in his memories and showed me as much as he could.

Adryen reading, researching, studying.

Adryen making plans and working himself sick to help his people.

Adryen secluding himself in his own kingdom and courtly duties until he was suffocating.

Adryen never had any fun.

Ever.

He showed me everything about his life in the last ten years. Adryen was forced to take the throne he never wanted and turned his duty into something that would make his parents proud.

This king had worked endlessly keeping his people happy and healthy.

Mother above, he is perfect.

The perfect ruler.

He pulled me out of his memories by releasing our hold and tears slipped down my cheek as I fell to the floor.

Adryen caught my fall and knelt down to me.

He was a good, natural king and cared deeply for his court. He was something I realized I could not claim to be. I was unruly, drunk, and wild. Despite loving myself for being those things, I could not allow myself to corrupt his purity.

We would not be an ideal match, and that sent an irrational spike of pain into my heart.

I was hurt and I did not understand why.

Adryen gently wiped the tears from my face and spoke softly, "I didn't mean for that to make you upset. I just wanted to show you that I have worked unceasingly on building a better future for my kingdom and people. I wanted you to know what happened to my family because when we form this alliance, I want you to know that you can trust me." Adryen looked into my eyes imploringly. "My people can't continue to live on this small slice of land anymore, Niya," his voice pleading for understanding.

He continued, "My brother's prophecy was fulfilled when he killed our parents. They tried everything to keep it from happening, but it hadn't worked."

I opened my eyes wide and shook my head in disbelief, "So what I saw was really your brother *killing* your parents?!"

Adryen nodded his head solemnly, "Yes, he was not in control of his powers, and they acted as if they had a mind of their own."

I placed my hand on his cheek, "I am so sorry for what happened to your family."

"It is in the past, Princess." He looked down, weary. "I have just had to move forward...one step at a time."

Thoughts of my own prophecy sprung to the front of my mind now. It was only a matter of time before mine came to claim me.

Adryen looked into my eyes and a small smile formed on his lips.

I believed him before he showed this to me; but now I wanted to just give him the land without any strings attached.

At this moment, the rebuilding of the lagoon was insignificant to the bigger picture.

I have been so self-centered.

His people needed to thrive—deserved to thrive.

Except the person who wrote 'death' on the windows and gave me that gruesome gift.

Crawling closer, I wrapped my entire body around Adryen.

I hugged him as tight as I could.

I was done fighting the urge to touch him.

He let out a strained chuckle and wrapped his massive arms around me, "You are going to suffocate me."

"Good," I tightened myself around him one more time looking at the door that was waiting for us, "What is that room?"

Adryen nuzzling into my neck, "Hmm?"

His warm breath sent prickled bumps all over my skin.

He smiled and kissed my neck.

I pulled away from him and asked, "The room, behind you, what is it?"

"Oh, that's the sculpting studio."

Was The King of Haldonia an artist?

I raised my eyebrow, intrigued, and released my hold on him, trying to get up. I used my hands to help me lift myself off of the floor and stood in front of the entryway.

Adryen grabbed my hand, stopping me, "It's late. I will show you that room another time. Honestly, I should probably take you on a proper tour."

Confused, I replied, "We just had dinner, what do you mean it's late?"

He got up and stated, "A couple of hours have passed. Sensory Projection takes hours to fully complete. It is probably close to midnight."

I gaped, "What?!"

He nodded, "Let me walk you back to my room. I will tuck you in all nice and cozy and then see you bright and early in the morning. We'll see that room first thing; I promise."

I scoffed, "I am not a child."

"You're right, but you are still healing, therefore, off to bed with you."

Letting out a sigh, I simply just gave in.

If he wanted to take care of me, *fine*.

Adryen started out of the hallway toward the main foyer and then up to the third floor. I trailed behind him in no rush to end our time together, "Please don't sleep anywhere else, it's your room. I should be the one going somewhere else," I hedged.

We were halfway up the steps and Adryen stopped, "No, my room is the only one suitable for you, Princess."

I frowned; I did not require much.

I would honestly be perfectly fine sleeping on the floor with a blanket, as long as he was with me.

Chapter 21
Niya

"I don't want to sleep in your room."

Adryen turned around to face me, eyebrow raised, "Why?"

I was not about to tell him what happened earlier.

"Well, your room kind of creeps me out."

Adryen burst into peals of laughter and mumbled something inaudible under his breath, smiling and shaking his head.

Suddenly feeling really uncomfortable, I looked to the floor as I followed behind him.

We continued our walk in silence and finally made it to the third-floor landing. Adryen guided us to his room and held the door open for me. I slipped in and stared at the room I had vigorously cleaned. I glanced up to where the goat had been and there was no trace. A silent sigh of relief shuddered through me.

Adryen murmured, "Sweet dreams, Niya," and started closing the door behind him.

I didn't want to be alone.

Not in this room.

I dashed towards him leaning on the open doorframe. Snatching his hand while the other clutched my tensed stomach, "Wait; don't go. I will sleep on the floor. Really, this is unnecessary, Adryen."

I was starting to panic.

He let the door swing back open and grabbed the top of the doorframe with his free hand, "It is necessary. You deserve the best, Niya. This is the best."

Looking up at him, I said smoothly, "Then stay here with me."

"I can't."

I pouted, "Why not?"

Keeping his hand on the doorframe, Adryen looked deeply into my eyes, "We aren't married, or even together. It would be...inappropriate. Also, you are very much a grown female; why would you need someone to accompany you while you sleep?"

I did not care what we were; I would not be left alone in this room!

I crossed my arms over myself, "But, I am a grown female that does not want to sleep alone. In this unnecessarily ginormous royal suite." I was about to get really nasty if he didn't agree to stay.

I dragged him inside, kicking the door closed behind him, "Stay. If you think that I care what anybody thinks, then you haven't gotten to know me as well as you could have."

"Oh, I know *you* don't care; but *I* do. I do not want anything negative said about you," Adryen paused, assessing me. His appraisal must've accurately determined that he would not win because he took a deep breath and rolled his eyes, saying, "Since there seems to be no changing your mind, I guess *I* will sleep on the floor, and *you* can have the bed."

That was easy.

Adryen went to the closet and rifled through his top shelf looking for foraged materials to make a makeshift floor bed. I gritted my teeth hoping he would not see my clothes from earlier. Grabbing, two thick sherpa blankets and a pillow, Adryen placed them on the bed.

Adryen looked around the room, "You should have some sort of clothes here."

I followed his eyes trailing and stopped at the office desk in the corner. A leather storage bag sat in the middle. Strolling over to the desk, I opened the bag and a plethora of clothing sat inside. I had a couple of silky, alluring lingerie for sleeping, and two outfits for tomorrow; both being pant suits.

I pulled out a kobi slip dress and smiled deeply. Doogan can really create masterpieces of fabric. The strapped sleeves lead down to beautifully knitted V-neck flowers. Turning the dress around, the back was complimented with multiple crisscrossed straps. I felt the silk and I instantly gaped.

Mulberry.

Mulberry silk was buttery soft and felt remarkable on the skin. I pulled the dress to my face and ran it down my cheeks.

"Do I even want to know what you're doing?"

I dropped the dress, "Why? Are you jealous?"

Adryen chuckled, "Of what? Rubbing your face on a dress?"

I whipped around and saw that Adryen stood by the bed shirtless, in the middle of changing.

I pointed at him, "No. Nope," and hurried to the bathroom.

I closed the bathroom door and pulled off my clothes, replacing them with this smooth dress. I glanced in the mirror to take a final look at myself. Snagging the hair tie from the sink, I pulled my hair up into a messy bun.

Walking out of the bathroom, Adryen had made his makeshift bed on the floor next to his actual bed and tried to get comfortable. He was so stubborn, but to be honest, I was so glad he didn't leave me alone tonight; I did not think I would be able to sleep without him being here.

I slipped under the sheets and his scent filled my senses. I breathed in deeply, smelling his birch and eucalyptus. Sinking into the feeling the smell elicited, my body grew taut and loose at the same time.

I scooched over to be closer to him and hung my head and arm off the bed towards him.

"You are going to freeze down there, Adryen."

A slight frown crossed his face then disappeared with a smile, "I will be okay. As long as you're comfortable, so am I."

I mumbled, "Why are you so annoying?"

Adryen's eyes were closed, and he hummed, "Hmm?"

I laid back on the bed looking up at the ceiling pondering so many things. My family should be searching for me. I had been gone for almost three days and nobody cared to notify Adryen or anyone else.

Garrin was more than likely badly hurt, and I left him behind. If anything happened to him, I would never forgive myself. I moved my fingers over the stitches through the dress. Considering Adryen had just restitched them today, my stomach felt significantly better than this morning.

I leaned back over and grazed my fingers over his, inviting him to my touch. Adryen's eyes shot open, and intrigue shown in them. I smiled at him, flopping my wrist around playfully for him to get the hint that I wanted his affection. He moved his hand up mine and grasped it. I closed my eyes as my mind started to relax.

A thought occurred to me, "Is it true that only males become wyverns?"

Adryen let go of my hand and turned to face me, "No. Anyone of high royal blood can be a wyvern. My mother was a wyvern."

My eyes widened, "What?"

Adryen sat up, nodding. There seemed to be much that I did not know about wyverns.

"How do females carry the wyvern child in their bellies? Wouldn't the child—like—break the mother's pelvis during birth?"

"Uhh...I have never talked to anyone about my wyvern before," Adryen trailed off and hesitantly replied, "No. Females who carry the wyvern child do not get harmed. Younglings grow into their wyvern. They are not born being one."

I tilted my head, "Did your ears always have the colors and scales on them or are they formed once you successfully transform.

"I was born with these blue tipped ears. It is how my mother knew I inherited her genes."

I sat back and moments passed before I replied, "Your wyvern is stunning, Adryen. You're really, really...miraculous."

I closed my eyes and dozed off. Slipping into deep sleep, my body jolted awake as I had the sensation of falling. I leaned over to look at Adryen on the floor and pouted. I couldn't sleep like this.

I slid my index finger down his stubbled cheek, "Sleep in the bed with me. I am lonely, and cold," I lied.

Adryen opened one sleepy eye, "I know for a fact that comforter is thicker than molasses and is keeping you well warm."

I smiled, "Please."

"I don't know if I should, Niya."

I breathed, "Please."

He slowly got up off the floor and moved around to the opposite side of the bed. He pulled down the covers and slipped in beside me, making sure his back was facing mine.

I grinned and my eyes fluttered shut, falling into a comfortable sleep.

Chapter 22
Niya

The rising sun shone through the glass as my eyes squinted open. A heavy arm was wrapped tightly around my chest and trailed up towards my neck. I slipped my leg in between Adryen's and snuggled into his warm chest. Adryen's eyes still closed, he moaned and placed his hand on my thigh, tightening his grip. I glided my hand up Adryen's arms as he shuddered in response.

Realizing what I was doing, I lifted my hand into the air to stop touching him and lightly squirmed away towards the foot of the bed, trying not to fully wake him.

I jumped out of my skin as a loud knock sounded at the door. I placed my hand on my heart and Adryen shuffled around behind me. He got up and rubbed his eyes, walking half asleep to the door. He cracked it open and a tall, dark-haired fae burst through the door.

"Adryen!" He sounded out of breath.

I quickly tried to cover myself with a blanket as the muscular male paused, looking me up and down.

Adryen mumbled, "What, Lorenzo?"

Snapping his attention back, "There was a breech," Lorenzo paused, "You need to come quick." He looked me over again and walked out of the room.

Adryen looked my way and smiled faintly, "I am sorry. I have to go.

"A breech?" I asked.

"I am not sure what he means and where," Adryen stretched and quickly gathered clothes to wear for the day. He slipped into the bathroom and came back out wearing a white long sleeved embellished tunic tucked into tan pants. Grabbing his leather baroque boots, Adryen sat beside me lacing them up tightly.

Walking over to the closet again, he strapped his scabbard around his waist, adjusting the sword to rest comfortably, "I will send Daphne up in a little bit to check in on you."

I nodded slowly, not really sure how to react. I was too busy taking in his breathtakingly beautiful appearance as he disappeared out of the room. I flung my body back onto the bed and looked at the ceiling.

Niya, you had a lot of self-control not touching him last night.

Looking down, I felt the stitching on my stomach through the gown. Shocked, I pulled up my dress to see that the stitches were no longer protruding but looked more like staples in the skin. I smiled in satisfaction at how fast Adryen's healing had worked since yesterday.

My stomach grumbled and I bolted out of bed. I snuck out of the room and down the stairs to find the kitchen.

I retraced my steps to the dining room and looked left and then right. A double door with two circular windows hung ajar; waiting for me, I supposed. Shrugging, I walked to the doors and looked through the glass. A bustle of chefs was frantically running around the kitchen cooking breakfast. I was welcomed by the smell of sizzling meat and the sound of the crackling fire.

I busied myself, looking through various shelves and pantries for dry goods and began checking the contents of the cabinets.

A cough ruptured behind me, and I slowly closed the pantry door. I turned around and smiled sheepishly at the now silent chefs.

I nervously chuckled, "Hello," and waved.

A rotund chef shoved through the others and pushed his belly into me, "You should not be in here! Take this and kindly get out."

The chef pushed a blueberry scone into my hands and aggressively pointed to the door. I raised my eyebrow and pressed my lips together in defiance. When the chef began yelling in an unfamiliar language, I decided to take my business elsewhere.

I stomped to the door and a thick accented voice trailed, "And put some clothes on! You are a guest; this is not your home!"

I scoffed, looking down at the dress I slept in last night, "It covers enough!"

Annoying faehole.

I left the kitchen, stuffing the pastry in my mouth. I walked through all of the hallways on the first floor. I had hoped that I would find marvels that only the Seelie court could know, but not a single door caught my interest as I explored.

This felt like a very boring labyrinth. How could a castle *be* this boring? Adryen needed to do some serious remodeling of this floor. He could have a training room, or even a lounge, or billiards—a bar.

An enormous, arched entrance came into view as I inspected what looked like the ballroom. I walked in and the golden floors shone under the glass windows atop the room. As I walked in further, I started to count the endless numbers of pillars.

Breathtaking, truly.

I sat in the middle of the ballroom and lay back looking at the circled windows above. In the center of the ballroom was a hand painted mural sitting inside wooden gold-plated coffer ceilings. I tilted my head and examined the figures in a frozen dance.

Finally satisfied with some reward for my efforts, I made my way back outside to the main common room.

I quickly climbed the stairs to the second floor. Yesterday, this floor seemed quite interesting so I had hoped this would go better than the first floor. I veered right and strolled down the wing. I heard voices behind a closed door and snuck up to the entrance. I loved gossip and Seelie gossip would be a new experience.

I put my ear to the door as a voice mumbled, "What do you mean there was a goat on the beach?"

Beach? Is that what the shore is called? My eyes widened at the realization that they were talking about the goat I had sent through the portal yesterday.

"Fin and Enzo, I need you to investigate this more, please. A goat, dead, does not just show up on our beach. Question all the staff and report back to me immediately."

That was Adryen's voice.

I gasped and backed up from the door, as I heard shuffling inside the room. I turned around and ran to the other end of the hallway. I read the placard next to the door, *Piano Lounge,* and slinked inside.

A maple grand piano sat in the middle of the room with booths covering every wall space except for the corner, where a bar sat. I ran my fingers through all of the booths and smiled at the extravagance. Red velvet tickled my fingertips as I made my way to the island bar. I sat in the bar chair and looked at the assortment of liquors. There was one in particular that I had never heard of before.

Vodka.

I went behind the bar and popped open the lid, smelling absolutely nothing. I raised my eyebrow and searched for a glass.

An alcoholic beverage that had no smell.

Interesting.

Pouring a small swig, I sniffed the vodka again, shrugged, and drank.

My tongue zinged as the clear liquid raked its way down my throat. I spat and coughed as I wiped my lips with the back of my hand.

"Dear gods! It tastes like fire!"

No wonder the bottle was still practically full. I stuck my tongue out and made a retching sound. I hummed to myself, pouring another shot.

I shook my head distastefully at the grand piano sitting there unappreciated.

My index finger trailed the maple as I smiled at the familiar touch. Playing the piano was my love. When I was not training or working on courtly duties, I was practicing with my music. I have composed many songs with the grand piano in our ballroom. I peeked at the soundboard and dusted pins waited for me to pluck them with their keys.

I sat on the bench and scooted myself in to reach the pedals. I pressed a key and the piano awoke. I grinned from ear to ear. My fingers hovered over several upper and lower octave keys and my hands took over.

Every note I hit was a beautiful sound that resonated inside my soul. I continued one of my original works and I closed my eyes, smiling at the familiarity. The sound coming from the piano grew louder, and the vibrations penetrated my skin. The harder I pressed the keys, the more movement the song gave.

My heart raced as I quickly glissade my fingers up the keys.

I repeated and played through many of my songs, and I lost all sense of time. My mind retreated as my body and soul took over and I sank into the rhythm.

Changing up the tempo, I slowed my fingers and played a somber tune. I pressed the keys as minor chords echoed through the room. My fingers moved unhurriedly as the song became dark and moody. I ended on a picardy third, to give that positive feel to the end of the song and a sound came from behind me.

I pushed back the seat when I spied Adryen leaning against the doorframe, beaming.

"I—I am so sorry. I just was exploring, and—" I stopped and huffed a breath, composing myself, "I didn't wait for Daphne. I wanted to see more of your massive castle, and I stumbled upon this room. I lost track of time."

Adryen pushed off the wall and strolled closer to me, "I would say so, considering you're still in your dress from last night and Daphne isn't anywhere in sight. I would say," Adryen leaned in to me, closing the distance between us, "that your explorations were successful. I should be the one apologizing for not taking you on a proper tour," and brushed his lips against my ear as a chill ran down my spine.

Adryen leaned back, placing his hands into his pockets, "You play beautifully, Niya." Adryen slowly circled me as he spoke. "This piano has not been played in many, many years. I was in a fairly important meeting when I heard your music. I left early to see who had bewitched me so. I have been enraptured for well over thirty minutes."

I whipped my head to look through the double-paned windows at the cloudless sky and shot my gaze back to Adryen.

"What time is it?!"

"Past noon," Adryen replied.

I blinked twice in shock, "Oh." I put my head down in concession. Adryen's rough hand caressed my cheek. The whole day seemed wasted at this point.

He squatted down next to me so he could look at my face, "It's okay, Niya. We all lose track of time sometimes, especially when we are doing something we love."

This was a deeply personal side of me that nobody ever saw, except Vallynn. We would spend hours in the ballroom; him telling me stories as I played and wrote music on our own grand piano.

"Do you play?"

Adryen smirked, "Oh, I can play. Not up to the standard you just set, but it's not bad."

His smile disappeared as he continued, "But I haven't played in," and dropped an octave, "years."

I instinctively grabbed his hand, "What's wrong?"

"I haven't been able to work up the courage to actually play since my brother left," he looked into my eyes, "it was sort of our thing. He was a wonderful pianist."

His pain was unfathomable. I didn't know what I would do if I lost Vallynn.

"Do you want to talk about it?" I asked, walking the line between concern and invasion of privacy.

Head down in desolation, "I don't really want to talk about him. It's hard for me. You understand, don't you?"

I scooted closer to him and really looked at him. At his pain, his beauty, his sad eyes. I patted the bench next to me; Adryen rose from his crouch and sat.

Without another word or look toward him, I reached up and started to play a few chords; sad and sweet, like Adryen. He gave a perfunctory smile. I knew that his soul was in need of comfort, so I played for him. After a few moments, his eyes began drifting higher and higher, his posture straightening. I could feel the mood lifting.

I reached over with a hand and touched his hand, encouraging him to play alongside me. He paused, "Oh, no, Niya. I'd better not. I am not really in the right frame of mind, and I am sure it wouldn't be very good."

Again, without a word, I began a calm and sweet duet. His head jerked up and his eyes shot to my hands. "I know this one," a small smile grew.

"Then play with me," I whispered.

Soon, the two of us played. Our hands and our hearts made beautiful music. I felt my own mood lighten and, as the song came to an end, I looked over at Adryen, drawing out the last note.

He stared at me in astonishment. My heart leapt when I saw what the music did to him; what I'd done to him.

"How are you feeling, King?" I asked with a quirk of my lips.

"Princess, you made me feel like a king this afternoon when I had so long felt like a failure."

His soul called to mine in that moment. I haltingly lifted my hand to the small curl that had fallen onto his forehead, combing it back off of his face.

I trailed my hand up his cheek, through his wavy chestnut hair, feeling every silky stand. His hair was cut short on the bottom and styled longer on the top where strands kept falling onto his forehead in an infuriatingly beguiling way.

A voice boomed from the hallway as it sounded closer, "Hey Adryen, I thought you were taking a quick look at who was playing the piano! It has been well over thirty minutes; we have a meeting to finish. Also, I thought this room stayed locked so nobody would have access. Who is in there?"

Adryen and I stared at each other, shocked, and began to laugh awkwardly.

I stole one last glance as Enzo peered around the door. Lorenzo stopped dead center of the doorframe, "Oh, well that explains the last thirty or so minutes."

Adryen moved away from me, "Enzo..." Adryen drew out.

Lorenzo threw his hands in the air, "What! I am just saying. You are in here, clearly making out with this beautiful female."

This was definitely not true.

Adryen paused to pull up to his full height, "What I choose to do with a female is none of your business."

I adjusted myself on the bench and perked up at the dominance Adryen radiated.

Gesturing between the interloper and myself, "Lorenzo Hemming, alpha of the wolf territories," He paused for a grand gesture, "This is Princess Niya Blackbyrn of Kaldamir."

The tanned male spoke, "Oh gods, I am an idiot. I am Enzo, Your Highness. First to King Adryen..." Lorenzo bowed, "It is so nice to meet you, Princess Niya," eyes darting between Adryen and me.

"Just, Niya," I smiled and gave a curt bow back.

Lorenzo moved in closer to us and I was able to get a better look at him. Wavy, faux cut blue-black hair faded down to his rounded ears. Hazel eyes met mine before darting away again. Lorenzo was very muscular and just as tall as Adryen. His arms were completely covered in tattoos that appeared to have gone up to his shoulder and onto his torso.

"That's a nice tattoo...Niya," seemingly unsure whether I'd actually meant for him to call me that. "Who did it? I might need to pay them a visit."

I shrugged my shoulders, "Um, it sort of just showed up one day," feeling embarrassed.

"Well, either way, Niya with the mysterious tattoo, it is a distinct pleasure."

Faking some composure, Lorenzo extended his hand to me. Smiling at his adorable attempt at courtliness, I reached for it. Lorenzo kissed my knuckles gently and a pang of jealousy flowed through me.

Going to reply, I scrunched my eyebrows together confused. I hadn't felt jealous. Where had that feeling come from? I looked over at Adryen, his face showing no signs of distress.

What in the dark realms was going on with my emotions?

I glanced back at Lorenzo and slipped my hand back to my side. Realizing that I was possibly underdressed for such a formal meeting with Adryen's first, "I should probably get ready for the day...that is...almost over," I started apologetically.

Both males looked at each other and smirked.

I walked to the door as Adryen called behind me, "Have lunch with me, Princess. I want to give you a proper tour afterward."

"What? Proper tour? What was wrong with the one I just gave myself?" I smiled slyly at him as a small frown creased his forehead.

Lorenzo chuckled as he tapped his hand on Adryen's shoulder, "The Princess does not enjoy your propositions, Adryen. She will get along perfectly with Malcolm and me."

Adryen shook his head as I gave a subtle wave goodbye, making my way back to his chambers.

Chapter 23
Adryen

Enzo and I made our way back to the meeting room where Finion and Malcolm sat on individual white barrel chairs swirling their glasses of liquor.

Malcolm seethed, "What took so long? Did the music entrance you into a stupor?"

I might've strangled him if he were not my cousin. He was often this blunt. Malcolm is the "no funny business" male on my cabinet. My cabinet was: Finion, my advisor; Malcolm, my cousin; and Enzo, my first in command; and of course, myself. The four have been running this castle since my parents passed away. It had taken all of us to successfully keep it functioning.

I sarcastically remarked, "Ha, ha."

Malcolm threw up his hands, exasperated, "We need to get this meeting done with, I have *things* to do. And quite frankly I am getting rather bored talking about this very dead goat."

Enzo blurted, "Like what? Sulk on the roof of the castle with those angelic wings, looking like a creeper?"

"These wings and I have helped notify you of a breach. I'd say *we* are very *non*-creepery; I thank you very much," Malcolm finished with his nose in the air and his head turned away from Lorenzo. Having another thought, "It's not every day that a portal opens up on the beach and spews a goat carcass," Malcolm seethed.

I plopped on the chaise and placed my two fingers on my temple while my thumb rested the weight of my head. This was not going anywhere. We had no idea who'd made the portal, or where this goat came from other than it must have come from the castle.

Somehow.

Finion inquired, "Who knows how to make portals?"

In that moment, the light clicked in my head, "Niya."

Oh, shit.

She could transverse; and when she did, a portal would sort-of form from her powers that she could step through. Transversing was more of a singular move through the void whereas portal making was a multi-step move. That was why when I transversed with her; I got sick.

Other than myself, she would be the only one in this castle who could create a portal to move something through.

"Niya?" Finion shuffled on his feet, looking uncomfortable.

"She can make portals?" Malcolm stood up.

I huffed, "Do I need to repeat myself?"

Enzo inquired, "But there is no way she would encounter a dead goat and be so calm about it. I mean, we would've *known*, right?"

"Maybe not; Niya is incredibly tough."

Finion stopped in his tracks and looked down, frowning deeply, "I don't see why this is such a big deal. It's just a dead goat."

I looked at Finion like he had grown an extra head and he returned the look, "What?"

"A dead goat came from a room in the castle and onto the beach. You think that is normal?!"

Finion shrugged his shoulders.

Malcolm interjected, "How do we know that the goat was dead when it went into the portal? Maybe it died after, or on the way," he cringed.

I needed to ask Niya if she knew anything about the goat.

I shook the tension from my fingers and made a fist, trying to calm my nerves, "I need everybody to leave; except you, Fin."

Enzo and Malcolm made their way out through the open door.

I quickly slammed it shut with the wind that bellowed out of me and stalked over to Finion, "There is no way that she would have seen any goat unless somebody put it in a room that not many people have access to. Fin, do you know what room does not have a lot of access?"

"There are many rooms, Your Majesty."

I angrily shouted, "The only place that Niya would be able to go into?"

"I—I. My King, I truly don't know," Finion backed up and had his hands in the air as to suggest he had no idea how this could have happened.

I sent out a golden rope and wrapped it around Fin's neck. Jerking the golden hued link towards me, he fell to his knees and whimpered, "Adryen, please! I would never hurt her intentionally."

This was not about Niya being hurt intentionally, so the fact that he'd said that told me that he was hiding something.

Rage coursed through me.

I tried to control myself, but it felt like I was having an out of body experience.

My anger was reaching the boiling point; I had never been so...mad...mad? Was I upset?

What was upsetting me, exactly?

I looked down at the golden grip wound tightly around Finion's neck, "Shit. I am so sorry, Fin," I took a long pause, "I don't know what has come over me."

Long moments passed as we stared at each other; the tight features of Finion's face relaxing.

"You are just under a lot of stress, and you need time to relax and not worry about the kingdom. Also, your power is manifesting. This is a reaction to it." He rubbed his neck and swallowed hard.

Unsure, "Thank you for your insight, Finion. You are dismissed."

Finion bowed deeply and slipped out through the doorway.

I stared blankly at the closed door for a few moments.

Shoes scuffed outside.

Reentering, Enzo spoke, "That was tough, my friend."

Shaking my head, trying to remember what I had just been doing, "What?"

"Fin just left here rubbing a gnarly red ring around his neck. Are you okay, Adryen?"

Finally remembering, "Oh. Oh! That fucker just mind manipulated the shit out of me to forget what I was doing and then calmed me down. You heard all of that?"

Eyes wide, "Heard that?! The whole kingdom *felt* that, Adryen. Not to piss you off, but the foundation might have had more cracks added to it."

I glowered at him, "Not helping, Enzo. I can't fix the cracks in my kingdom; my power is becoming too strong to withstand...and our land..."

Enzo shrugged and placed a hand on my shoulder, "You will figure it out. With your 'wonderful' Advisor and I, and," he shuddered, "Malcolm."

I chuckled and I gave him a light punch on his shoulder, "You love Malcolm, and you know it."

"Malcolm, after twenty years, continues to freak me the fuck out. Why is he so scary?"

"A winged male, scary? He is just a big, loveable, bird."

Enzo looked at me with a raised eyebrow and a boom of laughter erupted out of him, "Malcolm, loveable bird! Have you ever encountered real birds? They are little shitheads. Evil, vile creatures."

He continued to laugh as we made our way out of the meeting room.

Malcolm galivanted his way towards us and reported, "I already planned my next day. I will be perching on top of the castle and watching who comes in and out of the doors for potential suspects. Shall I chain them up and put them in the dungeon?"

Enzo whispered to me, "Loveable bird, right?"

Malcolm frowned, "I can hear you!"

I reached over to Malcolm and hung my arm around his shoulder, "We love you, cousin. Don't get your feathers in a bunch."

Malcolm was very self-conscious of how he looked and was perceived by the courtiers. Nobody else in this kingdom had wings like his: pure white feathers, and a wingspan double his armlength.

Enzo just had a really hard time not teasing him; it was his greatest joy.

"I have to meet Niya for lunch. I will see you two later." I winked at them and trailed down the grand staircase to the first floor.

Enzo shouted, "No more making out in public places that we *use*! Find a private room. Her scent is literally *everywhere*."

I rolled my eyes and smiled with contentment, "Our lips haven't even met yet, Enzo!" and continued walking until they disappeared from my view.

Niya saw my pain.

She reached out to me without words and touched my heart. She was truly a blessing from the gods that was sent directly into my life. I wondered if she'd felt that tug on her heart the way that I had. I truly dreaded the day when she would be healed enough to leave me.

I slipped through the common room and made my way to the dining hall where green gold-flecked eyes met mine.

Time seemed to stop.

Niya beamed at me, and time resumed. My heart leapt in my chest as desire rolled over me in waves. I quickly moved to Niya, not wanting to be apart from her for even one moment longer.

Chapter 24
Niya

Adryen moved lightning fast toward me and I stumbled backwards, "Hi," I whispered, and my smile widened in pleasant surprise.

He trailed his fingers up my cheek and whispered back, "Hello, my beautiful princess."

I backed away from Adryen to look at his face in amusement, "Again, how you move so fast is beyond me."

I'd considered telling him to stop calling me "Princess", but when Adryen said it, I kind of liked it. He said it in a way that was meant for a lover, and the thought of being that to him brought me too many nice feelings to give up.

The portly chef from earlier came out and stopped in his tracks when he saw Adryen kissing his way up my neck while I giggled, delighted.

Clearing his throat lightly, "Sorry, Your Majesty," the chef bowed, "Your lunch is ready."

Adryen whispered in my ear ignoring the chef, "Are you hungry?"

I felt his smile caress my cheek and all I could do was let out a small breath and nodded.

What is happening to me?

Adryen just found ways to make me feel like a young fae again.

The chef set the covered plate down and left...very quickly. Adryen grabbed my hand, guiding us to the table and sat next to me. He removed the lid with a flourish, evoking a courtier. Two sandwiches sat next to each other on their own little plates.

Adryen pushed one into the other lightly and made a small kissing sound with a goofy grin on his face. Adryen slid a plate to me, and I examined the sandwich. There was a layer of what looked like jelly, and a layer browner than the color of the bread underneath that.

I tilted my head in curiosity, and I pulled one of the sandwiches up to my nose to smell it.

Sweet and nutty smells hit my nose.

"What is this?"

Adryen stopped midbite and asked, "What?"

"This sandwich? What is it?"

Adryen set his sandwich down and swallowed hard, "You have never had a peanut butter and jelly sandwich before?"

I shifted uncomfortably in my seat, realizing that there was a lot that I did not know coming here to his kingdom. Starting to feel my glaring lack of experience in the world outside of Kaldamir, I frowned, "No."

It was almost as Adryen could feel my discomfort. He pushed our plates away and moved his chair to face me, "Please do not ever feel embarrassed around me. I would love to be there for all of your firsts. I know I might be selfish saying this, but I like seeing you this way. I want to continue showing you new things."

A sudden sense of warmth spread up my chest and neck at the implications of his words. These Haldonian experiences should not have been new to me, but they were.

I'd had no idea these things even existed. I tucked my hair behind my ears and shook off the tightening emotions, "I'm okay."

I turned my attention back to my lunch and bit into the soft sandwich, hoping to erase the stirring in my heart.

Strawberries hit my tongue, taking the first bite. I closed my eyes and smiled as the sensation of the jelly and this peanut butter mixed into my mouth.

The sandwich was amazing.

I had to have more of *this*.

"Niya, did you portal a goat from my chambers to the beach?" Adryen asked, abruptly.

I chewed my last little bit of sandwich, giving myself time to formulate an answer, and swallowed hard, "What do you mean?"

"My cousin saw a goat being portaled onto the beach last night and nobody else in this castle can use portals except for you and me."

"Oh," I trailed off and several moments passed. I knew that goat wasn't just going to go away. I should have used some different method of disposing of the thing.

Adryen scooted closer to me, "Why didn't you tell me?"

"I was afraid of what it might mean," I thought about my next words, "It's also why I did not want to sleep alone last night."

He growled, "Was there anything else in the room that you haven't told me about?"

His anger was not meant for me, but either way, that powerful surge of rage I was feeling was mighty, and constant.

I mumbled, "Yes."

Adryen started to get up and, realizing he had nowhere to go, sat back down slowly, catching his cool.

I continued, "There was the word 'death' written on your windows."

"What?!" Adryen shot.

"It took me forever to clean up," I continued, "but I managed to get it all done before meeting you for dinner last night."

Adryen's face showed conflicting signs of rage, concern, grief, and...something else I couldn't quite place.

I reached over and placed my hand on Adryen's. He looked at me and his facial expression softened, "Are you okay; really?"

"I'm not holing myself up in a closet, crying, if that's what you mean. I can handle myself."

Adryen stared, unblinking. After a small moment, his face broke out in a grin, "You cleaned all of that up *before* coming to dinner? I had no idea you were so efficient."

My lips flattened, "Ha, ha."

He ran his hands through his hair, shuffling the strands, then placed it on the table, "You really are beautifully stubborn, you know that? You should have just told me. You wouldn't have had to clean all of that up by yourself."

His eyes widened as the words crossed his lips.

Confused I asked, "What? Why do you look like that?"

"I—I just realized something that I had not before."

Impatiently, I waved him to continue, "Which is?"

He was staring into nothing, totally withdrawn from our conversation now. I did not understand what was happening, and it was making me uncomfortable.

I snapped my fingers in front of Adryen's face, and he didn't respond.

Snapping my two fingers together again, he would not budge.

I placed both of my hands on either side of his face and turned him toward me, "Adryen."

He blinked, "I, I am sorry," he got up and pushed in his chair, pushing out a hand to me, "I believe I owe you the grand tour."

I puckered my lips, uncertain as to what had just happened and refusing to touch him, "What just happened?"

"What do you mean?"

"You just spaced out, and then totally came back to real life, unphased and ready to move forward."

"Oh," was all he replied for several moments, "I just realized something a friend had told me, and I went into a slight panic mode. But I am good now," and smiled.

I took his hand, "Who is this *friend?*"

Adryen laughed, "You really do love to ask questions."

A small grin appeared on my lips, "Yes, indeed."

We walked out of the room and Adryen gave the full, official tour of the castle. We revisited places I had already seen and he showed me more, like his study, a common room, and other really interesting places.

Adryen stopped us at this massively carved double entryway, and I asked, "Now, what is this room?"

He gazed down at me, "It's my library."

I gawked, "I would very much enjoy going in there, Your Majesty."

"Adryen," was all I said before he lifted his hand and cupped my chin to face him. Moving in closer to me he whispered into my ear, "Maybe we can find a better smutty book for you to read that isn't about dull duchesses or ladies-in-waiting like *Lynora*."

I pushed his hand away and glared at him for several seconds. The tension grew palpable between us, "*Lynora*, was a perfectly respectable romantic character, thank you very much."

Adryen, heart pounding with sudden vigor, "You are beautiful, cunning, and have a sharp wit, Princess."

"Thank you—"

"—I'm going to kiss you," Adryen said breathlessly, eyelids at half-mast while he stared wantonly at my lips.

Taken aback and putting on my best flippant and sarcastic mask, I began, "Well, that's not something that you really need to an—"

As I was trying to act unaffected by his intentions, he leaned forward into me and reached his hand behind my neck and abruptly, but softly planted his lips on mine.

I could not think and my eyes widened. My body responded of its own accord, and I utterly melted into his kiss.

I know I'd insinuated this through subtle flirting, but he had finally just called my bluff. I did not intend this to...

His lips moved on mine in slow, kneading strokes. Feeling the soft warmth of him, my lips moved with his.

I wanted this.

Fuck.

Noticing the answer of my body, Adryen let out a breathy shudder and my mouth opened for him.

The kiss grew deeper, and our bodies grew warmer. His right hand began stroking my neck and he pulled back slightly from the kiss and said, "Right there," as he pointed at a spot on my neck. Before I had a chance to wonder what he was talking about, he had his full, wet, warm mouth and tongue on my neck in just the spot he had indicated.

I closed my eyes and quietly moaned.

Adryen took his right hand and pointed to my collarbone. Without uttering a single word, his mouth changed positions to begin gingerly kissing that spot on my body. I slid my hand up his neck and tugged at the back of his head with the pleasure of the simple gesture.

Just enjoying him kissing me from my collarbone to my neck and back again, I felt Adryen's hand move lower to the top of my breast and my eyes shot open in carnal need.

I tugged his shirt out of his increasingly tight trousers and guided our bodies onto the timber doors as I stole deeper kisses from him. He placed one huge hand on the doorframe, pulled back, and smirked at me. He continued kissing back down my neck sending even more pleasurable waves through me.

I wanted Adryen's mouth everywhere.

Adryen glided his hand off the doorframe and pulled my torso up closer to his mouth. I could feel his raspy breath on my skin and my nipples tightened from beneath my plunged neckline. Slipping his hand into the fabric that was barely hanging on, Adryen ran his thumb over my aching nipple, and I arched my back onto him as his lips replaced his thumb. Feeling his own arousal against my body, I moaned again. Feeling like my younger self indulging in such pleasures again for the first time, I slipped my hand over the evidence of his arousal.

A light chuff came from Adryen's throat in sultry amusement.

"What?" My eyes popped open in frustration.

He quickly remarked, "Nothing. Your body seems to like me is all."

My eyelashes lowered and with sensual admiration as I grabbed his hard bulging cock, "I could say the same for you."

"Mmm," Adryen hummed getting lost in his need.

Desire, sudden and immediate, zinged down my spine as anticipation made my breath catch.

I wanted all of him.

Fuuuck, yes.

My back arched even more as I realized that he'd nipped at the pink point barely slipping out from my now disheveled piece of fabric.

A jolt of pleasure sent me slamming us against the door causing it to swing open and we tumbled to the floor.

I winced in pain and Adryen caught himself beside me.

Not skipping a beat, I moved on top of him. I straddled my legs on both sides of his taut stomach and leaned down, whispering, "I think if we go any further, you might want to take me back to your chambers," I started kissing his neck in soft pecks, unbuttoning his shirt one delicate button at a time.

Adryen bolted upright, pushing me off of him and ran his hands through his unkempt hair, "I am—uh. This is inappropriate. I should go."

I stopped everything and breathed, "What?"

My body shattered in rejection. I peered deeply into his eyes, looking for a reason as to why we had just stopped.

He broke away from our stare and jumped up, bolting away from me and out of sight. I sat there huffing softly, trying to compose myself and my thoughts. After adjusting the top of my dress to fit correctly back on me, I sprinted up and looked into the library.

His library was as astonishing as mine, if not more so. He had to have several more feet of bookshelves with books just waiting to be read. There were endless amounts of varied colors of historical books on both of our Kingdoms. I touched the spine of every book, circling around the entire library in reverie.

In complete awe, I started toward the door to exit and a book sitting on a desk caught my attention. Raising an eyebrow, I sat in a cushioned chair and picked up the book.

The Stolen Love by Caroline Crawley.

My fingers lightly glided over the golden etched words and dark leathery binding, bringing me back to my first read of the book.

Oh, this was an amazing book!

I opened the front cover and a letter fluttered to the table. I tilted my head to the side curiously and unfolded the delicate parchment.

The letter was blank except for one word: *Princess.*

Setting the paper on the table, I put the pad of my index finger on the pen marking and felt every etch.

I eyed the book again and picked it up, placing my thumb on the pages of the book and flipped through them vigorously looking for any other notes or jots on the pages.

Nothing.

There were no other princesses in this realm except for me, so I had to assume the book was intended for me.

A gift, maybe?

Or just to borrow.

I smirked to myself. Either way, I could use this as an excuse to go see Adryen again. I would *have* to figure out why he had my title on an otherwise blank piece of paper inside of a book in his library.

I stood up and the floor started to shake beneath me. Placing two solid palms on the table, I tried to brace myself and planted my feet for stability.

Some of the books rumbled in their shelves while others dove to the ground under the aggressive shaking.

Several minutes passed and it would not let up. I ran to the door trying to keep myself balanced and not topple over.

I grabbed the doorframe and placed my hand on the knob, flinging the door open.

Adryen stood there grasping the door that was headed towards his face. His eyes were wide and terrified.

"Let's go," he spoke softly, grabbing my hand, he bolted us down the stairs and toward the exit.

"What is happening?!" I managed to say over the rumbling of the castle.

Adryen lifted his hands, and they were glowing magnificent shades of gold and yellow.

"My powers," was all he said before a huge block of ceiling cracked and stones fell from above.

Adryen wrapped his arm around my waist and pulled me backward, just in time before the ceiling fell in front of me.

I gasped and his power spilled from him, causing the castle to quake even more aggressively.

"Adryen!"

He was causing this to happen.

"We need to get out of here!"

Not ready to move, "Adryen!" I yelled again as little stone ceiling pieces fell all around us.

He snapped his head to me, and I felt this tug from inside of me. I placed my hand on his cheek, and he nuzzled into it. Looking down, his powers started to dim, slightly.

I spoke softly, "It's okay."

"No, it's not," he lashed out at himself.

Adryen pulled my hand down and we continued to push through the fallen stone toward the castle exit.

Chapter 25
Niya

Cracks crept up the walls as loud thuds came from falling stone.

I glimpsed down at Adryen's glowing hand and grabbed it again.

I whispered to him, "What is happening? I think this is coming from *you*."

The golden glow diminished as my grip tightened. The cracking of the castle began to subside as his tension eased. We looked at each other in consternation as the courtiers whispered amongst themselves pointedly looking at us standing there together.

He whispered, "I need my queen."

I could see hurt and pain behind the disquiet in his eyes. He couldn't control his power. Like myself, he held too much power within and there was no release valve. As much as it pained me, I knew that he needed to let me go and find his true queen to help him through this mess.

I couldn't be the one to mend this.

Could I?

Adryen looked deeply into my eyes and frowned, "I am so sorry, Niya." He tucked a strand of hair behind my ear. "You should be fully healed by tomorrow; then you can go home. I need to convene with my first and second and will come back later this evening to check on you."

His concern for me and the future of his kingdom were entwined in his heart; Adryen was trying so hard to help and protect all of us and I felt it as distinctly as if the troubles were my own. Adryen turned to meet up with a white-haired, angel-like fae with huge snow-colored, feathered wings...and Enzo. I had never seen this new winged male before.

Maybe he was the "second" Adryen had mentioned.

Something in my heart sank at the sense of loss produced when Adryen had walked away from me.

Again.

Daphne beelined toward me and pulled her arms out in front of her and landed them on both sides of my shoulders.

"Thank the gods you're okay! I have been looking for you everywhere since that craziness earlier. I attempted to sniff you out, but it seemed like every time I got your scent, you were no longer there."

I mumbled, looking around "Is it safe to go back inside?"

Daphne looked puzzled, "Of course it is! Adryen would not walk in himself if there was any concern. Come, let me set up a warm bath for you. I'm sure you need to relax after," Daphne waved an arm toward the castle "It's almost time for dinner. I hope it won't be too delayed; I'm already so hungry."

"I'm not hungry."

Daphne shrugged, "That's okay. I will send something up later once you've settled in for the night."

I looked down at the grass, in thought, and followed Daphne's footsteps back into the castle and up to Adryen's room. Daphne busied herself in the bathroom as I pulled out more clothes from Doogan's delivery. An assortment of colors and designs spilled out onto the table, and I sorted through them for some night clothes. There was not one piece that looked remotely comfortable to me in my need for solace. I walked over to Adryen's closet and pulled out a plain grey T-shirt and smiled.

This will do quite nicely.

Holding up the shirt to my face, the smell of him wrapped around me and I instantly relaxed. Not sure if this would cover up everything, but it was more comfortable than the clothes Doogan had made for me.

I found my way to the bathroom as Daphne was finishing up the preparations. She pressed a little button on the bathtub and bubbles started to rise as streams of water jutted from everywhere.

I jumped.

"Adryen installed this tub with bubble jets in here about a year ago. His mechanics and tinkerers invented it and wanted to try it out before mass production for the kingdom. This is the prototype."

"Wow," I gasped, "A bathing tub with powered sprays and bubbles!" I stuck my hand into the warm water and felt a hard stream. My hand wrestled with the water, and I beamed, "This is going to feel amazing!"

Daphne laughed, "I am sure it will. I will see you in a couple of hours to check in and I'll bring some snacks up."

I heard the door click shut; I pulled my clothes off, stepped in, and sunk down into the warm water. Oh, I was going to get my hands on one of these as soon as possible. My body was getting a much-needed massage from the streams of water pelting my skin. I closed my eyes and groaned out a sigh, leaning my head back against the porcelain frame.

I was not sure how long I lay immobile, but the water had started turning cold and I was ready to try out the shower. I lifted myself out of the tub and padded over to the shower in the corner of the bathing room. The shower had no glass to enclose it or curtains. It just hung there, waiting to be used in the open.

Fascinating.

The flooring changed from wood to a little white barrier and the gray tiles below the showerhead. I looked at the bath soaps and picked up the shampoo bottle and sniffed.

Eucalyptus.

I turned on the shower and let the water run until it started to create hot steam. I washed and rinsed my body thoroughly, turned off the water, and reached for a hanging towel. I quickly dried my body with the towel and then scrunched the towel in my long hair to soak up the majority of the moisture. Replacing the towel on a hook on the wall to dry, I put on Adryen's oversized T-shirt and slowly padded into the bed chamber. Water droplets from my hair trailed down my back as I stared at a sprawled out, half naked form on the bed.

I felt an undeniable tug. For a heartbeat, the instinct to claim overrode my senses. Adryen's body was lean, tanned, and perfect. The muscles connecting his neck to his shoulders were thick and corded. Seeing them on full display like this made me want to stroke every part of him.

And bite, just a little bit.

I licked my lips as I stalked closer to him. There was only him and me in that moment and the space between us. I couldn't help myself; the need to touch him, feel his warmth and strength, pounded through me. I reached out my hand and touched him lightly on his chest. His body reacted to my touch by creating tiny bumps under my fingers.

My body shivered and that shiver reached deep into my center. I continued guiding my fingers up through this chest to his neckline and stopped at the base of his ear.

Beautifully scaled azure tipped ears shone under the moonlight. A light puff of air escaped my lips in awe as I guided my fingers up the slight curve. I caressed up the point, feeling every scaly bump through the pads of my fingers, stopping at the tip. His ears fascinated me with their sensual beauty.

Eyes still closed in apparent sleep, Adryen jerked up and grasped my wrist. His eyes slowly opened. After blinking a couple of times, he understood what was happening. His beautiful mouth quirked in a wicked grin and flipped me over him so that he was now towering over me.

I was trapped.

Red flushing my cheeks, I gaped at him and gave a half-smile and smoothly stated, "Hi," waggling my fingers.

"If you touch me like that again, you will lose your clothes." He looked me over, "my clothes," he amended.

Eyebrows up in sensual thoughts, I chirped, "Oh, well in that case..." I used my other hand to start finger walking up his body. Adryen grabbed my walking hand with his free hand, slamming both wrists together pushing them above my head pinning them to the bed.

"What were you doing?" Adryen whispered, still hovering over me, wary.

"I got your book," I blurted.

"What?"

"The book that you left in the library....on the table? It had a card with 'Princess' written on it. It was for me, right?" I was starting to panic, thinking it hadn't actually been intended for me.

"Oh," he said, relaxing, "Yes, it was for you. I hadn't had a chance to give it to you yet with everything going on."

Earnestly, "Why did you leave so abruptly? Did I do something to upset you?"

Adryen let go of my wrists and rolled to the side, sitting up. He scrubbed his palm down his stubbled cheek, replying, "No."

I propped myself up on my elbows next to him and slid my hand up the back of his head and hauled his lips to mine. Adryen stilled with surprise and then he surged forward to kiss me back, deepening the kiss. It destroyed any illusion of restraint.

His glorious lips were just so irresistible. There was only his mouth; licking and tasting and biting. I wanted to claim him with my tongue and teeth and breath—all of it.

Deep purring sounds vibrated through his chest as he explored my mouth. Tender and coaxing sweeps of his tongue on my lips set my core ablaze. I knew that he could scent my arousal as his fingers wandered lower to find the wetness pooling there.

I gently placed my hand on his cheek. Slowly, my fingertips slid down his jaw and to the corner of his mouth. Releasing the kiss, I traced my fingers lightly over his red and swollen lips. I watched as my fingers drifted further down over the cords of his neck.

I stared into eyes that were beaming bright with preternatural desire. Adryen took hold of my retreating hand in his and brought it back to his lips in a slow and deliberate manner, eyes locked on mine. I watched our hands move closer to those lips and Adryen gently kissed the inside of my palm. I blinked and my fingers were being taken in one, two at a time into that soft, beautiful mouth.

I gasped; my pulse hammering in my chest.

He watched me as I writhed from the new warm and wet sensations both on my fingers and in between my thighs.

I pulled my fingers away from Adryen's lips and inched my way down the ridges of his abdominals.

The carved heaving muscle of his chest paused as he sat unmoving.

"What—what's wrong?"

Adryen planted my hands on both sides of his face, and I brought him in for a sultry and teasing kiss.

Confused, "Uh, Adryen? What're you doing?" I smiled playfully. "I would have chosen for my hands to go somewhere else." One of his hands moved firmly to my hip securing me to the bed and the other cupped around my neck.

Desperate for more of him and about to lose all control of this situation, I did the only thing I could think of.

I pushed Adryen off of me and in one quick motion, I spun and switched positions with him; he was now seated on the edge of the bed, and I was hovering over him. His face started to adopt a conciliatory air, but I was not about to stop before getting what I wanted.

I dropped to my knees in front of him and placed my hands gently on the inside of his thighs, spreading his legs wider. The look of concern and confusion on his face was comical.

He didn't know who he was dealing with. And I would not be denied again.

I reached up one hand to the top of his trousers looking for a way to unfasten them. His look of confusion turned into interest. Really struggling to unfasten this pair of ungodly pants, I huffed to myself in frustration.

Adryen's face softened into a smile and helped me unfasten them. He was either too stunned to realize what was about to happen, or he was giving me permission to continue.

Either way, I was going in.

I looked up at his tilted face and his right hand reached out to stroke my hair. Sweet heat filled me between my legs.

Permission it is.

My mouth started to water at the sight of his hardness bulging from his pants. I bit my lip in exhilarated expectation, pulling down the top, reaching in gingerly. I paused...

Holy mother of all things...*fuuuck*.

My eyes rolled with a silent prayer to the gods as I locked eyes with Adryen.

My mouth suddenly lost all moisture as I beheld him. His cock was beautiful; very possibly the most beautiful I had ever seen. Adryen's eyes went wide as I pulled him free. The sight of it knocked the breath from me. It was enormous; truly holding it now in my hand, I knew I was going to need both to fully encircle him.

His skin was soft; softer than silk or velvet. Adryen adjusted his loosened trousers to make more room for my attentions as I gave him a firm, but gentle squeeze, looking up into his eyes. The growl that came from his throat was guttural. I felt an answering growl come from my own throat as the saliva built in my mouth.

"How do you like it?" I purred. My own husky voice and the anticipation pounded between my thighs. Adryen was going to be a challenge to take in, but I would not balk. I was going to make it my personal mission to make him cum so hard, that he would see stars.

I squeezed gently as Adryen stared at the place where my hand met his proud member. He quirked a small smile and, maintaining eye-contact, slowly and deliberately shook his head.

"How about this...do you like this?" as I stroked and squeezed harder. Adryen bit his lower lip, raised his hips a fraction and shook his head.

"I know," I said with preternatural desire. I took both hands, encircling him, and twisted both fists on him.

"Oh gods!" Adryen gasped. "Don't stop," he pleaded.

A knowing smile grew on my lips and I knew I was gone. A small bead of moisture formed at the peak, and I thumbed it off just before taking the tip onto my tongue as I slowly licked across the broad head, tongue sliding into the slit there. His cock made a quick little jerk in response. He was so delicious that I sucked his tip into my mouth, sucking and sucking. My tongue glided down his shaft as the tip inched down my throat. I pulled him out nearly all the way before plunging him in again.

Adryen's hands speared into my hair, holding me to him. I removed my hands from his gorgeous shaft and with my left hand, I reached up toward his tanned and toned stomach. With my right hand, I cupped under the tight mound of flesh underneath.

Adryen shuddered. The feeling made a whimper escape my throat. I licked up his cock in one long motion, the tension building. I slid him between my lips and relaxed my throat so I could get every inch of him. I stroked and stroked him with my mouth, my tongue, my teeth, going farther and farther down his warm, hard length.

Yes, I had him right where I wanted him; or maybe he had me.

I moved my mouth and licked down the underside of him where a very thick vein lay. My heart ached from the need deep in my core. I wanted the full length of him inside me; stretching me and filling me. Adryen fisted the sheets as a sudden jolt of ecstasy rocked him.

I had to hold back. I wanted him to beg me to never stop again. Some small, quiet part of my brain told me that this would be about more than just tonight. He was magnificent; *we* were.

Adryen pulled my head onto him more forcefully and I gave in to him, allowing him to control my movements. I wanted him fucking my mouth. He sensed my submission and turned into a beast. Unexpectedly and crazily, he slammed into me with the insatiable hunger that I had been feeling for him. He thrust into my mouth, arching his hips again and again, losing all rhythm. Suddenly, one last spasm rocked him, and he hitched as he spilled his warm, thick seed down my throat; salty and sweet.

When his fingers had loosened on my hair and he sat, muscles beginning to relax, I wiped the corner of my mouth and kissed the tip of his still hardened cock. He jerked with the sensitivity of my lips touching him.

I was a queen, triumphant.

I got up off of the floor and made my way to the other side of the bed. I adjusted my drying, tangled hair into a loose braid over my shoulder and slipped into bed. Silently, Adryen willed his magic through him, turning the lights off and darkness filled the room. I felt movement, as Adryen settled into the bed beside me. He pulled me into him in a silent embrace and held me in the dark until a sweet sleep claimed us both.

My hand ran along the sheet to my side, feeling for a male that was not there and my eyes shot open from sleep. Regret and fear rolled through me.

He'd left.

Adryen must not have enjoyed himself this afternoon and sought an excuse to leave his own room.

I fiddled with my braid, worried I had messed things up between us. Getting out of the lonely bed, I walked toward the windows where the moon and stars shone bright down onto the beach.

A singular silhouette of a fae sat with their legs tucked into their chest looking out at the endless ocean.

I squinted my eyes trying to get a better look and planted my face into the window. After trying very hard, for several moments, I gave up. I backed away and the fae tilted its head revealing blue ears shining in the moonlight.

Adryen.

The moment I realized who it was, I zoomed down the stairs, not caring that I was wearing only a shirt and ran outside of the castle toward the beach; toward *him*.

Hot, and out of breath, I kneeled gingerly beside him. I clenched my jaw a little bit with how uncomfortable this was going to be, but I needed to be near him. Silently, Adryen pulled his shirt off and handed it to me.

"Thank you," was my only response. I grasped the shirt, wiped myself down and then set the shirt on the sand, placing my bare bottom atop it.

We just sat there for several minutes, staring into the darkness together. I slid my eyes over to see him through my periphery. He looked neutral, solemn even.

Almost as if he could feel my emotions, he slid a hand across to me and placed it on top of mine, grasping it.

My body immediately relaxed, and my fear and anxiety subsided.

"I forgive you," was all I could manage before turning my head to face him fully, "For the sprite sanctuary; I forgive you."

He squeezed my grasped hand, "I appreciate that, Princess."

A smile crossed my face, and I nudged his shoulder, "You're a great king, Adryen. One mistake does not define you."

It was true. I'd had so much hate pent up about this, that I did not even know why I had been angry for so long.

I scooted to face him and pulled him to do the same. We adjusted and our legs intertwined with one another, "What is really going on, Adryen?"

The moment of silence before his reply felt cavernous, "I am not enough." He turned his face away from me, silver lining his blue eyes.

He continued after a moment, "I have for so long not been worthy of this throne, of this kingdom. I am the second born, this was not meant for me."

"You didn't have a choice, Adryen." I placed my hand on his leg and rubbed down his knee, "You are doing a great job," my tone optimistic.

Adryen's eyes bore into mine, "I am not worthy of you." A slight deepening of his voice told me that he was allowing himself to be vulnerable with me in this moment.

It made me heart sick to think that this male didn't know how wonderful he was. "You are worthy of everything, Your Majesty. You have done so much for your kingdom, your people. The sacrifices you've made...I *saw* them. You *are* enough," I placed my hand on his powerful jawline and pulled his forehead to mine and whispered, "You are enough...for me."

His eyes closed and a silver drop trailed down his strong cheek, "And you, Niya, my Princess, are perfect...for me; In all ways."

Adryen pressed his full lips onto mine gingerly and we kissed deeply. I wrapped my arms around his neck and tightened into him, not wanting to let go. Pulling away from his kiss, I snuggled into his neck and hugged him tightly.

He had to know his worth. And if he didn't, I would make it my mission to remind him, even if it took every day, forever, that he was worthy of his crown, and his life.

I said into his neck, "Do you want me to let go?"

Adryen chuckled, "Absolutely not," and returned the tight hug.

Taking in a deep, cleansing breath and wiping at his cheek, "Tell me something about you."

"I don't like to talk about myself; I am quite dreary."

He put his hand on my neck and pushed me away from him gently, "You, are far from dreary, Princess."

"Okay, fine," I backed away from him, giving some space, "My life has always been my own. But it has never been the priority. Being the first born, I was molded into this person that was not me. Not the Niya that you know," I paused getting myself ready to open up myself to him, "I am never good enough for them. I would eat wrong, breathe wrong, sleep wrong and there would always be suggestions on how to do it better."

Adryen just looked at me and I looked away, "I don't want to be queen. I don't want to rule knowing I cannot possibly be up to the task. I am happy with the life that I have created for myself. I enjoy my independence."

Looking back to him, "That was of course before my mother told me about my proposed coronation and alliance with *you* and that independence sort of got ripped from me." I sighed, "I am glad at least one positive thing has come out of that."

"And what is that?" He finally said.

"That's you," I beamed, and kissed his cheek.

"Do you understand why the quake happened this morning?"

"I know that you caused it, but I am unsure how."

"I am proud to be something positive for you, but the earthquake happened because I could not control my emotions. The strong emotions that I have for you." Adryen touched my cheek, "You do things to me that I would have never imagined. It scares the *shit* out of me but excites me all at the same time."

I giggled, "I know you are being serious, but that is so adorable."

He gawked at me, and I got up off the sandy beach and brushed myself off, "It's late, we should go to bed."

"I don't think it's wise to sleep in the same room anymore." Adryen looked at the ground. "My emotions are in overdrive, and I am struggling to keep it together. When I am that close to you, in bed, I am afraid something worse could happen than the quake from earlier."

Normally, I would be offended, especially after what had happened today...but Adryen's face was pure worry. I did not want this, I wanted him with me, but I understood.

I looked at him with sad eyes, "Okay, I get it."

Adryen got on his knees, helping himself off of the sandy ground and grasped my right tattooed hand, "Thank you for this. For everything."

I gave a half smile, "And thank you," I kissed his cheek and we walked into the castle, bidding each other goodnight.

Chapter 26
Niya

The sun shone through the large glass windows as a light knock sounded at the door. I looked over and saw an empty bed beside me. Irritated, even though I agreed to Adryen not sleeping with me over the last several nights while I finished healing, I got up. Walking towards the knock, I rubbed my eyes.

I cracked the door and Daphne invited herself in.

"You are going on a picnic today!"

I looked outside to the sandy shore and replied, "A what?"

"A picnic. It's like you take your food and then pack it into this basket and you eat outside and enjoy the weather."

I squinted my eyes at Daphne, "And that is supposed to be enjoyable?"

"Oh, it is very enjoyable, Your Highness."

I questioned, "Who attends these 'picnics'?"

This sounded like a very inconvenient way to eat.

Where would the tables be; or the chairs?

"Well, it'll be nice, I promise."

I looked back at Daphne, who was fixing the bed, "Are you joining me, Daph?"

She smiled at the nickname I'd given her and shook her head, "No, I am not. King Adryen is making lunch for both of you now."

"Making it?"

"Yes; as in preparing, cooking, and packing," Daphne trailed off, finishing with the bed, "You ask a lot of questions, Niya."

I lifted my eyebrow at her curiously.

I plodded through the room to the bathroom to examine my hair. I groaned at the sight of the knotted mess, and shouted, "Daph, I need to shower again to fix my hair. Do you have any hairbrushes I can use?"

"Yes, Your Highness. I also pulled out a dress for you to wear today. I will be back with the brush before you know it."

"Daphne, please just call me Niya."

She nodded and continued tidying up the room and left.

Quickly, I jumped in the shower.

Once I was out, I wrapped a new towel around me and strolled out of the bathroom. A hairbrush and a short, ruffled, floral tied back dress was waiting for me on the bed. I searched for undergarments and slid them on under the dress. A pair of nude strappy wedges waited for me by the door. I pulled them to me and strapped them up my legs in a tight knot. I slipped Celeste on my thigh and tightened the strap.

Grabbing the brush Daphne had left, I walked back to the bathroom and detangled my wet knotted hair. I fingercurled the strands loosely over my shoulders and back. I pulled out two strands of hair that lay on my face and tied a loose knot at the back of my head, uncovering my ears.

This wardrobe was very different, but I loved it so much. The colors and fabric were so exotic from what I was normally used to.

I made my way out of the bedroom and down the three flights of stairs toward the castle entryway. I looked over at the grandfather clock.

Twelve-Thirty.

I looked around the common room where fae, dressed in burnt orange and alabaster smocks, busied themselves cleaning up from the castle's malfunction yesterday. I likened them to little flowers flowing in the wind, and dancing to their own music.

Eucalyptus and birch permeated the area around me as Adryen whispered, "Good morning, Princess."

Lightning danced in my veins. A smile quirked on my lips as I spun around to find him. Remembering our very singular sleeping arrangement, "I missed you these last days; where did you get off to?"

"After what happened with us and my castle's foundation cracking even more, I thought it would be smarter to keep as much distance as possible, despite our cuddling that night," Adryen finished his last words and held a wicker basket with a sheet on top of it in one hand.

In the other, he pulled out a crimson dahlia and handed it to me, "I really enjoyed the other night."

My eyebrows furrowed as a curl of a smile graced my lips. Without an ounce of shame, I said, "And I enjoyed every second of your thick cock between my lips."

A blush crept up his neck and cheeks.

I raised a satisfied eyebrow as I breathed in the fresh aroma of the stunning flower.

Deciding not to embarrass him more, I changed the subject, "This is my favorite flower—Eveline Dahlias. These flowers do not grow in the cold and are produced in greenhouses powered by Lord Zahar's earthly magic," My eyes closed remembering when I used to run through the city of Khine as a child, "I would beg Lord Zahar as a youngling to let me have all his *pretty flowers*."

"That's a pleasant surprise, Princess. My kingdom is absolutely overrun with these."

"Your kingdom has *wild d*ahlias? I *must* see them!" I enthused, "Our kingdom is *so* cold; most of our natural plant life is dreary. One day you will show me," I insisted.

Adryen smiled gleefully, "It so happens that day is today."

He moved in closer to me, putting his hand on my cheek and whispered, "I cleared my schedule for you."

I looked down as heat rose inside of me, "Thank you," and looked up at his sparkling eyes.

Adryen nodded and guided us out the front door. Our journey to the Dahlia fields took a while, but we spent the entire time talking and laughing with each other. These last couple of days had been truly magical. Knowing that I was going to have to leave today made me realize that it was not what I want.

If I could stay here with Adryen and forget everything that was waiting for me, I would.

"Adryen," I looked up at his sublime face.

"Yes?" He gazed back at me.

"I quite like this."

"Like what?"

"Getting to know you for you. I feel like the barriers and blinders have all gone and I can see you in your truest form."

"And what form is that, Princess?"

"Pure, and lovely. I see you for who you are and for who you will become. I see you trying your best. You are a natural king, Adryen."

His affectionate smile radiated as he looked away, "We are here."

I looked up and thousands of Dahlia's stood majestically in the field close to The Divide. An assortment of peach, crimson, lavender, and yellow flowers towered in an assortment of sizes. Running up to them, I walked the perimeter and attempted to touch every single flower.

Adryen chuckled, "If I'd known you loved flowers *that* much, I would have made sure you woke up to hand-picked ones every day of your stay."

"That is not necessary, and truly a lot of work."

Adryen flicked a sheet out and laid it down next to the wild Dahlia's, "Nothing is too much work when it is for you."

Looking down, my face heated.

I walked back to him, pondering, "So, you need to explain to me how this picnic thing works."

"Well, you make food. In this case, I made us lunch. After that, I packed it all in this picnic basket and we eat outside on a blanket, enjoying nature."

"That's it?"

"Yep," Adryen smiled.

Gods, why was he so damn perfect?

And why was I so imperfect?

I pinched my eyebrows together, trying not to get upset with myself, "Adryen," I started.

"You sure do like to say my name," he chuckled.

I shrugged my shoulders, "I guess so."

"Yes, Princess?"

"Was the other night a mistake?"

I needed to know his thoughts about us. I felt like it was so magical and right, but it also felt out of place. Considering everything that had happened with his home practically crumbling to dust for seemingly no reason.

I thought we might have a growing connection, and I really wanted it to continue.

I think.

Adryen thought about my question for a while, analyzing my facial expressions and worry when he was taking too long to answer.

"Do *you* think the other night was a mistake?"

Before even thinking, I replied, "No."

"Neither do I. In fact, I think the other night should be something that happens more often, Princess. I thoroughly enjoyed what you did to me; for me."

I looked at his beaming face and tugged at his loose strand of hair playfully, "What's my favorite color?"

"Uhh," he looked puzzled, "I am going to assume some shade of purple."

"Lavender is my favorite shade of purple."

Adryen pumped a fist in the air like he accomplished a great feat, "Yes!"

"Let me guess, your favorite color is green, or blue?"

"Blue? Do you say that because my Wyvern is blue?"

I turned my head from him, "No."

He placed a gentle cup of a hand under my chin and turned me to face him, with a steady hand, "My favorite color is gold, like the flex in your eyes."

I was speechless.

I was speechless at the fact that he had just complimented my biggest insecurity. I hated my eyes. I hated that I never got my father's blue eyes, or even my mother's. I hated that I looked so different than the royal family and that having this eye color made me stand out from them.

My thoughts and stomach suddenly turned sour as thinking about my mother led to thinking about my her plan. These thoughts sent my heart and head spiraling and flushed away every wonderful thing I had previously been thinking.

I needed to tell him my mother's plans before going, but I did not want to ruin a potentially amazing day. I'd loved every moment Adryen and I had spent together, and he did not deserve this; any of this mess.

It felt like my mind was playing tug-of-war with itself.

Maybe I could figure out a way to skirt her plans, altogether.

Adryen sat down on the sheet, and I followed suit, making sure my dress was neat around my crossed my legs, trying to stay proper, like any ascending princess would.

Adryen pulled out two closed dishes and empty plates, "I made something called rainbow pasta salad and chicken tortilla pinwheels."

I examined the food as he opened the containers. The delicious aroma wafted up to me. I looked down as the various dishes were laid delicately on the sheet.

And in that moment, an idea, crystal clear, if not totally sane, blasted into me.

A plan of my own.

I blurted, "I want to marry you, Adryen," and my eyes became saucers realizing what I'd just said.

Fuck.

Adryen choked on his first bite of lunch, hacking and wheezing to get the suddenly dry morsel down his throat. Finally composing himself, he slowly put down the rest of his food and stared at me, swallowing heavily one last time, "What? But you said you would never..."

It was too late to go back now, "Under one condition," I spat out, determined to power through my proposal.

He nodded slowly, trepidation and wariness filling his face, "And that is?"

"You seal a blood oath with me," I shot determinedly, nodding my head.

If I could seal a blood oath with Adryen, then I would have to do everything in my power to keep him alive. Killing him myself, per my mother, would *certainly* be out of the question.

And marrying him would indeed come with several advantages, despite my prior thoughts about this.

"I will marry you and provide Haldonia with more land and, in return, you allow me to protect you."

Adryen huffed a laugh, "I am more than capable of keeping myself protected, Princess. I do not need an oath to provide that."

"Adryen," unsure if my proposal was being dismissed.

His face suddenly severe, "Oh, you're serious. That's all you want? You don't want me to swear fealty to you?"

"No. Why would I do such a thing? I want you to swear to let me protect you, and in return, I will marry you and give you more land for you and your people," I responded, unsure how there was still some confusion.

"I don't know, Niya," Adryen paused, grabbing my hand, "Is this something you want? A marriage?"

"Yes."

No.

Not really.

But I wanted to be with him, for however long the gods willed it. I'd decided that in the shower this morning, recollecting all of our time together.

That wouldn't be possible if I was going to be forced to kill him. This was not *ideal*, but I needed to make sure he would live.

My power vibrated inside of me, preparing my magic for the blood oath. I slipped my fingers down the side of my thigh suggestively as I looked into Adryen's stunned face and pulled out Celeste to open the palm of my hand.

Adryen pleaded, grasping the wrist that held Celeste, "Please tell me this is one hundred percent what you want. Because you were very certain when we had first met that—"

"—Yes," I breathed, "One *thousand* percent."

Adryen took Celeste from my grasp and placed the cold bone knife on my skin, penetrating it just enough to release a sufficient amount of the ruby liquid. Droplets of blood dripped onto the blanket as Adryen did the same to his palm. We sat there for several moments, palms up, just staring into each other.

I was nervous. A nervousness I had never felt. I wanted him safe, and doing this blood oath would ensure it. I might be sealing my life to his, but it felt right.

"I swear to allow you to protect me in the darkest of days, and the brightest ones. You already have my heart, and my soul, Niya. I swear that this oath will not allow anyone or anything to hurt or kill me without you destroying them, first."

My heart tugged, "I swear, Adryen, to ensure you will live and thrive, happily in this realm or any other if you so choose. I swear that I will marry you and provide more land for your people upon our marriage."

Adryen whispered, "You don't have to."

I slapped our hands together before Adryen could change his mind. Staring at our clasped hands in awe, he smiled, grasping me more tightly. Just then, zaps of power zipped through us as phantom wind twirled around entwining our souls together. I could feel the emotions of Adryen as he refused to look away from me.

Love, power, and happiness.

This is not normal.

Blood oaths are just a quick twinge of feeling and the oath is set.

Our powers eddied and crackled against each other, as the earth around us shook uncontrollably. Adryen's hands glowed gold again as mine turned shadowy with power. His arm's golden swirls became a permanent entity as our powers became one.

Adryen strained, and his pain washed over me.

His arm looked similar to mine. His lightness complimented with my darkness.

I tried to break away but couldn't.

"Adryen, let go!" I shouted through the growing roar of wind.

"I can't!" His eyes darted around us, looking for something that could help break apart our bound hands.

I lifted my heeled foot up and kicked towards his chest, trying to force a separation. Nothing was working. I strained as I tried to use my other hand to pry his off of mine. An invisible cord grew taut between us; my eyes dilated with lust.

Adryen's eyes mimicked mine as we realized what had just happened.

No.

I screamed, with so much anger, hoping the sound would break this magical bond. Wind shot out like arrows and our hands fell. Power emanated from me as tears rolled down my face. Adryen backed up off the blanket and panic, that was not mine, rolled over me.

I grabbed Celeste and crawled over to him, pissed that our blood oath turned into something more...personal. Filled with sudden rage at the sense of betrayal, I lifted my knife and hot scorching heat jolted from my hand, forcing me to drop the knife.

I seethed in pain.

Well, the fucking blood oath worked.

My emotions overwhelmed me. All I could process was that I was sealed into something *more* than just a blood oath.

I was sealed into a whole fae-ass mating bond.

My powers rose up through me and started to boil over the edge, "Get up!"

Adren slowly got up, fear and concern lining his beautiful face.

I clenched my fists at my sides, "You owe me a sparring match, *mate*."

I felt Adryen's humor at the word that had escaped my lips and I scoffed, annoyed. I went in for a punch and he grabbed my fist, "I am not going to spar when you are in such a rage. I don't know why you are reacting this way. Shouldn't you be happy? Isn't this what you wanted?"

I was going to punch this handsome male in his stupidly perfect face, "No! Not a mating bond!"

I quickly slipped my foot under his, flipping him; he dropped to the ground like a stone.

Scowling and wiping the dirt off of himself, he retorted, "Niya, I didn't mean to —"

"Get up and fight me, Adryen!" I bellowed.

"Fine; have it your way, *mate*," Adryen's eyes glittered with humor, lust, and sport; my three favorite things besides music.

Adryen abruptly engaged, but I felt like he was still holding back. I had thrown several solid punches his way, and all he would do was simply duck out of reach.

Or deflect my fists.

He was enjoying this. This smug fae-hole was actually *enjoying* this!

I continued throwing punch after sweep and he was still able shake me off easily. I was giving everything I had! Adryen's eyes snapped wide, making me retreat a couple of steps. He bolted towards me, getting low; his full weight tackled me to the grassy floor. He tucked me into his arm to protect me from the impact as we rolled together.

More tears began pouring down my face as pain rippled through me. I conjured wind and pushed Adryen off of me, sending him flying through the air. Getting up, I adjusted the wind to keep him down, "What did you do?"

Adryen sounded out of breath, "Niya, you're upset, clearly. Why don't you just relax—"

I sent out a blast of wind into his face to shut up his stupid words.

"Why did our blood oath turn into a *mating bond*, Adryen?!"

"Niya, I—"

I jolted out another blast of wind straight into his annoying face.

Crying with rage, I screamed; a whirlwind whipping from me.

Adryen screamed through the heavy blasts of wind buffeting his prone body, "I cannot create mating bonds, Niya! You should know that; they are created by the gods themselves!"

Finally processing, "We are...this explains yesterday. You could feel the pull..." I huffed, "Why didn't you tell me?!"

I shrieked and stomped the ground, looking down at my arms and gray smoke billowed out from where my tattoo had sat. The tattoo shone in gold and black, as I pulled up my forearm to my cheeks, wiping off the tears. I looked over at Adryen's newly formed tattoo and it resembled mine of black and gold.

Fear and sadness replaced the anger that was growing inside of me.

Gods, I should have known he was my mate!

I had to leave. I needed to figure out how to break the mating bond. I didn't want this, I didn't ask for this, and I sure as hell wasn't going to keep it.

Standing up straight, I snapped my head down to Adryen as tears rolled down my face. Adrenaline took over and I grabbed Celeste from where she still lay on the blanket. Before I could think, my feet were guiding me away from him.

I didn't want this. This was supposed to be a *business* arrangement; nothing more. I ran as fast as I could from Adryen.

He called after me, "Niya! Please! For fucks sake!"

A light flashed and the sound of ripping cloth reached me as Adryen's wyvern hovered above me; blue fire billowing from his nostrils. I tried to push my wedges in harder to the ground and failed to outrun him.

I didn't really think I would be able to outrun a flying wyvern, but my mind was reeling from what had just happened. It took Adryen just two wing beats before he touched down in front of me.

Adryen shook the earth on his landing and blocked my progress. A short, sharp scream came from my throat as I fell backwards on my ass, dirt flying up around me.

He huffed out smoke; his eyes leveling me.

We couldn't be mates.

But we were.

I could feel every nuance of his emotions now. I thought I could sense them a couple of days ago. I was pretty sure I sensed them yesterday when his power shook the castle. This was all just too much, too soon. I just could not wrap my brain fully around this.

Everything made sense now and I had been *so* blind. There was a reason I felt so alive with him; I felt more whole than I had ever felt in my life.

I clenched my fists into the dirt and yelled, "I am so tired of you knocking me on my ass!" And hurled dirt at Adryen's wyvern.

The azure wyvern tilted his wedge-shaped head and bared his pearly teeth as his spiked wings moved in closer to me, blocking out the sun.

Mates.

Fuck.

I spewed, "Let me go." I got up and walked closer to him, pulling Celeste up to him as warm tears began rolling down my face once more, "Let me leave!"

My heart felt like it was breaking.

Blue eyes narrowed as Adryen huffed hot mist onto me. I put my free hand on his bowed head and glided my hand up his horn. A whole-body shudder erupted from Adryen as he submitted to me, nuzzling into my touch. My power felt so...calm, at peace, when I touched him.

My emotions felt like a calming storm.

It was like the magic in me yielded to his through our physical contact. Tears rolled down my cheeks at the conflict between my brain and my heart.

I found my second half. A fae equal to me in every way.

But...

A short, low growl came from Adryen, and I opened my eyes to see my already healing hand and light scuff marks from us sparring.

Was I healing myself? Or was this his magic?

A wolf's howl sounded in the distance, shaking me out of my reverie, as I dropped my hand to my side. Adryen huffed a sound of annoyance at the disruption and stepped back far enough for me to leave freely.

I side-stepped his bulky form warily and, once clear, I bolted again for The Divide. Pausing only to sheath Celeste, I ran. If I could just get back to Kaldamir, then all would be fine. I would have the time and space to figure out how I felt about all of this mess.

The Divide was coming into focus now; I pushed myself harder, muscles burning, to reach it. I wasn't sure why, but getting to the other side of this wall was as far as I was able to plan into the future.

The moment I neared the barrier, I realized that I had no way of escaping. I would either need to climb this monstrosity or go through it.

Neither was ideal.

Sahriah's suggestion of using my fire and ice magic in tandem to open a hole popped into my mind as I was looking at The Divide, crazed. My right hand chilled as blue sparks of ice flew from it and the left warmed as fire spit and spewed.

I roared as powerful magic spilled out of me, swirling and twining, into The Divide. Thickly vined branches fractured and tumbled to the ground before me. I dug in my heels to brace myself, pouring all of my fear and love and grief through my magic and the power grew until it covered the entirety of The Divide before me.

A voice howled behind me, "Niya, STOP!"

I pushed harder, as the fire and ice twined tighter into a beam of blue and orange. Pushing all of my will into that beam, my focus was on one thing only—getting out of this place—NOW!

Just then, a deafening *crack* sounded throughout the realm.

My ears rang and I shook the fog from my head as I looked up to see that The Divide had completely collapsed as far as my eye could see. In its sudden collapse, vines had scraped against my skin, tearing my dress and slicing gashes into me.

I backed up far enough to see the rest of the wall fall, and to avoid any more lashings. My eyes widened and, without hesitating, I started to dart through the fallen Divide to get to Kaldamir.

A hand grasped my arm and yanked me up into the air. White wings flapped in my periphery as I moved higher into the vast sky above.

Gaining my bearings from the instant shock of it, I rolled my head up to see vaguely familiar blue eyes staring down into mine, "You have caused such a mess, Your Highness."

I squirmed, trying release myself from his grip, "Let me go, you mangy bird!"

The white-haired angel growled, "Now if I do that, my cousin's lover will die. That would not be very kind of me."

I shrieked, "Lover?!"

He tilted his head forward toward me and smirked dropping his hand. My heart left my chest as the sensation of falling engulfed me.

I was exhausted, but I had to get away from here and *stop* my fall.

The winged fae laughed devilishly and I had had enough. I pulled Celeste out and jabbed him in the thigh. Pulling her out, he let go of his grip and I plummeted towards the thorns, keeping a tight hold on Celeste. I pushed out a puff of wind in an attempt to lessen my fall.

My powers pretty much shot, I hit the thorns roughly, groaning in pain. I lay there for several minutes as the angel figure hovered over me, stalking.

"What the fuck?! You did not have to drop me!"

The fae held his bloody thigh with one hand and the middle finger of his other hand raised to the skies.

He proceded to fly away, leaving me there alone in pain and bleeding.

I flipped up my middle fingers in response and continued through the broken wall. A roar rippled through the realm sending a jolt of anger into me. I couldn't concentrate when there were several different emotions flowing through through me.

Blue fire took to the sky as Adryen's Wyvern followed behind, flapping towards me.

I yelled, making sure my words hurt, "Leave me the fuck alone, Adryen!"

Dark magic swelled out of every inch of me as I tried to quickly make it to the edge of The Divide. After several moments of fighting the downed thorns and branches, I rolled onto the land of Kaldamir.

"First of all, I will not 'leave you alone'. Second, you can't keep running away when it's *convenient* for you!"

I peeked up from the mountain of thorns and vines where a very naked, and very out of breath Adryen glowered at me. I got a better view of the tattoo that creeped up to his neck and left side of his chest. It was absolutely beautiful.

I should just portal away; maybe he would get the hint.

I threw my hands in the air, almost in hysterics, "You think all of this is convenient?! I just sealed a blood oath that turned into a fucking *unwanted* mating bond. I also just obliterated the damn Great Divide! And I think I stabbed your friend. I don't know! Nothing is convenient for me right now, Adryen! I feel like everything we had built in these last days just shattered to tiny little pieces in front of me."

Adryen watched me, assessing. He just glared into my very being and I withered into nothingness as his stare burned into me further.

He had to understand why I was being like this. I was about to be Queen of Kaldamir and, if we were mates, that meant that he would have no choice but to be with me.

Forever.

My life, and everything in it was not what Adryen wanted. He was too kind, and too thoughtful, too pure for the likes of me.

This was a mistake.

Everything with Adryen was a mistake.

I wanted to cry.

But, the blood oath was to ensure our marriage. It needn't have been one of a true connection. Right? I was expecting more of a business arrangement born out of concern for the wellbeing of Adryen and his people. Despite our romantic interludes, I still didn't want him to feel trapped.

This mating bond.

This pull.

Changed everything.

I could hear his whispered plea, "Please, Niya. I want this." Adryen reached out a mental hand to me.

No, you don't.

I glanced up to the sky and said below a whisper, "I'm sorry, Adryen," and looked back to his dejected face.

I bunched my eyebrows together and frowned, trying to fight his overabundance of emotions jolting through me and transversed to Ca'Themar's temple.

I decided that it was finally time to see him.

Chapter 27
Niya

Bile rose in my throat, as I landed on the steps of the marbled temple, releasing the contents of my stomach.

I bent on all fours for a while before my stomach was completely cleared and I was ready to get up.

My magic was kaput. I used too much of it with that wall.

Rising to my feet and holding my stomach, I used one hand and banged on Ca'Themar's thick wooded doors, "Let me in, you old fae!" I covered my mouth, ready to puke again but got out, "I need to talk!"

The wooden entrance creaked open on its own and I invited myself in, stomping through the foyer screaming, "Ca'Themar!"

I wiped my mouth with the back of my hand as a voice boomed from somewhere inside the temple, "Gods child, all of Khine can hear *and* feel your rage! Whatever is wrong?"

Ca'Themar came into view with his old self and all my hateful emotions faded as he continued towards me with his bone-carved cane.

Grabbing his hand I held it, took a knee, and bowed.

This was custom.

Nobody outranked the ancient fae, even when emotions ran high.

"Oh, get up, you know you do not have to do that with me. Come, let's take a walk in my gardens, you angry little Princess." He cackled, guiding me by the hand for me to rise and we walked toward the luscious landscape he called The Gardens.

The Gardens were otherworldly. There were too many colors to count. A wide assortment of flowers filled The Gardens; imbuing it with vitality and warmth. Fruit trees and shrubs were lovingly placed along endless pathways. I wanted this garden. There was not one ounce of snow to be seen. The Gardens looked like something taken out of the Seelie courts and dropped right here in Kaldamir.

"Your garden is absolutely stunning, Ca'themar." I gaped with wide eyes as this was my first time visiting the elite space.

"You are here to ask questions about what just happened."

Turning around to Ca'themar, "Yes...how did you know that?"

"Child, you were born with magic you alone cannot withstand. You have found your counterpart, your mate, that can level you and help manage your magic. It's dark, and uncontrollable. Your mate will be able to store your power in his with ease. You cannot run away from fate, my dear. You have had enough time to play and avoid your duties. Take the throne and rule with the king, your lover, by your side."

The prophecy.

Momentarily stunned, "Ca'themar, he can't be my mate; can he? The last time our bloodlines mated, it resulted in the creation of The Great Divide and they did not produce an heir together."

Ca'Themar hit me on the head with his cane. I growled in frustration as fire swelled around my hands.

Gods damn it!

He spewed, "And look at what happened when the bloodlines mated again! The Divide collapsed. An heir will be produced to seal the Seelie and Unseelie fates. The Divide is only the beginning."

I whispered while rubbing my head, "Ow...why are you like this to me?!"

"Because you deserve it, you selfish female," Ca'Themar hooked his cane onto the sleeve of my dress and pulled me down to his eyelevel and whispered loudly to me, "There will be much more pain in your future if you continue this way, Niya. Get it together! Your prophecy is practically fulfilled." Ca'Themar was not having any of my nonsense; that's for sure. And he was also withholding this new information about the prophecy from me.

"I thought finding a mate and sharing power was all the prophecy was?"

Ca'Themar's eyes widened, and he burst into a wheezing laughter, "Oh, child! You know so little. It is not my place to tell you. Ask your mother for the full scope of your prophecy and you come back to me, and we will talk again."

I swiped his cane from my sleeve and threw my arms over my chest, tapping my foot vigorously, "Adryen and I cannot be mates. We haven't done anything to seal the bond other than make a blood oath."

"Not yet," Ca'Themar smirked, "In time, you will."

My insides screamed. I felt like a caged animal as I started to pace back and forth with all this new information. My prophecy is only partially filled now with Adryen being my mate.

My *mate*.

He would balance the levels of my power, which would mean I wouldn't die from having too much. But...there was more to the prophecy.

"I am confused," I thought out loud, scrunching my eyes, "If my power is leveled now with the bond developing, what else could be left for me to worry about?"

"Niya, your power is nowhere near leveled. Not until the mating bond is complete. You will know your magic has calmed when the black on your arm entwines with gold," He paused then continued, "Your fists are still running hot from your emotions."

I looked down at my hands and at Ca'Themar's cane. A sooty handle revealed itself and I moved my eyes to my flaming hands. I grunted in frustration as the flames grew larger. Concentrating on dimming the flame, it did not budge.

"You look constipated, Niya. Sit down," His words resonated, and I instantly sat, following his directions, "Good, now watch and learn."

I set my hands into the grass and adjusted my body to sit more comfortably.

Ca'Themar sighed, rather loudly, "Please watch where you are pointing those things! That grass is going to take a month to get back to normal!"

I rolled my eyes, and he smacked my head again with his cane.

"I will break that in half, ancient one!"

"You won't do shit; not unless you want to lose to me in a fight."

I squinted my eyes at him as he motioned for me to follow him through some breathing exercises. I huffed a sigh, and finally submitted. We practiced multiple calming techniques; many of which I'd never seen. My mind and body calmed to an easy simmer; I could work with that.

"Now that you have calmed your tumult, I am going to have to ask you to leave."

Shock and confusion zipped through me, "Why?"

"The meeting of the priests and priestesses will begin soon, and I would rather not have them see a distressed and *unkempt* Princess."

Ca'Themar really knew how to make a fae feel good...

Me leaving meant I must go back home—to Kaldamir. Which meant I would have to hear my mother's admonishments and questions as to why I could not finish the tour from almost a week ago.

I hurried back through the temple, head lowered, and onto the marbled steps outside. Walking through the silencing crowd, I bowed and tried my best to be as polite as possible to all of my people. I would have just preferred to blend, but how could I with my tattered dress and ragged appearance. Concerned looks grew on some of the merchants and traders.

I probably looked like walking garbage.

A little winged female child ran up to me and tugged on my torn skirts. I stopped walking and leaned down to her.

Her voice squeaked, "Your Highness, we missed you." She rummaged through her satchel and continued, "Please accept this gift from all of us from the orphanage," The little girl held out her hand and a wrapped cloth bulged outward.

I gently grasped it and opened the cloth to see a beautifully carved sleeping, blue wyvern.

"Our oracle said this is all she could see from your journey and spent all week carving it."

This was a spitting image of Adryen. From his blue hue, scales, and spikes.

Tears welled in my eyes, as I tried to hold them back, "This is beautiful, thank you."

The child nodded her head and started to shy away from me. I moved in closer to her and bent down, pushing her frizzy hair behind her ears. I kissed her forehead, "It means, everything."

She beamed and ran back into the crowd.

I walked the entire way back to the castle, examining and investigating this wooden figure and its beauty. Adryen must be livid. He would understand, in time, why I left him.

There was no way he was ready to settle down. I was over one hundred years of age and the thought of being with only one person seemed...

Unreasonable.

Chapter 28
Niya

The guard interrupted my thoughts, "Open the gates! The Princess is back!"

I looked up to see Garrin and Rose sprinting towards me. Pure panic swathed their faces as they fell just short of ramming into me.

Well, one of them at least.

Rose almost knocked me to my ass with the impact of her hug. I caressed her back and smiled at the familiar fondness.

I missed her so much.

Out of breath, Garrin interrupted our reunion, "Niya! Where were you? I have been searching for you on the border for the last week! The realm shook and a massive jolt of power surged through the cities. I didn't want to risk my team…"

We walked together back to the castle entrance.

I finally replied, "I was in Haldonia," paused, "and the realm shaking was me bringing down The Great Divide."

Garrin put a hand on my shoulder and pulled me back, "You were…you what?"

I nodded my head slowly and smiled up at him.

He whipped his eyes to mine as he grasped my shoulders, "Gods save us! What happened?!"

I shrugged my shoulders and Rose chirped, "I'm so happy you're home, Niya!" She linked her arm with mine and we walked inside the castle, leaving Garrin to follow behind us, gaping.

I reluctantly let go of Rose, "I should see my mother first before we talk. I just have to rip off that bandage." Putting on mock bravery, I pressed my lips into a line.

Rose and Garrin nodded slowly, but understood.

We parted ways and I trudged to the throne room. What should have only taken a couple of minutes, took several long minutes to get there. I had no idea what to tell her or how to explain myself. I was going to be punished for this, and I just had to accept that fact. Despite being an adult with my own set of issues to handle, my mother put the fear in me.

The sentry at the door looked down at me and his eyes widened, "Princess, shall I announce you?"

Garrin stepped in behind me, "Niya, are you sure you want to do this?"

I looked at Garrin and replied, "I guess so. There is no going back now." I took in a deep breath to steady myself.

"I am going in with you."

"No, Garrin. I need to handle this myself."

He stared at me stonefaced, "No, Niya. You have been gone for a week without my protection. What you *need* to handle is this, with a friend at the very least."

I quirked my lip up and inclined my head, "Fine."

The sentry held his hand on the pommel of his sword and announced my entrance. I slowly walked through the doorway and looked down until I approached my parents' thrones. My parents sat on the royal seats as I crept my eyes painfully slowly up to their eyes.

My mother sat there with her elbow on the arm of the chair, fingers propping her head up. She wore a devilish smile as I frowned at her, waiting for the room to fall on top of me.

"Hello, daughter."

I bowed deeply to the both of them, "Hello, mother."

"Garrin, you are dismissed."

Well, that was pointless. Garrin bowed deeply and walked out of the throne room.

She continued, "How was your tour?"

Wha—

I shifted on my feet, "Um, it was fine. Have you heard anything?"

Mother let out a bored sigh, "Only something about you almost being killed in Cleome and then something with a wyvern and you left," she spat out quickly.

"I don't really remember. It was not something that I cared to dwell on. I figured this tour would be tedious and grueling for you, and I needed you to see what it was like to speak to our people and listen to their needs. It's quite dreadful, actually," Rayven looked positively disgusted.

"I would not have been at all surprised if you had come home both exhausted and bored to death." She sighed, "But here we are; instead of that, I see," the queen waved her arm indicating my deportment, "*this.*"

Anger welled inside of me. I could never seem to please her. I was always less than what she'd expected of me. In this case, I'm *alive.*

Why stop now?

"I demolished The Divide," I shot like a petulant child.

She jumped up from her seat and slithered towards me. I tried to back up but her hands were around my neck, "You what?!"

I let out a choked attempt at breath as she tightened her grip on me. I started seeing stars as she continued to grip harder. Trying to grab and swat her arm away, my power surged from me.

She didn't budge.

She wasn't afraid.

My father retorted, "Ravyn, please. Think about it, this could be good for the marriage arrangement. She did half the work for us. All we need to do now is make sure Niya kills Adryen after the contract and the land is ours."

Ravyn dropped her hand as I fell to the floor, holding my throat. My tattoo glowed gold and my throat instantly healed, and I was back to normal; as normal as I could be in my current state.

I got up off of the floor and straightened my filthy and torn dress, "Dad," hesitating, "I...how...I thought you didn't agree with mother..." I abruptly stopped. I was lost for words.

He had always taken my side and supported me.

In everything.

This wasn't the father that I thought I knew.

"Niya, who do you think engineers these plans? Your mother? Nothing goes through her without going through me first."

A slice of pain entered my heart. A rumbling growl rose up in my chest, and ice-cold fire encircled my clenched fists.

My mother's circumspect tone stopped me from obliterating the entire throne room, "Interesting."

I looked up at the Queen staring down at me with eyes empty of all feeling. She grabbed my swirling black and gold arm, "Where did you get the healing magic?"

I lied, "I don't know."

Ravyn let out a deep growl, "I am not stupid, girl. Tell me. You weren't meant to have the power to heal."

"I don't know!" I was shouting now. Not really giving a damn how this would end. I was pissed. Pissed at my mother for keeping more of my own prophecy from me, according to the ancient priest. I was pissed that I reacted the way that I did when I found out Adryen was my mate. I was pissed that I had to explain myself to a family that only cared about themselves. I literally look like I came from the battlefield, and she could not give *any* fucks.

"Actually, I know a lot more than you think and definitely more than you, daughter," Ravyn moved back to her dais and sat victoriously on her throne.

"Please enlighten me, mother, since I have apparently been kept in the dark."

"No, I don't think I will, darling. I will let you explore the rest of this unknown part of your prophecy yourself until I decide the time is right. Plus, why would I give you *my* information if you won't give me yours."

Okay, we were acting like children.

I replied through clenched teeth, "If you'll excuse me, I would like to spend the rest of today *and* the week in the confines of my own wing. If you need me, please feel free to fuck off. Otherwise, you won't know I'm even here."

I turned on my heels, ready to go. But Ravyn had other plans. She laughed, "You still have that marriage contract my *darling daughter.*"

I whirled around as she continued, "He will be here soon, I am sure."

Fuck.

I put on the fakest smile and said through a clenched jaw, "Perfect."

I swung the door open before the guard could and stomped out of the throne room. Finding my way to the cellar, I grabbed a bottle of Moscato in one hand and whiskey in another, striding back up the stairs to my chamber.

Trying to fit both bottles in one hand, I managed to get the door open to my room and strolled in, kicking the heavy door closed behind me. I threw the bottles on the bed and plopped on my chaise lounge and let out a frustrated sigh.

Looking at my tattered clothes, I couldn't help but laugh at how ridiculous I's undoubtedly looked. My clothes were so ripped up from the thorns that I should just be naked at this point. I tried to undo my half up hair from this morning and my fingers got caught in the knotted mess. Standing up, I made my way to the bathroom and zoomed through the shower. It felt so nice using my own vanilla and jasmine scented soaps. My hair smoothed out and detangled once I ran my brush through it. Pulling it up into a messy bun, I slipped on some frilly silk pajamas and landed belly first on my bed.

I sent magic to pop the cork from the Moscato and held it up as it fizzed, "It is just you and me tonight, old friend."

I kissed the glass surface and started to chug. A knock sounded at the door and a frown crossed my face, "What?!"

Rose peaked her head in, "I *know* that is not you drinking wine without *me*!"

I shrugged my shoulders and took a couple more chugs. I pulled the bottle from my lips and looked at how much was left.

Half a bottle.

Rose glided in and stole the wine bottle from me, "You better explain yourself. I have been worried sick! I literally thought our oath was going to kill me. I was starting to feel the detachment and my heart was breaking."

"Aww, I missed you too!"

Rose plopped down beside me and leaned her head on my shoulder, "Don't ever do that again."

Kissing my friend on the top of her head, I laughed, "Okay, I will try harder not to get killed next time."

"What?!"

I nodded, "I was in Cleome and this shadow thing came from out of nowhere and attacked the village. I tried to escape, and it followed me. Adryen came in and saved me."

Rose smiled and squeaked, "And?!"

"And..." I stole the bottle back from her and drank some more, "He used his light magic to heal me."

Rose opened the whiskey bottle and took a swig, scrunching her face, "Niya, if you do not tell me the whole story now, I will literally throw this," waving the bottle in the air threateningly.

Trying to snatch back the threatened bottle, "Fine. He healed me, I learned a lot of new and exciting things about him and his people. He has a wonderful castle, Rose. Your picture is almost a perfect representation. You did an amazing job!"

She smiled, and I continued, "I was gifted clothes from his tailor, and they were absolutely beautiful. We need more colors here in our fashion district." Metrika had nothing on Doogan. "Maybe I can set up trade with his kingdom in the future," I stopped as Rose gulped harder.

"I mean...shit. Rose, his kingdom is perfect. Other than a little bit of foundational cracking...it is so perfect. Once my wound healed from that shadow thing, I kind of broke The Great Divide and now our kingdoms are one." I scrunched up the side of my face and cringed at that last part.

Rose did not stop sipping until I was done talking. I left out the part about him being my mate. I would tell her later.

"He is your WHAAT?!"

Oh fuck. I shot up my mental shields and she winced in pain, "Ouch."

"Are you okay?"

She rubbed her head, "No, as soon as you blocked me out, it felt like I ran into a wall."

I inclined my head to her, "That is weird. It might be my powers. They are kind of unpredictable."

"I'll be okay," rubbing at her temples. After a pause, "Adryen is your *mate?!*"

I let out a huge sigh, "Yes...and no, I am not ready to talk about it. I need to figure out what the Queen is scheming. Once I derail that, then I can move on to thinking about Adryen being my mate."

"Oh, come on Niyaaa! I want to hear more!"

Finishing off the last of the sweet wine, I let out a small burp, "We made a blood oath, and it somehow sealed our mating bond too. I am stuck with him, forever. So, I ran away."

Rose handed the whiskey bottle over to me and I chugged this alcohol as well. I turned on my back and looked up at the hanging bottle, "If I get bored with Adryen, swear you will figure a way to sneak in another male or two that will make me happy again."

"Maybe try not to run away next time, first. Second, I doubt you will get bored with that lump of sexy. He will figure out ways to satisfy you, and if he doesn't on his own, teach him," She shuffled her body closer to me and I leaned in on her.

"It'll be alright, Niya."

"I love you, Rose."

Rose capped the bottle, "I love you, too."

We talked for the next several hours and got very drunk. I looked over at my clock and it read two in the morning. Yawning, I snuggled into Rose and sleep claimed the both of us.

Chapter 29
Adryen

A week had passed since Niya had left me.
My mate.

My heart hitched every time I thought of her. I just wished she felt the same. Niya and I were bound together forever. I had never wanted someone as much as I wanted her. Niya was my perfect match; my person. She balanced me and made me want to be more loving and strong for her; my future queen.

A slight frown curved my lips as I remembered the blood oath and how disastrous that turned out to be. I looked down at my palm that I refused to heal with the new golden swirl tattoo that went up to my shoulder and overflowed onto my chest. The tattoo was almost a replica of Niya's. Beautiful, ethereal swirls that did not entwine with one another. Except, mine was gold and hers was inky black. I closed my eyes, sighing with longing. I didn't want to force a marriage or a bond. I asked her if she was sure because I knew I couldn't trust my own heart. My heart had been screaming at me for weeks that I needed to make her mine.

But, it was her idea. She practically begged to take the oath to marry me; and *protect* me—whatever that meant.

I didn't want this; not really. I wanted to build a relationship with Niya and form a bond through trust and respect. A blood oath is permanent and forced. I just couldn't bring myself to say no to her. I would do anything for her; even let her go.

I tapped my pen on the notice of invitation from Queen Ravyn. She was requesting my attendance for a formal contract signing tomorrow. I could always send my apologies that I would not be able to attend. Niya would be able to marry someone of her own choosing and she wouldn't be stuck with me. My heart and head ached and the only sounds were my heartbeat and the click of my pen. I clicked and unclicked the pen several times, reading the invitation over and over again until all I could see and smell and think was...her.

"If you do not stop with that clicking, I will break that pen in two," Malcolm pulled me from my thoughts as I looked over to him lazily laying on the chaise lounge sipping on some brandy and continued, "What are you so worried about? Signing that document, forever sealing your fate? She is already your mate, Adryen."

I clicked the pen several more times, not reacting to Malcolm's threat as I read the letter slower. Slamming the pen on the table, I buried my face in my hands.

This should not be this difficult.

Malcolm let out an annoyed sigh, "Cousin, I say you *don't* sign, and we just forget about her."

I looked over my splayed fingers, "Forget about her? My blood bound mate? Okay." I huffed, rolling to release some of the tension in my shoulders.

Malcolm smiled, his fangs protruding from his lips, "You know, maybe you could get conjugal visits every now and then without marrying her."

No sooner had Malcolm finished the last word, than I whipped my head around to him, baring my teeth and growling.

"I will flay you if you speak about her that way again, Malcolm. Niya would probably kill you herself if she knew you dared to...you didn't see her when we sparred at our picnic."

Putting up his hands in concession, "Oh, I saw it *all*. Being perched up in a tree playing guard duty has very few advantages, but watching you get your ass handed to you was definitely one of them."

I changed the subject, "Did you have to drop her, though?"

Malcolm shrugged, "She survived, didn't she?"

I lowered my eyelashes, throwing an annoyed look over at my cousin, "I am going to accept."

Malcolm choked, "Don't do it, cousin."

"You are not my advisor, and I am king. I make my own decisions."

"I hope you like steel for a wedding present. You'll likely get plenty of it in the gut on your honeymoon."

"Why would the Blackbyrn family want to kill me? I am providing them with access to our ancient magic; magic, might I remind you, that they have not accessed in several centuries. With The Divide down, their lands are probably going to go through some changes with Seelie magic starting to overtake them."

I did not want to tell Niya this part when we talked about it a week or so ago. We were having such a nice time and if she had heard about this, she probably would have cut all ties with me. I couldn't bring myself to ruin it.

I signed the invitation and the paper immediately disappeared into thin air. It never ceased to amaze me how their dark magic worked.

"It's done," I shrugged.

"And you're an idiot," Malcolm got up and patted my shoulder, "Congratulations, idiot, you have signed your death warrant."

"You know Malcolm, sometimes I really loathe you."

"I love you too, cousin. Now, let's go meet with Enzo about this Finion situation."

Finion.

Shortly after Niya left, we found out that Finion was the one who placed the dead goat in the room. One of the servers saw him dragging the thing to my chambers. It seemed that such an occurrence did not raise alarm bells around here.

Finion was a disgrace to the throne and to our people. What else had my trusted *advisor* done that had gone unchecked? When my parents passed, I allowed him to stay on as my confidant, and dare I say, friend. I felt like I had been utterly betrayed.

When Finion, Malcolm, Enzo, and I discussed the goat, he acted like he knew nothing about it and had the nerve to use his manipulation to calm me down!

Let this asshole lie to my face again.

Enzo burst through the study door and a cuffed Finion stumbled to the floor. Finion began blustering and acting offended to be treated in such a way.

Well, I guess we were doing this the hard way. Good. I cracked my knuckles and rolled my neck in preparation for a fight.

Enzo put his hands over his chest, "As requested, still alive. Barely."

Leaning against my desk, I scanned Finion looking for signs of treachery. He was vacillating between mewling like a newborn and grousing like an injured party. Bending forward to meet his eyes, I asked him if he had anything that he wanted to tell me about the incident with the goat. Finion had absolutely no idea what I was talking about; so, I reminded him with my fist.

Finion doubled over, clutching his stomach. Shouts of protest broke through his choked and wheezing breaths.

"Fin...I know that you know what I'm talking about," pretending to be the reasonable friend he had grown to know. "Now, tell me what I want to know," I smiled at him with a mouth full of gleaming and menacing teeth, "Please."

"I swear, majesty, I—" Another punch landed across his jaw, dropping the male to his knees.

"Mother, damn it!" Finion shot, grabbing his bloodied lip with a clawed hand.

Examining my fingernails, "Finion...I think you *do* know, and I think you *will* tell me."

"I'd do what he says, Fin," interjected Lorenzo, leaning against the doorframe.

"Stay out of this, wolf!" Finion shouted trying to save face.

"Finion," I shook my head in disappointment and motioned for Enzo, "Enzo, bring me the truth-bringer kit, please."

Enzo, from behind Fin, shot a confused look at me.

"The Advisor to The King of Haldonia is having trouble remembering the truth, so I think we need to bring in the kit to help him, don't you?" I quirked my lips conspiratorially at Lorenzo.

He got the hint and jumped in, "Yes, I'll send for the 'kit.'"

Finion was beside himself with terror at the mention of the "truth-bringer kit," even though he had never heard of it before.

He began to beg.

"Ah, Fin. You know that I have always liked you. It would be a shame to have to subject you to 'the kit.'"

Lorenzo shook his head and widened his eyes in agreement that Finion definitely did *not* want that.

"Okay, okay. I'll talk," Finion blurted.

I nodded to Enzo, "Don't worry about the kit for now, Enzo. It looks like Finion here is going to cooperate."

Enzo straightened into a parade rest, "Yes, sir."

"Smart, Fin; very good decision. Now let's see how *un*smart you were last week with the goat." Motioning for Finion to take a seat in the wooden chair in front of the desk, "Please, sit; get comfortable. I have a feeling this might take a moment."

Finion sat down with a plop, his shackles clanking with him.

Leaning against the edge of my desk again, I looked at him appraisingly.

Clearing his throat, Finion began, "Your Majesty...Adryen!" He hedged.

I eyed him, irritated.

"I have worked for your family for many, many years. I loved working for your family; and now, you."

I motioned with my hand to get on with it.

Finion continued, "I believe that I have proven myself to be a valuable member of your court and, dare I say, your team."

Finion paused for a moment.

"I had become almost a friend to you," he trailed off. Not knowing how next to proceed, but did, "I just didn't want that to end," he blurted out, releasing a heavy sigh.

"What?" I asked.

"Well, you know you have been spending so much time with the princess and I wasn't getting as much attention from you as I had been."

"Attention?" I echoed, incredulous.

"Well, I thought that I might pull a little prank on the princess; you know, make her think that there was a spirit or demon out to get her and maybe she would leave," Finn finished with a relieved smile on his face, "I actually feel so much better now that I've gotten that off of my chest. I know that things will go back to normal now that the princess has gone home, and it is just us again."

Power started to coil inside of me, "How dare you try to set up a 'prank' like that in hopes to scare Niya away; or whatever the fuck you planned on doing. How dare you sneak around the castle like a damn sly fox and think you can get away with it. You are supposed to be my Advisor, not my court jester, Finion."

"Your Majesty," Finion begged.

I knelt down beside him and spewed, "Oh, I'm sorry. Did you say something? Does my little *friend* miss my attention?"

"Enzo," I motioned to my first to take him away.

I started, "I banish you—"

"No!" Finion interrupted.

Continuing, "I banish you from Haldonia's castle. You threatened the crown and a royal guest. If I see your face here after the hour is up, Malcolm will dispose of you."

Malcolm chuckled, amused, from his chaise lounge as I waved my hand for Enzo to pull him up.

"One hour, Finion. I suggest utilizing your time wisely."

Finion grunted as he was pulled back to his feet.

"Oh, and Finion, I don't appreciate you lying to me about the sprite sanctuary attack in the Kaldamir kingdom. I have come to realize that you used your powers to manipulate me into that attack. You will never have the opportunity to do that again. I suggest you consider the consequences of your actions from now on, *friend*."

Enzo unshackled him and he bolted out of the room. I looked over at Malcolm and he nodded in silent agreement. Malcolm's wings flexed, as he followed behind Finion, keeping him in arms reach.

Enzo let out a relieved sigh, "So glad he is finally out of my guard. He would not break. Do you understand how hard it was to manipulate the manipulator? I'm assuming you don't need me to retrieve 'the kit' anymore."

"Thank you for rolling with it, Enz; and for the whole thing."

Enzo smiled and nodded his head, "That's what I'm here for," he looked down at the empty desk and continued, "I am assuming you said yes to the formal invitation...to your own marriage?"

"When you put it like that..."

"I don't think this is a good idea, Adryen."

I plopped back into the desk chair and let out a breath, "It is going to happen either way. I don't see what the big deal is."

"Why not just marry when it is right for the both of you?"

"Because our Kingdom is dying, despite The Divide being down. The claim to land has not been properly given."

Enzo slowly moved his head up and down, "So, when do we leave?"

"I am going alone, Enzo."

"The hell you are!"

I glowered at him as he crossed his arms over his chest in disapproval.

"You shouldn't go alone." Enzo spoke with concern.

I looked at him, then down at where the paper had been. I shouldn't feel threatened going back to Kaldamir, but both Malcolm and Enzo are making a fairly reasonable case.

"Fine."

Enzo grunted, relieved, "Okay."

And that was that.

We exited the study and parted company just outside the door. I crossed the hall to my room. Opening the door, memories of her hit me hard. I trailed my hands over the clothes left on the bed that Doogan had crafted for her. An assortment of colors and textures ran through my fingers, and I packed those into my luggage as well as clothes for myself. I asked Doogan to make a couple more outfits for her; I just hoped that she wouldn't reject them—reject me, again.

Chapter 30
Niya

Sahriah, cleaning a glass, "You know, Niya, you can't spend the rest of your life here. You are avoiding. You haven't even been home for a week, and you have been at the club every single night. Actually, where is your shadow? Where is Garrin?"

It's true, I had been at the club every single night.

I whispered, "Garrin is *indisposed.*"

She gawked, "What did you do?"

I smiled slyly, "I snuck away from him. He is probably running around the castle looking for me right now."

"You are cruel."

"Eh, it's fine. He will be fine."

When I was not working on my courtly duties and practicing the piano, I was at the Nyte Club. I had spent almost every night brooding and watching the guests—and bothering Sahriah while she worked.

I didn't feel like I belonged anywhere else, and I did not want to be in that castle any more than I had to. I felt haunted and so disassociated with my family after my mother had nearly choked me out.

I put my hand on my neck and swallowed hard.

Sahriah touched my wrist and flexed her wings, "Don't let it eat at you, sweets. She was just trying to scare you."

"Or straight up kill me..."

She shrugged her shoulder as Sayge came out with a plate of finger food. He set the tray down next to me and I nodded in thanks. A small smile covered his lips and he turned away, walking back to the kitchen.

I looked around, curious, "Where is Nik?"

"Don't know—don't care. I kicked him out after that night with you and he came back and paid me double what I was charging him."

"And you didn't tell him 'hell, no'?"

"How could I turn down ten thousand Kaldamirian Coins?"

My eyes widened, "You weren't charging him *that* much!"

Sahriah smirked, "Fuck yeah, I was. It just wasn't all on the signed checks."

"Damn," I giggled, "He is being ripped off."

Sahriah lifted her shoulders, "I was sending it all to the orphanage anyways. It is quite the bummer he isn't around anymore; they could really use the money."

"I saw that doing paperwork. I am shocked you got him to sign off on it as well."

She shrugged her shoulders and smiled. "Who could say no to the babes?"

I nodded and I sat there in silence, swirling my drink in front of me, "Have you ever heard of *vodka?*"

Sahriah smiled slightly, "Yes. Why?

I watched Sahriah cleaning a pilsner and replied, "I tried it at Adryen's castle, and it was absolutely horrible."

"What did you mix with it with; juice or elixirs?"

I tilted my head, "You're supposed to mix it?"

Sahriah let out a belly laugh, "Yes; gross!"

Rolling my eyes at my naivete, I took the last sips of my berry seltzer and slapped my palms on the table, "Well, I should probably get home. My mother has been sending her crows after me if I am gone for too long."

"Niya, I will pray to the gods for an uneventful return."

The crows.

Those cheeky bastards think they run this kingdom. They are nasty reprobates. Shapeshifters. They are only around when needed to cause trouble for someone; otherwise, they keep to the shadows.

I got up from the stool and walked outside to mount Blackstar. I craned my head backwards to pull all my hair behind me. Putting on my helmet, I strapped on the bracelet; he roared to life. Revving the engine, I spied a crow fluttering in front of me, disapprovingly.

I guess the crows are coming home to roost.

I lifted my middle finger and zoomed down the road trying to gain as much of a head-start as I could from the flying rat. I refused to look back, racing home. The ride took about twenty minutes from The Silver Expanse to the gates of the castle. The guard opened the gates with plenty of time for me to enter and circle.

The crow shifted into his fae form in front of me before I could come to a complete stop. Trying to avoid him, I swerved, and the bike jack-knifed; sending me sprawling onto the small stones of the drive. Fists engulfed in icy flames, I seethed, "What the fuck, you son of a grackle?!"

"What the fuck? You make me chase you home and you almost ran into me with that thing," pointing to my bike laying on the pebbles nearby. "My wings could barely keep up!"

I dismissed my scratched palms and knees and pulled the bracelet off of me. Shutting off the bedraggled bike, I stomped toward Talis, pointing my finger at him, and shouting through my helmet, "What the fuck to *you* for following me around, Talis! I am grown; I do not need you following me like a nanny."

I sent a rippling cobalt blue flame toward his black wings, and he stepped away from it. I caught one of his feathers as they turned to ice and fell off of him. He grimaced with pain, and I yelled, "I won't miss in the future, you stupid crow. Stop following me around or it'll be your favorite part next time."

With a slight jerk of his hands toward said favorite part, "It's your mother's orders, Princess."

"Stop calling me that! You and EVERYONE else know how much I HATE it!" Pointing a finger toward Talis, "Also, I don't need her fucking goonies— "

A cough cut me off, and I whirled around to see my mother, Garrin, and Adryen standing there.

Oh, fucking perfect.

Garrin gave me a stern, stressed look; he was *pissed*.

Adryen bore a huge smile on his face as irritation rested on mine. I threw up my mental shields. I didn't know how this bond thing worked and I didn't want him to feel any more of my emotions; or even hear my thoughts, assuming he could.

Pulling off my helmet, I fluffed my hair and walked over to my bike and sat it upright to hang both my bracelet and helmet from it. I wiped down my black pants and leather jacket to look more presentable.

If I knew he was coming today...

"Mother, I would love it if you would stop sending your crows on me," I curtly remarked.

She seethed, "I would not have sent them if you did not dismiss Garrin and force him to search everywhere for you."

"What is he doing here?" I asked my mother, strolling closer to them both.

"Niya, King Whitebourne is here to sign the contract."

The door to the castle creaked open and Enzo walked out, "What did I miss?"

I whispered, "Oh this is just divine..." rubbing my temples.

Adryen shifted on his feet, "Just yelling, name calling, and a threat to a certain favorite part."

I furrowed my brows. He must have been standing there the whole time. I pointed my dimming flamed hands at Adryen in an attempt to threaten him, but they just extinguished themselves. I threw my hands in the air and let out an annoyed sigh.

Adryen's eyes shimmered as he watched my impotence.

Was this a joke?

There was no way he had that much power over my magic.

Adryen chuckled and my mother interrupted, "I don't mean to interrupt, but we should get inside. I'd like to get the formalities out of the way and proceed with business."

I rolled my eyes and followed behind Ravyn, Garrin, Talis, Enzo, and The King of Haldonia. Adryen slowed his speed to walk alongside me, he whispered, "Hello, beautiful."

It was impossible to stay mad at him.

I looked up, meeting his gaze, and every fiber of anger burst into flame and turned to ash inside me. It had only been a week, but I'd missed him. I missed him so damn much my body was starting to ache. It was foolish of me to run away like I did that day when The Divide collapsed, and I had accepted Adryen being mad at me for a while for that. But, gods, save us when the mating bond was complete. We wouldn't be able to leave each other's side at all.

Mating bonds were sacred and special. Each one was different, and mates didn't have a choice of who they were destined to be with. And since the last known mating bond was hundreds of years ago...

Since The Divide went up.

My eyes widened; why had I never thought of this before... All the mates in our realm were between a Seelie and an Unseelie. With The Divide up, those who would have been mated could not be. There could have been mates walking around their whole lives with their other half just on the other side of a wall.

"Are you okay?" Adryen's concern cut through my thoughts.

I cleared my throat, "I am perfect," I lied.

"You can't lie to me. I can feel it, even with your shields up."

I tried to think of something that would get him off of the subject.

"Princess?"

"What?" I responded automatically.

He stopped and smirked, "Why don't you get angry at me when I call you 'princess', but you just yelled at the crow that you hated it and, supposedly, *everybody* knows it?"

He was not wrong. Adryen saying it didn't bother me; it felt natural. When he called me "princess", it was an endearment; loving.

Stopping to look at him and raised my eyebrow, "Are you trying to piss me off? Would you like me to throw something at you?"

He drew out, "Not particularly; unless it's your kink," and winked.

I lowered my tone, "You shouldn't be here, Adryen. My mother will suspect..."

"What? That we are mates?" A smile, so large, crossed his face as that singular word crossed his lips; mate.

Stopping dead in my tracks he continued a foot before realizing I was no longer beside him. Adryen looked over his shoulder at me and slightly pursed his lips, "I'm sorry. I—"

I cut him off, "Stop apologizing for everything," I paused and lowered my voice as we continued walking, "No, I could not care less if she knew we were mates. I don't need her thinking that I am scheming against her. When I got back from your kingdom, she put me in a chokehold. She has been insufferable. She has her crows tracking my every move. I can't step out of line."

Adryen tensed every muscle in his taut body, "She put her hands on you?"

"It's not like it was the first time."

Ravyn yelled from the hallway that led straight to the formal office, "We're not getting any younger!"

We looked at each other and walked through the office where Enzo was towering over a chair, waiting for Adryen to sit. My mother made her way to the opposite side of the table and gingerly sat down letting out a victorious and contented sigh, "I have been waiting a long time for this."

Adryen extended his arm to allow me to sit first and followed behind me.

I was feeling rather coerced and put upon with this entire situation. She could not force me to marry him. Especially since we had sworn a blood oath. The oath had contracted us to follow our own path and solidify our bond when we'd decided.

This marriage would happen if and when we were both in agreement that it is the right time. When we both felt ready to stand in front of a priest and exchange vows that would further seal our fates.

Which I am not.

Yet.

My mother slid the paper to me, and I snatched it up, reading the contract several times, very thoroughly. Each time I reread it, my anger rose more and more.

I couldn't do it.

Not right now.

It did not feel right. It felt like we were being forced into something devoid of love and true connection. I had decided that I wanted a marriage agreement to be meaningful and celebrated.

Slamming the paper back on the table, "I don't agree to this, Mother."

"Quite frankly dear, I don't care what you agree with. It has already been signed by King Whitebourne. It is just awaiting your signature."

I looked at him and his eyes hid nothing from me. He looked exhausted, and desperate and...hesitant. I could feel his want and need. I could also feel his hurt and reluctance.

Adryen was not ready either; not really.

I closed my eyes and a flicker of red and orange flame shot from my fingertips, "I don't agree."

Queen Ravyn's eyes darted to my fingers and then to the contract. Quick as lightning, she tried to snatch it away. Not quick enough; I touched my flaming finger to the paper, causing it to burst into flames.

Queen Ravyn howled.

Within seconds, the paper was nothing but ash and soot, lying on the desk. I smiled contentedly as my mother used every ounce of self-control she had to hold herself together.

Standing up, I smoothly stated, "Well, I think this concludes our business; I bid you a good day," I bowed and, as I started towards the door, an invisible grip tightened on my wrist. I tried to pull away and the hold jerked me back, sending shock waves through me. I winced in pain as I was pulled backwards, almost knocking me off my feet.

Enzo, eyes darting around looking for the threat, put his hand on the pommel of his sword, ready to attack or defend. Turning around, I let my mother reel me in closer to her.

"Your Majesty," My mother crooned through gritted teeth toward Adryen, "Please, excuse us. I need to have a talk with my daughter."

Adryen rose from his seat and moved toward the door; Enzo, with lifted brows followed behind him. Adryen stopped and looked back at me; concern shadowing his face. I lifted a corner of my lips in a small grin, and he returned with a frown.

Hoping my mental communication would reach him, *This is normal. I will be okay.*

Adryen grunted and nodded gently to my thought and clicked the door shut.

"Do you want to live, you idiotic child?"

I crossed my arms over my chest, "What I would like is to be allowed to make my own choices. You are controlling me! When will you let up?"

A burst of laughter cracked out of her like a whip, "You won't ever be free until you are sitting on that throne. Until then, you will do as I say."

"Why are we still on this stupid theme of me being on the throne?! Why can't Vallynn take it? I don't understand!"

I pounded my feet towards the exit and punched the door with all my fury.

My mother let out a weary sigh, "You know that your prophecy needs you to be on the throne. Once Adryen is by your side, and your powers are settled, you can kill him, and that will be that. The land is ours; the thrones are ours, and we can live."

This bitch.

"We?!" I snapped out, "What in the nine circles of hell does that mean?!"

"I meant you; of course, I meant you."

Lies. She was lying to me. I could feel it.

Looking over my shoulder, "Let me be very clear, Your Majesty. I refuse to follow through with your insane plans. I will ascend the throne on my designated coronation date, but I will not do anything else. If you ask me to sign a marriage contract again, I will denounce the crown and my title altogether. Then you will have no other choice but to have Vallynn as your successor. I hope you choke on your retirement," walking out of the room, I slammed the door shut.

Chapter 31
Niya

My body shook with the nerves that had overtaken me. Speaking to my mother like that was unnerving.

Glancing over my shoulder, I checked behind me to make sure she wasn't following me and crept out to the gardens. I looked out past the gardens to see the land defrosting as greenery covered the winter floor. Walking to the edge of the garden, I knelt down and touched the saturated ground.

The Seelie court's warmth was changing the season. With the winter solstice so close, I would have assumed the cold would have been here to stay.

Light footsteps drawing nearer perked up my attention, and I looked behind to see Adryen and Enzo advancing. I stood back up and dusted off my pants.

Adryen was inches away from my face as he whispered, "Are you out of your mind? Our blood oath, Niya."

"Did I ask you to sign that contract?" I raised my eyebrow.

"Wha—no."

"Then the blood oath is still active, Adryen. I will not marry you when the time is not right. My mother forcing it upon us makes it...*not* right."

Enzo interrupted, "I hate to break up this love fest, but she has a point. You know where Malcolm and I stand on this, Adryen. And now, coming from your mate, too..."

Adryen threw up his hands, "Fine," and then cupped my cheeks, "I will wait until you're ready, Niya. I don't care if it takes another hundred years. I will deal with the consequences."

"What do you mean consequences?"

When he pulled his hands down from my cheeks, I spied the scar on his palm from our blood oath. He had not healed it.

Adryen answered, "I mean, the mating bond. If the bond doesn't seal in a certain amount of time, it will start chiseling away at us."

Enzo made a downward whistle, "And then you die."

Adryen punched Enzo on the shoulder, "Shut up, asshole."

Enzo laughed and then turned around, "Who is *that?*"

I looked past Enzo and saw Rose walking toward us in a fitted silky v-line royal purple gown and heels. Her light brown, wavy hair shimmered in the sunlight.

Enzo stepped in front of her before she got to me and purred, "Hello."

She looked him up and down, "Uh," Rose snatched a glance at me. "Excuse you," and pushed him away from her with the back of one hand.

Enzo's eyebrows rose as he grunted and stumbled dramatically, making room for Rose to reach me.

He watched her every move, utterly entranced.

She walked right in front of me and whispered, "Your mom is livid. I think she incinerated part of the castle on her way out of that meeting. Do I even want to know?"

"She will be fine."

"She will, but *we* won't. You two are going to end up burning the castle to the ground. I enjoy living here, Niya; don't ruin my home for me because you two can't handle your shit like adults."

"This is Rose, my closest friend," I indicated to Adryen and Enzo with my arm.

"Hello, Rose," Enzo said with a low growl.

Adryen and I both looked at Enzo, curious.

Rose gave a small smile.

I wanted a little bit of alone time with Adryen, and Enzo had his eyes on Rose, so I blurted, "Adryen and I are going to go for a quick walk. You don't mind, do you? Get to know each other." I motioned to the two of them.

"No, Niya—"

I interrupted Rose, "Nope, we are walking away now!"

I grabbed Adryen's arm and we walked together into the gardens.

He let out a small laugh, "I have never seen Enzo stunned into silence before. I mean, 'Hello' is not his usual smooth talk."

"I don't know him like you do, but he looked like a little puppy just standing there giving her googly eyes. Has he never *seen* a female before?"

"He has been with many people. He is a wolf shifter, which means, naturally, Lorenzo has done a variety of things you and I probably do not want to know about. More than likely with more than one at a time. They enjoy sharing."

I raised an eyebrow, "Oh." Pink rose up in my cheeks at the thought of all the bodies moving together. I looked wildly around me in response to my pounding heart.

Adryen shot a glance at me.

"Princess....do you *like* the idea of Enzo doing a variety of things with more than one person?" Adryen bit his lip as he felt the excitement flooding through him. "I'm going to say that you do. Maybe, one day—"

"No!" I jumped in. "No, thank you. I mean, I don't begrudge him for doing whatever sparks his interest, I'm just..." I didn't know how to finish. I wasn't even sure it was the truth; I just did not want to think about that right now.

Warily, "Ok, princess; If you say so, it is so."

Glad to be off that subject, I pulled him along beside me. We walked and talked lazily; enjoying each other.

I inclined my head, "Adryen?"

"Hmm," he answered, languidly.

"Why didn't you heal your palm?"

Adryen looked down at the palm of his hand and we stopped walking, "I wanted it as a reminder of what we can accomplish as a team, as mates. Niya, I want to marry you, but I don't want you to feel dragged into it."

"Adryen," I put my hand on his cheek, "I feel the same way. I don't want you to be stuck with someone you are not going to want to stay by long-term."

He wrapped his fingers around mine and kissed the back of my hand, "You *are* my long-term, Princess."

I dropped my hand and looked at his swirling tattoos, "I guess I will have to slow down at some point, so you can catch up to me," and winked.

I had missed him so much. I missed his vibrant blue eyes and his tousled, wavy hair; his silly flirtations; his mouth; his body...I glided my fingers through his and I felt warmth and belonging wash over me. My tattoo turned golden again as we interlocked fingers. Adryen's golden tattoo was now joined by black swirls as my fingers tightened around his.

Home. Adryen felt like home. I wanted to stay in his arms, cuddled in bed, just filling each other with this feeling.

Adryen pulled up our clasped hands and turned mine up and kissed it, "I missed you too, princess. But, I can't stay long."

I frowned, "Why? I feel like that is your favorite saying," and I mocked him, "I can't stay long."

He chuckled, "You make it sound adorable," then continued more seriously, "With The Divide down, our lands are changing; I can't be away from my kingdom for too long. I am still working out how to connect to and balance my magic with the new land and it can get dicey if I am away."

Looking at him, I asked earnestly, "How can I help?"

"I'm not really sure right now. Without a queen on the throne beside me, I'm not exactly clear on what the next, best step would be." I felt his scattered thoughts. He was upset with me; he was disappointed that his plan for us had to temporarily be put aside; he was worried; he was lonely and a little sad.

"It was amazing of you to be willing to sign that agreement and come here, Adryen. I just wish the timing was better. I know you and mother made an agreement, but I'd tread lightly. Her intentions are only ever for her best interests."

I could not tell him she wanted to kill him. I just hoped that he would always keep one eye open with her, "I did not want to worry or upset you earlier. That has just been something normal, my entire life. I can never make her happy, no matter how hard I try."

Adryen, saddened expression on his face, simply nodded, "When you are ready to fully talk about your past, know that I will always be here to support you."

I leaned my head on his shoulder as we continued back to the clearing. Adryen placed his hand on my wrist with a surprised and cautious look on his face.

"What?" as I looked around for the possible danger.

"What is that? Over there?" Adryen pointed with his other hand off into the distance.

"I don't see anything—" I started to say.

"Oomph," he jerked back as if shot by an arrow.

"Gods, Adryen; what's wrong?" My heart pounded in my chest. Just then, Adryen quirked a saucy grin, took my wrist and twirled me out away from him and then back again into his arms. A shocked laugh erupted from me. Adryen held my body close to his and stared into my eyes. The closeness made my flesh burn.

This male was everything.

Being this close to him made me forget any issues I had earlier in the day and even earlier in my life. I pounced. I threw my arms around his neck and crashed my mouth into his.

Pausing, stunned, Adryen's fingers splayed out at my sides for a moment before melting into the kiss. My kisses grew ravenous as I devoured his tongue and his hands tangled in my hair.

Damn. What was I doing?

I felt his hardness press into me, and I had to fight the urge to climb him. My center grew hot and slick.

"Wait," I interrupted. "We aren't alone. Rose and Lorenzo are still out here with us."

Breathless, "Did you want them to join?"

"No!" I barked out a laugh as I slapped him playfully on the chest.

Adryen and I walked hand in hand back to where we had left Enzo and Rose, who were clearly enjoying themselves. Rose was twirling her hair as Enzo leaned over her with his forearm against a tree.

"Hello," Adryen smirked pointedly at Enzo. Jerking his head to the side, "Ready to go?"

Enzo straightened. His eyes shot back to Rose automatically and then back to Adryen, "Are you sure we have to go?"

I whined, "Yeah, are you sure you have to go so soon? I feel like you just got here."

Adryen reached up and brushed my jaw with a finger, "I have to make sure there is a Haldonia to come back to; I'm hoping to have a certain, gorgeous Unseelie princess over soon."

Enzo rolled his eyes at the display and Rose giggled, eliciting a huge grin from the shifter.

"When will I be allowed to come visit, King?" I purred as a zing of arousal shot through me and sent its echo into Adryen.

The King dropped his chin low and growled through lowered lashes, "Any time; every time; all the time, my princess." My heart felt like it dropped into my core as the butterflies fluttered much lower than the place where my heart should have been.

Adryen swooped in for a deep, sensual kiss that I could have held on to forever. I closed my eyes and wrapped my hands around his neck, not wanting to let go. He pulled away from me, dipped below my tightened hold, and kissed my cheek, "Goodbye, Niya. I—"

He cut himself off and I tilted my head, curious as to what he was holding back. He backed up from me and formed a portal big enough for a person to walk through.

Crackles and zaps emanated from it as my lips turned down in a frown.

He was really leaving me. My heart panged as I waved a small goodbye to both Adryen and Enzo. Adryen looked back and winked at me, smiling, and closed the rippling portal behind him.

Rose and I stood there in silence, watching the embers of the portal float into the sky.

"Rose," I drew out.

"Hmm?" She replied distractedly.

I nudged her side, "What the fuck was that with Lorenzo? I have NEVER..."

Rose giggled and then sat down on a garden chair, patting the lounge next to her, inviting me to join.

"Niya!" Rose paused. "That was the most beautiful male I have ever seen," she gaped at me as if I had intentionally kept something from her.

"Rose, I already told you that Adryen—"

"Adryen?! Um, no. Lorenzo..." Rose's gaze drifted off into the distance in thought.

"Enzo?" I asked, having been sure I had heard incorrectly.

"Niya, are you blind?!" Rose asked incredulously.

I wasn't sure how to respond to that, so I just kept looking at her as a sheepish grin scrunched up her face.

"Zoey is so masculine and tall...oh, Niya, and he smells *sooo* good," she gushed.

"When he was leaning over me, I wanted to just shove my nose into his chest," she closed her eyes and breathed in deep, "He's got wavy black hair, which I love, and cute little rounded ears. I could get lost in his hazel's eyes—and gods above—his tattoos!"

A little squeal escaped my friend's lips, and I could not hold back my giggle.

Rose's excitement made me happy. I loved Rose and I had never seen her so over the moon for anyone before. Had she just called Enzo, Zoey? Rose had it bad and I, very selfishly, wanted them to become a couple so Adryen and I would have them close.

Always.

We spent several more minutes chatting about Adryen and Enzo—oh pardon—Zoey. By the end of our conversation, I was going to make it my mission to get the two of them together. I wasn't sure how she would feel about the "sharing" thing Adryen mentioned...but that would be up to her to decide.

I had decisions of my own to make. I knew that I had really missed Adryen when we were apart and I missed him again now, the moment he disappeared from view through the portal. Adryen was sweet and so charmingly silly. That little prank he pulled in the clearing just to get me to laugh was perfection.

Just like him.

Trailing off into tangential topics as we walked back towards the castle, I hadn't really been paying attention to the full scope of my surroundings.

Suddenly, a voice shocked me out of my thoughts, "Niya."

I looked up and both my mother and Rose were watching me with tilted heads and disconcerted looks.

"Yes?"

"Might I have a word?" Ravyn asked me, her tone attempting to be light.

"Uh, sure," I shot a look to Rose, and she took the hint.

Rose quietly excused herself, giving my mother and me privacy.

Once Rose was out of sight and we were alone, I shot a look to the queen and scowled, "Are you looking to finish what you started before and *actually* choke me to death?"

The queen winced at my attack. She forced a softened expression and continued, "Niya, I wanted to apologize for my lapse earlier. I know that you and I both have done things that we are not proud of—"

"I have never attempted to murder you in the middle of the throne room, mother!" I shouted.

"Don't interrupt me, daughter!" Ravyn shot back. The queen quickly regained her composure, smoothing down invisible wrinkles in her gown. "I want to *fix* this *thing* between us, darling."

I wasn't sure what it was about the queen at that moment, but I wanted to believe her. I wanted to have a relationship with both of my parents that wouldn't lead to me getting married and moving forward without ever having them be a part of that life. What if I had children one day? They would never know their maternal grandparents and that might make them miss out on something that would have been important to them.

Sighing, "Mother, I know you are sorry about the *lapse* the other day and that you want to make things better between us...I am on board. What do we do now?"

"Well, Niya, I think we can just chat like friends for a start," the queen sat down on a nearby bench and straightened out her skirts around her knees. Patting the bench beside her, "Niya, why don't you tell me about The King of Haldonia—what is the story there?" The queen raised her eyebrows and waggled them a bit.

"Mother," I drawled. Crossing my arms over my chest, "I'm not sure how I feel about him right now."

"Oh?"

"I mean I like him...a lot, actually. I'm just not sure what kind of future we would have. Then there's the coronation...I am scared to death of that day," I spoke that last part in one quick breath, feeling utterly exposed.

"Niya," Ravyn chided, "Coronation day is a happy occasion. You will be thrilled on that day. Trust me," the queen said without an ounce of empathy. "How about this? What if we put one of those worries on the back burner for now? Wouldn't that take so much stress off of you?"

"What do you mean?" I responded, confused.

"I mean, daughter, that when you ascend the throne on your predesignated day, without any more complaints or vacillations, I will allow you to marry, or not marry, the king according to your own wishes since you do like him. You said you liked him, right? How's that?" The queen patted my knee, proud of the solution that she'd presented.

"I don't know, mother," I hedged.

"Well, luckily for us both, I do," Ravyn said, slapping her knees and rising from the bench. "Are you coming?"

"Uh, I think I'll just stay out here for a while," not sure what I was feeling after that *girl chat* I'd had with my mother.

"Suit yourself. Oh, and we will be having a family dinner tomorrow night. You will join, yes?"

"Sure," I said, all of the fight out of me.

"Good, my darling. We shall see you then." Ravyn turned on her heel, abandoning me to my ruminations.

Chapter 32
Adryen

We stepped through the portal back onto the castle grounds.

Enzo bent over and wretched.

"Oh, gods, why," he said ripping off his shirt and pants.

A light flashed, and Enzo lay on the cool ground in his wolf form, panting and whining.

"Does the puppy have a tummy ache?" I condescended, "Shift back, we need to talk," then demanded.

I walked to the beach, hands on my hips in thought. Enzo, still behind me, needed a minute to compose himself. I sat down by the shore, watching the waves crash ahead of me, attempting to calm my nerves.

Enzo sat down beside me on the beach, "What's bothering you?"

"I just cannot understand Niya sometimes. I thought she liked me—I *think* she does, at least."

"Yeah?"

"Well then why did she burn the marriage contract? I mean, I had *my* doubts, but I signed it; I didn't rip it up in front of her face, did I?" I'd started to sound hysterical, "She's got me all mixed up inside; I mean I'm baffled!"

"Oh, come on, Adryen; nobody knows why females do the things they do. It's best to just enjoy the ride," Lorenzo scratched his jaw.

"I know, Enz; I want Niya to be happy. I kind of thought she could be happy with me, y'know?" Lorenzo continued staring out at the waves, listening. "My kingdom is falling apart," I gestured at the castle.

"It's not that bad, Adryen. I've seen worse," Lorenzo consoled.

"Yeah, well, it will *get* worse if I don't marry soon," I looked down at my clasped hands around my knees. "I really like her, Enz," sighing. "I even brought her the clothes she left in my room. I left them with one of the footmen at her castle. Today was almost perfect," I began remembering aloud the events of the day. "Niya whipping in on her bike with a crow shifter hot on her heels," I laughed, "He obviously didn't know who he was messing with. She's so magnificent." A slow smirk formed on my face, "I just don't want to be without her." Looking up at Lorenzo, "What do I do?"

Lorenzo, eyes still on the waves, reached up his arm and clasped me on my shoulder. "I don't know," shaking his head. "I am not the one to ask about matters of the heart. I just met Rose and I already feel like I want to make her mine and have lots of little pups with her," he huffed a laugh. "What do I know?"

Lorenzo and I sat there watching the waves together until the sun set on the horizon.

Chapter 33
Niya

Yesterday passed quickly.

After having a long, somewhat awkward conversation with my mother, It felt like we might be able to mend things between us and move forward as a family.

When I'd noticed that Adryen had left clothes for me from Doogan, I picked them up and twirled around with them in my arms. He was so thoughtful, and so caring. I did not deserve someone like him.

I decided to wear one of his dresses today to feel like Adryen was still there with me.

A short, tight golden sequined halter dress. I matched it with black suede stilettos, and a high ponytail.

I walked through the hallways to the dining hall where my family awaited my arrival. It would be nice to see my brother. I hadn't seen him since I'd arrived back from my unexpected visit to Haldonia.

Garrin was waiting at the door, and he smiled slightly, "You look amazing, Niya. It is nice see you joining the family for dinner."

I smiled politely, not sure what to expect and hoping for the best.

Garrin nodded approval and opened the double doors for me, allowing access. He trailed behind me as Vallynn, mother, father, and Alman all waited at the table. I sat next to Alman and scooched in my chair nudging his knee on my way in.

He leaned into my side and whispered, "I miss our trainings. How are you?"

"I miss it, too," attempting to project ease and lightness. I had really missed my time with the old fae. My heart heavy and my stomach dropping, I forced myself to lift my head and smile, "I've been better."

Alman tapped my knee with his in a gesture of understanding. Dinner began arriving at our table carried on large ceramic platters. I looked down at the assortment of meats, vegetables, and potatoes, not sure if the heavy feeling of loss and longing that had overtaken me would turn the meal into ashes in my mouth.

I hadn't had a real meal since Adryen's visit. I grabbed my fork and started pushing the food around my plate until I could force myself to take a bite. The meal was quiet. The tension in the room was high. I had just looked over at Vallynn as he slammed his fork on the plate, sending out a ring throughout the room and making me jump out of my skin.

"So!" He started, "I think we should discuss my hundredth birthday."

Oh, shit.

I had forgotten that it was a week away. My eyes enlarged as his lips turned up reaching ear to ear.

Oh no, this couldn't be good.

Vallynn interlaced his fingers and extended them palms out, stretching them for effect, "I want to throw a ballroom *extravaganza* for my birthday."

"What?!" Alman and I shouted together.

Vallynn laughed, "Yep! And Alman, I want you to run the show. I want gold and red, everywhere. All the royals are invited, from both kingdoms. I am going to need a bartender, dancers, and our chef to create the best hors d'oeuvres in the realm. I also need live music, and the biggest cake."

Alman tented his fingers and propped his chin onto them. Letting out a long-suffering sigh, "Do I have to?"

"Obviously you *have* to, Alman. Who else would do it that has all this free time now? Niya is too busy getting ready for her ascension, otherwise she would be put in charge."

If there was one bright spot in this mess, this was it. At least I was not in charge of running the *extravaganza*.

I looked over at a very annoyed Alman and laughed, "You are going to have so much fun!" I said, with an exaggerated perkiness.

"I think that is a great idea, son." My mother chirped, "Just let me know how much coin you need, and I will make it happen."

"Fantastic; thanks, mom," Vallynn chirped back, not missing a beat.

Staring agape and alternating my glare between the two, "What?!"

The audacity; this was utterly unfair. I always had to budget and work for what I had.

"Niya," Vallynn hummed.

I raised an eyebrow as he continued, "Would you like to help?"

I smiled, approvingly. I knew he was spoiled and always got what he wanted, but I could not be mad at him.

I loved my little brother.

"Yes, I can help with the drinks and hiring a bartender. Ooh—I'm going to play the piano; is that alright?"

"Are you going to play one of your original songs?" Vallynn inquired.

I nodded, "Sure. Maybe I will write one just for you for your birthday. What would you like? Upbeat? Slow?"

"You choose! You are the musical genius."

I beamed as a little squeak released from inside of my throat.

My appetite back, I emptied my plate with vigor as we continued discussing our plans for the party. Garrin, playing butler, made sure that our glasses stayed full throughout, in an effort to keep the tone light and happy.

Alcohol always worked well as a buffer for our familial disagreements and mitigated any outbursts. Maybe it was just an Unseelie thing. I got up from my chair and gave a slight, tipsy bow, dismissing myself. My head was beginning to turn the conversation into a drowned-out mess of sludge.

I tottered out to Bellow's shop and stopped to look up at the night sky.

Cloudless.

Beautiful stars glittered majestically. With how forbiddingly cold and snowy Kaldamir had always been, I had never truly seen the night sky. I stood in the cold, occupying myself by letting out hot, steamy breaths for several minutes before the steel doors to the shop clanged open.

I looked down and Bellow walked out, giving a slight upward jerk to his head at me, "Blackstar is touched up from the tumble yesterday. Enjoy your night!"

This male needed a raise.

His hard work never faltered.

I strolled in behind him, grabbing my helmet and bracelet off the work stand, and roared my bike to life. Counting my fingers and toes to make sure I was good enough to drive, I hopped on, hiking my dress up to my upper thighs. Zooming off the castle grounds toward The Silver Expanse, I shifted through gears, speeding up my motorcycle as I zipped through empty roads. I pulled up to a red light and downshifted, coming to a stop. Looking down to adjust my feet, a horn bellowed from beside me. Almost jumping out of my skin, I looked over to see a blacked-out vehicle revving beside me. I pulled my helmet shield down and revved my bike.

Challenge accepted.

The light turned white, and I placed my feet back on the footholds and shifted as fast as I could to gain some speed. The car next to me kept up as my bike continued shifting through gears. The stranger started to outpace me, and when the black vehicle was far enough ahead, it whipped around into my path.

I pressed down on the front and rear brakes as hard as I could, but my bike went skidding sideways. I braced my hand below me for impact and the bike rammed into the car as my body ate the hard gravel. My helmet braced the surface as it made contact, and I groaned in pain. The bike shut off as my body lay on the ground, sore.

"You stupid ass, power hungry, mothers above *fucker*," I whimpered in excruciating agony.

I lifted my arms up as the blood spilled from various scrapes and gashes. Whipping off my helmet, it slammed it to the ground. Power crackled at the surface of my body as the sky thundered in its wake. I looked up as lighted clouds started to form in the sky sending bolts of energy around me.

Gods above.

I hadn't seen lightning here.

Ever.

A male slipped out of the black vehicle and strolled over to me. All I saw were black pants with large hands in their pockets. A familiar, velvety smooth voice resonated through the emptied streets, "Hello, gorgeous."

I snapped my head up to the sound and then automatically regretted the quick movement. The silver-eyed vampire, Nik, smirked at me bloodied on the road.

I shouted, "You could have killed me!"

He countered, "Nice powers. I would not have thought that a female like *you* could harness electrical energy. That is normally a Seelie power."

"What the fu—a female like *me?!* I am the Princess of Kaldamir, I will harness whatever I please, Niko."

In a pure rage, I stomped towards Nik and glanced down at my golden arm, healing my body. Thunder continued to rumble as I closed in on Nikolaj. I pointed my finger at him, ready to burst, and before I could start spewing obscenities, he grabbed my wrist and pulled me into him.

He chuckled, "You really enjoy being angry, don't you?" Then he growled in a low tone, "And do not call me that."

My hand was electrified with every color of the spectrum as lightning hit down all around us. I tried to push away from Nik, but his grasp was too strong. Taking my free hand, I punched it to his rock-hard chest, not budging him an inch.

I gave up. I went limp and leaned against his blacked-out vehicle, letting out a dramatic sigh.

My galvanic powers receded and the storm clouds disappeared. Fully aware now that the storm was me, I couldn't help but smile at the impressive new magic that I now had in my arsenal.

Nik continued, "You know, you keep fighting, and it is not going to work, Your Highness," he laughed, "I knew there was something so familiar about you. I just could not put my finger on it. Your family did such a great job hiding your beauty from the world. It's a shame, honestly. I might not have done what I did with you if I'd known you were my *Crowned Princess*."

"That is the most disgusting thing anybody has ever said to me. Don't call me your 'Crowned Princess'."

Nikolaj sighed, "I can't make any promises," He loosened his grip on me, and I seized the opportunity.

I had to get away from him.

I pushed Nik off of me, sending him stumbling back. Bolting for my helmet, I slipped it over my head and ran to my grounded bike. Standing it back up, I straddled the bike touching the amulet on my bracelet, roaring it back to life. I squealed the wheels as I headed straight for the Nyte Club.

Tires screeched behind me, and we were back to the race. Panic rolled through me in waves as I shifted through the speeds as fast as I could. Blackstar was fast, but only as fast as two wheels and a motor could go.

What did he want from me?

I jumped the bike onto the sidewalk, and pedestrians shot out of the way, screaming. The bike rolled to a stop as Leer turned around, eyes wide. I threw off my helmet and shook my ponytail loose. Leer did a quick bow and motioned me in.

I left everything outside except myself and made quick work of adding to the distance between Nik and me.

A voice yelled, "Let me in you brooding elf!"

Leer responded, "M'lord. Not tonight."

I quickly whipped my head around and spewed, "Lord?!" I ran up to Leer, blocking Nikolaj from coming in, "I should have known you were Morelli's son. I assumed it was a fascist vampire naming you after him."

Nikolaj's body went still, "I guess there are no more secrets."

I looked at Leer, "Let him in."

"Sahriah—"

"—Let him into my club, now!" I turned on my heels toward Sahriah manning the bar, per usual.

I plopped down on the barstool and Nikolaj swiftly joined me snapping his fingers for a drink. I gawked at him, "You do not run this establishment, *Lord-in-waiting*. And last I checked; you got kicked out. The only reason you are here now, is because I am *allowing* it."

Those three words cracked like a whip as Nikolaj physically shuddered.

Sahriah looked over at the snapping and stopped dead in her tracks, brows furrowed. I genuinely smiled and waggled my fingers in a greeting toward her. She frowned and shook her head, disapprovingly.

"Why did you track me down? What is so important that you needed to continue to follow me?" I adjusted my dress in the seat, making myself comfortable.

Nikolaj looked at me and trailed his eyes all the way down. I snapped my fingers, and his eyes snapped back into mine.

"I..." He smirked, "I thought this would be another good opportunity."

"Opportunity for *what* exactly?"

Sahriah stopped in front of me and set down a perfectly separated red and orange cocktail garnished with a dainty cherry and orange. She backed up, crossing her arms over her chest.

I smiled and started to drink.

"Oh, come on, you don't want to have another time like the last?"

I spit out my drink all over the table and onto Sahriah. She let out a scowl and mumbled to herself about "this bullshittery" and she "doesn't get paid enough for this," as she stomped away.

"I thought I was just a fae who enjoyed one-night stands?"

"You didn't enjoy it?"

I didn't remember it!

"It's not that...it's just that—"

Sahriah cut me off and continued, "She is seeing someone, Nik. Back off."

Nikolaj hissed, "You mind your business, Riah."

"Oh, my great mother above! You both are possessive little bats!" I pushed off the table and got off the chair, sauntering to the bathroom with my drink. I pushed through the door and stopped in front of the mirror, looking into it.

Into me.

Damnit, he was making me uncomfortable with those silver half-mast eyes.

Lord Morelli's son was the fae who made himself cozy in my club and set up business deals from my booths; probably for his shady-ass father. I would never understand why that male was still in my mother's circle. He had done nothing to further the interests of the crown.

I readjusted my high ponytail and fixed any smudging makeup. Adjusting my breasts in my dress, and the length to sit right under my butt, I walked back out to Sahriah pouring Nik a drink.

Sneaking up on him, "You owe me an explanation as to why you have been using my club as a meeting place to do, I am assuming, your father's exporting business?"

Nik took a swig of his drink, "And what exporting business is that?"

"Illegal exporting across the border," I sighed, "And now that The Divide is down, there would be no need to keep it private anymore; am I correct?"

Nik raised an eyebrow, "Why would I answer any of the above?"

I rolled my eyes. This was going nowhere and quite frankly I was getting *annoyed* at all of the questions being answered with questions.

"If you are not going to answer me, I am going to have to ask you to leave, Niko."

Nikolaj growled, "Fine," And got up, heading toward the exit.

I took the last swigs of my cocktail and headed to the dance floor, shaking off the stresses of the night.

Several hours passed and my stilettos were putting a strain on my feet. I slowly hobbled to the bar and plopped on the stool, "I am so tired," I whined.

Sahriah remarked, "I would be too if I danced in sky high stilettos. How in the ever-loving hells do you do it?"

I shrugged my shoulders, "I don't know. I have always worn heels. It feels weird not wearing them. However, right now, slippers sound divine."

She laughed, "Your dress is amazingly original. I have never seen that fabric here in our kingdom. Is it one of Adryen's designers' dresses he made for you?"

I smiled to myself, "Yes." and pushed down on the sequined dress, "Can you take me home tonight on your extended bed? I don't think my feet will be able to shift the bike properly."

Sahriah chuckled, "Sure, Niya. Would you like another drink?"

"No, a water is fine. I am going to fae watch until we are closed," continuing, "Hey, do you want to bartend for my brother's birthday celebration?"

"I don't know...who will bartend here?"

"Really? I can close for the night. It will be fine. You will make a lot more at the party than here, anyways."

"It's not about the money. It's about the customers."

"Sahriah! More than likely these males and females," I waved towards the bustling club, "will be at Vallynn's birthday."

"You're right. Fine, I'll do it."

I squealed in excitement, "Thank you!"

Chapter 34
Niya

I sat in the ballroom at the grand piano, staring at the blank sheet music. I tapped the pencil on my temple and squeezed my eyes shut, hoping for some muse to flow through me.

Letting out a huge sigh, I leaned back and glanced at the pile of scrapped music on the floor, making my sigh heavier.

I whispered, "Why is this so damn difficult?"

"Because you have no energy. You have been at this for days now, Niya. Eat." Rose demanded.

"I don't know what I would do without you, Rose."

I grabbed the sandwich and munched.

Rose, covered in paint, sat next to me at the piano. I looked her over and shook my head.

I said through a mouth full of food, "What are you painting now?"

Rose let out a breath, "Your *brother* has commissioned a welcome painting for this weekend," and ended with an eye roll.

I chuckled, "And I am assuming he did not guide you in any way."

She shook her head back and forth, "Nope."

Rose stared at the pile of crumpled music on the floor, "Want to go dress shopping for the *extravaganza*?" Rose quirked her lips ironically at the term.

I could always use a new ball gown. I didn't have a lot of dresses that went past silk or cinched waisted sequined clubbing attire.

I replied, "Why yes, yes I do."

"Be kind to me with what I'm about to say," Rose paused, wincing. "Garrin has to come with us."

"Why? I thought my mother had dismissed him from his babysitting duties." It was going to be my kingdom soon and I was deemed incapable of shopping without a grown-up. I'd assumed that after I put up a fight about letting him go, that all would be well and settled.

Rose giggled, "You don't have to be the biggest badass all the time. I *asked* him."

I quirked my head to the side, "Are you afraid you might get *hurt*?"

"No, it's the fashion district. When your people see you there, they are going to bombard you, Niya. They love you that much."

It was true.

Metrika Bazaar was one of the busiest cities in our kingdom. There were tons, and tons of people bustling around in clothing shops, coffee shops, and anything else one could think of. When anybody from the royal court went there, it was bedlam. Every seamstress or tailor begged to have us go to their shop to be fitted.

Garrin cleared his throat behind us, "Are we ready?"

I got up from the piano seat and gallivanted my way to Garrin, wrapping my arm around his, "Aren't you just *so* excited to go dress shopping, Garrin? I wonder which color will suit you best."

Rose laughed out loud and came up beside me, looping her hand in mine, "I'm going to say...periwinkle," Rose joked.

Garrin groaned and raked a hand over his face and eyes, "Niya, not today."

I kissed his cheek, "It will be okay, a dress will definitely cheer you up. Let's go!"

I transversed us to the busy streets of Metrika and let go of them both as we safely landed. Garrin let up a little gagging sound and I pointed my finger at him, "Don't do it!"

He managed to choke out, "I'm trying..."

Rose smirked, "Be nice, Niya. They can't all have steel stomachs."

We waited patiently for Garrin to compose himself. As he did, we perused several different boutiques, but nothing really caught my eye. This season's dresses seemed dull compared to what Doogan had presented to me in the short amount of time we were together.

Rose however, could not decide which dress she wanted. She tried on every style of dress imaginable. We had one boutique shop left: *Momma Mel's*.

Momma Mel made the dresses I'd preferred and was usually my first choice when shopping. But I'd felt like today was really more for Rose than for me. Rose did not get out much and rarely attended parties. I wanted today to be special for her.

"This is the last shop!" Rose excitedly blurted, "Once we are done here, I am going to make my decision on the dress."

"I'd hope so. The party is in two days," I replied.

I looked over at Garrin who was silently holding a couple of bags in his hands for us. He was such a good sport. As much as he hated doing anything other than combat, he was extremely patient with us.

We walked into the shop and Garrin took a seat on a plush ottoman, setting the bags down beside him, "Sweet gods, I am so glad this is the last shop," he whispered.

I smiled and patted his head, "Just wait. Rose might want to go back to some of the other shops again after only narrowing down her options this round."

"What?" Is all he could get out before Rose started pulling dresses off the racks.

"Niya, you have not shopped at all today. Here!" She pushed red and gold dresses toward me. I grabbed as many as I could, but the weight was pulling me down.

A female voice resonated throughout the the shop, "Niya, it is so nice to see you!"

Mel swooped in, giving me a gracious hug. I hugged her back and smiled, "I missed you too, M."

"To what do I owe the pleasure? I see you brought a friend," glancing at Rose.

I cleared my throat, "Yes, this is Rose. We are looking for ballgowns for my brother's birthday party in two days."

She frowned as she looked up, thinking, "You came to the right place. Give me one second."

Mel snuck into the back of her shop mumbling to herself. I set down the dresses Rose threw on top of me, and we looked at each other, confused.

"I still think you should try those on."

"These are my usual, Rose. I want something special, and different. I am going to be inviting Adryen to the party, and I kind of want to impress him."

Rose replied, "I'm sure you already have, Niya."

I smiled and Mel came out with two thickly zipped bags on hangers.

"I feel like I have been waiting a lifetime for you to say those words to me." Mel placed the two garments on the back of a chair with a cautious smile on her face. "I made two dresses for you, with the hope of you wearing one of them to your coronation or any other special event."

"Mel, I..." I trailed off, "Thank you."

She grinned, "Go try them on!"

Rose took a seat by Garrin and nudged him in the shoulder, whispering something just out of earshot. I grabbed the bags and lugged them to the dressing room.

Closing the door behind me, I unzipped both bags and pulled out a beautiful glittered red ballgown and a slick pink ballgown. I stared at both for several minutes then opted to put the pink one back.

I pulled out the red dress and the glittered tulle on the bottom started to spill out. I lifted up the corseted bodice where beautifully embroidered lace hugged the entire frame, sweeping into the shoulders.

I slipped on the dress and tightened the back the best that I could. Fluffing up the tulle, I got the best picture of it. Red laced, plunged V-neck bodice that trickled down into a lightly shimmered tulle. The off the shoulder straps hugged my arms perfectly.

Walking outside the fitting room I looked at Rose, her mouth gaping and eyes wide, "That is nearly the most beautiful thing I have ever seen, Niya. Holy smokes."

Garrin replied, "I have to agree, for once. Red is your color."

I looked down and fidgeted with the tulle.

Mel sniffled, "Prayers to the holy gods have been answered; this dress is perfect."

"Then I guess it is mine, M. How much?"

She waved her hand at me, "Don't be silly. You do not pay."

Tapping an annoyed foot on the floor, "I will support your business, M. Tell me how much."

Garrin started pulling out money and handed a wad to Mel, not worried about counting it. She graciously accepted and bowed. Mel and I walked back to the changing room, and she helped me get undressed, pulling the dress off of me carefully so as to not snag the tulle.

"I will have this steamed immediately and hand deliver it to you by tomorrow evening. I want to add one more layer of tulle to give it the true ballgown look as well," Mel smiled and exited with the dress.

I slipped my clothes back on and walked to the waiting room where Rose and Garrin were waiting by the door.

I asked, "Rose, did you want to try anything on?"

Rose shook her head, "No. I do want to go back to the shop where the gold dress was. I think that will complement the decoration and color scheme of the party."

I shot a look at Garrin, knowingly, as he slowly closed his eyes. Nodding my assent, we walked back to the shop that had the gold dress. It took entirely too long to purchase the dress and head home, but we finally made it.

Garrin, hands completely filled with bags let us go inside before him. I opened the door and Alman was standing there with his foot tapping rapidly on the floor.

"Yes?" I snapped, ready for a fight.

He looked over my shoulder at Garrin, struggling to hold on to the bags while closing the door.

Garrin turned around and saw Alman, annoyed. He let out a sigh, "Rose asked me to join them in Metrika Bazaar for protection."

"I don't care who asked you. I needed you here helping me decorate for this freaking party."

I cut in, "Alman, no need for foot-tapping. Damn, who shoved a stick up your ass?"

"Your brother, that's who!"

Rose and I looked at each other and burst out laughing.

Garrin handed Rose and me the bags and we turned to head to my rooms. Poor Alman was not meant to coordinate formal things like this. He was a warrior, and an advisor. This should have been for our event planners.

I smiled at Rose and took my things upstairs to hang up.

Shortly after, I grabbed a snack from the kitchen and practiced more of my new voltaic power before sleep finally claimed me.

Chapter 35
Niya

The next day, I was looking forward to hand-delivering my brother's invitation to Adryen. I dug through the bag of clothes Doogan had made for me in hopes of finding something interesting to wear for my visit.

I happened upon this strange item with a green and pink floral pattern. It looked sort of like underclothes, but the two parts were connected together at points on each side. It had long ropes that looked like the back of several of my dresses, so I figured that I knew where that part went. I turned it over and over, trying to figure out how it would go on. The material was different than anything that I'd worn before; it was slick on one side and had a light gauze on the other.

I assumed the garment was something that one could get wet in. I worked myself into it, tightening, and pulling at the straps and strings until I felt like it was on the right way. I looked at myself in the mirror and I was seriously impressed. These two swaths of fabric fit me like a glove—a very intimate glove.

Choosing a light blue dress with a square neck and ruffled hem, I put it on over it. I felt an interesting combination of sexy and sweet. I was hoping my assumptions of the fabric were correct because I really wanted to visit the water with Adryen. I had never been to open water before ending up at the one in

Haldonia and I thought I could convince Adryen to go into it with me.

When I transversed myself into Haldonia, the first thing I saw was Adryen and the angel-fae sparring several yards from me.

Sweet rapture.

They were both shirtless and gleaming with sweat. Forgetting my purpose for the moment, I reached behind me, keeping my eyes on the spectacle, feeling for a place to sit and watch.

Watching the rippling muscles straining and bulging did something to me that I was not willing to stop or ignore. With each powerful stroke, a memory of Adryen above me shot through my head. Each dodge had me remembering the several times he'd slipped out of my embrace.

My fantasies must've shown on my face because when Adryen noticed me sitting there, he was distracted from the fight and the winged-fae took that opportunity to sucker punch him, making him clutch his middle momentarily. Adryen popped back up and grabbed his opponent and they began to grapple.

The fae tapped out, conceding defeat, as Adryen strutted over to me, perfectly pleased with himself.

"Good morning, Princess. To what do I owe the honor?" Adryen asked in his best courtly manner, sweat rolling down the muscled planes of his back.

Struck stupid, I didn't remember how to form words as I watched a rogue droplet rolling lazily over the ripples of his abdominals. I got a better look at his nearly replicated tattoo of mine on the left side of his chest that swirled across to his shoulder and down to his wrist. Not realizing how much more prominent it was compared to mine, I smiled in amazement.

"What is that in your hand?" Adryen asked, nodding his head to the invitation in my hand.

"Oh! Here," I shot my hand up to deliver the notice. "I totally forgot why I'd come here," I shook my head to clear the fog.

"What is it?" Adryen asked, turning it over in his hands.

"It's an invitation to my brother's hundredth birthday party tomorrow; his *extravaganza*," I made quotes with my fingers. "It is going to be a lot of fun; Queen Ravyn has placed an unlimited budget on this little soiree. We could even ditch the party and just spend time alone together if you want," I said sheepishly.

"I'd love to go, Niya. Wow; thanks for inviting me. What colors are you wearing? I want to match," Adryen's grin wide.

I reached up my hand to him and wiggled my fingers. Still grinning, he grabbed my hand, bracing his feet, and pulled me up to stand. I popped up excitedly and pulled him along with me toward the open water of the beach, running and laughing. Adryen held my hand and pulled me to him. I put my head on his shoulder, and he put an arm around my waist. I wrapped an arm around his back, rubbing lightly at his salty, damp skin.

"I'm going to be wearing red," I whispered.

"Red is a hot color. I look forward to it."

"You're a hot color."

Oh, gods Niya.

You idiot.

Adryen chuckled and tucked hair behind my ear, "That was adorable, as you always are, Princess." He pressed a quick kiss to my lips.

"I hate myself right now, don't judge me." Trying to avoid any more conversation on this, I pulled off my dress revealing the attire that I still prayed to the gods was meant for the water. I breathed in the crisp, salty aroma of the ocean and walked towards it.

Adryen grabbed my waist and pulled me into him again, inhaling a sharp breath, "I forgot to breathe for a moment. This bikini looks fantastic on you. I mean..." taking my hand and twirling me for a full view.

I blushed, and looked down at every inch of my revealed body, "And this is normal? To be showing this much in a public place that's not a club?"

Adryen trailed his hand down my hips and onto my ass, gripping it tightly, "I am not sure what you mean by 'not a club', but if the choice were mine, I would much rather have you naked." A surge of desire hit me square in my center. "But, unfortunately, we are in a public place...for now."

He frowned slightly at his own comment, truly disappointed.

"Can I go in?" I glanced up at Adryen, questioning.

"I mean, yes. Do you know how to swim?"

With a light awkward laugh, "No."

Adryen slipped off the pants he was wearing to reveal his undershorts, tightly wrapped around his muscular ass. He grabbed my hand, and I trailed him to the ocean. My feet splashed in the water as the waves crashed lightly against our legs.

The water was cool and refreshing as Adryen pulled us further in. Once the water hit our hips, he knelt down, and I followed suit. I had no idea how to swim, and this was making me very nervous. I did not want to drown, but I trusted him.

I trusted him with every part of me.

Wrapping my arms around his shoulders and legs around his waist, we ventured out further into the ocean as he carried me. My hair had gotten heavy with the water as Adryen calmly walked farther out. The sun was beating down on us, and I could feel my cheeks reddening.

I stared, for what felt like eons, in Adyren's eyes, admiring his perfection. Those cornflower blue eyes, perfectly framed face, and arched eyebrows were my entire world at this moment. He was amazing, and I had been cruel. I slid my hand through his messy, sweat-glistened hair.

"I am sorry, for everything," and followed it up with a kiss, "I just..." I stopped when a croak escaped my throat.

Adryen kissed me back, "You just what?" He whispered on my lips.

"You really deserve someone with their shit together, Adryen. I couldn't even put my anger at my mother aside to sign that marriage contract. I am selfish, and not nearly the lover, or queen, you deserve."

"Stop talking," was all he could get out before gently placing his lips once again on mine.

My arms and legs wrapped tighter around him, pulling him in close. I reached a hand up to the back of his head and clutched it by his hair, guiding the kiss. Adryen licked up my neck and I pulled him back by his hair. He let out a sharp cry at the removal of his prize. I quirked a smile and tsked, "You're mine."

Still clutching his hair from behind, I kissed and teased his lips. One moment, I plundered his mouth with my tongue and the next moment, I bit and licked his lips. His body hitched with his restrained arousal. I was in control this time and all he could do was stand there, holding me, and let me do whatever I wanted to him.

He clutched my ass and I let him. I didn't want him to drop me. I kissed up the side of his neck, nipping at an earlobe. A hiss escaped him as he arched his back. I could tell he enjoyed this little game of control and I just enjoyed being anywhere and doing anything with him.

I pressed my heated core into him as I flexed my legs, tightening their hold. He grew rigid under me. "Oh gods, Niya. Don't do that."

Smiling, "What? This?" squeezing again, eliciting a lunge from Adryen's hips.

He tightened his grip on my ass and pushed me into his cock, grinding me on it. "I thought you didn't want me to do that, Adryen," I purred, coquettishly.

"Niya, I want you so badly; fuck!" Adryen spat, losing himself in the moment.

Adryen kissed down my neck, salty water flowing onto us, as his lust melted into longing, "You mean more to me than you could ever imagine, Niya." I stared into the limpid pools of his eyes. "My life was not nearly full, until I met you. Properly. I don't care how much you self-sabotage. Just know that I will be here to help you heal through any and all of your wounds, whatever they might be."

I wrapped my body around him tightly and the only thing I could say was, "Thank you."

He understood me and listened when I needed to vent. He was not deterred by my quirkiness or weird comments. He had his own. Adryen was, in fact, the only male, that cared to get to know the real me. I wanted to be like this with him forever, and never leave him to be alone again. As much as I believed that he deserved more than me, he was meant for me. He was my rock, my person, my mate.

In time, I hoped he would be my husband, my king.

Adryen nuzzled into me again and we bobbed on the water until our stomachs growled. He carried me out of the water and set me down next to my dress. I picked it up, looking at it and then looking down at my dripping body. Opting out of putting it back on, I followed him back to his castle.

Daph waited in the entryway with two towels. Adryen thanked her and grabbed them both, handing one to me. He dried off the best he could and slipped his pants back on. I set the dress down and patted myself as dry as I could. I slipped the light blue dress back on and handed the towel back to Adryen.

"I am going to set this down and grab a shirt. I'll meet you in the kitchen," Adryen kissed my forehead and took the stairs in two's up to his wing of the castle.

I strolled toward the empty kitchens and placed my hand on the marbled island, breathing a contented sigh.

Two, very large hands swept their way from my hips and down my thigh. I turned around, ready to attack and Adryen's lips quirked as he said, in a low octave, "Hi," and lifted me onto the island, trailing his hands up my torso and to my neck.

"Are you hungry?"

"Yeah, for you," I whispered as his hands made their way to the back of my neck, pulling me into him.

He let out a growl that sent my toes curling and responded, "I guess I'd better start seasoning myself if I am going to be your main course."

Adryen kissed my cheek and walked past me towards the cabinets. He pulled down various spices and my mind started reeling, wondering if he was literally about to season himself.

Did he have kinks that I didn't know about?

I'd sure like to find out.

I adjusted myself on the island to watch his movement throughout the kitchen. Walking toward the fridge, he pulled out some meat and set it with the seasoning.

I frowned.

Adryen chuckled as he started fixing a meal for us, "No, I do not have *those sorts of kinks*, Princess."

"How do you do that?" I questioned.

"Do what? Read your thoughts?" He looked over at me and I nodded my head.

"I dunno. It kind of started popping up when the mating bond revealed itself. Can you hear my thoughts?"

"No. I can feel your emotions, though."

"Huh," he simply replied.

I'd watched Adryen prepare our meal and just simply enjoyed every moment with him. I had been living for well over a hundred years and I could not cook a meal as delicious; it might have been the company.

Adryen prepared our plates and handed me mine, and I asked, "What is this?" Looking at what looked like chicken but there was something stuffed inside of it.

"It's stuffed chicken breasts. There is garlic, cheese, and broccoli, inside of it."

I looked down at the plate again and smelled the sautéed garlic as I dug my silverware into the chicken, "Where did you learn to cook? I am so terrible at it, and I have been alive much longer than you."

"My mother taught me as a young child. It was her hobby, and one of the few my father did not deny me. He believed that cooking was meant for the female, but my mother resisted, and I was allowed to share this with her. If I wasn't cooking, I would have been training in combat, or working with my father on tactical warfare. Besides, cooking with someone you love always makes the experience better."

"I think this is a wonderful hobby," I dug into the food the rest of the way as we spent the entire time conversing about his family and his life growing up.

I jumped down from the island, and Adryen grabbed my hand, kissing the back of it, "Thank you for visiting today. I missed you."

I embraced him tightly and closed my eyes, "I missed you more. I wish we could just merge our castles, so we are not so far away from each other."

"You wouldn't want to merge with my deteriorating mess."

"What do you mean?" I inquired.

"Let me show you," Adryen pulled me out of the kitchen and out to the castle grounds.

I looked at the castle's foundational cracks and hoped to the gods they did not get worse around the corner. Adryen stopped us at the furthest right side of the castle, and I looked at the crumbling walls and shattered glass windows.

"We don't use this side of the castle anymore," Adryen whispered.

Letting go of him, I walked in front of the walls in disrepair and placed my hand on it. My powers roared to life as the ground started to shake and the fallen stones levitated off of the ground. I gasped as my magic had a mind of its own, fixing the broken disaster. Adryen backed up, his gasp even louder than mine. Wind whirled around me, and the stones fitted themselves into their original places. After several minutes, sweat poured from my face and the wall in front of me was back in order; the cracks and missing stones were fixed.

Completely intact.

Tears ran down my face as a wave of exhaustion hit me. I started to fall to my knees with sudden weakness as Adryen caught me, guiding me down.

"Niya? Are you ok?" Adryen's voice was shaking. I looked up at him through lowered lashes and smiled sweetly.

"How...did..." He was speechless. He pushed the hair out of my face and kissed the sweat from my temple, "Thank you," and embraced me in a tight hug.

I returned the embrace, and my depleted power returned to me, "I don't know. I just touched it, and it was like my magic knew exactly what to do."

"Niya," Adryen started, "It's the mating bond, and your prophecy..."

I wiped my face and stood up, "I have to go. It's getting late and I need to prep for tomorrow. I still haven't gotten my task done for my brother."

Adryen followed behind, grabbing me and pulling me to him one last time, "Niya, are you sure you're, okay? That was a massive amount of power you just expended. Stay with me so I can take care of you," Adryen paused waiting for a reply that was not happening, but suggested, "I still want to show you my sculpting studio."

Very unsure about staying, "I don't know."

"Please, stay a little longer."

I couldn't say no to his company. I really wanted to be with him longer today, "Okay, only if you promise to show me the studio and then I can leave."

"It is a deal, Princess," he stuck out his hand and I grasped it, shaking on it.

I watched him move back toward the castle, motioning for me to follow. I trailed him, enjoying the view of his wonderfully muscled backside and tattoo.

I was unsure if I liked it or *loved* it.

We followed the same path as we did that night he showed me his parent's death. We stopped in front of the single room. Adryen put his finger to the doorknob. It glittered silver; the bolt clicked and unlocked.

Adryen turned to face me, "This room is a favorite of mine. I come here when I want to pretend that I am an artist; really, it lets me let off steam. I hope you like it."

He smiled and opened the door wide.

I peaked in and rubbed my eyes to confirm what I was seeing.

Chapter 36
Niya

I t is *literally* a sculpting studio. I was not sure what I thought Adryen meant by "sculpting", but I was not imagining a room where a person sculpts.

I walked in and Adryen closed the door behind me. I gasped at all the figures hanging on the mantle and wall shelves. There must have been hundreds just sitting there waiting to be painted or finished. The room was lit by the windowed wall. A sheer curtain covered half of the window, letting in full sun. The room was cream-white and had several working tables. I walked the perimeter and perused every lovely piece.

I said, in amazement and joy, "Did you sculpt all of these?"

Adryen hummed in agreement from across the room. I continued to an alcove where I noticed a beautifully shaped, sculpted female body. It wasn't a body, but just a torso. I gently lifted it, turning it to investigate every detail.

Suddenly realizing, "This is my body." I whipped my head back to see him blushing.

"Yeah, I..." Adryen stammered.

He was embarrassed.

That was so cute.

I looked down at the breasts that I had known for nearly a hundred years, "You have an amazing memory, Adryen."

"I wish I could do all of you."

Raising and eyebrow, I set the torso down and sat on a clay-stained lounge, "Do it."

Adryen, taken aback, "What?"

"Sculpt me," striking a pose on the lounge.

I started to pull down my dress from my shoulders and Adryen hovered over me and snarled, "You do not want me to sculpt you right now, Princess."

Almost a whine, "Why not?"

"I am not—I can't—I am not sure it is a good idea."

I continued, pulling the dress up instead, teasing him as his eyes trailed down to my very bare thighs, "I am."

Adryen growled, scenting my arousal, as he tore the dress off of me. He stretched out the fabric and had surely ripped it in a few places based on the accompanying sounds.

"Gods, I've dreamed of getting my hands back on these gorgeous breasts again," Adryen said like a prayer.

His eyes struggled back up to mine; the longing there sent my heart hammering in my chest. My own need for him sudden and vital, I grabbed Adryen by the back of his neck, pulling him down on top of me on the sofa.

Desperate for any skin, I tugged roughly at Adryen's shirt. All the lessons on propriety went flying from me. I gave in to the impulse to taste him. His neck, salty and sweet, was the very nectar of life. I raked my teeth over a spot just below his ear, sending a thrill through me as he tightened his grip. His shirt untucked, I ripped it up over his head and threw it far away onto the floor.

Adryen slid his hands around me, gripping my ass and I pushed my hips up into his thickness. At the first push of his hips into me, all illusions of restraint were destroyed.

My breasts ached with the heaviness of my desire as I traced my tongue in a line up the column of his neck. Adryen's heart beat against my chest and, I could not be sure, but it felt like it beat in time with my own. I had to feel his hardness pressing into my hand, my mouth, or my body; I needed him NOW. I cupped Adryen's length through the fabric of his pants.

I was aching for every inch of him; so wet that every seam down the center of my suit was torture. Dragging the heel of my palm upward to the tip, I watched as Adryen's eyes rolled up into his head.

"Take off your pants," I ordered huskily.

Adryen paused, eyes popping open. A smirk showed on Adryen's face, the portrait of male arrogance, "Are you back for more?"

"More, yes, more," I breathed.

The smirk left his face and was replaced with predatory intent, as he moved his hand up my thigh to the bottom of my bikini.

"May I?" Adryen inquired, biting his lower lip.

"Please," I begged as I put all of my effort into convincing his hand to travel further up to the inside of my thigh.

He gave me a smile that was pure fae as he kept his eyes locked on mine. "You never have to beg me, Princess," a deep rumble rolling through him. Slowly, he started moving his hand in lazy circles on the inside of my leg, reaching ever higher until he slipped underneath my bikini bottom from my thigh. My entire body pulsed in time with the beating of our hearts. Adryen had become a predator and I was his prey. I nearly climaxed at the sight of him so powerful with all of his attention focused on me.

I had never felt so seen; so wanted. I was hungry for him; ravenous.

"The way you look at me sometimes makes me think such filthy things, Niya," Adryen purred into my ear. "I have been thinking about all of the places I want to touch you and fill you."

He closed his eyes and took a long, luxuriating sniff of the air between us, noting my readiness and the wetness pooling in my core.

I pulled him down onto me with a quick pull to his hair and pressed our mouths together. I wanted to claim. I plundered Adryen with my tongue, madly taking all of him for myself. Adryen tore his mouth away, brows furrowing.

Placing my hand on his cheek, he kissed the heart of my palm as he moved to push his hand further up my leg.

Adryen didn't take my bottoms off, he just slipped his hand up into them, reaching up to my drenched center.

"Are you always this wet for me, Niya?"

Skipping a breath, "Every time I think of you."

Adryen let out a soft growl and gently moved the small cloth aside more and slid his finger down the slick center of me.

Adjusting my position on the sofa, I laid back and Adryen dropped to his knees between my legs. Sliding his hand under me to cup my sex, he groaned.

His breathing became short, little pants.

"Adryen, I want you to fill me. I want to feel you inside of me."

The sound of my plea was his undoing.

He pushed a finger into my warmth as I shuddered. He repeated the movement again and mimicked the movement with his hips. If only he would use that thick cock of his. I lifted my hips in invitation as he replaced his first finger with two inside of me. I rode his fingers, rocking back and forth to hit all of the spots that I wanted him to fill.

Adryen began pumping me harder, licking those juicy lips of his. I wanted to devour him.

I wanted all of him; I wanted him seated fully inside of me.

"Adryen!" I shrieked. "Please, I want more of you. Let me take this off," I begged as I bucked my hips, freeing myself from the bikini completely.

Top and all.

I threw the wretched thing across the room with Adryen's abandoned shirt, and it landed with a *slap*.

Adryen stared at my naked body with worship on his angelic face, "Niya." He looked at me like a lover.

"Your body is the most beautiful I have ever seen," Adryen said with pure astonishment on his face. "I want to make offerings to all of the gods in thanks that I get to see it; be with you."

Adryen tried to look away from my naked body spread before him but couldn't bring himself to do it.

I reached up to touch his face, "I think that the gods made me just for you."

I was not quite sure where those words came from, but I was not about to take them back. He looked at me in a way no other male ever had, and the mix of emotions inside of me made my heart ache.

Palming his chest with one hand and reaching to his pants with the other, "Take off your pants. Now!"

"I am sorry, Princess, but I can't do that." A disgruntled sound came from my throat. He chuffed, "Not until I've made a thorough offering." His slow blink and sultry lips told me that I was in for something very interesting; and thorough.

Adryen's eyes dipped, noting the hammering of my pulse at the side of my throat. He raked his gaze over every imperfection, every curve, every freckle, and every dimple I had on my body. "Beautiful."

I wanted to grab him; I wanted to always have this level of intimacy in my life. I'd never known anyone that made me feel as truly beautiful as he had. I couldn't breathe under his burning stare.

I whimpered; my breasts straining up toward his touch. Adryen grabbed my leg gently and lifted it to roll me over onto my hands and knees on the lounge in front of him. Adryen's hands tightened on my bare thighs, spreading them further apart for him.

I bowed my back, lifting my hips up to him in invitation.

Yes, please, yes.

I felt a movement of wind behind me as he dropped to his knees again, gaining better access to the offered sex. He gripped either side of my ass with both hands, pulling me open wider. He leaned in and I noted a sudden huff of a sigh as he began his long, languid drag up my center all the way to the top.

A jolt of newly experienced sensation had me bowing deeper, pushing my face into the sofa. Oh, gods. Adryen dived deeper than his exploring tongue that I would have ever thought anyone ever would. I was not complaining. I was on board for whatever Adryen had planned for me; happily.

"You taste even more delicious than I'd dreamed," Adryen's low growl sounded like a whimper. Another flick of his tongue all the way from the lowered front of me to the top backside sent me involuntarily undulating my hips and pushing myself back into his tongue.

"You are so wet," as he pushed his thick thumb into my center, pushing it in to the meat at the base. He slowly pushed and swirled the thumb until he added his index finger to my swollen and aching bundle of nerves. I rocked into him as he worked me in a way I had never known; his hand felt like several hands at once and his skill was unimaginable.

"Adryen," I wailed as I lost all rhythm pushing harder and harder into his hand.

"My gorgeous, princess; I love it when you say my name like that. I want my name on your tongue always like I want your beautiful body on mine."

I slammed my body back into the hand that Adryen had braced against his thigh. Sensations were everywhere. I felt him release his grip on my hip, and after just a moment, he'd replaced that hand on my extreme lower back. In one unfaltering movement, he teased the sensitive exit at the top as he continued the swirling and pounded with his other hand.

A sudden, mind-shattering release rocked me; rolling over me and through me for what felt like eons. The reverberations echoed through time and space as he held me through the spasms.

This sexy, caring, and skilled male was my mate. Mine. Emotion welled in my breast as I felt an immovable desire to show him how much he meant to me.

Adryen wrapped an arm around me as I lowered myself to my stomach; his chest pressing against mine in solid comfort of the bond we shared. He kissed my neck and my spine lovingly.

"Adryen," I whispered.

"Yes, Princess?"

"Please take off your pants," my voice grew louder.

"Yes, Princess," he smirked.

Adryen quickly sat down on the lounge beside me and yanked off his boots while I fumbled with the clasp of his pants. This time, it took me only a few tries before I got it undone.

Thank the mother!

I yanked down and his throbbing member sprang free from its torturous cage. Adryen quivered and took a deep breath in as I licked tantalizingly up his throbbing cock.

"Oops, sorry; I couldn't help it," I offered shyly as I bit my lower lip in admiration. I gestured for him to continue as his stayed hand rested on the waist of his pants.

He managed to pull them all the way off in one smooth, whipping motion, not wasting anymore time.

He was truly impressive in many ways.

Adryen leaned one knee onto the sofa beside me and drew in close for a soft, languid kiss. The kiss was so gentle and sweet; like real lovers.

I could not remember ever having a kiss like that in my century of life.

Oh, damn, I was in trouble.

Raking my hands through his hair, deepening the kiss, I pulled him onto me; our bodies fully lining up. His taught muscles flexed so as not to crush me. I wanted him to crush me; I wanted it all.

My breaths grew ragged as I reached my hand up between us, looking for purchase. I grabbed at any bit of muscled flesh I could, desperate and on fire. Adryen did the same with one of his hands on my backside and one between my thighs.

I reached between us and tweaked his nipple; A hiss of pleasure made Adryen jerk his head back.

Oh, yes. I had found his sexual weakness.

I took his tiny nub between my thumb and forefinger and squeezed again, reaching up with my mouth and claiming his lower lip with my teeth.

"Oh gods!" Adryen gasped. "Oh, Princess. I want to do terrible, wonderful things to you right now."

The corners of my lips rose as an all-consuming pride filled my chest.

My mouth watered as I beheld him. Looking up at Adryen's face beneath my lashes, I reached down between us and gripped with one hand as I used the other to hold behind his neck, keeping him in place.

I stroked him as I licked down the column of his neck, leaving a trail as wet as I was in my core. My teeth nipped and sucked at his earlobes and chin. I closed my eyes and just felt for him; mouth moving with blind need.

Entangling my hand within his hair, I pulled his head back, exposing the strained cords of his neck to me.

One hand on his velvety smooth cock and the other tugging his head back, left him completely exposed and vulnerable to me. I kept my hand pumping in rhythm to the explorations of my mouth as I kissed down his muscled chest.

Opening my eyes again, I gazed adoringly at a tiny pebble of nerves on his gorgeous chest.

Taking the tip of my tongue and making lazy circles around the outside, the skin broke out in goose flesh. Smirking with satisfaction, I swirled my tongue around faster and faster as I pumped him below.

Gasps of pleasure broke from Adryen's throat as he began to pump into my hand. Adryen's heart beat so hard, I could feel it in my hand and my mouth.

Suddenly stopping, Adryen pushed me against the back of the sofa. His predatory gaze and swift, decisive action were a show of dominance that I relished in this normally sweet and calm male.

Getting onto his knees in front of me, Adryen gently lifted my leg and stared adoringly. A feral grin crossed his lips as he leaned in to kiss the inside of my knee. Placing my knee over his shoulder, he turned to my other knee and did the same. With both of my legs draped over Adryen's shoulders, he stared at my body spread before him.

I ran my fingers through his wavy hair, tousling it. A moment later, Adryen dipped his head down and made one slow stroke of his tongue up my center. The first lick of his tongue set me on fire.

Gasping, I gripped his hair tighter.

Adryen kissed the inside of each of my thighs and grabbed my ass with both of his large and capable hands as he lifted my hips up to his mouth. He slid his tongue inside me, working me in great, sweeping strokes. Pulling his tongue out to lick up my center and then going back in; it was a whirlwind of sensations.

He bared down on me, pushing with his tongue hard against me and pushed and pumped until I groaned. He lowered me slightly back to the seat so he could place a finger inside.

He glided in and out, pumping inside me. Adryen leaned down to lick and suck, his teeth scraping ever so slightly on the apex.

A guttural rumbling erupted from him, "Princess, you are so incredibly wet."

I felt the rising surge of release, moaning.

Adryen pounded into me faster and harder until I went over the edge, trembling and half-sobbing with ragged emotion.

"You're mine," he said with no sense of self-consciousness.

Adryen's eyes raked down my body as he shifted above me.

Adryen moved me over on the sofa. He reclined back, placing his head on the arm of the lounge. He guided me on top of him and I turned to face his knees.

Putting my hands on his thighs, I placed my knees on the other side of taut obliques.

"I want your ass in my face," Adryen was utterly scandalous, and I loved it.

I whispered seductively, "Yes, My King," and backed up slowly, wiggling for him.

He grabbed me tightly. His breath was a warm gust of air as it hit my dampness. He palmed my bottom, squeezing and kneading; spreading me open with his thumbs. I was already moaning, my body ratcheting tight with desire. I was on fire with how close his breath, his mouth was to the most sensitive part of me. All I felt was a delicious ache; a sumptuous pulse inside.

When he dipped his head, my fingers spasmed open. He lifted me, and his mouth quickly explored my most sensitive areas. His tongue sliced over my very center; he devoured me, capturing my flesh with his mouth. I was consumed; I was lost in the raw sensations. Fierce heat built. My back arched as I grasped the cushions.

The sharp graze of his teeth scraped the bundle of nerves, and I screamed as I shattered again.

That sound, that raw truth of my unraveled desire made Adryen's cock twitch in front of me. I repositioned myself to get a better perspective. I was very much in need of reciprocation.

I tongued him; licking, sucking, feasting, touching him while my mouth worked. Relentless sensation was everywhere. My heart, body, and mind all burst with feeling.

I pulled my mouth away from him and wrapped my fingers around the broad width, taking special care to tease beneath the tip. He was a slave to my caresses. Combining the efforts of both my hands and my mouth, I worked him until I had him tensing; pushing harder into my mouth and fisting the pillows.

He tried to pull me back to feast on me again, but I was on a mission.

I was a female possessed.

Adryen came with an explosion, grabbing my ass hard and thrusting into my mouth one last time, spilling his seed down my throat.

Adryen and I were a sweaty mess. My swollen core wanted him inside of me—needed it. He pushed my hips down his sweaty torso, lifting his abdomen to drag through my slickness. The touch of him at my swollen entrance had me whimpering.

A strong rattling began behind us. The windows started shaking vigorously. I let out a small whine, "What now?"

Adryen shifted me off of him and jolted up. A frustrated groan escaped me.

We were so close!

My body was hot with need as the room continued to reverberate.

I looked up behind me, and the glass panes warped and bowed; a crack spidering along the bottom edge.

"Oh, shit," I got off of the sofa and grabbed our clothes.

He yelled from behind me, "My magic! The windows are about to shatter," and stuck out a glowing hand towards me.

I grasped it and the bowing of the windows made a painful warping sound, straining to hold the tension.

"We need to go, now!"

Nodding in agreement, we were mere feet from the exit and the windows retracted one last time, exploding into tiny shards. Adryen covered my head and pushed me in front of him, forcing me out. He scowled in pain as the glass tore up his bare back. Closing the door behind him, I slipped on my dress and handed him his clothes.

He looked at me with contrition in his eyes, "I am so sorry."

"Turn around," was all I could say as I grabbed his shoulder, forcing him to move.

His back had many small pieces of glass stuck in and I let out a puff of disapproval, "I need to get the glass out of your back."

Adryen slipped his pants on, "No, please don't. That is going to hurt like hell."

I placed my hands on my hips, "Do you want them to stay in there forever?! Don't be a baby."

Daphne and Enzo huffed their entrance as Enzo blurted, "What happened?!"

Daphne threw her hand toward Adryen's back, "Look at our king!"

We didn't have time for the exposition. I grabbed Adryen's hand and guided us past the both of them, "We need to be alone, please," as I pulled him toward his room.

Adryen attempted to open his chamber door, but his injuries were too severe. I moved around him and opened the door for us, "You need to lay on your stomach on the bed so I can take out the glass."

He looked at me with a frown, "No."

"Yes."

"No, I will not allow you to heal me when I am more than capable of doing it myself," Adryen placed his arms around his chest, trying to hide his pain.

"I—what? Are you serious, Adryen? After what we just *did?*" I poked his chest with my finger.

He flexed his chest, rolling his head to the side; he had no argument.

I let out a hysterical laugh, "You are truly a masterpiece, you know that?"

Adryen let the air out of his lungs and his chest deflated, "You think I am a masterpiece?" He pulled a strand of my hair from behind my shoulder and toyed with it, admiringly.

My laughter turned into a giggle then just a beaming smile, "I do."

Pulling his finger up my strand of hair and towards my ears, Adryen caressed them in between his thumb and first finger, "If I am a masterpiece, then you are the goddess that created me," Adryen's palm cupped the back of my jaw and he moved me to look up to his eyes, "I will submit to you. Please, be gentle with me."

I glowed, "I will," and Adryen walked to the bed and lay on his stomach, back toward the ceiling.

Climbing on top of him, I used his arched bottom as a cushion to perch myself on and started delicately pulling out the individual shards of glass from his back.

I struggled with the smaller pieces and was unsure how much more he could take.

Closing my eyes, I gently touched the pads of my fingers to his beautiful golden tattoo. This somehow conjured a tool to use to pull out the tinier pieces. That was amazing that a single thought brought it into being. I looked at the newly formed golden tweezers in my fingers and smirked, "I could really get used to wielding Seelie magic," and strategically pulled little hidden glass pieces from him.

He tensed and seethed with every pull, and gripped the sheets as I carefully plucked all the pieces from his skin.

Chapter 37
Niya

A spark of inspiration hit me the other night with Adryen. I spent the entire night writing this beautiful ballad about our love story and the future I want with him going forward. This piece was for Vallynn, but it was really for Adryen.

He was my muse.

My, everything.

Sitting on that piano bench this morning, I finished the final touches with vocals that I would only share with Adryen, when the time was right. I practiced several times and once satisfied, I collected the music.

Walking back to my room, I opened the door to find Rose sitting on the bed with hair extensions and hot tools in her hands.

"Are you ready to blow everyone's mind?"

I laughed, "My hair is already so long, I do not need those extensions."

"Girl, you are getting more hair. Take a shower, it's time to get ready."

"Yes, ma'am," I saluted her and hopped in the shower. I double washed every curve of my body with my vanilla and jasmine soap. I stepped out and threw on a strappy shirt and shorts and went back to see Rose.

Rose had everything laid out on the bed: make-up, extensions, hair pieces, hairspray, gels, earrings, and strappy lingerie. All of which were ready to go on either her or myself.

"I hope that thong is for you. That is not going to fit me. There is barely anything to it!"

"Niya, it is red, it is obvs not mine. If Adryen is coming tonight, you are going to rock his world," Rose wobbled her eyebrows.

"Oh, gods," I whispered.

"Oh, gods is right! Let's get to it! Vallynn's birthday is not going to wait until you are ready."

"What about you, Rose? When are you going to get ready?"

She pushed her hands towards me, "Pfft, this dress is best with an updo. So, I am going to do a formal messy bun with glittered embellishments on the hair. It will only take a couple of minutes."

"And your make-up?" I questioned.

"Uh. Um," Rose trailed. She was never good with make-up, and I knew she would go to the ball without it.

"Sit down. Let me put your face on," I motioned her to the chair and pulled a light closer to her so I could see every angle of her perfectly delicate face.

"Thank you," She breathed.

"There is no way I am going to let you leave this room not looking like a whole snack."

She giggled, "I love you."

I simply replied, "I know," and got to work on her face. I gave a beautifully golden smokey eye to match her sparkling, formfitting golden dress. Since this event was in the evening, her make-up was contoured to reflect prismatically with the dimmed lights, and sparkling attire. I finished her face with a white, shimmering highlight on her high cheeks, nose, and between her arched eyebrows.

"What lipstick do you want?" I asked as I showed her the finished look. She screeched in excitement, turning her head this way and that in the mirror.

"Do you have a dark red, or pink?"

I looked at her, "You know I have any color you could think of." I quickly made it to my vanity and brought back my lipstick bag for her to shift through and decide, "Just don't forget to put on a lip liner first. You don't want to have to keep applying the lipstick throughout the night or have it smudging."

She nodded and started sifting through the small bag. I started pulling back her hair, putting it into a low ponytail. Grabbing individual strands, I placed them strategically to look like a messy bun, pinning them in place. I plugged in the curling hot tool and waited for it to heat up.

After several minutes, Rose finally pulled out a lipstick shade and handed it to me. I smiled, "This shade is perfect. I love me a deep, vibrant red. It's going to look fabulous on you. Don't move, I am about to curl your loose strands, and then set it with hairspray. Then you'll be ready to go!"

I grabbed the strands of hair framing her face and loosely curled them. I pulled my fingers through, to provide more of a bounce, I spritzed her hair with the holding spray and stepped back, placing my fingers on my lips and making a kissing sound, "Muah. Perfection."

Rose jolted up and ran to the bathroom, looking at her reflection. A loud squeal came from her, and she stood in the doorframe screaming, "I love it so much! This is so perfect!"

"Woah, I cannot reach that level of intensity right now, calm down," I giggled.

"I can't, I am just so excited! We haven't had a royal ball in *ages*. Sit down; it's your turn. I can't do your makeup, but I *will* make sure your hair is perfect. I was thinking a half up, half down to compliment your tiara.*"

I looked at Rose as she waved her hands for me to sit. I sat in the chair, and she grabbed the extensions, and started clipping them in various places, making sure none could be seen. She spent at least an hour just styling and clipping the hair to my head. I was getting restless and anxious to see the final product.

After several mumblings to herself and a shit-ton of holding spray, she backed up and looked at me with an expression of pride on her face, "I'm done."

I got up slowly and walked to the bathroom mirror. I turned the lights on to see my hair and my eyes widened.

Holy Gaia herself.

Rose placed several loose strands to frame my face and the rest of my hair was pulled back. It started at the very top of my head and swooped down to the loose hair in the back. It almost looked like a waterfall. The different variations of silvery blonde stood out as the strands of hair that were pulled back were placed in a way to show all the dimensions.

I turned around to look behind me and my hair reached almost to my ass. Damn, these hair extensions match beautifully. She left huge smooth curls in my hair that bounced with every movement creating that half cascaded look.

I have never.

"Rose," I called from the bathroom.

"Oh no!" She whined, "You hate it, don't you."

I ran out of the bathroom to see her pouting on the bed, "What; I freaking love it!"

"Oh," she perked up, "I am so happy that you're happy!"

A knock sounded at the door, "Ladies," a deep voice resonated from the hallway, "You have half an hour before the party-guests arrive, and you have a delivery, Your Highness."

Rose got up and opened the door, bringing in the garment bag accompanied by a small gift bag, "It looks like your dress is here, along with, a gift?"

She walked back, pulling out the red dress so it would not get wrinkled and hung it up on the closet door. She handed me the gift bag and I read the label:

> I can't wait to see you in your dress
> tonight, Princess.
>
> With Love,
>
> Adryen.

I arched an eyebrow, curious. I pulled the contents of the gift wrapping out and two velvet boxes laid one on top of another. I pulled out the smaller box and opened it up to see dainty, diamond earrings with pearl drops on the bottom.

I gasped, "Rose, he bought me pearls. Do you know how hard these are to come by? They must have cost a fortune."

"Well open the other box!" She pushed.

I pulled the larger box out from the bag and opened it. My eyes could not widen any further when I saw that an embellished matching pearl necklace lay in the box.

"I...I can't wear these." I put my hand on my chest, trying to stop my rapid heartbeat, "Nobody has ever given me something so spectacular before."

"Niya, if you don't wear those, that male is going to be utterly heartbroken. Plus, white is complimentary to red. They will match your dress perfectly. You will wear them; I've decided for you."

Pulling the necklace out of its box, I stared at the perfect imperfection of each pearl. There was no way he'd spent as much as I imagined on these. Pearls were an anomaly. I guessed since he lived so close to the ocean, they might have been easier to come by, but I was still in awe of the extravagance of it.

I applied my makeup, going for a more natural look with light eyeshadow and contouring. I pulled out a mahogany-colored lipstick and placed it on my lips after lining it with a similar shade.

I fitted Rose first, tightening her back corset and tucking in the laces so we couldn't see them. She turned around and the gold in her dress shimmered with her movements.

I pulled my dress down from the hanger and stepped into it and pulled it up to my chest. I slipped my arms through the shoulder straps and Rose adjusted the bodice and tulle for me. She tightened the lace corset and left the bow to lay where the bodice met the gown. I fluffed the front of the dress to see the shimmering underneath. I placed the pearl earrings on my lobes, as Rose helped with the necklace, making sure it would not travel throughout the night.

Turning around, Rose gasped, "Gods, Niya. You look stunning. If I were not crazy about di..."

"Do not finish that," I interrupted and placed the onyx tiara on my head.

Ready to leave, Rose opened the door. Vallynn was waiting there, hand raised to knock.

"Damn," is all he said as he adjusted his long sleeve embroidered red and gold tunic, "You both look amazing. I am a little jealous considering this is *my* birthday party."

Rose sneaked out of the room first and I followed behind her, closing the door. Vallynn cleared his throat and gestured for my hand. Instead, I wrapped my arm around his and tapped his shoulder, "You look wonderful tonight as well, brother; very dashing."

We walked together to the ballroom, Rose trailing behind us.

I looked at my baby brother, "I hope you get everything you ever wanted this birthday."

"Listen, I will be happy to have more than one Seelie female in my bed tonight."

"What...Val...oh my gods," I shook my head, "What is with you and the Seelie court females?"

"They are a whole different breed of beauty. I made sure to invite all of Adryen's courtiers here. I hope he accepted your invitation."

"He did," I smiled, "and hopefully you get all the girls you want tonight." I cringed slightly as I said it.

Garrin stood at the entryway and nodded to us, "Evening, Your Highnesses; all of the guests have arrived."

"Perfect," Vallynn smiled, "I will enter first since you both have clearly out-dressed me. I would hate for them to see you both first and then me."

I laughed, "Vallynn, you are so weird; although, I imagine we would be a tough act to follow," I winked at Rose. "Have a good night, little brother. Come see me when you're ready for your song," and kissed him on the cheek.

Garrin nodded toward Vallynn and made his royal announcement. Vallynn threw up his hands in a gesture for the party to commence.

Rose and I gaped at each other and stifled a nervous laugh.

Butterflies took over my stomach as she entered the ballroom first.

Chapter 38
Niya

"**A**re you ready?" Garrin questioned.

No, not really, "Yes," I replied.

Garrin made my formal announcement, and everyone in the ballroom stopped, and stared. I felt all of their eyes boring into me.

I shifted uncomfortably, and scanned the room quickly; for *him*. I smiled at no one in particular and moved away from the entrance and into a spot where I could further survey the room. I walked towards my parents' dais and looked at every fae dancing, conversing, and walking in and out of the gardens. Not one of them was him.

Adryen didn't come. He'd dropped off jewelry and abandoned me...or, maybe he just wasn't here yet.

Oh my gods, Niya.

I should have known he was too busy for this. I toyed with my dress, trying to hold in my spiraling emotions. I spotted Vallynn getting cozy with what looked like twins, wrapping one hand around his waist and the other around his shoulder. They both placed their hands on his chest, coming in for a kiss.

I closed my eyes and breathed through my nose, trying to compose myself.

Tonight is not your night, it is Vallynn's.

Rose peaked into my view, holding two drinks.

One of those had better be for me.

She stepped over to me and handed me a glass of pink bubbly, "This is for you."

I snatched the glass away from her before she could finish her sentence. She raised an eyebrow and gracefully drank from hers. I chugged mine and the bubbles burned on the way down.

"What in the entire realm is this?"

Rose replied, "I don't know. Sahriah said she was experimenting tonight and wanted us to try her first drink. She said with the borders down, she was able to get some vodka? Whatever that is."

I looked over at Sahriah's set up and left Rose behind,moving toward her.

I leaned against the bar, "Who gave you vodka?"

"Haldonia."

"How?" I seethed.

"King Whitebourne sold me a case earlier today and said to mix it with whatever I had on hand. I wanted you to try some mixtures before I distributed it to the guests."

"Well, it tasted like shit," I snapped.

"Damn, Niya. What's wrong with you?" Sahriah crossed her arms over her chest like she always did when I upset her.

I breathed out, "I'm sorry. I was expecting someone, and it seems that he came to drop off alcohol and jewelry...but didn't care to say hello to me."

"Who? The King? He stepped outside a while ago with some handsomely tall, dark fae. I am sure he will be inside soon."

I spun around and spied two males; coming from either side.

Enzo.

Adryen.

My Adryen.

Both of them seemed to be headed my way at the same pace. I moved my head to look at both and confusion took over. Adryen invited a plus one. I watched as Rose walked past my view and met up with Enzo who immediately began playing with her loose strands of hair.

I stormed towards that familiar eucalyptus and birch scent, not paying any attention to either Enzo or Rose.

Adryen smiled widely and all that pent up anger disappeared completely.

He put his hand on my cheek and came in for a kiss, "Hello, Princess."

Smiling, I opened my lips for him, not caring who saw.

"I could feel your anxiety through the bond and came inside to see you before you absolutely exploded with rage," he chuckled. "You are so fiery when you don't get your way. I like it," waggling his brows.

I mumbled, "I thought you could only hear my thoughts...your power is evolving." I paused and looked up at his contented smile, "And, I wouldn't have to get like this if I had known where you were. But it's fine. It was a *slight* overreaction."

He chuckled, "That was not *slight*," Adryen stretched out his tattooed arm to me, "Dance with me, Niya."

I looked over his attire. A red button-down shirt covered by a black tuxedo and matching bowtie. His hair was side swept perfectly, and his facial hair was nicely groomed. His azure-tipped ears were hidden by glamour, but his entire physique was...*breathtaking.*

True royalty.

And he is all yours, Niya.

He smiled and took my hand, "I *am* yours, Princess."

Hand in hand, he led me to the dance floor.

Adryen put one hand on my waist and held the other, "I could say the same thing about your beauty. It's a shame you have to keep that dress on all night. I could rip it from you right now and fuck you in so many different positions. Leaving those pearls on you, of course."

Adryen's arousal brought my own arousal to whole new levels. I could feel every ache in his body yearning for me. Needing me.

And I sunk into it.

"Adryen, these pearls are decadent. I could have never imagined such a thoughtful gift. Thank you," is the only thing I could get out before he pulled into a waltz.

"No, I am not waltzing tonight," I said moving Adryen closer to me and bending our arms to be closer together. I slid my other hand around his shoulders and his head was inches from mine, "Better," and smiled.

"I don't know what dance this is," Adryen trailed off.

I tilted my head towards him and let out a little shush as he slid his hand over my waist, tucking me in close. I reached up and placed my arms around his neck. We moved as if our very breaths were timed to the music. Each movement of my body, loose and taut in all of the right places. Adryen responded to every one of them. He twirled me around, my head snapping to meet his gaze with every one. I was positively giddy with all of the spinning and Adryen's eyes never left my face.

Adryen twirled me one more time and I found my center, moving in closer to him. He dipped me low, placing his lips on mine, smiling onto them as he brought me back up.

He looked nervous, and sweaty. Something was on his mind that he was not telling me.

"What's wrong? Did I do something to upset you?" I questioned.

"No," he stopped his words and said carefully, caressing my cheek, "I love you, Niya. I have loved you since you placed that damned dagger to my throat."

I backed away from him and the gleam in his eyes dissipated and his smile faltered.

No.

I wanted Adryen. I wanted all of him, but him saying those words to me sent fear spearing through my body like an arrow.

It scared me.

Love was dangerous, and the unyielding and the perpetual nature of it confused me.

Love was not for me.

I was Unseelie.

A sudden, irrational part of my brain told me to flee. I brushed past him and ran outside to get some fresh air.

Adryen called after me, "Niya!"

I threw up my mental shields, blocking him out.

This dress suddenly suffocating me and making it extremely hard to breathe. I made it outside and I grabbed at my neck, hoping to get the air back into my lungs.

"You look terrible, Niya." Vallynn bellowed from a bench where he had the Seelie twins laying all over him.

He shooed them off and patted the now empty bench next to him, "Come, sit with me for a moment."

I obliged, and sat down with a *huff.* I placed my elbows on my knees and rested my chin on the inside of my palms, "I hate myself."

"How could you possibly hate yourself? You have everything you want. You're about the ascend the throne, and you have a very viable male ready to marry you and rule by your side."

"I guess when you put it that way," I replied, annoyed.

"Oh, come on, don't cocoon on me. What's wrong?" Vallynn nudged my shoulder.

I rolled my eyes all the way into my head, fluttering my lashes, and let out a deep breath, "I am an idiot."

"That is very unhelpful. But I get it, you don't want to talk. I *would* like to hear that song you wrote for me when you are done feeling sorry for yourself out here. I can't wait to hear what my big sister has cooked up."

Vallynn kissed the top of my head and walked back inside, shouting to the party guests to "party harder!"

I placed my face on my palm, regretting walking out on Adryen in such a vulnerable, beautiful moment.

Unsure of how long I sat outside on the bench, I composed myself and walked back inside. I made eye contact with Vallynn and he nodded towards me with a thumbs up, face beaming.

Scanning the room for him, every face in the ballroom seemed to blur as I took a seat on the piano bench, where my sheet music was waiting for me.

I looked up and a wash of black covered my sight. Panic rose inside of me and I felt frozen to the spot.

A voice rang in my ears, "What you know as true, is no longer." The voice repeated, "What you know as true, is no longer. Niya, elemental queen, the end is nigh."

The room fell silent as I pulled my head down. Looking around the room at all of the staring males and females, overwhelming performance anxiety permeated me.

It was eerily quiet.

Too quiet.

I must have zoned out for several minutes. That voice shot through my head again and I held my ears and eyes shut.

Get out. Get out! GET! OUT!

Vallynn, next to me, whispered, "Are you unwell?"

I looked up at Vallynn, "What?" That is all I could reply before he backed up to give me space.

"Thanks, Vallynn." I gave a wary smile, "I am fine."

Vallynn nodded his head slowly, unsure; he backed up, rejoining the crowd.

I looked towards the gardens and Adryen stood there with Enzo and Rose. Adryen was tense, and his hand rested on the pommel of his sword. He murmured something to Enzo and moved in closer to me.

Stop, I communicated through our bond.

Adryen hesitated, but eventually stopped; unease rippling through him.

Turning my attention back to the piano, I shuffled the sheet music and got myself ready to play. Putting my hands on the piano keys, I let out a deep breath and closed my eyes.

My fingers flitted over each note; beautifully struck chords resonating. I lost myself to the music, and the guests started to dance slowly to my song; Adryen's song. Emotion and music flowed through me; slow chords that allowed the guests to dance and sway in time. I peeked over at Adryen leaning on the doorframe, entranced. Ending in a crescendo, I mouthed, *I am sorry,* to *him.* He didn't soften to my declaration; he didn't even *look* at me. Gracefully, I held onto that last note as long as I could, giving the guests the emotional hold that they all needed; the emotions I was feeling shooting straight to the many hearts in the room.

My song ended and Vallynn clapped as loudly as he could. I looked over to him and tears were rolling down his face, "Brava sister! Truly amazing! Everyone, the night is still young, let's get back to partying!"

The fast-paced music chimed back on, and I stood up and took a slight bow and sprinted towards the exit.

"Niya," I heard my name from the crowd.

I turned around and Adryen yelled again, "Niya!"

I slipped out of the door and ran through the castle, trying to make my way to the front gates.

I need to see Ca'Themar.

That was an auditory hallucination.

Terror filled me as those words echoed in my head again: *What you know as true, is no longer.*

"Niya!"

Twirling around, Adryen put his hands on my cheeks panting, "What the *hell* was that voice in your head. It was not yours."

Panting, "I don't know, Adryen. I'm scared."

Like the beat of the drums, the voice kept panging:

The end is nigh.

The end is nigh.

The end is nigh!

I bawled and lightning buzzed all around me. My power surged and Adryen's eyes glowed with fear and concern.

I pressed the palms on my hands onto my ears again and pleaded, "Stop!"

And it all went quiet.

The thunderous sky was no more, and Adryen fell backward on his ass holding his chest.

His heart.

He whispered, "Something is not right. I will be back with a firestone. It should help you with your power overload. Please, be careful."

Adryen kissed my cheek platonically and quickly looked away.

A flash of blue light flickered, and he took to the sky as his wyvern.

"I'm sorry," I cried after him, "What is a firestone?!"

I watched as his wyvern disappeared into the night sky. A howl bellowed from the distance and my mind ran rampant. Now *determined* to see Ca'Themar, I turned to face the gates of my castle.

Running down the streets, I made it to the temple steps and forced myself to plod upward through my fatigue.

I banged on the door and it opened automatically.

Ca'Themar was standing there with a grin on his face, "Your mother must have told you the second part of your prophecy."

I towered over him, "Which is what? You're the oracle and our priest, you should be able to just tell me!"

This was not what I came here for, but maybe it would help me with the answers to some of my questions.

My mother hadn't told me anything. The voice in my head was driving me to distraction. I needed it out; now!

Ca'Themar smirked, "That you are of elemental blood. *Your* truth is not *the* truth. Once you found your mate, your powers would manifest into something godlike. What you know as true, is no longer."

Those words rang again in my head and this time it took me to the floor. I fell on my hands and knees and groaned in pain, "Make it stop!"

"It will stop when you accept what you are. Who you are."

"Please!" I begged, "What does that even mean?!"

"You can only help yourself, Niya, Elemental born. What you are is very rare; the last sighting of an Elemental was ten years ago."

I looked up from the floor towards Ca'Themar and the voice in my head diminished, "What do you mean?"

Ca'Themar laughed, "I mean, that you are special. Child of the gods. And, that you are not the only one."

I glared at Ca'Themar.

This old male was out of his mind.

Or I was.

It could be both, if I were being honest.

Ca'Themar coughed, "You need to leave."

My magic boiled inside, and I growled, forming a powerful wind encircling us, "No," I demanded.

Ca'Themar snapped his fingers and my magic suddenly just shut off with no trace of it ever being there, "Yes," he insisted. "You cannot be here with your heightened emotions. You need a more...open space," he waved me goodbye as his own gust of wind pushed me out of his temple, a foot away from the staircase and boomed from inside, "Tread lightly, child! Your powers aren't your own. Not yet."

I stormed down the stairs, through the empty streets, and back to the castle; furious.

Child of the gods, my *ass!*

My parents are Ravyn and Edmund Blackbyrn.

I am of Royal Unseelie descent.

There is *no* possible way I am a child of a god.

Especially one of the Elementals.

There were many Elementals.

Elementals were our gods; the creators of this realm. They had sacrificed and created this land so we could flourish away from the human realm. The Elementals were the most powerful fae. They lived thousands of years without showing a single wrinkle, or loss of hair color. When the Blood Wars ended, we were no longer deemed worthy of them, and they left us to our own devices.

Part 3:
The
Manipulation

Chapter 39
Niya

The castle gates were left open, and the trickling of vehicles were on their way out. I wended my way through stopped extended beds, four door cars, and motorcycles. My hands became engulfed in fiery, orange and red flames as I reached the entrance to the castle.

I was pure rage and anger trudging back to this damned castle.

Walking up the steps, livid, I flung the entrance to the castle open, and my parents stood there, talking to Lord Morelli.

"What is *he* doing here?"

"*He* is one of your lords, child. Have some manners," Morelli spit out.

I pointed my conflagrant hand toward him, and Lord Morelli threw his hands up in concession. He quickly stepped aside, and out of the way.

"Let's take this outside," My father insinuated.

I stomped to the grassy area of the castle as people, trying to leave, stopped to watch us.

Not giving a damn who was listening, I rasped, "I will pull you of your rank if you talk to me that way again, Morelli."

Lord Morelli stepped into the worrying crowd, and I turned my head to my mother and father.

"Darling," my mother started, "What has you so upset?"

I looked at both of them, and everything made sense. I didn't look like either of them. My personality was one of its own. My powers outranked everyone in this entire gods-forsaken kingdom. I did not belong. I never truly did.

I was not them.

"I am not yours," I said lower than a whisper.

"Sweetie, please speak up, you know I hate when you mumble."

Looking at my father, "I am not yours."

"Of course, you are, my darling," My mother cut in.

"Ca'Themar told me everything."

A sour twinge altered her facade, "What did that old excuse for an oracle tell you?"

I quipped, "You know very well what he told me, *mother!*"

"Enough!"

"Fine," I spewed, but continued, "I am talking about the both of you. You are not my real parents."

Ravyn and Edmund looked at each other. My father's countenance grew distant and empty.

My patience was wearing thin, and I was not about to stand staring in silence any longer before taking matters into my own hands.

"You are mine," my father said, finally, "But you are not hers," he put his hand on the Queen's back.

The Queen chimed in, "It took you way longer than we anticipated for you to figure it out," she smirked, "You are illegitimately born, Niya. Unfortunately, though, you are still a firstborn, which means you are the rightful heir to the crown. If it were my choice, you would have been dead when Dreya abandoned you. She was quite upset with your lack of god-like abilities. We had to keep your prophecy at bay for as long as possible. But here we are! Could you imagine if you had all the powers of a goddess." She sent a sneering glare to my father.

My fists changed from oranges and red to fire of hot blue and white.

Magic oozed out of my pores.

It had felt like I did, in fact, have all the elements of a goddess. I was able to harness every element, besides the magic from the ground itself.

I thought more on this, Dreya, who was being maligned as a being who would abandon her own child.

Dreya was *the* goddess of this realm.

I could not fathom why she would ever just abandon a child.

Me.

Exhausted emotion escaped my eyes as hot tears rolled down my face, "You lied to me."

My father looked into my eyes, "No, we withheld the truth. For your own safety."

"But you withheld something so important! I am not even of Unseelie blood!"

My life was a lie.

The voice started chanting in my head: *What you know as true, is no longer.*

My prophecy was not to just ascend the Unseelie throne and be queen. I was supposed to be ruler of this entire *realm* and of *both* kingdoms. That was why my mother needed Adryen. To ensure that I would be in a position to realize my destiny. As the daughter of Dreya, I was born to sit on a throne of my own and rule.

Everyone.

Oh, gods.

"Half-blood, actually," Ravyn pitched into my thoughts.

I curled my upper lip, "The books never mentioned Dreya having a child."

"Why would she mention it? You were unwanted; a disgrace."

"Shut up," I said out loud to the voices.

"Excuse me," Ravyn snipped.

"Shut up," Now I directed it to her, "I am not a disgrace."

"Oh, but you are. You have done nothing for this crown, or our people. You have lived a perfectly selfish life doing as you please, Niya. How dare—"

I snapped out a golden chord that replaced my fired hands, and wrapped it around her neck, tightening the grip, "How dare *you!*" I pulled the golden cord down and she fell to the floor.

"Niya, stop!"

Jerking my other hand, a second gold chord wrapped around my father's neck, and he tried to claw free. I clenched my jaw keeping a firm hold on the both of them.

All I could see was white hot anger, and the grief of knowing that my entire life, my entire being was a lie.

And at the moment, in complete shambles.

They choked and coughed, trying to speak.

"Say that again, please. I didn't hear you over your choking," I rejoindered loosening the hold on their necks slightly.

My mother spewed, "Let us go!"

"Fine," I retracted the golden chords and backed away from them.

Lord Morelli ran to their sides, helping them up. I watched as my mother rubbed her neck in vexation. Looking around, the crowd had doubled, and all eyes widened as they trailed me.

I was not a killer, but in that moment all I could see was red.

My blood boiled as I turned to walk away.

The voices spoke in my head again:

What you know as true, is no longer.

The end is nigh.

"Okay!" I screamed finally into nothingness, "I understand."

The voices said one, simple, word: *Yes.*

And that was it.

The voices shut off like a snap as power surged and raged all around me. Every element that I wielded sparked and billowed to life. Water seeped up from the ground and circled around me with the wind. Fire emanated from my body as if I was a walking torch. The clouds covered overhead, and thunder boomed above, causing lightning to spark in the sky.

I forced myself away from everyone, fearful that someone would get hurt. I couldn't control the forces raging inside and around me. They were too powerful.

Suddenly, with a mind of their own, my powers shot out from behind me. Two lightning bolts struck the floor, followed by a huge *crack* from the skies. I fell to the floor, hands first from the bolt hitting so close to me. The ground shook and I turned around.

Terrified screams resounded; the guests were scurrying away from me, from us.

My parents.

Two bodies lay behind me, unmoving.

I shrieked, "No!"

My powers were still amped up as I crawled over to them to check their breathing.

Both my father and Ravyn lay askew on the grass.

My heart raced as I jostled their shoulders, "Wake up! Please, gods!" I placed my cheek under my father's nose to check for breathing.

Nothing.

I did the same for the Queen, who was not my mother.

Nothing.

Their bodies smoking from where the bolts hit them.

Oh, gods.

"Guards!" Lord Morelli yelled, "Seize her!"

My magic finally dropped to a simmer, and it was once again, just me.

I was in control.

I tried to send healing magic that I thought I may have gained from Adryen to them to see if I could heal them, but nothing would work.

"No!" Was all I could get out before I heard Morelli yelling false accusations and decrees.

"This is treason, of the highest order!"

"No, I—" I started to breathe heavily as my thoughts were sent scattering. "I didn't mean to, it wasn't me. I mean—"

Garrin ran up and stopped inches from me. I started crying uncontrollably as a somber and betrayed look crossed his face.

He whispered, pulling me off the ground, "Did you," and could not finish his sentence.

"It was not me. I was not in control of my magic. I swear! Garrin!" I choked out "I—"

He frowned at me, and all I could do was stand there paralyzed.

A roar came from the distance and Garrin and I looked over at the blue wyvern.

Adryen landed near us, and I snapped my pleading gaze over to him. I looked back at Garrin who was shaking his head back and forth at me.

"Don't run, it will make things worse."

"I can't be taken prisoner."

"Don't run to him, Niya," Garrin repeated more firmly.

Instinct had me running toward Adryen, causing Garrin to follow behind me.

Adryen would be my salvation; an oasis in the desert.

He was safety.

My comfort.

Gasps sounded from all around us, as Adryen shifted back into his very naked fae form for all to see.

The crowds, that were trying to escape, stopped and looked back at the cornflower blue eyes that were searching mine.

Niya, he sent through the bond.

I, I did not do it, I cried. Tears rolling down my face.

"He is a wyvern," said one voice coming, closer to us.

"The King of Haldonia," commented another following behind.

I was halfway to him, and a brown and white wolf stopped me in my tracks. He snarled and I backed away.

"Enzo?" I questioned, "I need your help. Both of you."

Adryen said out loud, "Don't come any closer, Princess."

Confusion and heartbreak hit me square in the chest.

The realization of being utterly alone in this world cracked me open wide.

Enzo continued snarling at me, and I attempted to approach them, but I was too late.

Two large hands grasped my waist and turned me around.

"Gorgeous," a smooth voice resonated in my ears as two painful jabs went through my wrists and chains clicked into place. I screamed, as agony swept through me.

I fell to the floor and Nik was grasping my wrists, making sure they were chained and locked properly.

The ground shook angrily as Adryen growled from across the grassy field. I looked over at Garrin who was talking with Lord Morelli; every sound echoing without meaning in my skull.

I glanced at Adryen whose fists were clenched so hard they were turning white.

What a mess I had gotten myself into.

A prisoner.

In my own fucking kingdom, because I could not let something go.

But, I couldn't let it go. Not really. My whole life I thought I was just Niya, Crowned Princess of Kaldamir. Not Niya, daughter of Dreya, Queen of the elementals and quite possibly this entire realm.

Looking back to Nik, I shouted at him, "Where did you come from?!"

"Familial call," is all Nik replied.

"Let her go!" Adryen shouted from across the field; gaining speed, light flickered, as he transformed back into his wyvern.

He was ready to fight and defend. A deep roar escaped his scaled breast, and his nostrils flared with blue flames.

I looked over at Garrin, who was now trying to get my lifeless parents off the grass and back inside, not concerning himself with Adryen and his wyvern form. He was shouting for a medical fae or a witch to see if they could revive them. Garrin was also shouting for his guards to subdue Adryen and get him back to his fae form. The four guards grunted in acknowledgement and quickly bolted toward Adryen, unsheathing their swords.

Everything had happened so fast that my head was spinning. My new chains depleted my magic and made my head swoon.

I groaned in pain and Nikolaj hauled me up to my feet. Blood spilled from my punctured wrists, and I screamed in pain. Adryen let out another deafening roar and everyone around pressed their hands over their ears, trying to dampen the sound.

Adryen had begun forming a fire ball, but before he could release it at my would-be captors, shadows overtook us and everything went black within a blink.

Chapter 40
Niya

I yelled out of my nightmares. My eyes flexed open to a completely enclosed room with iron bars to the left. I put my hand on the brick wall to help myself up, and groaned in pain.

My gorgeous red tulle dress, that I had been so proud to wear hours before, was now in total disrepair. The tulle was ripped in various places and I was missing a sleeve. I wanted to run my fingers through my hair, but they kept getting stuck in between the various pieces and pins.

I began to pull out the hair pieces from the mess atop my head and dropped them next to me on the floor.

I was caged.

I looked at my freed hands, turning them over to check all angles, and raised an eyebrow. I thought I would run toward the iron bars in hopes that I just might be able to slip through, but I immediately felt the excruciating pain in my ankles. I screamed in anger and impotence.

Pulling my dress up to my calves, metal shackles shown from below, were my bloodied and ruined feet throbbed. These shackles were meant for the highest security prisoners, but I wasn't a threat to anybody.

Nobody but myself.

Where was I? The red, deteriorating brick walls indicated that I was no longer home. If I even had a home anymore. I was an outcast, shunned and left to die. I was supposed to be queen and now I was a prisoner.

This could not be happening.

I sat back on the floor and tried to examine the shackles looking for a way to remove them, but all I got was the iron pole. Touching the metal, my ankles received renewed unbearable pain.

I could feel that my bones had been shattered.

Bringing my knees up to my face, I dug my head into my thighs and leaned against the rough wall. Endless tears rolled down my face until I slipped into oblivion.

Chapter 41

Adryen

The tension was palpable. No one knew where to look. Eyes darted from one to another to the space formerly occupied by Niya—my mate.

The Kaldamir guards mandated that I withdraw my wyvern. The wanted to talk in hopes of understanding what had happened and exact proper punishment for all involved in the treason; including, possibly me. I would much rather have fled with Enzo. This was not going to be a fireside chat.

"Why is the Seelie King here?" said one Lord.

"Lords, please," Lord Morelli suggested placatingly.

"But he is *her* consort!" seethed another.

"And *he* was just about to use a fireball on us!" There were murmurs of agreement amongst the throng. They all turned to look at me.

All of these angry and fearful faces and I knew none of them. I looked over at Enzo and we began slinking deeper and deeper into the entryway, my hands up to indicate that I meant no harm.

I should not be here.

The throng started turning into a vexed mob. I lowered my eyes, backing toward the exit, "I will look into this, I promise," and slipped out the door with Enzo trailing behind me.

I snapped a portal into place and jumped through it. Enzo followed behind, treading lightly as he jumped through.

Ignoring Enzo's retching, I ran through the palace grounds and through the castle's common room where Malcolm sat, lazily sipping whiskey and reading.

I ran up to my room, to slip on a new shirt and comfortable shorts to meet back with my team in the common room.

Entering, I started to pace back and forth, dragging my hands through my hair and scrubbing my face with them.

"Cousin, stop," Malcolm brows furrowed with anxious concern. "What has happened?"

Enzo busted through the door, "I fucking hate portals so much. I would rather run back home than travel through that damn void again."

Malcolm disregarded Enzo's comment and gestured towards me, "I'm afraid to ask."

"Niya killed her parents," Enzo choked out.

I growled at Enzo, wanting him to take it back, "Don't say that. We don't know what happened."

"She did *what?!*" Malcolm's voice strained with the higher pitch.

"Malcolm, stop talking," Enzo countered.

"Both of you need to shut the fuck up so I can think," I growled, "I need to process what the hell just happened, and I need to get Niya back."

"Get her *back?*" Malcolm spasmed.

Enzo, completely ignoring Malcolm's question, "We're lucky we got out of there alive!"

So many hand movements came from Enzo as he attempted to fill Malcolm in on the pertinent events. Malcolm just nodded his head periodically as the wolf rambled.

"Uh-huh," was the only noise from Malcolm after the retelling was complete.

I went to the bar and poured myself an entire glass of whiskey, knowing I would need it for the discussion and planning ahead, "I have no idea where they took her. There was a vampire who pulled her into the shadows, and they were gone. I don't know who he was or where to start looking. Which lords have holding cells?" I shot a look to Malcolm. I inhaled and then exhaled deeply, "I can't feel or hear her anymore. It is like our connection was cut as soon as she disappeared," I choked back tears.

My heart was breaking.

"How can I help?" Enzo perked up and put his fist to his chest.

"Can you ask your pack to get acclimated to her scent so when we have a plan ready, they can start looking for her?"

Enzo nodded, "I will notify my brothers of the need. It would be an honor for them to help you find your mate. They can stop by tomorrow to familiarize their noses with her scent. What are the next steps?"

"I don't know yet, but keep your pack on alert. I need to think."

Enzo slipped out the door, shutting it behind him.

I topped off my whiskey and plopped in a chair next to Malcolm.

"Why?" Malcolm cut in, "Why only figure it out on your own? You have three very capable brains. We are here to support you, Adryen. You don't have to do this alone."

"Last time I had either of you help me figure something out, it became the shittiest night of my life. So, don't come for me if I politely decline."

The shittiest night being the one where I was left by my parents to learn my lesson stuck in the thorns in The Great Divide. I was coerced and encouraged at ten years of age by my equally young and stupid friends into thinking that I could bring down the barrier, and Seelie and Unseelie could live in harmony together. Well, all I got was a night outside where nobody was allowed to bring me anything or help me until the morning; which I would not recommend.

"Adryen," Malcolm looked at me.

Staring back, "Malcolm."

"I will help you get her back. It is the least I can do," then mumbled, "I can temporarily put her stabbing me aside; for you, cousin."

"Let that go, Malcolm."

Malcolm lost his lover a decade ago to a band of rebels who tormented her, raped her, then beheaded her. My parents tried everything they could to stop it and save her, but before they could reach her, she was already dead. She was the closest he'd ever come to a mate.

Malcolm sipped his drink, "I can't just let it go. You went behind your parents' back to try to find her above and beyond what they were doing and put yourself at risk of exposure or death. I am forever in your debt."

I looked down at my whiskey and gave it a swirl before sipping and replied, "Why do I feel like I would die if anything happened to Niya? I feel like my heart would literally rip apart and I would bleed out for days."

"It's the mating bond," is all he said before standing up to leave, "Let me know if you need me to do anything. Spy, kill, torment. Just say the word, and I'll be there, cousin."

Malcolm put his hand on my shoulder and walked out of the door, leaving me to my own thoughts.

I slung the glass backwards and chugged the alcohol that had, by that time, numbed every bit of my throat on the way down. Getting back up, I filled another glass and chugged that one as well.

Pouring one last glass in efforts to actually feel a buzz, I wandered through the common room, trying to shake the feeling of suffocation while I thought.

I had all these books and documents; there had to be something in here about Kaldamir and its lords and ladies. I placed my hands on dusty tomes and leafed through the pages.

Looking for something.

Anything that might help.

I peered up at the top shelf and pulled down everything I could reach. Not one thing had a title indicating anything about Kaldamir or its people. There was no way that my parents did not have secret documents about their kingdom. My family was wonderful, but they were not innocent or naïve. They had secrets and schemes.

Sitting down in the desk chair, I sat the glass down and placed my head in my hands, letting out a muted growl. My foot kicked the inside of the desk and a compartment popped open on the right-hand side. Raising an eyebrow, I peeked around to see a little door opened to show an enveloped document. I reached my hand around the table to grab the paper, and my eyebrows rose.

Kaldamir.

Frantically opening the envelope, I found papers haphazardly stored. I pulled them out in a single clump and began to shuffle through them. I scanned every page looking for everything that I could use that would help find her.

I sighed, relieved.

There was everything!

Maps, documents, research, royal lines, lords and ladies.

Every one of their districts and approximately how many people inhabited it. My eyes flew through the different types of fae and where they lived, until my eyes snagged on *Vampires*.

The Silver Expanse.

I flipped the papers around to check for any more information on the back. There was a date indicating twelve years ago.

I groaned and placed my head on my index finger leaning against it for support. Separating the map from the rest of the scrambled papers, I leaned in closer to investigate.

Gods.

This was very poorly drawn.

Some of the lines and symbols were hard to decipher, but I thought that I could make it work. This should be exactly what I needed.

I scanned the map for The Silver Expanse. It sat in the southern corner of the many districts of Kaldamir. This Silver Expanse was located just west The Wastelands.

Pulling the map closer to me and using a magnifying glass, I noticed that there was a little label for a club that sat in the middle of the district.

I smirked and chugged the rest of my whiskey. Setting the glass down, I whispered to myself, "I guess we are going clubbing."

Chapter 42
Niya

The sound of clanging metal jerked me from my sleep as a guard stood at the cell bars. Chuckling to himself, "Well, well, the lovely princess is finally awake. It only took an hour." He quirked a menacing smile, eyes piercing me.

I rubbed my aching head and the guard, somehow, said even louder, "Here, I brought you water and dinner," and threw it on the floor, splattering everywhere, "Enjoy, *parent* killer."

How long had it been? I feel like I had drowned in sleep for the last several days.

Hours?

Weeks?

Months?

I didn't know anymore.

But what I did know was that the little show of dominance was the same, every damned meal. A guard would come in, throw my food and water, then leave me to figure out how to eat and drink in my condition.

It was almost impossible to move around with the iron penetrating my bones. Crawling to the bread, I picked it up off of the dirty ground and wiped off what filth I could.

Stale, like every other meal. I turned up a sour lip at the bread and set it back down. I opened the bottled water and drank greedily.

I didn't know the last time I'd eaten, but I'd made sure I was hydrated. I lay on my back and sprawled out, looking at the cracking bricks. I counted them over and over again until I thought my mind was dripping out of my ears.

Tilting my head, I found a rather more interesting thing to watch. Water dripped slowly from the gap in the ceiling. I counted each of those drops until a small cough drew my attention.

I looked over to where the sound originated and I spied Nik standing in the shadows, keeping his distance from my cell.

"I am truly sorry you are stuck here, gorgeous," Nik slurred, saddened.

"No, you're not; you are the one that brought me here. Are you drunk?" I barked, looking at the bottle of alcohol in his hands, "And you did not bring one for your *prisoner*?"

"Now, why would you be *my* prisoner? I would not have you here in the cells, if it was me. You would be in my bed," he smirked, "And yes, I am drunk, thank you very much."

"This is your home, isn't it?"

Not far from home; I just need to find a way out.

"No, this is my father's house. I am just his son, who he has given no rights to," as he took another swig.

"Aw, it must really suck doing what you would like all of the time," I remarked sarcastically.

"Niya, I really have no part in this."

"Again, you brought me here; so yes, Niko, you did have a part in this."

"Niya," Nik drew out.

Nik and I had talked several times since I had been here. It was always the same response. Quite frankly, I was getting tired of his half-ass excuses.

"Then help me escape," I said shortly.

"You know I can't."

"Remind me again why, Niko?"

He lowered his eyes and stepped out of the shadows, capping his bottle, "Because, if I help you, my father will have my head on a spike. Then he will find *you*, and a spike through your head would be a sweet dream compared to what will happen to you."

"He can't touch me, I am the princess," I gestured to my invisible crown on my head and waved my hands like I was bowing, from the floor.

Nik laughed and then lowered his eyebrows, "You are stripped of your title now; you know that, right? You cannot kill your parents, the King and Queen, and expect to maintain your status."

I razzed my lips, "Just one parent. That female was not my mother."

Nik's eyes squinted like he was about to talk, but I countered, "Your father is just a lord, what makes him think he in is a position to sit on *my* throne?"

"Are you an idiot, Niya? That *throne* is no longer yours. You forfeited it when the King and Queen died at *your* hands."

"My *powers* weren't working upon my wishes." I surged.

"They are still yours, controlled by your *wishes* or not. And they are very powerful," Nik paused, "I have never seen one fae hold as much as you, Niya. It almost seemed...godlike."

I sat up quickly at that remark and pointed my finger at him, "Watch your tone. I might be immobilized, but I *will* remember this conversation."

Nik let out a loud, annoyed sigh, and slid the alcohol bottle across the floor towards me. I grabbed it and uncapped the lid.

I whispered, "Thank you."

"Don't say I didn't do anything for you, gorgeous," Nik responded, and walked out of the confined, musky room.

I watched as the door clicked shut. Screams rolled through my parched throat as loud and as long as I could until my lungs couldn't hold any more. I flung the alcohol bottle against the bricks, and it shattered into a million pieces, liquid spewing everywhere.

Tears rolled through the dirt on my face, leaving tracks. I cried and screamed and cried some more until, wiping my face with the back of my hand, I gathered my anger, my will, and my stubbornness back to me.

I needed to find a way out. I was not going to be this weak thing that I was becoming.

I didn't know how long they'd planned to keep me, and I was starting to doubt I would ever leave here alive. My growling stomach was a constant distraction in my efforts to formulate an escape plan, and the scant amount of water provided by lecherous guards was never more than enough to dampen my tongue.

Was I going to be allowed a trial, at least?

Glancing over at the shattered bottle, I frowned.

I should *not* have thrown that bottle. Any taste other than dirty water and stale bread sounded so good to me in this moment and I had literally thrown it away.

I whimpered dramatically as I bent back down to lie on the floor. I continued counting the painfully slow water droplets from the ceiling.

It was water droplet two thousand, eight hundred, four before I was visited by the next guard bringing me my rations.

At least this time, I was provided warm bread and soup that was not thrown to the ground. Thank the eternals and all of the gods I would get to eat *real food.*

Chapter 43
Adryen

Enzo, Malcolm and I spent the last week creating a plan to visit the Silver Expanse and explore the club that resided there. Enzo rallied his pack and they stayed close to the border, waiting for his command. Malcolm made sure the sentries were practicing their hand-to-hand combat and getting all their training in for worst case scenario.

The three of us stared at the old, historic building as fae were lined up down the street to be let in. We walked together to the end of the line.

"What do we do now?" Enzo questioned.

Malcolm glanced over at Enzo, "We wait in line, dummy. It's a club. The bouncer has to approve your entry. We dressed up nice tonight so we should have no trouble getting in."

I gawked at Malcolm, not quite understanding how he knew what a club was. We did not have these establishments in Haldonia. I had to do more research after finding the map to know what it was.

"Do you think we are going to walk into fae stripping to nothing?" Enzo inclined, eyes wide and sparkling.

I guess they both had done their own research. We inched closer and I responded, "I don't think this is that type of club.

From the documents my parents had left, this is an upscale establishment. There are private rooms, a bar, dance floor, and lots of booths to just talk or hang out."

"Must be a boring owner," Enzo shrugged and continued, "If it were *my* club, I would have *all* the employees be naked."

Enzo nudged Malcolm as he laughed and the two continued their conversation about their alternative club visions.

My mind wandered to Niya, once again. This last week had been the worst week of my life. I missed her terribly and the worst part was that I didn't know if she was being exposed to any number of tortures that the Unseelie could cook up.

I missed her warmth; her scent; the way she called me on my bullshit; and most of all, the way she made me feel.

I missed her so much; it was hard to think clearly. I had been almost to the point of confining myself to my room and refusing to leave from panic and grief, but my first and my second would not let me destroy myself with brooding.

A spark of her pain trickled down our bond, and I froze, wincing.

Niya?

She must be close. Oh my gods; my mate was close...and in pain.

I nudged Malcolm's shoulder, "I feel her."

Malcolm raised an eyebrow, "Huh?"

More insistent now, "I *feel* her, Malcolm. She's nearby. I think she's in pain."

"It is probably just your imagination. There is no way they would keep their princess this close to their palace," dismissively.

We were closer to the brawny elf bouncer now.

"I don't think that I am. I haven't felt anything all week. And now—this," I waved to my ankles, "I can feel her pain in my ankles. They must have her in shackles, or something similar—"

"Names?"

Our conversation was cut short. The fire haired elf tapped his clipboard and repeated, exasperated, "Names?"

Enzo peaked over to the clipboard and the elf pulled it away growling, "What...are...yer...names?"

"Sheesh, fine. I am Enzo, this is Malcolm, and this is..." Enzo trailed off.

"Liro," I smiled sheepishly, "Hello."

The elf growled and tilted his head in, "Yer names an photos aren't on my list, so yer good to go in. But...this one," looking at Enzo, "looks like trouble. Watch yerselves."

Enzo saluted the male and sauntered inside as the elf flipped the papers back on his clipboard. I nodded politely and followed behind.

This place was immaculate. Everything looked spotless.

There had to be constant cleaning while the club was open.

No drinks spilled on the floor, nothing sticky, and not a speck of dust.

I didn't think this could even be consider a club.

I scanned the Nyte Club looking for anything or anybody that might hold some insight into finding that vampire I saw. I looked over at the bartender, who was also the same one from Vallynn's birthday party.

Short, glossy black hair and black leathery soft and stretchy wings shifted to face me. The glass she was cleaning dropped to the floor, letting out a shattered *crack* throughout the loud club.

Enzo and Malcolm split off in different directions while my feet moved toward the bartender.

She *had* to know Niya. They were chatting very familiarly during the party. I only briefly talked to her when I dropped off the vodka. She was very curt with me, so I didn't really get to know her.

I sat on the barstool as those sharp, golden eyes stared into mine.

Maybe tonight she would say more than one or two words to me.

Smiling slightly, I went to speak, and she cut me off, "What the *fuck* are you doing here?"

I pointed to myself, "Me? What do you mean? The bouncer let me in."

She looked around and lowered her voice, "What the hell is The King of Haldonia doing here? In The Silver Expanse. Shouldn't you be looking for—"

"Shh, my name is *Liro.*"

The vampire burst into laughter. I felt like curling up into a ball and rolling under the bar. Her booms of laughter suddenly made me feel very self-conscious.

"Okay, *Liro.* What are you drinking tonight?"

"Whiskey on the rocks, please," I paused, "I came here because this is a busy establishment and I wanted to get information on Niya's whereabouts."

"I'm Sahriah, by the way," she poured the whiskey in a small glass, "If I knew Niya's whereabouts, do you think I would be here pouring you a drink, Your Grace?"

"Um," I trailed off, "I don't know. Do you have an affiliation to her?"

"Do I? Affiliation?" She burst into laughter again, "She never said how embarrassingly funny you are."

Oh gods. Was this female a sister? A lover?

Sahriah must've been close to her for her to react so incredulously to my question. I let out a frustrated sigh and rubbed my head on the palm of my hand. Pain jerked through me, and I winced.

Sahriah's look softened, "Are you okay?"

"No," I grunted, "Niya is in pain. I can feel it...literally."

I took a swig of my whiskey. As soon as I'd placed it on the table. I looked up at the bartender and I saw her eyes wide and her jaw dropped.

"What?" I asked, not sure what I'd said to illicit that response.

"You can *feel* her *pain?*" suddenly very serious.

"It's a long story," I said, trying to avoid that topic for now.

"I don't know where she," Sahriah said softly, still shocked. "I miss my fierce friend; it has been too quiet without her around."

Ah, so, friend.

"What do you mean? Does she come here often?"

Sahriah shrugged a shoulder, "Something like that."

I needed to just get to the point. I blurted, "Does Lord Morelli have a son?"

"Why?" Sahriah questioned, appraisingly.

I growled, "I am trying to find her, help me out!"

"Are you normally this spastic?"

I had started to feel panicked again. I had gotten pulses of her emotions, and it was making me confused and petrified.

"You need to calm down. I cannot disclose information about our patrons."

"Are you saying that because you are helping her captives?" I accused.

Sahriah growled showing both of her fangs, "Fuck you, Your Majesty. You can take your crazy somehwere else," and she turned on her heels leaving me behind.

"Fucking perfect. Great job, Adryen," I scolded myself.

"Great job? What did you find out?" Enzo spoke up behind me.

In despair, "Nothing, let's leave."

He pouted, "Why? I was just having some fun. There are these two females over there," he pointed to the dance floor, "and I just wan—"

"—Let's go!" I cut in and stood from the bar, "This was a royal waste of my time. Niya is not here."

"But you said that yo—"

Annoyed, I cut Enzo off again, "I am leaving, with or without you, Lorenzo."

Enzo sighed dramatically, then grumbled, "Fine, but I am not portaling home with you, I will take the long way."

I rolled my eyes and walked out of the club to see Malcom leaning against a wall, rubbing his chin.

He replied, "No luck?"

I shook my head back and forth, full of hopelessness.

"Well, you would not believe what I just saw."

Raising my eyebrow, "What?"

"Finion is here, and he was carrying some weird ass kinky shit like rope, ball gag, and some iron shackles. He stuffed them all into a bag and started rushing down the streets."

"Which way did he go?"

Malcolm shrugged his shoulders and then looked over to me, "That was like an hour ago."

"Did you just decide to leave the club when we all split? You're such great help, *cousin*."

"What? There was nothing of interest inside of the building. Everything seemed normal. Nobody was talking about the princess, so I just left."

I groaned, and leaned along with him, watching a crowd pass.

Across the street, two dark hooded figures ran down the pavement, pushing others out of the way. People yelled after them, but they ignored the commotion. I looked down to see bare feet on one of them moving swiftly on the stone, trying to gain momentum, but straining.

I whispered, "This place is weird. Everyone is either yelling, grumpy, or running suspiciously through the streets."

"Did you find where Lord Morelli lives?" Malcolm questioned.

I looked back and the hooded fae were gone.

"Lord Morelli? The *High* Lord Morelli?" A voice chirped.

Enzo got between us, "What is it to you, neonate?"

The young, male vampire responded, "Lord Morelli's is the mansion at the end of The Silver Expanse. It's where all the roads meet."

A sentry bolted down the sidewalk, interrupting us while yelling, "Find her! She killed Vlad and escaped with a hooded male. He wants her back, *now!*"

Feeling the tug on my mating bond, I raced through people trying to find the two hooded figures. I looked down every alleyway and dark corner and found nothing.

She was here.

And that was *her.*

Chapter 44
Niya

I stared at the ceiling of my cell unabashedly wishing for *anything* to happen. The only thing that did was the need to blink; I counted and blinked.

At this rate, if the lack of nutrients was not going to kill me, the boredom would. I had lost track of how long I had been held captive, but it felt like months.

Nik sighed from inside of my cell, "You are becoming so boring to talk to, Niya."

"Well, when you leave me to count water and bricks, it doesn't exactly make for scintillating conversation, Nikolaj."

"What can I do to help?"

I growled, "I could use a bath."

"Sure," was all he replied.

Leaning up on my elbows, I snapped my head up to him, "Really?"

"Yes, really; I will get Vlad to come down and watch you. You won't have any privacy, but I can at least get you cleaned up. No one else needs to know. Just, please, don't do anything reckless."

Pouting, I asked, "Why would I be reckless? I am a good fae."

Nik chuckled, "*Good* is not a term I would have thought anyone could use for you. How about just don't get into any trouble, huh?"

I folded my arms over my chest, "Fine. You don't have to treat me like a child, Niko. I am far from that."

"Oh, trust me, I know that all too well," he winked at me.

Thinking on my feet, "Whatever happened to us?" I implored through lowered lashes.

"What do you mean, Princess?" The term from his lips sent a shiver of nausea into my gut.

"I *mean*," I continued, "that with our one encounter that night and all of the flirting afterward on the street, why didn't we ever have another go at things." I was looking for a possible out and was using the tools the gods had given me.

"I was told that several times that you had no interest in me, anymore," Nik spoke through lips curling on the edges. "You had found another male to warm your bed."

Bile rose in my throat as the thought of Adryen and the fear that I would never see him again burned my insides.

Without a response, I looked down at my ripped dress; I had pulled apart most of the fabric that had remained out of boredom these past days or weeks. My dress length sat above my knees and the tulle was pretty much gone, in tightened knots strewn across the cell.

Nik gestured with an outstretched hand, "Get up."

I groaned, putting my hands on the floor to help adjust myself to standing. Everything hurt; the iron spikes though my ankles were suffocating me inside and out. I was honestly shocked I had not gotten any type of infection yet.

The magic inside of me had been rendered moot, and I was not sure how the iron affected all the magic that had been coursing through me. It was still very much questionable if the iron could hold back all of it. I could still have a chance of escaping. Standing up slowly, I wobbled to catch my center and my knees gave out.

Nik grabbed me from under my shoulders and hauled me up, "I got you."

I sneered, "I can handle myself."

"Fine," and he let go.

Dropping to the floor again, this time my knees smacking hard with the fall, I growled, "Fine! Owwww," I whined.

Nikolaj leaned down to me, pulling unkempt hair from my face, "I am trying to help you the best that I can, Niya. You don't have to play big tough female with me. Let me take you to the bathtub, please. It is the least that I can do for you."

I nodded slightly and Nik swooped me up in his arms and carried me out of the cell and up the stairs. I took in every single view. The winding steps, the change of colors in the walls. Being kept in a windowless cell, with barely any light did a number on me. The sunlight shone through the windows, and I squinted, trying to adjust my eyes.

Nik scrunched his nose.

My smell was probably rancid. This male was doing everything in his power to keep calm around me.

I murmured, "Sorry."

"It's not your fault. I should have asked my father to let you bathe sooner. I should be the one that's sorry."

We entered a doorway to the sound of running water. Nik set me down on the bench in the bathroom and tensed when my feet hit the floor.

"You have twenty minutes. Get cleaned up as fast as possible, so I can get you back to your cell. I have one of my shirts sitting in the sink for you to put on," Nik let out a sigh, "It's all I could find on short notice."

"Nik," I looked down at my ankles, "Can you take these off me so I could bathe without the pain?"

Nik said hesitantly, "No, but I can unlink the chain to give you more mobility. Niya, please don't make me regret this."

A smile crossed my face, "Of course."

A large light-skinned sentry walked in and grunted at Nik. Nik nodded and slipped out of the door, closing it behind him. I looked back at the brooding guard and his black eyes stared into mine, "Hurry up, prisoner. I haven't got all day."

I can escape this. I am strong enough. I am powerful enough. I am a goddess' daughter.

I can do this.

And I will.

Looking up at the sentry seductively, I tsked, "Don't rush me, I have twenty minutes to enjoy myself; and you have twenty minutes to watch," I winked.

Stripping down to nothing as quickly as I could while attempting to look enticing, I put on the show of my life.

The guard watched my every move, shifting on his feet as I pulled laces, clasps, and fasteners all while keeping eye contact with him. I loosened my bodice, shimmying it to the left and to the right, tempting him with the tiny peekaboo's of my breasts. Once I could see the bulge in his pants indicating I had done my job well, I dropped the dress down to my ankles, revealing everything.

Smirking, "Why don't you come closer, so you can get a better look," I teased.

I will kill this male and not lose a moment of sleep afterward.

The guard blinked and straightened like he'd snapped out of a trance, "No," Vlad grumbled.

I hobbled to the tub, doing my best to look sultry instead of lamed, and let my body sink into the...

Oh, my fucking gods the water felt *amazing!*

Dunking my entire body under, I relished the memory of the privileges I'd once had; like hot running water. I pulled myself up out of the water to catch my breath and breathed in deeply, eyes closed, letting the warm water sluice off of my face and bare chest.

I missed this.

Not as much as I missed him; my mate. The iron bindings cut off my communication through our mating bond. I could not feel or hear anything from him, and it felt so incredibly lonely. I felt the loss of him greater than anything I'd ever experienced in my life. It was greater than any physical pain.

I frowned.

Niya, you are strong enough and powerful enough

You can do this.

And you will.

I looked over at the guard, and with renewed intent, I snatched the soap board that was sitting on the edge of the bathing tub. I started rubbing myself down slowly, making sure to lather every curve of my body; paying special attention to my breasts. I lathered them in lazy circles, biting my bottom lip, and making sure to appear as if I'd had no idea what I was doing to him.

The guard, Vlad, began to inch forward, licking his ample lips. Moving in closer, he grinned, "I would be careful how you wash yourself, Your Highness. You are my prisoner."

I wasn't *his* anything.

"Oh yeah? Why is that?" I placed my leg up on the porcelain and began to lather it, wiping in up and down strokes, suggestively.

Vlad groaned and dropped to his knees at my eye level, absolutely unable to stop himself.

I smirked, handing him the soap, "Could you get my back for me?"

Vlad, to one side of me, rubbed my back with the soap, making sure to get every single speck of dirt; even the invisible ones. Dirty bubbles ran down my body and I splashed the water up, making sure to rinse myself as best I could.

I turned my face towards his and put my hands on his cheeks, "Thank you," I whispered.

He nodded and licked his thick lips again, starting to move in for a kiss.

With my hands on his cheeks, I used all my strength to slam his lascivious face onto the rim of the tub. He growled in pain and grabbed his bloodied face with both hands. I fumbled out of the tub, smacking his head against it again. This time, he screamed at me, "You bitch!"

The searing pain in my ankles was distracting, but I knew that I had one chance and I had to push through this.

I curled my fingers into the hair at his nape and dunked his head in the water, putting all of my weight into ensuring that he would not be coming up for air.

He struggled and scratched at my forearms and hands. Vlad tried to pull away, but I pushed and pushed as if my life had depended on it; because it had. Vlad's legs started the flail and I stepped on his calves, securing them in place. Only a couple more seconds passed before he went utterly still.

After several more seconds of no movement, I fell backwards and finally let out a breath that I felt like I'd been holding as long as Vlad had. I looked at Vlad's limp body and just watched in shock.

Horror.

Realization of what I'd just done.

Vlad was one of my citizens; my sentry in The Silver Expanse.

Panic overtook me.

I was a killer, and I would lose sleep over this. I could just stay here and let Lord Morelli run a spike through my head which may be deserved, but I decided that I didn't feel like dying today.

Limping over to the sink, I snagged Nik's mahogany and dark oak scented shirt and slipped it over myself. It sat right above the bottom of my rear cheeks. Great, I was going to end up escaping practically naked.

Desperate and no longer caring about my unbecoming state, I felt around Vlad's pants for keys, I snaked my hand in every pocket until metal hit my fingers.

"Yes!" I let out.

Not sure how much time I had left before Nik came back, I looked around for something to bite on. A small towel lay on the toilet; I grabbed it, placing it tightly rolled into my mouth in preparation for removing the iron shackles. I'd tried unlocking them with almost every single key and none of them were working.

Punching the floor, I looked at the last key and closed my eyes sending a silent prayer for this to be *the* key. I slid the key into the lock, and it did not turn.

No.

I slid it back into the lock, fiddling with it and wiggling it every way to see if maybe it was user error. The lock still did not budge.

I pushed the towel further into my mouth and screamed into it.

Fuck!

A second scream rolled through my chest.

A knock sounded at the door, and I whipped around to face it. I was dead. I was *beyond* dead.

"Hello?" A raspy male voice echoed.

I backed up onto Vlad laying halfway in the tub and the door swung open. A blonde-haired male came in and smiled.

"I have been looking for you. I heard screams from the hallway and ran here to make sure you were okay."

I tilted my head. This was not a sentry. He did not even look remotely familiar. I ripped the towel out of my mouth, "Who are you?"

"Oh," he perked up and bowed, "I am here to save you. Adryen sent me."

My eyes watered, "Thank you," is all I could let out before my throat closed up from a mixture of happiness, relief, and sobbing tears.

The male pulled out a key and reached down towards me, "We don't have much time, grab that towel and bite into it."

Nodding, I did what I was told. He placed his key into the lock and my shackles clicked open. My eyes closed with relief as sobs wracked my chest.

"This is going to be incredibly painful, but I am going to try to make it quick," He patted my shackles. I winced at the jolt of pain that the pat had caused.

I stared into his chocolate brown eyes and tried not to cry anymore while traitorous tears rolled down my face. Ripping out the shackles was going to hurt like hell.

"This is going to hurt like hell," he echoed my thoughts.

I remarked, ironically, "No shit."

He chuckled and then pulled both iron bars out at the same time. Pain engulfed me starting from my ankles and moved swiftly up my body. I shrieked and bawled at the same time. Magic started flowing through me again as the healing muscles stretched and knitted.

The pain of my body attempting to heal itself was excruciating. It felt like I was regrowing limbs.

My world was getting hazy, and I just wanted to sleep. I closed my eyes and breathed steadily.

"We have to go, *now!*" The male grabbed my wrist and pulled me up. The weight shifting onto my feet sent another shot of anguish through me. I seethed and twitched, trying to keep my balance.

"Your powers are going to heal this wound faster than you realize. It has already started to close your skin, but we need to move."

I nodded, "I will be seen, though."

"No," he reached into the pack on his back and pulled out a black, hooded cloak, "Put this on, and keep your head down. You will look like a commoner passing by."

"This is not going to work," I said as he pushed fabric onto me.

I whirled the cloak around my shoulders and snapped the clasp in place, pulling the hood over my head. Looking over at the male, "What's your name?"

"That's not important at the moment," the male grabbed my wrist, and we started running down the hallway. Swerving through male and females, I made sure to keep my head down as we moved.

The male stopped in front of a door and looked back at me breathing heavily, "You need to stay close to me as we go through the streets. There will be people that want you back in that cell if they see your face. Keep your head down and try to keep up."

Looking down at my ankles then back up to those chocolate eyes, "Okay."

We bolted off into the streets. I kept my head down, but a sense of familiarity hit me. I *knew* these streets. We were in The Silver Expanse!

That Vamphole.

He kept me in his own fucking mansion!

Rage surged through me, and my power started to boil. I took a deep breath in an attempt to calm my nerves.

"We need to get to an alleyway," I whispered.

A guard yelled, "Find her!"

"What?" He said in front of me, still running.

Grabbing his wrist, I jerked him into a dark shadow within the alley and a portal crackled vibratingly in front of us.

"Go!" I seethed.

The male looked back at me, "How do I know where we are going?"

"Just trust me, please! I will get us as close to Adryen as possible without being seen."

The male hesitantly nodded and walked through the portal.

I followed behind, leaving no trace of ever being there.

As we walked out of the portal, Cleome's beauty shimmered in my eyes.

Chapter 45
Niya

The male's eyes widened as I walked past him to the people gawking in the streets.

Delilah ran to me, hands outstretched, "Niya!"

She suffocated me with a hug and whispered, "You can't be here, they will find you."

I returned the hug and did not let go, "I am so sorry," is all I could manage before getting choked up.

"Sorry for what?" She pushed away from me, "It was not your fault; anybody who knows you believes that. I told you that your powers held a great deal of death and destruction. I am truly sorry about your family."

"Lilah, what do I do?"

She backed away from me, "You need to leave. Go into the forest until things settle down a bit. The entire kingdom is going to know that you've escaped and will be searching for you. I will make up a little tote for your journey, but you need to make haste to Haldonia, girl," she paused and looked at my companion, "You are not Adryen. My poplars did not mention brown eyed fae in their travels. Who are you?"

The male had our rapt attention, "Fin," he replied finally.

"Well, Fin, come with me to get some supplies for your journey. Niya," I looked over to Delilah who continued, "Go to the stables, there is a friend waiting for you."

A smile crossed my face as I ran to the stables. The workers shot out of my way as I ran, flailing, toward Nero, who snorted at my arrival.

"I thought you were dead!" I breathed, knowing full well that the damned horse did not understand a word that I'd said. I placed my hand on his neck and he snickered, pushing his snout into me. I kissed his nose and hugged him.

Whispering, "I missed you," and started saddling him up for our journey.

Several minutes later, Fin's cool and mellow voice chimed in, "Are you ready?"

I whirled around to see him with a satchel of food and water. There were the clothes left over from my trip here a while back, so I had time to change into something more comfortable, that actually fit. I kept the black cloak clasped around my neck, pulling the hood over my head, "I am."

"You look good; healed," the male, Fin, said eyeing me.

I smiled and nodded my approval, mounting Nero, "The healing powers, thanks to Adryen. Honestly, I feel so good in my own body at the moment." I slid my hand down Nero's mane, "We can take turns riding, so you're not walking all day. I can't use any more of my portals to get us to Adryen. They may be able to track them. Traveling on foot and horseback would be safer."

"That sounds perfect, because if I have to jump through another one of your portals, I might lose the contents of my stomach."

I smiled and we left Cleome behind in silence as we trekked through the heavily wooded forest. Last time I'd been here, I was being chased by a shadow. The shadow that gutted me.

I still could not feel Adryen.

I should be able to feel everything from him. Unless something was blocking my powers, or his.

I looked over at Fin and he was staring intently at me.

Squinting my eyes, I whined, "I can't feel him."

"Why would you be able to? Doesn't the bond cut off after being so far away."

"No, because we aren't far from his castle, I should feel something."

Fin stopped Nero and faced me, "Give me your hands," he demanded.

"Why?"

"I am trying to help, Niya. Please allow me."

I waited several moments and then finally gave him my hands.

"This might hurt, but it will ease your anxiety," Fin placed his hands on mine.

Suddenly feeling dizzy and weak I managed to reply, "Wha—?"

Darkness enveloped me.

∞∞∞∞∞

I jerked awake to see Rose and Fin hovering over me with concern in her eyes.

I rubbed my head, "Where am I?"

Rose blurted, "Oh my gosh, Niya! Are you okay? Finion here was trying to help you and you fell off of your horse. He had to bring you back here to Cleome."

Placing my hand on my head, I felt for any bumps or cuts.

Nothing.

The healing powers I'd obtained from Adryen must have worked very quickly for me not to feel any pain at all.

"Delilah sent for me as soon as she found out," Rose breathed.

Not really caring how'd she had gotten here. I got up and pulled her into a tight hug.

She released a small breath, "Oh," from her lips and eventually hugged me back.

"I missed you," I stated calmly.

She giggled, "I missed you too, Niya."

Looking over at Fin, "Could you give us a moment please?"

Fin nodded and exited Delilah's familiar home.

Rose stood there with her hands behind her back and smiled, "I am so happy you are okay."

"Yeah," I rubbed my head, "Me, too."

We stared at each other for several moments before I asked, "How is Vallynn? Kaldamir?"

"Oh, Kaldamir is great! It was a little rough when you got captured, but things are running smoothly now with Vallynn on the throne."

"Wait, Vallynn actually took the throne? I am shocked!"

Rose replied, "Yeah, it is quite shocking, to be honest. We were not sure with what happened and all."

She chuckled and I reached out to touch her hand, "Rose," I drew out.

"Hmm?" She replied.

"How are you? I know, with our blood oath, being away from each other was hard. It was probably better that I was so far away. I was in so much pain in my captivity. They put the high-security shackles on me."

"Oh, that is dreadful. On a positive note, you look great!" She motioned toward my attire and gave a forced smile.

I furrowed my eyebrows at the strange focus on my appearance. Rose was normally very concerned about my wellbeing. I must be absolutely glowing with renewed vigor for her to shift to this topic so completely.

"Tell me more about Vallynn," I gave a wary smile, "Does he truly enjoy his new life?"

"Yes, he does. When he claimed the throne, he couldn't have been happier. He has even put me in his court. He says that I have the most brilliant mind, and he could use me as his bookkeeper."

I leaned back and my voice elevated an octave higher, "Bookkeeper? You, a bookkeeper? Rose," laughing, "That...is a choice."

Rose smiled at me, "When you come home, I would love to prove to you how amazing I am!"

"I need to find Adryen first, then I can find a way to come see you without getting captured again. I think I am on Kaldamir's shitlist right now."

"Maybe; nothing has really been said."

Interesting, considering I was the Crowned Princess.

"Niya, it is getting late. You should rest up for your journey back to Haldonia tomorrow."

"Oh," I looked down, "I had forgotten."

A little spark of happiness zinged at the realization that I would see Adryen again...tomorrow.

"You will have to tell me everything when you come back to Kaldamir. When it is safe, of course."

"Why don't you come to Haldonia with me?"

"I just got promoted to bookkeeper, I can't let Vallynn down now. Besides, wouldn't it look weird if I just disappeared?"

I thought about this for a while, and finally concluded, "I guess you are right. I am going to miss you Rose. I love you."

Rose's eye twitched and then she smiled, "You too, Niya."

She walked to the door where Fin was waiting to reenter.

Fin bowed slightly at Rose as she disappeared. He walked into the living room where I sat, "Get some rest, Niya. We have a long journey tomorrow."

Nodding my head, I moved over to Delilah's wooden couch and laid down flat, deep sleep capturing me.

Chapter 46
Adryen

I paced back and forth in front of the massive windows of my room. I peered out onto the ocean and the sunset on the horizon. I felt like I couldn't breathe. My lungs were collapsing and the only thing that might save me...was her.

My mate.

I was getting restless trying to figure out ways to find her. It seemed damned near impossible. Malcolm had nothing new to report and neither did Enzo.

This search seemed doomed.

All I could think about was her, and my mind could not leave her. Not one second passed without feeling the quick glimpse of pain down our bond that day.

I put my hand on my heart, the pain was real.

My heart was aching for her.

If I didn't find her, and have her back in my arms soon, I might literally die.

This mating bond had latched its claws in too deep and I was too emotionally connected to be away from her for this extended period.

Our investigations were at a standstill. We had no advancements or clues to where Niya could be. I hated myself for just missing her in The Silver Expanse. After that moment, she had just disappeared.

I turned my gaze to the left and noticed that the poplar trees had started growing faster than normal around the castle.

I growled out loud, "What could Delilah possibly want now?! I have given her everything!"

With The Divide down, her land was significantly warmer. Her poplars should no longer need to creep further into Haldonia.

Walking down the stairs, I stormed out of the castle and to the poplar trees blowing in a phantom wind. I turned my hand into fists and stopped in front of the single poplar standing tall. I was unsure why they were here. I had given them everything they'd wanted but they started showing up more often; as of several weeks ago.

My mind and body were very out of sorts, and I was not in control of myself. The leash on my anger was long and loose since she'd been taken, and my patience had worn thin.

I was a walking storm.

I peeked off to the side to see a straight row of poplar trees and stared down the perfect line they made. I shook my head at the strangeness of the sight.

"What do you want?" I seethed, "I have given you and Lady Delilah everything you could have possibly wanted. Why do you intrude on my personal space when you have your own plot?"

I was aggravated, and impatient that this poplar would not turn into their fae form.

I did not have time for this.

A shudder came from the tree. I backed up as the tree transformed into a beautifully green curly haired female.

"You stepped on my roots, rude." A little whimper escaped her.

"Oh my gods," I threw my hands in the air, "I wasn't intentionally trying to! I needed your attention, and I got it, didn't I?!"

The dryad cleared her throat, "I guess so..." she paused and looked me up and down, examining me for truth and continued, "We tried to help you, Your Majesty." She pointed down at the line of poplar trees, "We made a path for you to follow, but you just ignored us. What else do we need to do; draw you a map?" She spat and then paused, noting my disheveled and distraught features, "Are you okay, Your Majesty? You seem unwell."

Being honest with myself, I was unwell. My days, and even weeks were blurring together. Everything without Niya was just a blur.

I slowly replied, "Please forgive me, I did not mean—"

She looked at the ground, "Please stop apologizing and listen!" She was screaming now, which stole my attention back to her words.

I stared at her, blinking.

The dryad continued, "Niya stopped by a couple of weeks ago, and when we realized she never made it to you, we started planting ourselves in hopes you would follow us to our village. Our Lady is expecting you. She thinks she can help you find her."

"What?" I asked, trying to shake my stupor, "Why couldn't you just walk into the castle and tell me?!"

She frowned, "Because you have been beside yourself, Your Majesty. We were afraid of you lashing out at us," pausing, she backed up a little from me, "We will be expecting you tomorrow, yes?"

I responded, "Yes, should I come alone?"

"You don't have to," is all she said before turning herself back into a poplar.

A soft thud sounded behind me, and I whirled round to see Malcolm.

"Well, that was interesting."

"What?"

Malcolm laughed, "I was on top of the castle keeping watch and saw the dryad. Super interesting, those fae. So, when are we leaving?"

We walked back to the castle, "Why is it always a '*we*' with the both of you. Can't I just do things alone?"

"Absolutely not," Malcolm started, "You are king, and you are in a very vulnerable state right now and Kaldamir knows it. With Vallynn denying the throne and the Fae appointing Lord Morelli, they are waiting for you to mess up," he sighed, "And your temper, cousin; you are a mess."

"I probably shouldn't go to their lands tomorrow, should I?

"No, but the poplar seemed adamant, and truthful. We will go as the three of us."

I nodded, leaving the heavy lifting of decision making right now to Malcolm.

∞∞∞∞∞

I spent the rest of the day in the sculpting studio working on the pottery wheel; constructing, deconstructing, and remaking the same piece over and over again until all thoughts were drowned out.

Exhaustion overtaking me, I laid on the couch that Niya and I were so close on and took in a deep breath.

Her scent was no longer in this room, or my bedroom, or this castle. I still tried, every time, to see if I could smell her.

But I couldn't. It sent me to the depths of despair, and I felt hollow inside my chest thinking about the loss. I looked up at the cracked ceiling for a while and eventually closed my eyes, passing out from exhaustion.

∞∞∞∞

The next day, we took an incredibly long walk to Cleome, despite my instinct to just portal there. Enzo, in his wolf form, trailed behind me as Malcolm followed from above.

Sweaty and annoyed, we finally reached Cleome.

A dainty jade dryad came out with a solemn look on her face. She held her hand out to me and I took it in my grasp, kissing her knuckles, "Thank you for allowing us to visit your beautiful home again, Delilah."

A soft thud came from behind me, and Malcolm quickly came to my side.

I pointed down and said, "This is Enzo. He is my first in command. If it is okay with you, he will stay in his wolf form."

She nodded slowly, eyeing me warily, "That's okay. Please come in."

She gestured inside of the familiar house connected to a very large tree and we walked in. It was so much more magnificent than when I'd stopped by the first time. Malcolm struggled with his wings but tried not to show any discomfort in front of the lady. I sat on the bench, and she made some tea and poured it into three cups.

She handed the both of us a cup and then looked down at Enzo.

I quickly responded, "He is fine, thank you."

"I am so happy you're here. Once I heard about Niya's affiliation to you from her friend, Rose, I sent my dryads to search for you and bring you to me." She took a sip from her tea, "I am Delilah, Lady of Cleome," she gave her hand to Malcolm, who obliged to grasp it and provided a gentle kiss.

Malcolm and I both sipped the tea and we instantly warmed from the liquid. I raised an eyebrow, "What is this?"

"Magically enhanced calming tea. I hope you don't mind."

"No," Malcolm stated smoothly, "It is delicious!"

Delilah laughed, "I am glad you like it," she steadied herself and continued, "Niya was here a couple of weeks ago with a male. We gave her Nero with the hope that he would get her to you, Your Grace. But, when she left, the horse came running back to us. I should have known something had gone wrong. I feel terrible."

"Who was the male with her? What did he look like?" Malcolm questioned.

Delilah took another sip, "Golden blonde hair, chocolate brown eyes, muscular, but not like the both of you. Pointed ears. He had this nasty demeanor about him. Very pushy."

"Fin." Malcolm and I said at the same time.

Shit!

Enzo whined from the floor, and I scratched his ear reassuringly.

"Yes, that was his name. You know him?" Delilah questioned.

I spoke up, "Yes, and we need to cut this meeting short. I need to gather my troops and send them out on a rescue mission. Finion is dangerous. He has the power of mind manipulation and there is no telling what he is doing to her."

Delilah abruptly stood up, "Is she going to be okay?" Concern blanketed her features.

"I don't think he would do anything to harm her. He is probably doing this to get back at us; but we *have* to find her—now."

Delilah put a hand on my shoulder, "She is powerful, Your Majesty, but she is also very vulnerable. She has just had everything taken from her. When you find her, be gentle with her heart."

I gave a slight bow to Delilah and the three of us stepped outside. I looked at Malcolm, "Send the spies through every inch of this kingdom. Question everybody. If you see Finion, don't kill him unless Niya is with him. We may never find her if we can't torture her location out of him," I looked at Enzo, "Can you rally your pack and have them search up and down the borders and through the woods to get his scent?"

Malcolm took to the skies and Enzo chuffed in response and ran through the woods back home.

I turned around to Delilah, "I will bring the Unseelie Princess back."

Lady Delilah nodded her understanding as I created a portal. I jumped through without any doubt or trepidation that I was going to bring *my* queen home.

Chapter 47
Niya

It was an incredibly long journey from Cleome to Haldonia's castle, but Fin and I finally made it through the forest to Adryen's massive home.

I took in the beautiful white hues of his castle, and the high spires that reached for the heavens.

I missed this place, with all my heart.

Looking back down, Adryen ran up to me and smiled, "Niya! You are home."

Adryen embraced me with a light hug and continued, "You must be exhausted, come," He motioned for us to walk into the castle.

Fin kept pace behind me as the three of us entered.

This place was exactly how I'd remembered, except, it was empty.

"Adyren, why is nobody here?"

"Oh, I told everybody to take time for themselves, Adryen cleared his throat and gestured toward Fin, "You are dismissed, Fin. Thank you for finding her and bringing her back. I don't know what I would do without you."

I gave a small wave to Fin, who nodded his dismissal, as he made his way out of the castle.

Adryen pecked my cheek, "I am so happy to see you."

I grinned and held my cheek, "I am, too, Adryen."

Leaning in, I grasped his neck and pulled him into me for a kiss.

He chuckled and pulled away from me, "You are tired, I am going to draw a bath so you can relax."

Shocked, and slightly upset, "Wait. I thought we would talk."

"I figured you would want to clean up first."

"No," I barked and sighed, "I'm sorry, but no; I want to talk to you. I missed your voice. I missed you Adryen." My need for him felt unfulfilled.

"Niya," he laughed, "It's okay."

We walked to the bedroom and Adryen opened the heavy door for me.

I'd missed this room. The stupidly large windows, the ginormous bed and accompanying furniture. We sat down on the bed together and I looked into his eyes.

Adryen's distinct medium blue eyes met mine. A little whimper escaped me as the nearness of him began to soothe my soul.

I talked about everything. How I'd gotten captured, and the spikes in my ankles. I looked down and showed him the scars and how my magic was able to fully repair, through ossification, the separation of my ankle. I explained who Nik was and how he'd tried his best to make me as comfortable as possible. I also told of how Fin's efforts were heroic in saving me.

"He really planned a great escape. Thankfully my magic was still strong enough to portal us out of the alleyway."

"I am sure my advisor did everything he could to make sure you were safe and comfortable."

"Fin is a great advisor, Adryen. Don't let your friendship ever falter. I really don't know where I would be without him."

Adryen chuckled, "He is great, isn't he," Adryen put his hand on my shoulder, "Are you ready for your bath?"

Unsure of how long we'd sat there talking, I felt ready to wash away my capture and imprisonment.

"Yes, I think I am ready," I smiled and reached for Adryen's hand.

He quickly got up and walked toward the bathroom, "Niya, I hope you enjoy this."

An awkward laugh escaped me, "Why wouldn't I enjoy it?"

Adryen was not responding to my quick remarks like he normally would. I had to question if he was still mad at me from before the capture.

Something was off.

"Adryen," I called as he turned on the running water.

He breathed out a sigh, "Yes, Niya?"

A frown crossed my face, "Are you okay? I feel like I did something to upset you."

Adryen walked out of the bathroom and gave a sheepish smirk, "What do you mean? Everything is fine, Niya. You are just tired. You just need a warm bath and some rest."

Quickly accepting his reassurance, "You're right. I'm sorry."

I walked to the bathroom behind Adryen as turned off the tub faucet. I looked down at the bubbling water and a little squeal of excitement left me.

"You know, I am honestly shocked you dismissed everybody. I would have thought Daphne would've refuse," I said grinning.

Adryen ran his hands through his hair, "I dismissed everybody, even the biggest help. Even though she had been basically absent since the queen died. It wasn't until you arrived that she'd become helpful again."

That was really rude. Daphne did an amazing job taking care of me in this castle.

Adryen knew that.

"Adryen," I looked down, "Daphne is a great help, I don't think you truly meant that."

"You're right, Niya. I did not mean that. She is fine," he retorted, "Daphne is with her family."

Shyly, I questioned, "Do you want to get in with me?" I motioned toward the bathtub and winked.

Just imagining Adryen without his clothes sent spikes of excitement through me.

He was too beautiful, and I *needed* him in this tub with me.

"No, Niya," he replied, "I am okay," and walked out of the door, closing it behind him.

I'd had had enough of his aloof attitude. I stared at the closed door for minutes, thinking about what I wanted to say to him.

He said he'd loved me in the ballroom, and I knew he did.

I must have hurt him deeply.

Determined and confident I would help him with his mood, I walked to the door and flung it open.

A flash of light pulsed from the bedroom and my eyes squinted closed.

∞∞∞∞

The light vanished as quickly as it shone, and Adryen sat in front of me in new clothes. He was adorned in royal garb. I smiled and giggled at how handsome he was. He was holding a bouquet of colorful wild-picked flowers in one hand and a clenched fist in the other.

Seeing Adryen wear such formal clothing was a sight to behold.

"You look very dashing, Your Majesty," I bowed delicately.

"Thank you, Niya, but there is no need for formalities from you."

"I feel like I am underdressed," looking down at my body wrapped in a towel.

"You look fine; don't be silly."

Blushing a little, I inclined my head slightly and asked, "What are those flowers for?"

"Goodness, how rude of me," he handed them to me, "These are for you; wild-picked from this morning."

Grasping them in my hand, I attempted to take a good solid sniff, but I could not smell anything. That was strange; maybe I was unwell. I continued, "But it's the afternoon? I was only in the bathroom for a couple of hours."

Adryen beamed, "What do you mean? We just got up an hour or so ago and I went downstairs to pick some flowers for you," he moved in closer to me.

I did not know how this could be true, but I trusted Adryen and went along with it. Maybe I had fallen asleep and waking up had me a little groggy.

Adryen put the palm of his hand on my cheek and gently kissed my other, "Niya, I love you," he bent down on one knee and opened his clasped hand, "Will you marry me?"

My breath caught, "What?"

"We have a blood oath, Adryen. I thought we agreed not to marry until we were both ready."

He was confused at first but then responded, "Yes, which we are. You don't remember talking about this?"

"No," I murmured, "I guess I am having trouble remembering things lately."

Trying to remember when we'd had that conversation, my body started feeling very light and weak. Suddenly, I felt very tired and was not able to think any harder about this.

I smiled faintly, "Adryen, this is so sweet, but unnecessary."

He pushed the box at me with a pear drop diamond ring, "It's really not. Marry me, Niya."

"Okay, yes. Yes!" I kissed his cheek and sat on the bed with my towel still wrapped around me.

"Will you lay with me, *husband?*" I smirked as that word escaped my mouth.

Adryen did a slight body twitch after my question, "Yes," and sat next to me.

I pulled the blankets back and slipped under them, snuggling into the comfort of his large bed, patting the spot next to me, "I missed you."

Adryen chuckled, "Why is that? We just saw each other."

Letting out a breath, "I don't know. I just really miss you," running my fingertips down his arm, "and your touch."

He placed his head on the pillow beside me and I swept my hand up his stomach, to his chest and planted it on his masculine jawline.

Adryen tensed and his tone went dry, "I don't think I am tired right now. You should rest, and I will see you—"

I shouted, "No! Adryen," pausing to really think about my next words, "When was the last time you touched me, truly? You blow me off, and continue blowing me off until I get pissed and shout at you. What is going on?"

Shock.

Shock shown on both of our faces as my brows pinched together, "I want this so badly that it hurts, Adryen. We are mates, but why do I feel like you don't want me."

"I," Adryen moved away from me and lifted himself off the bed, "I do want you, Niya. That's why I asked you to marry me. Do you not want that? A marriage?"

"Of course I do! That's why I sealed the blood oath with you."

My heart was breaking into tiny little pieces. I really did not understand why Adryen was acting this way. I don't even remember the last time he'd kissed me on the lips.

"I feel unwanted," I mumbled.

"You shouldn't," Adryen's footsteps trailed to the door.

I looked up at him and a nefarious grin crossed his face, "Everything is fine, I promise," and opened the door, slamming it behind him.

I flinched at the anger that boiled to the surface and closed my eyes, trying to take long, steady breaths.

When I was finally ready to open them, the most singular thing happened.

Chapter 48
Niya

A knock echoed in my ears, and I was standing in Adryen's bedroom in front of his large mirror. I tilted my head to glance at my hair moving stiffly behind me. Touching the bump right above my forehead, I ran my fingers to the gold crown. Trailing my fingers further back, my hair did not move.

Immobile and lifeless curls stuck out from my head.

I growled, "What the fuck is this?"

Straightening my silk button down pajama shirt and shorts, I quickly moved to the door, cracking it open to see Adryen peeking from outside.

Giggling, "Why did you knock? It's your room."

"I wanted to make sure you weren't startled when I walked in," He pushed the door open all the way and entered. He was holding a clothing bag over his shoulder, being careful not to bump it on anything.

Adryen's appearance was magnificent. He was wearing a black tuxedo with a white dress shirt underneath and his hair was beautifully groomed. He trimmed his facial hair down to a shadow. I lifted my hand and put it on his cheek, "You look ravishing, Adryen."

He chuckled, "Thank you, I would hope so considering we are getting married today."

Wait, no. I was not supposed to see him before the wedding. It was a bad omen!

"You can't be here! It's not good," I pushed on his shoulder, trying to force him out.

He laughed, "What do you mean? You told me you did not care if I saw you or not. You asked me to fetch your wedding dress."

I don't remember ever saying something like that. Actually, I would never say something that absurd.

He held out the nude, zippered garment bag, "Doogan just finished it this morning."

I wanted to be excited, I really did. But something just did not seem right. I was just coming from the bathroom and his proposal happened in a blink, and now it was our wedding day. Was I on elixirs? A sound escaped from me as I tried to hold back my perturbation, "Thank you! I am sure he did a wonderful job."

I grasped the bag out of Adryen's hand and walked to the closet to hang it up, trying not to wrinkle it, "How long has it been since the proposal? It feels like it was yesterday."

Or even twenty minutes ago.

Adryen's eyebrow rose, "Don't be silly, you should know how long it has been."

I mumbled, distastefully, "If I knew, I would not have asked. Now, would I?"

I turned away from the dress and faced him in exasperation.

Patronizing, Adryen asked, "Have you been heavy drinking again?"

I sneered, "What?"

Adryen moved closer to me and kissed my forehead, "It is a year today since the proposal, Niya. Don't get all worked up over nothing," he smiled, "I will see you in a little bit."

There was no telling when he would actually return; a minute, a year, ten years...

He walked out of the room, and I felt like I could throw something at him with my anger and frustration. I tried to create something, anything with my magic and nothing would happen. I was devoured by my impotent rage.

Breathing through my nostrils and closing my eyes, I composed myself and thought through my next steps.

Adryen was my mate, and I did in fact want this with him. We sealed a blood oath, and even if I did not feel like right now was the right time, it was still happening.

Also, drinking heavy again? I would never do such a thing around Adryen like that. My party days were over. Every now and then I would ask Sahriah to top me off, but I was not an addict.

Turning back around to the zipped-up dress bag, I placed my hand on the zipper and pulled it down to the floor.

The contents of the bag spilled out. I scrunched my nose distastefully as a pure white dress flowed in front of me. I didn't wear white as snow clothing. I'd had enough of the snow and, besides, it was unheard of for the Unseelie.

Grabbing the bottom of the dress, I pulled it out completely and slipped the hanger from the bag itself. Hanging it up on the door of the closet, I took in my wedding dress in all of its glory.

A curve-hugging style, mermaid wedding dress hung before me. I shuddered a little bit at the fact that this white dress was not my style; at all. Tugging at the lace bodice, the strapless sweetheart neckline struck me next.

I frowned, deeply, "This is not my style," and trailed my hand down the skirt. Layers of cascading organza ruffles fluffed out as the sweep train touched the floor.

I groaned, "Please at least have a slit, or even a strappy back."

Turning the dress around, the back was centered with a zipper and covered with pearl buttons. There was no slit to be found.

Adryen didn't even know me. Panic rose to the surface as I pondered this hideous dress. I couldn't get married in this!

Right?

I sat on the bed for what felt like hours just staring at this monstrosity. A gentle knock sounded at the door and pink hair with bright eyes peeked in, "Hello," Daphne waved.

"You're back from visiting your family?"

She stammered, "Oh, yes. That was fine. I wanted to be here for your special day," she said with a smile that didn't reach her eyes.

Giving a slight smile back and throwing my hand toward the dress, "This can't be serious, right?"

Daphne fully entered the room and walked toward the dress, "It's not terrible. Doogan worked hard on this."

"Yes, but Doogan knows how much I love a good slit."

Daphne sighed, "Oh, come now. Don't get all down and mopey about it. You helped pick out the fabric. Adryen did the rest," and she smiled, motioning me to come to her.

Like hell I did!

I pushed up off of the bed and walked over to Daphne who was taking the dress off of its hanger and opening it up for me to step in.

"I will help you step in, just leave your undergarments on."

I raised an eyebrow, "Why would I take them off? This dress doesn't have any support."

"Let's go! Adryen is dying to see you in your dress," she smirked.

It was just a wedding so I guess I would have to start learning how to compromise. I was getting married because Adryen was my mate, and we had a blood oath. I could sacrifice *this*.

I pulled off my sleeping clothes and stepped into the dress. Daphne helped shimmy the fabric up my body and position it to sit correctly. She zipped up the back and looped every pearl button. Backing away, she smiled as I pulled up the frilly skirt and attempted to walk toward the mirror.

This thing was suffocating my hips. I could hardly move. Finally, I stood in front of the mirror and looked at myself. My sky-high hair that moved together as one piece and this dress combined, made me feel like I was about to be presented to a panel of judges; and I would be deemed unworthy.

I was so uncomfortable.

Daphne chimed behind me, "I have to go, Niya. We are by the beach when you are ready to walk out," she smiled and exited Adryen's bedroom.

Letting out a long, frustrated sigh, I followed out of the door behind Daphne, ready to just get this over with. Daphne must have moved fast, because she was nowhere to be seen.

Pixies.

Lingering on my way down the staircase and out of the castle doors, I headed to where the ceremony was being held in front of the waves crashing to the shore. I wanted to love this scene so much, but I couldn't. This just did not feel right.

Looking at all the heads turning to face me, I saw two very distinct fae. I stopped walking, and ran to my parents. Both of their very alive bodies sitting down and looking at me.

I touched their faces for reassurance and tears rolled down my face, "How did you—you're alive!"

"What do you mean, child?" My mother cooed, "Of course we are alive."

The realization hit me. It hit me straight across the face and knocked me on my ass. I stumbled backwards and wiped the tears from my face, "No, you died. I killed you."

"You thought you killed us," my father pitched, "But, our advisor saved us."

"Advisor?" my eyebrows pulled together, "No. That isn't what happened."

This must have been a sick joke. Was it the chanting and echoing voice in my head? Or was it my own imagination so far gone from reality that I created this...world.

I was stuck in a different version of reality. I looked around to see Adryen frowning at me with squinted eyes.

I whispered, "You are not real," and snapped my head back to my parents, "I killed you with my magic; you are dead. Alman did not save you. Nobody did."

Ravyn's laugh bounced off of the inside of my skull.

∞∞∞∞∞

I blinked and my eyes adjusted again. I was in a light pink room with a white crib that appeared welcoming, and quaint.

There was a cream nursing chair on tracks to allow a gliding rocking back and forth while holding a child.

Walking to the chair slowly, I sat down.

Tilting my head, I glanced over at all of the children's toys and nursery items. Diapers were organized on a table with wipes and a couple of stacks of neatly folded clothes.

Whose baby room was this?

Looking down, I glimpsed my very round, very far along pregnant stomach. I beamed as I realized that this was a nursery; for *my* baby.

I breathed, "Oh my gods, I am going to be a mother."

Adryen and I had been successful in conceiving a child.

Placing two delicate hands on my belly, I rubbed for a long while, just enjoying the bump. In my most authentic thoughts, I had always wanted a child. Even despite being brought up the way that I had, motherhood seemed to be an honest yearning of mine.

And now I had it. Joy washed away any doubts or insecurities.

Outside of the window, the sky seemed to be getting darker, inordinately quickly. I got up and waddled to the door, suddenly exhausted. I turned around, taking one long last look at the nursery when two large arms swooped in behind me, cradling my lower stomach.

Adryen kissed my neck and whispered, "Are you excited to be having a child?"

"I turned around and held his cheek in my hand, "I am so excited to be having a child with *you!* Adryen, you have given me everything I could have ever wanted."

Placing my hand back on my belly for confirmation, I giggled, "There is an actual baby in me, Adryen. We did this!"

I beamed, "I hope it's a girl, so I can teach her all of the things I learned growing up. She can learn how to defend herself and be a lady all at the same time."

"What if it's a boy?"

"I will still teach him how to fight and defend for his kingdom, his crown," I paused, "I hope they inherit your wyvern blood," and turned my head over my shoulder to glimpse Adryen.

He smiled and twirled me around, bending on one knee. He kissed my stomach gingerly and the memories flashed back into me from when he proposed.

That god's awful proposal that I somehow allowed and continue to let happen.

"Adryen," glancing down at him.

He replied, low, "Yes, Niya?"

"When did we get married?"

He stood up from his bent knee and towered over me, "What do you mean?" Adryen grabbed a strand of my loose hair and tucked it behind my ear, "It is the same day it has always been."

He never gave me definitive answers anymore and I was starting to get agitated whenever we spoke.

Playing coy, I inquired, "I am having a hard time remembering, How long have we been married now?"

Adryen's face turned down as he growled, "You don't remember our anniversary?"

Backing away from him a little bit, "No, that's why I asked."

"Niya, it is today," he barked.

"You don't have to get loud with me, Adryen; it was just a question!"

Another wave of exhaustion rolled over me and I grasped my stomach; attempting to ground myself in the feeling of comfort of carrying this child.

My child.

Ours.

I breathed, "I need to know what's going on with you. You seem aggravated and disconnected. If we are going to have a child together, I need to know that we are a team. You getting loud with me feels like you do not care about me or my emotions; or this babe," as I touched my roundness.

Adryen charged at me, yelling, "Are you accusing me of mistreating you?"

I screamed back, "No! That's not what I said! You are not listening!"

"I don't appreciate your tone, Niya!"

Adryen never raised his voice with me, this is not right.

Something is *not* right.

I looked around for an escape and he had me trapped in the corner of the room.

Adryen moved in closer and I backed away, falling backward on the crib, hitting my head hard.

Chapter 49
Niya

"Niya," a voice rasped, "Niya!"

I squinted my eyes, and the sunlight blurred my vision.

"Are you okay?"

The scenery was different. The nursery was gone and replaced with snow.

Desolation surrounded me.

"What happened? Where is Adryen?"

I started to sit up, but the voice interjected, "Slowly, Niya."

My vision clearing, I saw where we were.

How in all the gods did we get here?

I immediately reached for my pregnant stomach, and there was no bump. No belly. No child. Just a flat stomach. I rubbed my stomach again and it was the same. No belly. Just a smooth plain.

Looking again at my surroundings and keeping my hand on my stomach, I saw nothing but snow. This was a tundra. Snowy lands, with no life. I looked around and felt the whipping wind and saw nothing.

Fin was hovering over me, his attempt to hide his disdain on his face.

"Fin, where are we? Where is Adryen? My baby?"

"I don't know, Adryen called me into the nursery, and you were passed out with a busted head. Don't worry; we had a witch come deliver your baby. It is fine. Afterward, when I touched you, a portal formed, sucking us into this," He waved his hands around, "But, we will find our way back. I am familiar with this land."

This land was barren, with no trail markers. Fin must be really good at directions.

I scrambled to my feet and looked around, "Oh gods, my magic is completely unmanageable. I am so sorry. I don't know how I could have formed a portal passed out like that." I felt back down to my empty stomach, "Where is Adryen and the baby?"

Panic rose; I had to get back to the both of them! He was probably worried sick!

I ran in one direction, then changed course and ran the other. Endless snow-covered grounds surrounded us with nowhere to go.

Panting, I realized out loud, "This is The Wasteland. I have never been here before. How was my magic able to portal us here? I am not going to be able to get us out until my powers can regenerate."

This was a nightmare. I continued pacing around back and forth and my body started to sweat.

We were going to die.

I was going to die.

Adryen was going to have a *dead* mate and my child was going to be motherless.

"Where is my baby?" I asked out loud, again. My fear and anguish completely overtaking me, I dropped to the snowy floor and started hyperventilating. Tears rolled endlessly down my face, and I wailed, "I need to get back to my child!" I grabbed into the snowy tundra and gripped at the ice-cold ground as tight as I could, screaming in pain. My fingers started to numb and hot tears dropped into the snow.

Fin blurted and I looked up to his hand on his hip, "Follow me," and started off in a direction, "We need to get to shelter, Niya, or you will freeze to death and your child will be motherless."

Pulling myself together somewhat, I used my hands to get off of the white, blanketed ground and sniffled, rubbing the back of my hand over my snotty nose, "Are you sure my baby is okay?" I placed my hand on my empty stomach again.

Fin growled, "Your baby is fine, Niya! You need to get inside and warm up. There is this place where we can do that and then plan an action on how to get home!"

I nodded hesitantly and trailed behind Fin. Walking in this wet snow was tiring.

I was so tired.

Fin broke the silence, "I came here on trips with my father to collect exotic gemstones. There is an outpost around here somewhere."

I felt like I could not move anymore. It felt like Fin had my body in a halter and was dragging me through the snow.

I felt like I was a prisoner again.

With a whole new level of torture.

"This does not feel right," I yelped, "I am uncomfortable."

The whole situation did not feel right. My magic, especially my portals, should not go further than where I know. I looked around at the snowy landscape and shivered. I closed my eyes, trying to warm my body.

A jolt of warmth filled me up like a glass and I relaxed slightly at Fin's touch.

We walked in more silence over the unforgiving terrain.

Exhaustion was a friend to me and I was accepting its embrace.

Nobody could truly survive in this place. There had to be a really nice home, or shelter for someone to live out here.

Unsure of how far we'd walked, I kept pace with Fin as we trudged through the snow. Fin stopped and I looked up from the ground. This massive two-story building disguised as the white tundra came into view. If I did not see the lights coming from inside, I would have assumed this was a rock, or tree covered in snow.

"Is someone in this house, Fin? The lights are on."

Fin looked up, pondering, "Huh, I guess Adryen must have found us. He probably brought your baby."

Holy gods.

We made it to the door and Fin pulled out a key, unlocking the entryway to the house.

"Where did you get a key?"

Fin looked over and smirked, then looked back toward the house.

The house was cold and musty. It did not seem like anyone had inhabited this place in many years. I trailed my hand along the tabletop and dust covered my fingers.

Looking around at the open floorplan, I shot up the stairs, looking through every room for Adryen and our child.

The bathroom; empty.

The bedroom; empty.

The hallway; empty.

There was not one piece of furniture in this house. Everything was...empty.

I began to cry as I opened the door to the last of the empty rooms.

Utterly devastated, I trailed slowly down the stairs, trying to hold back the hysterics building inside.

"I apologize for the dust," Fin responded, pushing his fingers through his golden hair.

I yelped, "Where are they?"

"Like I said, you pulled us both through a portal. It's just us."

"What do you mean?"

"You said the lights were on because Adryen was here with my baby."

"Oh, I did?" A sly, ugly smile reached ear to ear on Fin.

My mind started to recall the events and it felt like there was a haze in my brain. A fog that would not clear. I held my head and closed my eyes.

Think.

Think!

No, there was no way this could have happened.

I had truly gone crazy.

"Why did you bring us here, to The Wasteland?"

Fin questioned back, "Bring us where?"

I looked around and a flash of light illuminated everywhere around us. There was a living room on the right, and a kitchen with food cooking on the stove on the left. I wandered off to the left to look into the kitchen. Fin followed in behind me, working at whatever was boiling on the stove.

Fin breathed, "I started to cook us some dinner."

"What?"

I was beyond confused. Maybe a little manic.

I retraced my steps in my head.

We were in Cleome and Fin was helping me calm my nerves and I blacked out, waking back up in Cleome. Then Rose was there and we stayed the night to regroup for the next day. I was finally able to make it back to Adryen and we spent days—no, weeks—years possibly, together. We got married and I was pregnant. I woke up here, in The Wasteland, with Fin.

My eyes became saucers.

My baby...

What year is this?

I am going crazy.

I am crazy.

But, we were just in the snow, in an abandoned home...and now, how could he have been cooking already?

Nothing made sense!

Fin cut through my thoughts, "I am making beef stew."

I ran to the window to see clean green fields and a castle in the distance.

"How did we get here? I thought we were in The Wastelands. Where is my baby, Fin?"

"Oh, there is no baby," Fin chuckled waving his spoon around then going back to stirring the pot.

No baby?

"WHAT THE FUCK IS GOING ON?!"

I was pregnant; the baby was *real*. This was not real. He stole me. Fin took me from my family, my home.

I looked over at the counter where a knife lay and I snatched it.

Pointing it at Fin, "Where is my baby, liar?!"

Fin turned around and crossed his arms over his chest, "I am many things, Niya, but a liar is not one," he frowned and continued, "In the keen state you're in, it is probably better you not have that knife."

I looked down at my clenched fist; it was empty.

"I will scratch your eyes out! What have you done? Why did you say my baby was not real?"

"Oh, Niya. It's not," he smirked.

"No," I trailed off, feeling like I was losing my mind.

I felt back down at my stomach for reassurance, and it was still, very smooth.

Fin came closer to me, "It's okay, I will help you remember."

He placed his fingers on my temple and shooting pain went down my spine.

I closed my eyes and screamed, falling to the floor.

Tears rolled down my face and my breathing quickened.

I was so fatigued. I didn't think I could go on.

I needed to get back to my child and away from this monster.

I looked up and we were back in the dusty hallway of the house in The Wastelands.

I shouted, "What are you doing?! I don't understand," tears trailed down my face again as I came to realize that I was indeed out of my mind.

"Parlor tricks," is all he said as he leaned down, clamping my wrists into iron bands, "I have had you for longer than you know, Niya. You will never see Adryen again. You're mine."

"How long? Where are we?" My mind was so fuzzy.

I didn't know what was real and what wasn't.

"That vision in Cleome, was only partially true. That was, I don't know, maybe two months ago. Maybe three. Once you found your horse, we started in the direction of Adryen's castle. I had no intention of stepping foot back in Seelie territory. So, I manipulated you into portaling us to the very edge of your kingdom where The Wastelands are. You have been in this vision for a very long time. I feel like I did a pretty damn good job keeping you distracted."

I backed up from him, squirming with the intrusion into my mind, "No."

"Oh, yes," he slithered, "Once we got to The Wastelands, I found this shack, abandoned and took it upon myself to make it into our little home," Fin snapped his fingers and the world around me faded to a small, dreary, rotting four-walled shack. "I made...*improvements* as you can see."

Fin continued, "See, I *take* what I want, Princess." His smile didn't meet his eyes and I felt a slimy feeling in my gut.

"We are almost out of food, so I figure that we will stay another night, then we will travel into the human realm; where we will create a new life for ourselves."

"The realm of the humans?"

"Yes, I heard rumors that when you get to the very edge of The Wastelands, there is a barrier you can cross, putting you into a new realm where these said humans live. They are very similar to us, except they have shorter lives and no magic."

"Wait," I couldn't wrap my brain around what he was saying fast enough, "You are telling me, you rescued me from my previous captor, to then take me and imprison me again? You manipulated me, with your mind, in hopes that I would just forget my life and stay with you? In an *entirely* made-up world? Where nothing is real?!" I was screaming now, "Nothing was real!"

Lowering my voice, trying to recollect myself, "But I had a life with Adryen, and my baby."

"You were never pregnant, Niya!"

I closed my mouth and pressed my lips together in anger, "You are lying."

"Now, what did I just say? I don't lie," Fin put his fingers on my temples, "Calm down, Niya," and suddenly, my tight muscles went lax and the world faded away.

Chapter 50
Niya

The next morning, Fin began stuffing everything into a bag; readying for our trip to this supposed, "Human World." He had rope in one hand and a ball attached to leather in another.

I did not know what was real anymore.

This felt real, and looked real, but I had begun questioning if this was all in my head.

I barely slept last night, tossing and turning on the floor. I was beyond tired. My powers felt like they were in constant use, and I could not relax to recharge.

"What is *that*?" I asked drowsily.

"Stop talking, or I will send you through the manipulation plane again."

Not really caring anymore, "Do what you want," and I looked around me, searching for any possible weakness to exploit if it had turned out that this was real.

I closed my eyes and breathed in the muskiness of the house. I just needed to get back to Adryen. Fin was lying; I have a baby out there somewhere. It really seemed like Fin also did not know reality from his own machinations, so even his truths could be false.

He stopped fiddling with his bag and walked over to me, on the floor. Fin grabbed my jaw and tightened his fist, "I could blow your brain up from the inside out, if you would like. I would thoroughly enjoy the look on Adryen's face when he realizes his mate is gone and it was me that did it."

"Oh, I am *so* scared," I laughed hysterically.

Fin's lip curled, "What the hell is wrong with you?"

I giggled, "I am unsure, actually."

Fin growled, "Stop, or I will gag you with this."

"Oh, I might like that, be careful."

Fin rolled his eyes and pulled me up from the floor, "You can't use your magic to warm yourself, so bundle tightly in your cloak, and hope frostbite doesn't kill you."

Fin was all over the place. He wanted to kill me, he didn't want to kill me. Cared for me, didn't care for me.

Maybe he was the crazy one.

"Why are you doing this, Fin? Did Adryen do something to piss you off?"

"You are lucky I found you at the right time. That lord would have killed you when he found out what you'd done."

Fin was not listening to me, very much like Adryen from my memories.

Oh, wait.

Was that Adryen?

I shrugged a shoulder, "I could have taken him."

Fin wrapped rope around my wrists alongside the iron bracelets as I asked, "What is the purpose?"

"Of what?" He grumbled.

"Of the ropes? I can't use my magic. I'm useless."

Fin looked at me crazily, "You're a fucking fighter. I am not so stupid as to let you walk with me unbound," he eyed me and tightened his lips.

"Do you not see these?" I raised my wrists to show the iron.

"Better to be safe than sorry," he said, not looking at me.

"You know, I was going to just submit and follow you, but fighting you is a really great idea, too," a wide grin covering my face.

Fin tightened the rope on me, and my grin morphed into a smirk. He mumbled to himself and turned away from me.

I got up off of the floor, using my hips and knees, and walked to the open door. Looking outside to the white expanse of nothing, a white blob moved on the horizon. I squinted my eyes to the movement and jerked my head backward to see Fin messing with the bag again; not paying any attention to me whatsoever.

Glancing back at the movement, my legs bolted into a jog and then into a run.

"Niya!" Fin yelled behind me, "Niya, fuck! Come back! You will die out there!"

I didn't care. I would rather die than stay in limbo any longer.

I continued pushing through the wet and icy terrain. That moving thing was either food, or help. I would take either at this point. Losing my footing, I tumbled forward and fell to my knees. I seethed with pain but got back up and continued running toward the figure. Getting a better view, it was not an animal.

It was fae!

I kept running to the figure, and it seemed to look directly at me.

Male.

"Help," I shouted to him, "Please, help!"

The male started toward me in a sprint, and we met in the middle. I looked behind me to see Fin stopping in his tracks to see who—*what*—was with me. He turned around, eyes wide, and ran back to the shack.

I moved my head forward and a warm breath caressed my cheek. I fell backwards, not expecting to slam into him.

"What are you doing here?" His voice was low, and raspy.

Panting, "I, what? What are *you* doing here?"

Fuck, I was so tired, and these iron bracelets were not helping.

He pointed behind me, "That is my shack, Miss. You and your friend are trespassing."

I let out a laugh, "That is *not* my friend! He kidnapped me."

"From whom?" The male questioned.

I looked into his blue eyes, "Can I be honest with you? I think I have had a really rough month or maybe two. I don't know. I just want to go home. I have a child waiting for me. Can you please help me?" That came out as a beg.

I didn't beg, but I was beyond desperate.

I missed Adryen.

I needed him.

Needed my baby to be real.

Scrabbling myself off the ground, I got a closer look at the white-coated male. He pulled his hood down to reveal delicately pointed ears met with a too-long unkempt beard, and long ruffled hair.

He squinted his eyes, "Why are you looking at me like that?"

"You just...you look so familiar," I straightened, "Do I know you?"

I reached for his reddish-brown hair, and he smacked my hand away, "Don't touch me, Princess."

Shock rolled over me, "You know me. Okay, I can work with that."

"Niya!" A voice interrupted us. I turned around to see Fin holding something.

A knife?

A weapon?

I could not tell, but it was probably something that I did not want a closer look at.

The male stepped in front of me, his powers radiating from him. A massive, crackling portal formed right in Fin's path. Fin had not expected it and could not stop himself in time. He ran right through the portal, and I could hear his scream as it began to close behind him.

I shuffled backwards, not knowing if the next one mightn't be for me. Out of pure desperation, and without any other ideas, I pushed my hands in the air. He looked at my iron and rope bracelets and grabbed my wrists.

Fear, relief, and submission; his touch felt so real.

Warm on my very cold body.

"Fuck these wretched things," he snarled and broke both of them off with his bare hands.

Rubbing my wrists, I gaped at him, "Thank you. Who are you?"

He examined the iron bracelets thoughtfully and then flames shot from his hands, melting the iron to liquid, "I am nobody. Just a traveler."

He walked away, and I quickly followed behind, "I need your help," I stopped to see if he would respond. But he did not, so I continued, "I can't transverse or portal myself out of here because I don't know my location."

The male kept walking, ignoring me.

Desperately, I needed his voice to reassure me that this was real. His touch alone was not enough. Fin had done a stellar job of making me actually feel things in my mind.

Looking down to my stomach, my heart sank into my gut.

Working up enough energy to do something, I leaned down and slammed my hands into the snow, forming a snowball. Putting all my weight behind it, I threw it as hard as I could to the back of his head.

And I did not miss.

He stopped briefly, but shook the snow off, and kept walking.

I growled and formed a ball of ice with my powers, making sure it was a perfect circle. I aimed for this male's head and extended my arm, propelling the ball through the air. The male turned around and caught the ball with a fire-hot hand, and it melted.

"I haven't played children's games in many years, Princess. If I'd wanted to play them with you, I would have asked," he sneered.

"Then talk to me! I have been alone with my own thoughts for however long; and just when I think I'm safe again, this male uses mind magic on me and I am not sure if my thoughts or what I see are real. How do I know you are real, and you aren't one of *his* games?" I shouted, panicking.

The scraggly male trudged to me and stopped, looking down, "This is real," he grabbed my tattooed wrist and my powers emanated and glowed, "If it was not, you would not have access to your powers."

"What?"

Oh, my powers. Even if I wanted to tap into my powers, I was beyond that at the moment. The male put his hands on my shoulders, illuminating my magic. It danced and skittered all around me.

I inclined my head, "How are you doing that to my magic?"

He tilted his head, "Doing what? Disturbing it?"

The male released my shoulders and the bone-tiredness hit me again.

I just wanted to sleep.

Forever.

"Lots of practice. When you are alone in The Wasteland for as long as I have been, you would have all the time in the world to master your abilities; enough time and you'll begin to master everyone else's, too." He looked down, forlorn, "I've been here a long time."

He was crazy.

I was crazy.

The blue-eyed male turned on his heels and continued walking through the snowy expanse.

I yelled after him, "Can you help me get home?"

He stopped in his tracks and looked over his shoulder, "And where is home?"

Where was home?

Kaldamir probably had a death warrant for me and Haldonia would not accept an outcast, or a killer.

I whispered, "Adryen."

He was my only home now.

I'd hoped.

"Who?" The male's voice went up an octave.

I said louder, "Can you get me to Cleome?"

The male moved in closer, "Whose name did you just say?"

"Nobody," I needed to get to a place not a male, so I asked again, "Can you get me to Cleome?"

His eyes darkened and he placed his hand on my jaw, clenching it, "Adryen is your destination? Adryen who?"

Yes, I wanted to beg, but instead I responded, "What?! I thought you could not hear me?" A childish snicker laced my words, "No, Cleome is."

The hold on my jaw was strong and he was not letting up, "I don't know where Cleome is, but I know where The King of Haldonia resides, if that is the Adryen you are talking about."

"You can portal me to Haldonia?"

"So, it *is* King Adryen," he smirked, "What is your affiliation to him? I don't see a ring, or a tattoo marking you of significance." He looked all around my body.

I placed my hand on his chest and pushed him away from me; he let go of his hold and dropped his hands.

"My affiliation is none of your business, sir." We stared at each other, "How do you know so much? You look and smell like you have not been around anybody in a very long time. How are you able to keep up with the politics of this realm."

He said simply, "I haven't," then continued, "I will help you get to Adryen. But I need you to reciprocate in a deal with me."

"I am not making a deal with you until I at the very least know your name!"

"Okay," He drew out, "My name is Ryktor."

A smile crossed my face, hopeful, "Well, *Ryktor,* what are your terms?"

"I am lonely, and life here is very scarce making it hard to hunt." He stopped for a moment to look into my eyes.

"I am not going to sleep with you; I don't care *how* lonely you are," I balked.

He pushed past my comment and continued, "I would like to make a deal where you bring me supplies once a month so I can continue to live here in peace. The company might be nice as well."

He had no desire to leave this barren place. He was content living alone in The Wasteland, "No," I replied out of pure stubbornness.

"Okay," he shrugged, "Then I cannot help you, Princess," and continued walking.

I just stared, and stared at him until he was a little figure in the distance. The way he said princess struck me in a very familiar way and made me ache for Adryen more. He did not have that *tone* like everyone else did. Ryktor said it like Adryen said it and it tugged at me.

Everything swirling around me had gotten to be too much; my mind and emotions were a mess.

I was having a hard time believing any of this was real. Someone could not just sound like Adryen, unless I was still being manipulated.

But, if I was being manipulated, I didn't think he would really just leave me here.

Right?

Fuck Ryktor, I needed to figure this out on my own. I looked around at nothingness, and as quickly as I was motivated to try, I gave up. My insides started churning and my nerves started taking over.

Deeps breaths, Niya; in...and out...

This is as real as it is going to get.

I closed my eyes and tried to center myself. I thought that it would probably be the wiser decision to just give this male what he wanted, even if that meant I would sacrifice my time and resources. In reality, I needed to get back to Adryen and that was all that mattered to me.

I opened my eyes, and I felt his emotions had started coming back to me. For the first time in however long. Oh, I missed this. They were faint, but they were there.

Adryen was worried, angry, and stressed.

I bolted into a run. The icy wind hit my face and snow started to fall, landing everywhere. I finally caught up and grabbed his wrist, pulling him back.

Very out of breath I spoke, "Fine."

"Fine?" he questioned, pausing in his steps.

"Fine! I will make a deal with you! But you have to make one with me."

Ryktor grunted, eyebrow raised, "Which is?"

"When I come to visit you with supplies every month, you have to help me control my magic. I recently...was not in control of them, and they lashed out in my defense and killed two of our kind," I looked down, "Two of my family members."

The male looked at me, more alert now, "Did you hear voices in your head chanting something? And were those family members your parents?"

I bobbed my head in answer to both questions. His questions were uncanny; it felt surreal.

Ryktor had a look of concern on his face. Those crystal blue eyes showed so much pain, and so many secrets. Ryktor seemed kind, and caring, but the only thing keeping him here was himself. Me making this deal with him would give me time to build his trust, and eventually bring him back to Haldonia with me and help him through whatever issue he was running from.

Nobody deserved to live in solitude, despite whatever they'd done in the past.

Ryktor continued, "Yes, it's a deal then," and stuck out his hand.

My hand reached his and they smacked each other. Ryktor wrapped his hand tightly around mine. He chuckled and two flesh toned ancient symbols appeared below our thumbs.

They looked identical to one another.

I raised an eyebrow, "What in the entire realm is this?"

"A sealed bargain."

"How the hell did you do that?"

"It is one of my powers."

"You're fucking crazy, Ryktor. I like it," I laughed.

He ignored me and asked, "Haldonia's castle is your destination?"

"Yes."

"Come visit me next month at the shack where you were held captive. With your powers, you should be able to jump through the void to me now, yes?"

"Yes," I replied again.

He grunted and a portal appeared in front of me.

I looked over at Ryktor, "Come with me, please. I won't know this is truly real if you don't."

"No, I can't."

I whined, "Why? I can find you a place secluded from everyone; it will be fine. You can't be here alone anymore, Ryktor."

"I can't," His voice turned firm and dark, "Go home, Princess. I am sure that Adryen is eagerly awaiting your return. The portal will take you to the front lawn of the castle. Now, go."

Looking at the crackling portal, I took in a deep breath and held it.

I was terrified.

This could not be real; it seemed too easy.

I rubbed my temples, trying to pull apart what was imagined and what was tangible.

I hesitated and stared at the portal for several minutes. I started replaying all of what happened since I'd been taken by Fin. So much was manipulation that I was not sure, even now, what was facts and what wasn't. The worst part was that I didn't know if I would ever be sure again; including this portal.

Faltering, "I can't do this."

Ryktor replied, annoyed, "Do you want to see your baby or not?"

Hurt stabbed through me and tears welled in my eyes.

My thoughts were spiraling: What if this whole thing was a lie? What if this is just Fin in my head again? I am not ready. I can't do this. This is too good to be true.

A hot breath caressed my neck and goose bumps rose.

"I'm sorry, Princess, but you can't stay," Ryktor said, and a push came from behind.

I fell through the portal with a scream. I closed my eyes, hoping to everything holy that I did not just get manipulated again.

Landing hard on the green grass, the portal snapped closed and a familiar deep, smooth voice sounded from above me, "Niya!"

I snapped my head up and saw him.

Oh gods.

This wasn't real.

Chapter 51
Niya

I looked around and there were wolves and guards surrounding me. I started to breathe hard and squeezed my eyes closed, trying not to panic.

This is real, I am okay. I am not going to be imprisoned again.

A rough hand touched my shoulder and I squirmed backwards, looking up at those beautiful, entrancing, cornflower blue eyes.

Adryen's face was solemn, sad, and unkempt. He looked miserable and torn. Like someone ripped his whole world apart and refused to mend it back together.

Please, gods...please.

Adryen did not just let himself go like this. He looked as if he had been locked up for months.

A sudden surge of remembrance, *My baby...*

I felt down to my stomach with a gentle touch, and it was just a flat surface.

I did not understand, and I was scared.

My whole life was ripped away all in one night.

I threw a wind shield around me to protect myself against possible threats. I looked around, seeing concerned faces from every angle looking at Adryen who was talking slowly to them. His people nodded and they all dispersed in their separate directions, afraid to make eye contact with me. I could not hear anything, but I could *feel* his emotions.

He was hurt, confused, and very, very sad.

My emotions mirrored his; my mate.

Was this truly real? Am I free from both Lord Morelli and Fin?

Hot tears rolled down my face and I curled myself in a fetal position, letting my shield down, not able to hold on anymore.

I was *so* tired. Mentally, physically and emotionally drained.

Large arms wrapped under my knees and around my back, lifting me up off the grassy floor.

I didn't dare open my eyes.

The smell was enough.

Eucalyptus and birch filled my nostrils, and, oh gods, I knew I was home.

Tears poured unchecked down my face.

Adryen.

Wrapping my arms around his shoulders, I tightened my grip and nuzzled into his neck, refusing to let go.

Refusing to believe that this was anything less than absolutely real.

Adryen tightened his grip around me and whispered, "You're home. I won't let anything happen to you, Princess."

His heart was racing, but it felt calming and grounding.

A lock clicked open and, quickly, a door shut causing me to jump in Adryen's arms.

The locking sound reminded me of my shackles and the key to Fin's imaginary home.

Adryen tensed with me and I could feel his head shaking, "I'm going to put you down, Niya, and start a shower for you." His cornflower eyes pierced into mine and I slightly melted, "While you're in there, I am going to start a hot bath for you to relax when you're done."

This was not real.

This happened once before, in my mind.

But, was this in my mind?

He walked away and I just stood there, staring out of the large windows of his room.

This felt like an eternity.

Adryen pushed the hair out of my face and grazed my jaw, "Are you okay?"

All I could do was stare back at him, and watch.

I was paralyzed.

Shocked.

His touch was supposed to mean everything to me, but right now, it felt like a betrayal. A betrayal of myself, and of him. I could not embrace his touch like I had before being held prisoner. He was gentle and kind.

I was so broken.

Adryen frowned, "I can feel you, Niya," He paused, "I'm real," he kissed my forehead and then my cheek, "I'm real."

I needed to move my feet, but I couldn't. It felt like my body was frozen in place and my mind was not awake enough to make it move. I was in the darkest part of my mind, not able to escape.

Not wanting to.

Adryen's eyebrows furrowed and he closed his eyes.

He whispered something to me, but I was so far into my darkness that I could not hear anything that he was saying. Adryen helped me undress and carried me to the shower. He set me down gently and I wrapped my arms around myself.

I looked at the running water and just stared.

Stared into the flowing drops.

Refusing to get under, I pushed back against the wall. Adryen reached his hand over me and shut off the water.

He was talking but nothing was getting through.

Nothing.

He was so patient and so...perfect. I shouldn't be here. I should be with Fin in the depths of his manipulation.

I didn't deserve Adryen.

Adryen moved around behind me and grabbed my hand. Finally looking at him, tears rolled down his rough face as inaudible words moved on his lips. His soundless lips stopped moving and he guided me to the bathtub that was filling up. Adryen scooped me up and set me down in the tub and my body instantly curled back into itself.

Inaudible words floated around my head, *Niya.*

I looked at Adryen, who was getting soap and washing the dirt and grime off of me.

He smiled faintly before I dropped my face onto my knees and started to sob.

That was real.

Him talking to me through our connection...

Real.

Fin would not have been able to do that even if he'd tried; which he never would have thought to do nor cared to do.

I was not sure how long I'd cried, but Adryen managed to get into the bathtub with me fully clothed. He did not care; he'd just wanted to comfort me. We sat there until the water got cold and the tears ran dry. Adryen stepped out of the bath and walked outside of the room. Moments later he came back in with a new set of clothing and an extra shirt of his. He smiled, faintly, and dried me off. Only concerning himself with my needs and comfort, he pulled the shirt over me.

I just stood there and allowed him to take care of me.

To love me.

He brushed through my hair as gently as he could, as I sat there, numb.

Numb was better than the pain that I felt.

Tears rolled down my face again and he wiped every single tear away with his kisses.

I was just waiting for this beautiful dream to fade away. I was expecting to find out that this was all an illusion to break me.

And it *would* break me.

I reached up and touched his overgrown, bearded cheek. Each little prick of his beard sent renewed sensations of reality through me.

I really saw him this time. Saw his sad eyes, his broken heart, and every ounce of emotion he'd tried so hard to hide from me. He did not give up. He pushed through...for me.

Adryen was broken.

We were broken.

Both snapped in half like a dried twig removed from the nurturing tree.

And this, this pain was real.

And this was the rawest I had ever seen Adryen.

He was in pain, and desperate.

Desperate to find *me*.

I finally found the words to say, "I don't know if this is real or not." A small, choked sound escaped me.

Adryen placed his hand on mine. He pulled my hand to him and kissed the heart of my palm, "This is real; *We* are real, and I am never letting you go again. You are mine, forever. I love you, Niya. I love all of you. You, being taken from me was...I could not function without being able to feel you and know that you were okay," Tears rolled down his face again, "I couldn't handle you being taken away from me again; not ever."

I wrapped my hands around his neck and hugged him tightly. A relieved sobbing sigh wrenched from him as he snuggled into my neck, wrapping his long arms around my torso.

His voice low and tender, "I love you so much, Princess."

I melted into nothingness. I had waited so long to really touch him again; to be with someone that would see my stubbornness and love me anyway. I had waited so long for him.

I missed his voice.

I missed his touch.

I missed *him*.

My entire soul felt like it was wrapped around his, and I sunk into the pure bliss of it all.

And *this* was *real*.

Made in the USA
Columbia, SC
04 November 2023

8627e87d-531d-49d8-b6f5-31503028f36eR01